DATE DUE

AUG 0 4 2011			
SEP 0 2 2011			
OCT 14 2011			

GAYLORD   PRINTED IN U.S.A.

What The Heart Knows

What The Heart Knows

Kathleen Eagle

AVON BOOKS NEW YORK

AVON BOOKS, INC.
1350 Avenue of the Americas
New York, New York 10019

Copyright © 1999 by Kathleen Eagle
Interior design by Kellan Peck
ISBN: 0-380-97705-2

Library of Congress Cataloging in Publication Data:
Eagle, Kathleen.
What the heart knows / Kathleen Eagle. —1st ed.
p. cm.
1. Indians of North America—Fiction. I. Title.
PS3555.A385W48 1999   99-14876
813'.54—dc21   CIP

First Avon Books Printing: July 1999

AVON TRADEMARK REG. U.S. PAT. OFF. AND IN OTHER COUNTRIES, MARCA REGISTRADA,
HECHO EN U.S.A.

Printed in the U.S.A.

FIRST EDITION

QPM   10   9   8   7   6   5   4   3   2   1

www.avonbooks.com

To Honor the Memory of
Robert Eaglestaff
Fort Yates High School, Class of 1971
and
Sidney D. Pierson
my father

Two strong, fine athletes whose good hearts gave
out too soon.

*"The race is not always to the swift nor the battle to the strong
—but that's the way to bet it."*
DAMON RUNYON

What The Heart Knows

$\mathscr{R}$oy Blue Sky had heard the owl's warning call for three nights straight.

He would not have stepped outside his house after midnight on the fourth night if it hadn't been for Crybaby, who had gotten himself locked out of the yard again. With a sad, whimpering howl, the dog begged to be let in. Roy flipped the switch for the yard light. Nothing happened. He kept forgetting the damn thing was burned out.

"Quit your whining, now. Where were you when I called before?" The chain-link gate squeaked on its hinges. The dog skulked past, brushing against Roy's jeans. "Damn, you smell like you rolled in something dead. Good thing you stayed away while that woman was here. You come around a woman smellin' like that, I'll pretend I don't know you."

But since it was dark and the woman was gone and it didn't matter how Crybaby smelled now, Roy leaned down to ruffle the black-and-white shepherd's stinky fur.

Then he noticed something else out of place.

"Who left that gate open? Did you do that, you stinkin' old mutt?"

He was sure he'd hooked the latch on the pasture gate after he'd shown his two flashy paints off to his visitor. The horses had gotten out on the road by now. They couldn't resist an open gate.

He glimpsed a flicker of white up the road before it disappeared below the rise. The dog whined and wagged his whole butt, looking for more petting.

"What did you do, stand there and watch them walk away?" Roy closed the gate to the yard and headed down the rutted approach toward the highway, dog at his heels.

It was a black-velvet Dakota night, and the two-lane county road was not well traveled, even less so since the casino had been built on the Bad River cutoff, twenty miles south. But the night was never silent in the summertime. The tall grass housed night-song creatures, and the whispering cottonwoods gave perch to the owl, whose call struck old ears as an ominous thing.

Roy wasn't thinking about the owl as he walked, but about his visitor and how pretty she was for a fair-skinned *wasicu* woman. This was a thought he would not voice, not even to the dog, so he kept up his grumbling as if he'd turned on a recording. "You're supposed to be a stock dog, you know. Your father before you was a damn good stock dog. You quit whinin' and start usin' your instincts, you'll see it's in your blood."

The dog was spoiled, of course. Spoiled from the time he was a pup, and Roy had nobody to blame but himself. He'd spoiled his dogs the way he'd spoiled his sons, by not expecting a whole lot. He hardly saw Reese anymore, and Carter wouldn't have much to do with him since he'd called his son's employers "just another pack of thieving gangsters" at a tribal council meeting.

It had to be said. Wasn't anything personal. Carter was always telling Roy he had to start thinking like a businessman if he was going to lead the Bad River Sioux into the twenty-first century, but officially calling the Ten Star Casino Management Company mobsters was straight-tongue business. Nothing personal. Personally, he liked some of those guys. White guys, most of them, but you'd have to be white to be able to come up with the money it took to get a casino going. They were friendly enough, and they'd given him some nice gifts. They gave a lot of people nice gifts. But the casinos weren't bringing in the money they should, and nobody could tell Roy any different. He knew damn well there were some shady dealings going on somewhere.

"Hey! Get over here, mutt." The dog was slicing through the ditch grass, getting ahead of the game, but he turned tail when Roy clapped hand to thigh. "You stick by me until we can see them from the hill. We'll pull a sneak-up on 'em. You rush in and spoil it now, I'll be eatin' dog soup tomorrow."

The dog ducked back and got behind him. Roy laughed. Crybaby was no dummy. The woman had made a big fuss over the mutt, called him pretty puppy, old as he was. Old as Roy was, she could have had him wagging his tail, too, had she called him pretty. Pretty smart for an old buzzard, pretty funny, pretty spry, pretty anything. She was the kind of a woman who made a man think about what tricks he still might have left in him to impress her with, just to get one of those devoted-daughter kind of smiles. Storytelling was about all he could come up with, and she liked his stories. Stories about the old days always pleased young white women.

She was a dealer down at Pair-a-Dice City, the casino his younger son managed. Carter hadn't hired her himself, but the boy sure turned on the old Blue Sky charm full blast whenever he got near her. That bothered Roy a little because the woman had been around before, years ago. She'd been Reese's girl for a while, so it didn't seem quite right, Carter's behavior. It was no good, brothers trying to wear each other's old shoes. Somebody was sure to feel a pinch. His sons could act tough and independent, but underneath it all, they both were touchy over matters of the heart, each in his own way.

"There, see?" They'd topped the hill alongside the road and spotted their quarry. "Grazing the right-of-way, lookin' for a chance to play chicken with some trucker." Roy could hear one coming, or feel it maybe, even before the headlights came into play. "This one goes by, we'll cross over and get around them. Then you'll stay on that side, and I'll come back to this side. Got that? Walk 'em home easy. Like cake, like pie."

The expression made him smile. He'd said it to the woman when he'd shown her how to play Using Hoofs, demonstrating how easy it was to spear a string of deer foot bones on a wooden pin on the first try—"like cake, like pie." He'd shown her the old game before he told her one of his stories about gambling, about how the Lakota had been gamblers long before there were any casinos, before any of them had seen a deck of cards. She'd wanted to try her hand at the game right away, and he knew he had to get her into it first, before he could get her into the story. She was that kind of a woman. The do-it-herself kind. She'd gotten the hang of it pretty quickly. She had good hands. Dealer's hands.

Woman's hands. Deft and delicate. Watching those hands find just the right grip on the fat end of the stick, the way she tested the feel and the balance, made a man wish and wonder and remember while he watched. Universal, eternal woman's hands. Necessary hands. Pretty hands. Her name was Helen, and she was quick and lively and fun to be around. And she had something on her mind, something she wanted Roy to know. She hadn't told him what it was, and he didn't think she would, not just out-and-out. He wondered whether it would still be weighing on her next time he saw her. He wondered how forthright she really wished she could be.

If it was about her job, he knew she wasn't supposed to tell him anything, but she didn't have to. She'd been a teacher before, worked for the Bureau of Indian Affairs. Not too many teachers took up dealing blackjack. He figured her for the one who had been sent to investigate. Who else could she be? How clever they were to send a woman. Roy himself had filed the complaint with the gambling commission. He suspected some kind of cheating, big cheating, but he didn't know who was involved or how. Indirectly he had sent for her. He didn't want her to tell him anything, just to do her job.

"You think she's a plant?" he asked the dog as he eyed the grass beyond the blacktop. "She smells like one, don't she? Stay here, now, and don't let those horses cross the road. *Ssst. Hiya.*"

4

Roy smiled against the dark and trotted back across the highway. He was trying to figure out what sort of plant the woman smelled like. Must have been some garden variety, the kind he didn't know too much about. Reese would know. Reese was a city boy now, and he probably knew plenty about the smell of garden flowers on a woman's skin. Once the boy had started playing basketball on television, seemed like there was no shortage of women hanging around him. No wife, but plenty of women.

Carter, on the other hand, had been married three times, twice to the same woman. Roy felt bad for his two grandchildren. They were pretty confused. Some fathers had a way of doing that to their kids, and Roy himself had been one of them. Thinking about it touched off a vague, all-over ache in him. *For their own good* was so easy to say these days. A hundred years earlier he'd have made a good father, but in this century he was a flop.

A flip-flop. Got started later than most, which was probably why he hadn't been much of a breeder. No staying power. Finally they'd managed to get Rose, who had been her mother's special flower until Reese had come along. Roy hadn't seen Rose in a while. She lived in Oregon, never came home anymore. Reese was next, and then came Carter, and then . . . ah, that bone-deep ache again. Then he'd given Carter away, and later, years later, he'd taken him back again. No wonder the boy had two faces. And Reese, well, Roy had shortchanged Reese, pure and simple.

But his boys were men now, and there was little he could do to help or harm them. He figured he had one more chance to do right in this life, and that chance had begun to take shape with his reelection to the council. Some people were already saying they'd like to see him run for chairman next time around. Maybe he would, but with age, he had gained the wisdom to take one go-round at a time.

"That's the beauty of it, ain't it, you ol' whiner? The reward for living this long. Stay back, now." He was herding the two horses along the right-of-way while the dog guarded the flank from the opposite side of the road. The mare tried to make a break for it, but the dog yapped as he moved into position to head her off. "That's right, you talk to them. They got a lot to learn yet."

The woman with the pretty hands. She'd asked about Reese. Doing real good, he'd told her, and she'd seemed a little disappointed until he told her the boy had never married. That sure had surprised her. She'd tried real hard not to show it, but it pleased her. So he'd given her what she was looking for, spread it on thick about how hard it was for Reese when he couldn't play basketball anymore because his body couldn't take it. Didn't tell her any medical details—Reese was real touchy about his privacy—but she didn't ask too many questions, even though she was hanging on every word.

He'd watched her hands, stroking the smooth game stick he'd told her she could keep, but he'd gotten a furtive peek at her face, gone soft and serene, as though she'd suddenly draped herself with a sheer, somber-colored scarf, the kind the old women tied way down over their tired faces. She'd said she'd read about Reese's retirement, and she'd known it had come too soon. But still, she said, Reese had done what he'd said he would do, and few dreams as lofty as his were ever realized.

"What do you make of lofty dreams?" Roy had asked her then, and she'd confessed that she didn't much like being up in the air herself, but she thought they were fine for some people. Tall people, like Reese. She made more of the dreamer than the dream, Roy thought, remembering how curiously hard it had been for him not to be rude, hard not to invade her privacy by looking her in the face when her tone turned melancholy. Hard not to wonder what memory she cherished behind those wistful-woman eyes. They had connections, he and this woman. He couldn't define all of them yet, but he could feel them as he watched her thumb trace a small groove in that game stick he'd carved long ago. Such grace in those hands. Roy had to wonder what his son had done to chase her away.

"And everyday, dirt-common stories told by dirt-common old men? What do you make of those?" he'd asked.

"Sense," she'd said. "Your stories make sense to me. Old

stories are dependable, good for everybody. Dreams are tricky. You can't depend on dreams. I can't, anyway."

He'd thought about suggesting to her that dreams weren't meant for depending on, but who was he to say? In dreams he saw images that were both familiar and strange, things that beckoned and taunted, often played on his fears. He liked stories better, too. The woman was right—stories made sense. People were people, no matter what century they lived in. He couldn't say much about dreams.

"But tomorrow I'll have plenty to say about those crooks at Ten Star," he told his dog, his voice sounding bold in the dark. "I'll have a story or two to tell. Might just make a few people squirm, but . . ." He noticed a light swelling below the hump in the highway to the south. He signaled the dog as the headlights plunged over the hill.

But Crybaby wasn't there. Roy whistled. "Where did you get to now?" The headlights were closing in fast, too fast.

Up from the ditch on the opposite side of the road, the dog's eyes shone, too. He'd missed a beat, but he was there now. His master had called him, and he was coming. So were the headlights, hurling through the dark on the force of a roaring engine.

"No, stay back now. *Hiya!*"

Roy threw his arms out and waved wildly, thinking surely the driver behind those high beams saw him, but maybe he couldn't see the dog, he might hit the dog, don't hit the dog. *Damn you, don't hit my dog.* He pointed. The shepherd whimpered and crouched in the road, eyes gleaming like stars, caught between listening to him and being with him.

The shepherd was the last thought Roy Blue Sky had and the last thing he saw.

*D*eath had a way of screwing up the best-laid plans.

Helen Ketterling was a heavy-duty plan maker. Keeping things in order required a plan. She very much resented any form of plan bomb, and death was atomic.

She stood next to her car in the graveled parking lot across from the Bad River tribal offices and puffed on a cigarette as she watched a trio of old Indian men mount the steps to the front door. Two of them were older than the man they'd come to visit for the last time, but the third one might have been a classmate of Roy's in about 1940 or so.

In the brief time Helen had known Roy Blue Sky, she hadn't gotten around to asking him whether he'd finished high school. She didn't want to offend him by asking the wrong questions. He was a wonderful storyteller, but he preferred folk tales to personal reminiscences, although she'd managed to get a few of those out of him, too. She now knew that he'd fought in the Battle of the Bulge and that he'd been married twice, to young wives, both of whom had died much too soon. He'd told her less about the second wife, the mother of his children, than he had about the first, which was how she knew that the memory of the second loss still pained him.

Or *had*. Nothing pained him anymore. He had found peace now, and as a member of the Bad River Lakota Tribal Council, he was lying in state beyond those bright blue doors.

He was also her son's grandfather, but no one knew that. No one but Helen.

She turned her back on the building and the mourners mounting the steps as she puffed madly on her cigarette like a sneaky kid. It was the only way she ever smoked. The only good cigarette was a secret cigarette. Sidney had caught her at it a couple of times, and he'd read her the riot act, saying, "You're supposed to be a *teacher*, Mom." She'd been proud of him, the way he'd whipped those health-class facts on his mother, who still called herself a teacher even though she'd gotten into this other business because . . . well, partly because it paid well. But Sidney was always holding her to her own high standards, and she'd felt guilty about her lame claim that this was such a rare indulgence that she could hardly be called a smoker. He'd asked her what it did for her, and she couldn't tell him. She hated it when she needed a good answer and realized there wasn't one.

Helen had come to Bad River to look for answers. She had a job to do, and she told herself that learning everything she could about the Blue Sky family was simply part of that job. She needed to know about their involvement with the casino she was investigating. Roy had asked the Bureau of Indian Affairs for an investigation, a fact that was particularly interesting because his son Carter was Pair-a-Dice City's general manager. In the time Helen had spent around the two men, she had observed, as was her habit, she'd listened, and she'd put a lot of pieces of a still patchy picture together, which was her job.

But she had motives beyond the duty to her assignment. She had a duty to her son. Sidney had always been *her* son, hers alone. It was a necessary selfishness on her part, but now that he was barreling headlong into adolescence, she had to start thinking about who he was *besides* her only child, and who he would become. He had questions, and God only knew how she was going to answer them when the time came for a mother's full, unambiguous explanation of the ways of the real world. So she was angling for family history, and she had been reeling it in quite nicely since she and Roy had become friends.

There were times when she was sure he knew what she was up to, and she decided he didn't mind. She sensed that he actually approved. Tacit approval counted as approval in Helen's book. It wasn't such a huge leap from knowing to not minding to approving, one small hop at a time. She wanted the old man's approval. She liked him and she knew that Sidney would like him, that they ought to meet, that Sidney ought to hear his grandfather's stories; and knowing these things pained Helen, *still* pained her, for she was very much alive. Her secrets were very much alive, as was the risk she was taking just by coming to Bad River. The risk was huge.

The risk was over six and a half feet tall. Thirteen years ago she had known Roy's other son, who must surely be waiting behind those blue doors, too. She turned and stared at them, tried to bore a hole through them, tried to see how he looked now, how much the very public end to his illustrious professional basketball career had changed him, and how he carried his grief.

Helen had loved Reese Blue Sky once.

She had lusted after him, anyway. From the moment her craving for him had hit her—and it had hit her hard—she had told herself that this was the Romeo-and-Juliet kind of love that could never last and should never be declared unless you wanted corpses lying all over your personal stage. Reese believed, even if no one else did, that he was on his way to becoming a sports star. Helen was on her way to graduate school, after adding Indian-reservation teaching experience to her résumé. She was too busy for love, and he was too young, too unsettled, too quiet, too sexy, too improbable by half.

But he was a powerful temptation, and she had made little attempt to resist. She had denied love and fallen headlong in lust because he was the essence of her secret, silly female fantasies. The American West was etched on his angular, rough-hewn face, and he moved like a wild and natural creature, wondrously agile for his size. She knew full well that her fanciful fixation with the myth of the noble warrior had followed her into early adulthood, and it embarrassed her to think about it.

She was an intelligent woman, mostly. Responsible to a fault, but when her faults shifted and her shield cracked, she had a bad habit of folding in on herself and tumbling into the fissure. That tiny vein of romanticism was one of her weaknesses. She indulged in a private love affair with the myth and mysticism of the stark plains that rolled beyond the little clutch of boxy brick buildings across the street. Behind the tribal offices, the Bad River flowed between the Missouri and the Badlands, and beyond the river, the hills harbored history, the buttes remembered days of triumph and tragedy. She loved this place, and she was enchanted by its history. She had read about a man named Touch The Clouds, a name that had flashed inside her head the first time she saw Reese.

He'd been shooting hoops against an old backboard with a group of children who had been chased off the playground by the high school boys. School wasn't in session, but one of the elementary school teachers had complained about the bullies on the playground. Helen had gone in search of the dispossessed youngsters with the intention of championing them in their claim to their rightful territory. But the little ragtag group had found its champion in the form of a lean and lanky giant who could lift them close enough to the netless hoop for even the smallest child to score. He was Touch The Clouds, dressed in snug, threadbare jeans, a black tank shirt, and shoes that looked like ordinary Nikes until she'd seen them, two weeks later, lying beside her bed next to her own size sevens. A small child could have canoed in Reese's shoe.

He was a very big man with very big dreams, and, oh, what a very big time they had had that summer. What a short, sweet, grand and lovely season.

Now she would see him again after almost thirteen years, and she would offer commonplace condolences, and she would be collected and polite. It was the proper time for collected and polite.

To go in there and see him in the flesh again after all this time would be foolish, but she'd made up her mind. She ground her cigarette into the gravel and waved to her friend Jean Nelson, who'd just gotten out of her battered Bronco. Jean was still teaching at Head Start, still seemed to enjoy her job as much as she had when Helen had first met her, when they'd been young and idealistic and questing. Neither of them had gone back to school as they'd planned, but Jean was now in charge of her program. Helen was working hers.

"Let's do this together," Helen suggested when Jean drew close enough to link elbows.

"Have you seen him?"

"I haven't gone in yet. I just got here."

Jean gave her a knowing look. "I meant Reese."

"No, I . . ." Helen glanced at the blue doors. "I just got here."

"Nervous?"

Jean thought she knew how Helen felt about Reese. She was one of those frustrated would-be counselors who was always trying to pick the emotional garbage cans of her friends' brains. She was too damned intuitive to suit Helen, who returned a blank look.

Jean tightened down on the elbow link as they walked. "How long has it been since you've seen him? In person, I mean. For a while there, he was all over the—"

"Since I left," Helen said, cutting her off. "I haven't seen him since then."

"We didn't see much of him around here, either. Once in a while he'd show up at a high school basketball game, but that was rare. And it sure created a stir."

"He's a celebrity." Helen said this with an easy shrug, but the concept wasn't so easily managed. "No, I'm not nervous. He probably won't even recognize me. I'm here for Roy Blue Sky, Jean. This is about him."

"He and Reese were sort of estranged lately, I guess."

"That's too bad. I was just getting to know Roy." And what she knew was that if Reese had shut his father out in recent years, his loss would be magnified. The old man had been a delight. He'd had a dry sense of humor and an anecdote for every situation. "He said I could come over and ride his horses anytime, and that's what I've been doing for recreation."

"While you played cards for a living," Jean admonished.

"It actually pays better than teaching summer school."

"Almost anything you can name pays better than teaching."

"Roy was hoping to change that. He wanted to use some of the casino profits for education." Except that there had been scant profits. A little-known fact that Helen had not discussed with Roy, even though it concerned them both.

"He'll be missed," Jean said as they threaded their way among the parked vehicles, most of them sporting a dried crust of summer bug guts and South Dakota clay. "He was a man who was just coming into his own, late in his life. There was talk that he was going be the next tribal chairman."

Helen had heard the talk, and she'd mentioned it to Roy. Just talk, he'd said. He wasn't sure old age was much of a qualification for office. "We need an educated man," he'd said, and then he'd laughed and amended his last word with a gender-neutral noun. Then he'd told her that he'd heard Reese had gone back to school. *He'd heard.* And what she'd heard in his voice was the distance mixed with a father's heartache.

"Roy will be missed," Helen echoed quietly as they passed through the blue doors.

She spotted him immediately. Surrounded by people, he stood head and shoulders above all of them and could easily see over their heads. He looked straight at her when she came in the door, but there was no change in his face, no sign of recognition or welcome or displeasure. He simply looked at her, kept on looking at her in a way that drew her directly.

She made an attempt to smile, then let it slide away. She'd thought about what she would say if he didn't recognize her right away. Something witty and flippant. A casual quip, some sweet, private little joke to jar his memory and maybe throw him slightly off balance. Then she'd have the upper hand. But he was still looking at her, his dark eyes completely unreadable, and she couldn't think of a single clever thing to say.

So she offered a polite and collected handshake. "Helen Ketterling."

"I remember." His big, warm hand swallowed hers up completely. "It's been a long time."

"Yes, it has."

"Ten years?"

"More than that. You're looking—" Casting about for her wits had left her suddenly short of breath.

"Yeah, I'm looking." His smile was slow in coming, but finally his eyes befriended hers. He wasn't releasing her hand. She wasn't drawing it away. "You haven't changed."

"Yes, I have. I'm really very . . ." She shook her head and glanced away. She was going to say "sorry," but it felt like a pale, simpering word, and it had little to do with his comment. *Different.* She was really very different, but she didn't want to say that, either, because part of her wished she hadn't changed so much.

He'd changed, too. She'd known him when he was raw-boned and edgy, when his everlasting hunger burned in his eyes, but now she beheld a cautious, confident man who had made his mark. "I've only been back for a short time," she said quietly, suddenly noticing Jean's absence and wondering when she'd moved away. "But your father had become a friend."

Reese looked surprised. "To you?"

"He remembered me from . . ."

His surprise turned to expectancy. Would she say it? From the time he'd introduced her as "his girl" and she'd teased him about using a schoolboy's term? She'd used his greenness against him at times, embarrassed him in a shameless attempt to gain the upper hand in their impetuous courting game.

Unable to look him in the eye, she sidestepped, withdrawing her hand. "He invited me to ride his horses anytime, and of course I jumped at the opportunity. We visited about politics, history, folklore, all kinds of things. He had so much life in him, so many stories."

"What brings you back?"

"A job. The quest for the perfect job."

"And you came back here to Bad River?" He chuckled, shook his head in disbelief. He'd always worn his hair long, neatly trimmed, touching his shoulders in back. "Well, it's good to see you."

"Not like this, though."

"Why not? It's good that you came to say good-bye to your friend. You forget to do that sometimes."

A stab. So unlike him. She had to remind herself that she really didn't know him anymore. She had to remind him. "We said good-bye. In the rain that night. Remember?"

As soon as it was out, she was sorry she'd said it. She could feel the cold rain on her face, his wet shirt beneath her hands, his warm, promise-making breath in her ear. He'd said he figured he had one shot and now was the time to take it. He would call. He would be back. He would catch up with her.

Cold rain, she remembered, shivering inside as she noted the cooling in his eyes. "It was a long time ago," she said quietly.

"I didn't realize it was meant to be a final good-bye."

"It wasn't meant to be. As it turns out, it wasn't." She lifted her chin and offered a tight smile. "Hello again."

"Hello again." He stepped around her, turning his back to the room, as though he was putting her in his breast pocket to keep her to himself. She'd always liked the subtle way he had of positioning himself as her protector. "You never know, do you?" he said quietly, his gaze drifting to the coffin that stood several steps away. "Which good-bye will be the last."

"No." She laid her hand on his dark blue sleeve, and she realized she'd never seen him in a sport jacket before. She wondered whether he'd bothered to own one back then. "I guess the gods think they're being charitable, keeping us in the dark as we go our merry way."

"It's shadowy," he told her. "It's never completely dark. But if you pay attention to the shadows, you can get along pretty well." He shifted his big body again, turning her attention toward a pass-through window and tables laden with kettles and trays full of food. "Did you get something to eat?"

"No, I . . ." She looked up, all set to excuse herself. *Uncollected. Impolite.* "But I will."

"Good. The frybread's great. I haven't had any in a while." He shoved his hands into the pockets of his slacks and inhaled the aroma of deep-fried yeast bread as he edged her toward the table. "Ah, the smell of home."

"That was the first thing I looked for when I came back. I went to a powwow just to find a piece of . . ."

With a subtle chin jerk, he signaled one of the women who was tending the table. "Gramma, Helen needs some food. Some frybread to start with, right?"

"You come with me," the old woman said.

He touched Helen's shoulder, and she turned and found gratitude in his eyes. "It really is good to see you, Helen."

She was more interested in helping at the serving table than eating. From that vantage point she watched the people pay their condolences to Roy Blue Sky's sons. Roy had been a community leader, and there was a kind of honor due that was readily understood and easily managed. But Reese was a hometown hero, and that honor was not as easily managed. Not by Reese. It surprised her to see the underpinnings of his shyness in gestures she remembered so well. Surprising to see a man as big as he was, as physically imposing and adroit, fumble over an old man's handshake when the recollection of a particular play during a particular game was mentioned.

"No one could touch you that night," the man said. "You were unstoppable."

Shoulders back, head bowed, Reese gave a small nod and muttered an acknowledgment.

"We've got something we want to talk to you about later," the man said. "Not now, but pretty soon. *Toksa.* Me and some friends. Friends of your dad's, relatives, friends of . . ."

Reese lifted his chin, questioned with a look.

Somehow the look connected with Helen, although his eyes did not stray. He knew she was listening, even as she made a production of scraping the last of the potato salad from one bowl on top of the fresh mound in a bowl she'd just set out on the table. She scraped louder, faster, but still she listened. It was part of her job.

The man tapped Reese's chest with the back of his hand. "Not now, but before you head back to the Cities. We have things we want to say."

"Sure. You know where to find me."

"Out to your dad's place?"

Reese nodded, and the man motioned to a small boy who was wearing a T-shirt emblazoned with the name Minneapolis Mavericks, Reese's former NBA team. "This is my grandson. He wanted to meet you."

Reese shook hands with the child, then squatted to the boy's level and gave his full attention, as though they were the only two people in the room. The child had a story to tell, his small hands describing shapes and sizes, and Reese was right there with him for every detail. Helen pictured Sidney standing in the boy's place, his lanky arms measuring the size of a fish he'd caught or the length of a pass.

Reese looked up and caught her smiling. She turned away quickly. She knew what a silly look she'd permitted to cross her face and what sentimental notions were bound to follow, and she could allow herself none of that now. Just seeing him, even after all this time, was risky enough, but seeing how open he was to the child's interests, how he made the boy's whole face light up . . . *oh, lord.* She hadn't intended to see him again, not until Sidney was older. Her son's grandfather, yes, even his uncle, but his father wasn't part of the plan.

Reese's warm smile pricked that pouch of guilt she swore her obstetrician had stitched into her belly during her C-section. He'd probably been a basketball fan. A fan of the man who stood beside her now because she'd been eavesdropping and he'd caught her at it.

"How was the frybread? As good as you remembered?"

"Almost."

"For me, too. Almost. They say you can't go home again." He took a piece of frybread from the blue roaster pan on the table, tore it into two pieces, and offered her half. "Do you think that's true?"

"Not always. I think it depends on how long you've been gone and where you've been." *Whether you had the good sense to insist on a female obstetrician.* "And maybe on what you're looking for."

"Just a little taste of home." He ripped off a big bite of the chewy bread. She nibbled at the piece he'd given her. He swallowed and smiled. "Can't get it anywhere else. Why did that amuse you before—me and that kid?"

"Just the way he was so starstruck."

"That is funny, isn't it? I was probably all done by the time he could even say the word 'basketball.' His grandfather and the ol' man used to hang out together."

"They were on the council together, weren't they?"

"Before that." He waved frybread at their history. "They go way back."

"Do you . . ." She was about to play her hand unwisely, and she knew it, and she couldn't stop herself. ". . . have children?"

He shook his head. "Haven't had time for any of that. No wife. No kids. You?"

"I do have a son, yes. But his father and I are no longer together." It sounded so funny and formal, the way it came out. Cover-up came with the territory she'd ventured into as a casino investigator, and she'd gotten pretty good at it, but this was rough. Reese was looking at her with too much interest, and her stomach was getting itself in a twist. "And he's not with me. My . . . my son isn't."

"That must be hard."

"I miss him." He was looking at her with some new feeling. Sympathy? Oh, Lord, not that. She found a sunny smile and pasted it up front. "He's in camp this summer. He loves it. He loves . . ." *If you're smart, you'll say anything but . . .* "Sports."

"How old?"

"Ten." She'd said the number too quickly, and it reverberated, mocking her. This was more than custodial cover-up now. She was back to telling those "necessary" lies. "Almost eleven." He'd turned twelve.

"What sports does he like?"

"Everything. You name it. Swimming, hockey, baseball, anything involving . . ." Games, games. Oh, God, the man was tall. Looking right down into her devious brain. "Horses. He loves to ride."

"Like his mom, huh? How about basketball?"

"Any kind of ball. He loves . . ." Part of her didn't like the way this conversation was going, while another part of her was dying to go there with this man, to tell him, show him, and let him share in her parental pride. It was past time to get a grip, to clamp down on that foolish second part. "Well, he's an active boy."

"That's good."

She nodded, the words *Yes, you'd get along fine* burning in her brain.

"You have to share him with his father?" When she didn't look up at him, didn't answer, he quietly apologized. "None of my business."

"That's not it. I just . . . it's complicated."

"Seems like it always—"

"Hey, Blue!"

They'd both been so absorbed that the interruption startled them. It was a tribal police officer, stopping to help himself to half a bologna sandwich on his way over.

Reese scanned the room, looking for help. "I don't know where my brother is. I gotta talk to this guy, but . . ." He touched Helen's arm. "I want you to meet my sister. She's around here somewhere. Don't go away."

She didn't. She still had a job to do. In fact, she used his request as an excuse to stay within earshot of another of his conversations. She didn't catch all of it, but she gathered that the driver who had killed his father had still not been found and that the police had plenty of questions but no answers.

They were questions she'd already been asked. She had left Roy's place at about ten the night he died. She was the last person known to have seen him alive. She had already recounted much of the discussion they'd had, explaining to the police that she and Roy had become friends, that she enjoyed his sense of humor and the stories he told her. She sensed some skepticism on the investigator's part. Why would a young white woman be paying a social call on an old Indian man alone at ten o'clock at night? He was telling her stories? Strange he should turn up dead.

But then, Bad River was a strange place. An unusual place where the people were living in the detached backwater of the mainstream and where they had gotten by on so little for so long. Policy after policy, one government program after another, had failed to do much except compound the problems that isolation, lack of resources, and a history of injustice had caused.

Then, suddenly, the Indian Gaming Regulatory Act arose in the East like the promise of a new day. Here was new possibility for new enterprise, although, according to Roy Blue Sky, gambling was not a new enterprise for his people. But the form it was taking now was new. In the form of casino gaming, the pastime had taken on some new wrinkles, and Roy was suspicious of wrinkles. "Trouble can hide in the folds," he'd said once. She'd waited for him to elaborate, but he had given her a fable instead. Finding trouble was her job. He must have known, she thought as she gazed down at the inanimate mask that had once been his warm face.

Coyote loves to gamble. They say he lost his whole tribe one time to the Knife River People. So he turned himself into a really good-looking man, and he talked Gray Badger out of three of his daughters. Then he took those daughters back to the Knife River village, and he said he wanted to play a dice game. And he said he would bet his fine new brides, who could breed some muscle into those bandy-legged Knife Rivers. Got them all snorty, talking like that. But all the while, Coyote had this little bird hidden in his thick hair, right behind his ear, and when they got to playing—

"They did a good job, didn't they?"

Helen looked up as Carter Marshall joined her at his dead father's side. Carter favored his father more than Reese did. Carter and Roy were closer to the same height, same build, and she now saw they had exactly the same ears, turned out like half-open doors. It seemed ironic that Roy had given this likeness of himself away when Carter was a baby, given him up for adoption and later taken him back. She knew little about either deed except that a change in the law had permitted the latter. The Indian Child Protection Act had returned Carter to his father's house when he was a teenager. She knew all about that law. She had a copy of it tucked away at home.

"He looks peaceful, doesn't he?" Carter said.

Helen nodded as she extended her hand. "I'm so sorry."

"Thank you." He smiled, but he was already looking around the room for something or someone else, as though he'd been signaled. She was tempted to check behind his ears for birds, but Carter was like a bird himself, always keeping an eye out for the next perch. "Just got here. So many details to look after, you wouldn't believe it. I had to stop in at the casino, plus call my wife and make sure she's bringing the kids over." He squeezed her hand quickly before drawing his away. "You're on the schedule tonight."

"I know."

"Everything's going to be closed tomorrow for the funeral. Even the casinos. He'd like that. Show of respect. His favorite word." He glanced at his father's corpse again, then back to Helen. "Did you get something to eat?"

"Yes, thank you."

"Well, look at this. Isn't that Rick Marino, the basketball player?" Carter nodded toward the door, where the man who had just entered with a small entourage was turning heads. If he wasn't a basketball player, his height had gone to waste. He was the only man in the room who stood taller than Reese, who was welcoming him with a handshake.

"He's got a hell of a nerve," Carter said. "He wants to build a big casino over by Spearfish. He's trying to get the state to change the laws and up the betting limits to suit his plans. Must be nice to be famous." He shoved his hands in his pants pockets as he eyed the two giants. "We'll have to raise the roof to accommodate my brother's friends, won't we?"

"The door frames at least."

"I gotta meet this guy. Come on, we'll get an autograph." This remark made Helen draw a quick scowl. "Just kidding," Carter said. "A handshake's plenty."

"But you just said he had a hell of a nerve."

"So do I. Hell, *we* were here first. We're established. We've got Ten Star behind us, and Ten Star has deep pockets." Carter smiled, still watching the two once-famous rivals, who were plainly exchanging friendly words. "Let him pay his respects to both of us. And to my father." He tapped her on the arm. "Don't be shy, Helen."

"I'm not. I have to be on the floor in . . ." She checked her watch, even though they both knew she had plenty of time. It was a good opportunity to quietly withdraw.

"On second thought, I don't think I want to introduce my best dealer to a prospective competitor." Her boss excused her with a nod. "Thanks for coming."

She left without saying another word to Reese or to Jean. Suddenly there was only one person she wanted to talk to, and he was five hundred miles away. She found a phone at the Standard station.

It was suppertime at camp, the best time to get hold of her son. She tried not to call too often, but staying away from the phone wasn't easy. This was the first time he had been away from her for more than a week, and a week had seemed interminable. Yet he'd wanted this particular summer camp for his birthday. It had been a major expense for Helen, but he was such a gifted child, and gifted children needed special gifts, special opportunities. Helen wanted to make up for what was missing in Sidney's life by giving him more opportunities, often expensive ones. It was right that she should pay. It was the way of the modern, guilt-ridden parent.

She managed a casual greeting when he came on the phone. He'd been too old for a gushy mother since the day he'd started kindergarten.

"Everything's great, Mom. Tomorrow we're going backpacking up in the San Juan Mountains. We're only going to eat what we can harvest on the trail."

Across the road, three boys were playing marbles in the dirt. She didn't know kids still played marbles. She smiled. "What if there's nothing to harvest? It's pretty late in the season, isn't it?"

"There's always food, Mom. This is a survival test."

"But you'll have a little trail mix along just in case."

"No way. That would be, like, wimping out. The counselors might have something stuffed away in their bag of tricks, but I'll just be roughing it."

"I sent them a boy; they're sending me back a man?"

"That's what you're paying them for. I scored fourteen points in basketball last night. I'm getting pretty good."

She closed her eyes and nodded, picturing him in his over-sized shorts, his hair sweaty, sticking to his neck. He wanted to let it grow, maybe wear it in braids. He'd suggested that when he'd been mad at her for a remark someone had made at school. Someone who was white, like his mother, had made a remark about his being a half-breed, and he'd told her he didn't like the word, didn't like it that he never seemed to be or have or do any more than half of something. He just didn't like the sound of "half," so he was going to go the whole way and the hell with the white part of him that didn't count for anything because it was the Indian part that showed more. She'd asked him not to swear, and he'd ignored her. Hell, he was almost *twelve*.

"Sounds better than pretty good to me. How about your writing?"

"I'm keeping a journal, which is, like, part of the program. I try to write in it every day."

"I was thinking about a letter."

"Jeez, there's so much going on, Mom. I haven't had time for any letters."

Good Lord, his voice was changing. He sounded so much older, so much like a man, like . . .

I haven't had time for any letters. The words could have been Reese's echo.

"So what have you been up to, Mom?"

"Just dealing cards, sweetheart."

"Not *just*. You're on a case, right?"

She laughed. "You make me sound like 'Bond. Jane Bond.' " Sidney did the accent better than she did. "Yes, but I'll have it wrapped up by the time your program is over."

"You're letting me stay through both sessions, right?"

"Is that what you want to do?"

She heard her own hesitancy, and she wanted to attribute it strictly to the fact that this would be a long separation, the longest she and her son had ever experienced, and it was too soon for him to be easy with it. He was still a boy. She wasn't Mommy anymore, but she was still Mom. And Mom didn't want that hesitancy to come from any place but her lonely heart. Her son was so far away, and at this point, she knew she was going to need more time to get her job done. *Mom* would not allow Helen's slightly shady job to cloud her noblest instincts. But Helen had a job to do. Helen was the bread-winner.

"You know what's really cool?" Sidney was saying. "Everybody else in the program is Indian. I'm not the only one, you know? There's guys from Alaska and Florida and Montana and New York. They're from all over the place, Mom. But we're all at least part Indian, and it's cool."

What had been even cooler was that Helen had not had to provide proof of tribal enrollment for this program, which was partly funded by federal money. Sidney's teachers had recommended him, and all she'd had to do was sign a statement that he had at least one Native American grandparent. She hoped she hadn't risked any kind of exposure by signing the document and filling in the word "Lakota" under tribal affiliation. That seemed vague enough. There were many Lakota tribes.

There was no documentation of Sidney's affiliation. In the first year of a twelve-year history of haunting lies, she had put "father unknown" on his birth certificate. She had never come any closer to overturning that lie—other than explaining that the reason he looked "different" was that he was half Indian—than she had when she'd signed his application for the summer program.

It had been a good move. He was having a ball. She could hear it in his voice.

"You can stay, but I want at least one letter a week. Deal?"

"There's a big deal for parents at the end."

"I'll be there."

"You won't believe how much I have to show you."

"I can't wait."

The boys across the road had finished their game, and the smallest one was claiming the winnings. *Something was always wagered*, Roy had said. *Even the young ones learned to bet what they valued against what they hoped to gain. As long as you draw breath you will gamble. Everyone does.*

"I miss you, you know."

"I know. I'll try to write sometime. Listen, I gotta go." But he hung on, and she did, too, hoping there was more. He cleared his throat. "I miss you, too, Mom."

The following day Helen attended the funeral of Roy Blue Sky. She stayed at the edge of the crowd. She waited in line to shake hands with his family. His two sons, his grandchildren, the daughter Helen had never met but whose stature and features and regal solemnity were unmistakably Blue Sky.

An eagle hovered above the mourners as they lowered the casket. It circled when they dropped gifts into the grave, and it circled still, resplendent against the clear cerulean sky, as they took turns at the shovels. Women trilled, men pounded a drum and sang their ancient song, and male and female tears flowed generously. Helen kept to herself, but she would hold the memory for her son. He should have been there. By all rights, she knew he should have been there.

She also knew instinctively, while she listened to the heavy clay fall into the hole, that Roy's death was no accident. The old man had not been afraid to blow the whistle, to call for an investigation that could implicate some of the people who stood around his grave. Management, employees, tribal officials, even Roy's own son. How many of these people knew about the investigation? Roy had bypassed Ten Star's in-house monitors and contacted the Bureau of Indian Affairs, which was the reason Helen was involved. Roy's suspicion that somebody was taking the tribe to the cleaners was no secret, but had he told anyone that he'd done more than just make some local noise? Nobody loved a whistle-blower, and Roy no longer had breath to blow.

But Helen did. She had breath, skill, and mandate. And she had duty to a friend.

2

*T*he woman still made him feel like King Kong peering over the treetops at Jessica Lange. He knew damn well she was a different breed, but just the smell of her hair made him feel like turning cartwheels. The thought of Reese Blue Sky turning himself into a windmill over a woman made him laugh. Now *that* would sell tickets.

He didn't remember exactly how long it had been since he'd seen her—he generally wasn't one to count the years too precisely—but he hadn't forgotten her. She was the one who got away. He'd been backward and boyish, desperately hanging onto the illusion of cool, and she'd walked away when his back was turned. He should have tied her to a tree when he'd had the chance.

He pulled the rented Lincoln Town Car up to the casino's main entrance, under the sprawling portico bearing the Pair-a-Dice City sign, which was impressively spotlighted at night. But it was early afternoon now, and the parking lot was two-thirds empty, so he figured this was a good time to drop in. He'd just come from the Rapid City airport, where he'd put his sister, Rose, on a flight back to Eugene.

Maybe he wasn't exactly dropping in. He knew Helen would be there. He'd called a friend who worked in the front office and asked for her schedule. Truth was, he didn't much like casinos, but he was curious about Helen's quest for the perfect job. He was curious about *Helen*. Damn, it had been good to see her. After they'd gone their separate ways, it hadn't taken her long to hook up with somebody else and have a kid, but he wasn't going to get hung up on details. A dozen years would add up to a lot of details. He was just curious about the big picture. How was Helen, the unforgettable woman who had stolen his young heart?

The uniformed valet who opened the car door had finally found his ideal job, if not the ideal uniform. Elvis Spotted Dog's paunch was about to win the battle with his shirt buttons, but Reese remembered the way Elvis had loved nothing better than getting behind the wheel of someone else's car when they were in high school. He still had the aviator shades and the slick black pompadour. Without much facial hair, he had never had a serious option of sideburns, but whenever anyone called him "the King," he fell right into character.

"Hey, Blue, how's the Big Gun?"

"Still hangin'. How's the King?"

"The King lives. Tell the *Enquirer* you saw him yourself on the Indian casino circuit." Elvis grinned and patted his belly. "Tell them he's still just a hunk-a hunk-a." With a laugh, he whacked Reese on the shoulder. "Or a hunk-a *hunka*." With the nasal Lakota inflection and a shift of emphasis, the word meant *ancestor*. "Ol' El played an Indian pretty good in that one movie."

"We're all related, son." Reese's Elvis imitation had the King cackling as he claimed the driver's seat and immediately started testing out buttons on the control panel. "You'll be a hunk-a Graceland grits if I find any dents in this barge."

"This is one fancy buggy, Blue."

"It's a rental, and I waived the insurance, so take it easy."

"Mind if I adjust the seat?"

Reese laughed. "Don't get yourself wedged in."

The car started rolling. "Mind if I pop in a tape?"

"Are they paying you by the hour here?"

Grinning, the King leaned out the window and adjusted his shades, his chunky Black Hills gold ring flashing in the sun. "Bet red."

Reese nodded and tapped on the car roof to send Elvis on his way. It was good to see people working. He'd lost count of the number of people he'd visited with during the vigil over his father who had talked about their casino jobs. If the gaming industry could put a dent in unemployment on the reservation, he was all for it.

But he still didn't like casinos.

He didn't like the flashing lights or the drifts of smoke or the random *cling-cling-cling* announcing a slot machine payout. He especially didn't like the eyes of some of the players seated at the machines. Some looked as though they'd been watching TV for a week. Others resembled those of guys coming off a four-day drunk. But the eyes that bothered him the most were the brightest ones, the ones that looked cornered and scared, the desperate ones. A desperate player was a sure loser. Reese didn't like losers. When he was losing, he didn't much like himself. But he loved playing the game, and he sure loved winning. Cards and dice simply didn't enter into it.

The feeling that he'd lost something with Helen Ketterling had nagged at him periodically over the years. The nagging had become distant, like somebody calling to him once in a while from a back room. But now she'd opened the door and peeked in. Of course, she'd disappeared without a word from his father's wake, as she had in the past. He had to come looking for her, but that was okay. Pride wasn't such a big deal to him anymore.

He rounded the corner on a bank of quarter slots just as an elderly man in bib overalls and a faded Cargill cap hit paydirt. He looked up at Reese as though his score was something they might have in common. Reese smiled, gave the guy's row of cherries its due nod.

"You stick with her long enough, sooner or later she'll put out," the man said cheerfully. He bracketed the machine between his thighs while a gush of quarters tumbled into the tray.

Reese felt like someone who'd caught himself peering

though a keyhole. He turned away. "I'm looking for the black-jack tables."

"Some in the middle, some straight back. Depends on what kind of betting limit you're looking for."

"I'm looking for a dealer."

Reese was pulling away, but he could hear the old man raking his change into a plastic cup. "Not too busy this time of day," the man was saying. "You can probably have one all to yourself for as long as your chips hold out."

It was unsettling to see her standing there, waiting, arranging fans of cards on the green table. He imagined a forsaken hostess absently playing with the unused table settings for a party that had never got off the ground. A strand of summer-gold hair that had escaped from the clip at her nape sketched a long, lazy s from her forehead to her delicate chin. Soft, polished, elegant. She was just as compelling to him now as she had been the first time he'd seen her coming toward him across the school playground.

Reese was no card player, but if she had been selling fruit-cakes from last Christmas, he'd be pulling out his billfold.

"What do I need to get into this game?"

"Money to burn." She met his gaze, then lifted her chin. "And time."

"Got those bases covered." But the handful of bills he offered without counting might well have been aflame, the way she waved them off. "It's perfectly legal tender," he told her. "Best kind of tinder. Or do I need chips? They burn, too, but they've gotta be—"

"I can't take it from your hand. Put it down and I'll exchange it for you." She counted his cash and announced the amount to the pit boss as she slipped the money into a slot on her side of the table. She gave him two stacks of chips. "Is this another one of your games?" she asked quietly, sliding over two stacks of colored chips.

"Not unless I get points for flipping the cards into some kind of a hole."

"This is a twenty-five-dollar table."

"So the sign says. One of these, right?" He placed a green chip in the box before him. "Where are you staying?"

"I've subleased Carmen Benzinger's place. Are the cards to your liking?"

He remembered he was supposed to see that the required components of all four decks were there and they weren't marked, a gesture he considered a formality, like tasting the wine you'd ordered for dinner. Hell, it was . . . "Fine." She flipped all of them over with a neat domino trick, and he grinned. "Excellent." He didn't care if she had an ace up each of her crisp white sleeves.

"You're not looking."

"Sure I am. Show me the Ketterling shuffle."

Her fine-boned hands fascinated him, so deftly did they handle not one deck but four. She made it look as though the cards had a life of their own and she was just keeping them contained while she made conversation.

"You remember Carmen, don't you? She still teaches biology. She's up at UND for the summer."

"I remember her. Your sidekick. I saw her once when I was home, and I asked her about you." He waited until she glanced up at him. "She said she'd lost track, never heard from you anymore."

Helen offered a tight smile. "I'm not very good about keeping in touch."

"Guess I'm not, either."

"I saw you on TV a few times, playing basketball."

"You never watch TV," he recalled.

"Did I actually say 'never'?" He nodded once, challenging her to admit it. She handed him a colored cut card. " 'Never' is such a bad word. A surefire liar-maker."

"Not if you like double negatives." Which she didn't. He remembered that she'd corrected him once or twice. He eyed the stack of cards, picked a spot, and stabbed with the cut card. It figured to be his best move of the game. He smiled at the dealer. "So you *didn't never* see me play basketball on TV?"

"Didn't never."

"Two negatives equal a positive," he quoted.

"It's kind of exciting when you actually know someone who's playing." She dropped the cards into the plastic box, or "shoe," from which she would deal. Then she "burned" the top card in the discard rack. "I think I've even dropped your name once or twice."

"Dropped or drop-kicked?"

"Dribbled." She brightened as she demonstrated in front of his nose, her pretty hand tickling the keys of an air piano. "Sprinkled it like holy water when I thought it might raise the dead. You know, during an uncomfortable lull in the conversation."

"And did it?"

"It worked if there were any serious basketball fans in the room." She shrugged off any illusions he might be harboring. "Well, your name isn't exactly Magic."

He laughed. "Still easy on the eyes and hard on the ego."

"Only because your ego always seemed invulnerable."

"Really." He remembered being invulnerable once upon a time, but it was ancient history. He chuckled. "You didn't know me very long. A piece of a summer."

"Not very long or very well, really. Except in the biblical sense."

"Is that what that was? And they said I didn't learn anything at the mission school."

They shared a laugh, surprisingly as easy as it was intimate, the response to sweet memories that were theirs alone.

She dealt him a ten of clubs.

"What are you doing in this joint?" he asked. "I thought you liked teaching."

"I did." The cards were down. She was showing a nine. "I do. This is the part where you tell me what you want and I give it to you."

He looked at his hand. "I want an ace, but a ten or—"

"Tap the table for a card." He did. She gave him less than he wanted, so he tapped again. "I love teaching, but this is what I'm doing now."

He stood on eighteen. She ended up with nineteen. "You're good at it," he allowed as she claimed his bet.

"I know the game, and I enjoy getting paid by the hour to play it. The odds favor this side of the table." He was still waiting for an answer. She smiled. "This is just temporary."

"You're just here for the summer?" He anted up again.

"I left abruptly before. Transferred. Took a job closer to Denver, which is . . ."

"Where you came from," he finished for her.

"I've always wanted to come back to Bad River, though, at least for a visit. I think I needed closure."

"Closure?" He glanced at the cards she'd dealt him, then quickly sheltered them, creating a roof over them with his big hands. He didn't remember what they were except that one had a face. "Like nailing down the lid on the box?"

What he wanted from the opposite side of the table in that instant was a real hand, a human hand, her hand touching his. According to the sign on the table, it was against the house rules. No contact, no touching. What kind of a game was this? Sterile at best. You looked down, and there was a cold face, some face of hearts. The house was cold, the heart was cold.

But, damn, they weren't his. They were not his shabby house, not his faulty heart, not *his*, these cold things that created gloom.

I don't care what's in the cards, just touch my hand.

"I'm really sorry, Reese."

His back stiffened. "For what?"

"I liked your father a lot, and I'm so sorry he's gone."

He couldn't look at her just now. He nodded. "But now we get this closure thing, right?" In the absence of touching, sarcasm felt good. He looked at his cards again. Good hand. Cool, stiff hand, a breaking hand. The kind a cool guy would play cool, offer a cool smile, cool talk, like, "Put the body in the box, close the lid, say a few words, and drop him in the ground. Case closed." Cool, dismissive gesture. "And what a case he was."

"You still have some issues with your father," she said carefully, still waiting for his decision on a card. "But as far as the case being . . ."

"Issues?" He shook his head, admonishing her with a look, then a laugh. "Closure and issues. You want to be careful about throwing that kind of psychobullshit around. Somebody might mistake you for a therapist. Or is that part of a dealer's job?" He signaled, finally, that he would stay. "Gamblers cry on your shoulder much?"

33

"No. I'm just a machine. Almost as impersonal as a slot."

"As a . . ."

"*Slot*," she said with a coy smile. "Machine."

"Ah." He sat back, smiling because he was enjoying this exchange and because he had a winning hand this time. "They don't talk back."

"And I'm not supposed to. I'm supposed to shut up and deal the cards." She had to draw to her sixteen, and she broke with an eight.

"I'm more interested in the dealer than the cards, but please go ahead and deal. In my game, when you're tied you have to keep playing."

"The odds are against—"

He glanced past her at the man who'd just appeared on the landing near the bar. "Better shut up and deal. Your boss is looking."

"Your brother?"

"I have issues with him, too." He placed his next bet, the signal for another hand. "My head is all messed up, Doctor Dealer. What I need is a new deal. All new cards. Can you help me out?"

"The best I can do is hit you."

"As cold as that sounds, it's still real tempting, coming from you." He looked at his cards. "But I can't take much of a hit. Pretty close to the edge here, Doctor. Can you advise me?"

"No."

"I'll take what I can get, then. Hit me. Hard, if you want." He looked up, offered a slow, enticing smile.

Left him feeling pretty silly when she didn't bite.

"What you said about your father's case being closed, were you . . . I mean, it isn't really closed, is it? The police . . ." She gave him a card, which they both ignored.

"It was hit-and-run. They figure the hitter had been running for a good sixteen, eighteen hours by the time they found the body. Had a good head start. They won't catch up to him."

"But they're trying, aren't they?"

"They say they are, but this is the rez. Crimes go unsolved here all the time. Our own cops and courts don't do the big ones, the felonies. That's federal, which is another world." He shrugged, glanced away, swallowed some resentments he figured he'd inherited, the ones that came wrapped around your neck when you were born on a reservation. "Anyway, what difference does it make? If they find the driver, what, we've got more closure?"

"At least you'll know for sure what happened. It's a terrible thing to just drive away."

"You're right about that. I'm good with this hand." He signaled that he was staying with his cards, and he was working on a follow-up to the hand hint when he noticed his brother ambling down the five carpeted steps as if he owned the place. Damn, he was about to butt in and likely take over. Good old Mr. Smooth.

Helen turned over the card they'd both lost interest in seeing. "And the thing is, your father was an important man who had a lot of"—she glanced up at Reese as she claimed the bet he'd just lost—"irons in the fire."

"How're we doing over here?" Carter asked, moving in next to Helen. "I do believe this is the first time my brother has actually set foot in our establishment. What do you think of all this? Not too bad for a little halfway-to-nowhere rez, huh?"

"It's . . ." Reese made a pretense of taking a survey. "Flashy."

"Not like what you're used to in the Cities, but for around here, this is excitement. Not so much this time of day. Nights and weekends we draw quite a crowd. This lady right here draws a crowd." Helen questioned the claim with a look, and Carter grinned like a proud papa. "You do. The cowboys wait in line for a seat at your table." He slid Reese a sly wink. "One guy told me he just liked watching her hands."

"Good way to lose your shirt," Reese said.

"Not here. We're only interested in your money. Right, Helen? Gotta watch this guy. If he starts betting his clothes, you call me."

"Yes, I will, Mr. Marshall."

"Didn't anyone offer you something to drink?" Carter signaled a woman with a tray. "What's your pleasure? You know, you ought to take a look at the lodge, brother. You'd be more comfortable here than out at the ol' man's place. I stay here a lot myself. You don't know what kind of restless spirits might be wandering around out there. *Gigis*, you know."

Reese accepted a soft drink since the young woman had gone to the trouble of making the detour. "When did you start worrying about *gigis?*"

"After my big brother left me with no protection." Carter washed the dry joke down with his own drink, then hoisted the glass in his brother's direction. "He went away and left me stranded with a bunch of ghosts. The old man was stuck in the past. It was getting to the point where all he really wanted to do was hold us back."

Us meaning the tribe. Reese still thought it remarkable that Carter had been able to turn around so completely. Their mother had died shortly after Carter was born, and a priest had persuaded their father to give the baby up. The church had placed Carter with a white family in New York. Rose had gone to live with their grandmother. Reese was old enough to go to school and make up his own mind, and when his father had asked him whether he wanted to go away, too, he'd said no. So he had stayed and looked after Roy. In his mind, that was what he was doing, even though he was only about six.

Years later, when Roy had dragged Carter back kicking and screaming from the Marshalls of New York, Reese couldn't help wondering what the point of it was, besides the fact that Carter was some kind of whiz kid and Reese was just another Indian ball player. Roy had said that it was important for Carter to know who he was, and since he'd been instrumental in getting the Indian Child Protection Act through Congress, he was bound and determined to use it to get his son back. Carter had been so miserable in Indian schools that eventually Roy had let him finish up at a private school. But when he'd gone to Harvard and discovered the term "Native American," Carter had stopped kicking.

And now he was managing the casino. Good for him, Reese thought. He looked good in his blazer with the Bad River Sioux symbol embroidered on the breast pocket. He was obviously pretty proud of who he was now and what he did, and

Reese didn't doubt that he was successful at it. His brother was smart as a fox.

But the idea that the old man had wanted to hold *us* back inexplicably rubbed Reese the wrong way.

"When are you heading for home?" Carter asked.

"I don't know yet."

"Not before we play a little one-on-one," Carter said. "Sarah says if I bring you along I can have Sunday dinner with her and the kids. I've been living pretty much in the doghouse lately, but you could help me get back in her good graces, and the kids would get a charge out of watching their dad play round ball with their uncle."

"Yeah, *now* you want to play me."

"Hell, you can still play an amateur like me, can't you? You're not *that* damn stove up."

Reese laughed. "Stove up" wasn't a Carter Marshall kind of expression. "I'll bring the blindfold, little brother. How bad do you want me to make you look in front of your kids?"

"You're coming out, then? Hey, great." Carter nodded to a man with a walkie-talkie on the upper level, indicating he'd be there soon. "You come, too, Helen. And Rose, let's make it—"

"Rose left. I drove her to the airport. Her flight was this morning, remember?" Reese smiled when Carter whacked his forehead with the heel of his hand. The truth was that Carter and Rose hardly knew each other. "She said to tell you good-bye. You gonna help me with the ol' man's stuff?"

"You're not serious, are you? About burning it?" He tapped Helen on the arm with the back of his hand. "You'd think a guy like this would have given up the blanket a long time ago, right? He thinks he has to torch the personal effects or one of our local *gigis* is gonna get him."

"It's what he would want. There are times when you just do it out of respect. But anything you want to keep, other than . . ." Reese glanced at Helen. This wasn't something they needed to be discussing in front of her.

"He left it up to you," Carter pointed out. "He even put it in writing, which sure surprised the hell out of me, that he'd bother with a will. But he did, and it's out of respect that I'm leaving it all in your capable hands."

Reese shrugged. "I didn't know you two were on the outs."

"How could you? You haven't been around enough to—" Carter started backing away. The guy with the walkie-talkie was still waiting. "This isn't gonna come between you and me, Blue. You're here, and that's good. For however long you can be here, that's great. You're coming for Sunday dinner. Both of you." He headed up the stairs.

"Sunday dinner," Reese mused. "Sounds wholesome, doesn't it? Sunday dinner, family gathering, nice, big Blue Sky. What do you say, Helen?"

Her hands were folded, looking prim and patient next to the chip rack. "It's hard for me to get away."

"From *this?*"

"I have a crazy schedule," she said, and he knew *she* knew exactly how lame that sounded. He looked her in the eye and waited. "I don't think it's a good idea, Reese."

"Whatever you say." He wasn't going to ask her twice. "I'll be staying at my dad's for a while. He dumped a lot of loose ends in my lap by leaving the place to me. Said Carter wouldn't want it. I don't know what made him think *I* would, but . . ." He tapped the edge of the table with a fist and rose from the stool. "So that's where I'll be."

She nodded.

"Looks like that line's forming." He jerked his chin, indicating the approach of a couple of those cowboys Carter had mentioned, and he'd be damned if he was going to share her with them. "Thanks for the lesson. You're still a good teacher."

Getting out of the casino turned out to be trickier than getting in. Reese hadn't been home in a while, and it felt good to be recognized and remembered by old friends and newly discovered shirttail relations rather than just basketball fans. He was greeted by a cousin who used to help his father put up hay in the summer and was now eager to tell him about his job in the casino restaurant. He remembered going to school with one of the security guards, and there was a cashier who had been a cheerleader back in the old days. "Hey, Titus is here," she told him, and she pulled out her walkie-talkie. "Have you seen him yet?"

"Titus Hawk? He was at the funeral, but there were so many . . ."

So many faces, and some had surely changed more than others, but Titus still had that hook-billed nose and the scraggly goatee the team used to razz him about. He'd been a quick, feisty guard, and he was still lean and wiry, still took a boxer's stance, threw a playful punch, finally offered a handshake. Yeah, Reese said, he could use some coffee. They found an empty table in a corner near the bar and sat down to relive the glory days. Titus gave Reese a glimpse of himself in terms of contemporary Bad River folklore. Once merely bigger than average, he was now stronger, smarter, richer, cooler, better, and badder. He owned the world.

"Might as well pop that bubble right now," Reese said with a laugh. "I own a limo service, some interest in a small chain of sporting goods stores, some property that needs developing, some property that I never want to see developed, a condo, and a cat that somebody dumped on me."

"What, no yacht?"

Reese shrugged. "Got a pretty nice canoe. Oh, and a Cherokee."

"A Cherokee? What are they good for?"

Reese caught the twinkle in his old friend's eye and bounced it back to him. "Hell, she irons my shirts."

They shared another laugh, proving to each other that some things hadn't changed. Then Titus said, "Why don't you come home? We could use a limo service. I don't like the idea of Reese Blue Sky chauffeuring them rich eastern Sioux around."

Reese chuckled. "They're not all rich."

"That Mystic Lake bunch is, though, south of the Twin Cities there."

"They did their time being poor."

"Like you?"

"What, you gotta be poor to be Sioux?"

"*Lakota*," Titus chided. "We're Lakota again, man. Didn't you see the sign when you crossed the river into Indian country? We took our real name back. Bad River Lakota Nation."

"I know who we are. The ol' man drummed it into me good." He'd been thinking about it, too, couldn't help thinking about it with his father's hoard of stuff surrounding him out there at the place and that voice that was like a damned recording in his head. "He missed out with Carter, so I got a double dose of Lakota history. I don't know how we could've lost so much ground the way we kept 'whipping their asses,' to hear him tell it."

"Here lately he was on TV almost as much as you used to be. All them Indian history shows they've been making?" Titus sketched the titles in the air. " 'Roy Blue Sky, tribal elder,' written right across the bottom of the screen, with him sitting there dressed up all snazzy and telling it from our side. He was getting to be more famous than Russell Means."

"I've got some of the videotapes."

"Ordered them off the toll-free number on TV?" After Reese nodded, Titus said, "I called, too, but you gotta have a credit card."

Reese had almost forgotten how difficult it was to get credit when you lived on a reservation. But this casino was a different story. A new story, one that might have some gold teeth.

"What do you do around here? What's a gambling commissioner?" Reese smiled and raised an eyebrow. "You got a job, or just a title?"

"I'm like the watchdog. I'm looking after the tribe's interests. Ten Star—you know, the management company the tribe hired to set this thing up—well, they look after *their* interests pretty good. Me, I'm on the Bad River Gaming Commission. When I walk through that door, these people better be shifting their asses into high gear. There's not much that gets past me. Hell, you know that." Titus stabbed a finger across the table. "We were a team, Blue. This state's never seen anything like us, before or since."

"I know."

"You won more games with us than you did with the Minneapolis Mavericks."

It wasn't true, but Reese nodded anyway.

"You were great with them, too. First year?" Titus

shrugged that one off. "You were just startin' out. After that, those next few seasons? You were something else, man."

Reese nodded again. He knew how to deal with this now. He had plenty of practice at sitting there and letting it wash over him while he thought about something else, like maybe he ought to polish up his blackjack game and take Helen on again.

But Titus was wound up on coffee and glory days. "All that time there were seven of us guys back here living those years with you," he was saying, "helping you get your mileage out of it. Four times seven, that's twenty-eight years, man. That's a damned good career."

"But after that . . ."

"After that you got the hard-luck trophy for us a couple of times. I got a hell of a load of sympathy because you were hurtin' so bad, and I was hurtin' for you. I got laid more than once on your account."

"No shit?" Reese laughed. "I sure got the short end of that stick."

"*Tuwale*," Titus admonished. "You worry about your stick, I'll worry about mine." He sat back, grinning. "You really like that city life?"

"It has its advantages."

"I ain't lyin', we could use a limo service. We've got a lot of competition in this business. We could use some of those advantages. Even one. Even one advantage would help."

"You've got that federal gaming act. Some people out in Atlantic City claim that's a hell of an advantage."

"It's an advantage for anybody who knows how use it. Outfits like Ten Star. And maybe for those hundred-member tribes all of a sudden popping their heads out of the woods. But, hell, we've got some jobs out of the deal. We've got this place. It's a nice place to go have a little fun, get a good meal. And it's *ours*. The Bad River Sioux Tribe welcomes you."

"Lakota Nation," Reese amended with a smile.

Titus looked him in the eye. "Come on back home, Blue."

"I'm back in school," Reese averred. "One more semester, I'll have my degree."

"You already went to college."

"Started. Didn't finish. All I could think about was playing basketball and making a pile of money. When I started having problems with—with injuries, all I could think about was myself, you know, how my whole body was . . ." He looked at Titus for a moment. Injuries, yeah, he'd understand bone chips and torn ligaments. But some muscles were more vital than others, and a guy hated to talk about those over coffee. He dismissed his body with a quick gesture. "Now I'm back in school, and I'm getting that degree this time so I can do something with myself."

"The limo business ain't workin' out?"

"You know why I started that?"

Titus shrugged and leaned closer to find out.

"A driver refused to take my check. I went to an ATM, got him his cash, told him to start looking for another job 'cause I was gonna buy his car right out from under him."

"Didn't he know who you were?"

"Hell, Titus, I ain't exactly Magic."

The laugh they shared was interrupted by a ruckus in an alcove close by.

"No!" a woman shouted. "No, I can't go home without that money!"

Titus turned around in his seat to see what was going on. Reese had a feeling he didn't want to know, but he asked anyway. "What's back there?"

"Offices," Titus said. "Crying room."

"Crying room?"

"That's what I call it. People win big-time, you wanna put 'em on display. People lose big-time, you kinda wish they'd tough it out quietly, you know? Like we've been doing for how long now?"

A plump, middle-aged, red-eyed woman backed into view through an open door in the alcove. "I need to see the manager. I just want to talk to him." Somebody in the room was talking to her, but she was having none of it. "No, you get me the manager first."

Reese counted three employees in the immediate vicinity getting on their walkie-talkies. Two security guards appeared, each quickly taking hold of an arm, but the woman hauled back on them. "No, I'm not leaving. Not without my money."

Carter emerged from another door and said something to her in a low tone.

"But I didn't know what was happening," she said, trying to square herself up and claim some semblance of composure. "I don't know what came over me. I didn't realize I'd lost that much. I thought—"

Carter's quiet response wasn't what she wanted to hear, so she turned to the white security guard. "See, I thought I'd put most of it away. Right here, see?" She thrust her hand into her shoulder bag and brandished a small pouch. "This is my safe keeping. I always—I *never* dip into . . ."

The three men were moving the woman a few steps at a time, Carter walking and talking with his head bowed. They'd almost reached a "Staff Only" door when she balked again. "I want my money back."

"We can't do that, Marilyn," Carter said. "We can't refund your losses. You know the rules."

"It wasn't fair." She was wild-eyed now, and Reese could almost feel her heart pounding, which made him very uncomfortable. "The game wasn't fair. It wasn't . . . and I wasn't even playing that long. I just came in—"

"You were in here yesterday, Marilyn."

"I know, but . . ." Her voice became a small, sorrowful, squeaky thing. "Paul's gonna kill me."

"Where is he? Is he at home? I can call him if you want me to."

"No. Please, just give me *half* of it back."

"I can't do that, Marilyn. It isn't in my power to do that."

"That was our whole . . ." The woman grabbed Carter's sleeve, raised herself on tiptoe, and whispered something to him.

"I'm sorry, Marilyn. I don't know what to say, except that I'm really sorry." Carter motioned for more assistance. "Next time you come in, you'll have better luck. You're one of our big winners."

"Not since last winter. I haven't won big since . . ." She was cornered, with still more uniforms moving in. Carter didn't seem to mind her death grip on his arm. "You have to give me some of it. Otherwise I can't . . . I can't . . ."

She was trapped. Reese wanted to tell the poor woman to use her elbows, get herself out of there, and he didn't realize he was on his way to his feet until Titus laid a hand on his arm.

Then, out of nowhere, Helen glided into the pack.

"Take Marilyn in the office and help her call someone," Carter told Helen.

Helen put her arm around the woman, wresting her from Security's muscle power and Carter's authority. "Is there a friend we can call for you? Someone who—"

"No! I don't want anybody knowing about this. It was a mistake. I made a mistake. Please, *please* help me get some of it back."

"We'll talk about it in the office," Helen soothed.

"It was . . ." The woman latched onto Helen now, clearly hoping she finally had an ally. "We ran some bred heifers through the sale ring last week. I picked up the check. I cashed it. I was going to pay some—some bills. I *have* to pay those bills. Otherwise we won't have any—"

"Jesus," Reese muttered to Titus, but he was looking at his brother, who was beyond earshot. "Just give the woman her damn money back."

"Is that the way they do it in the big city?" Titus wondered.

"I don't know how they do it. And this isn't the big city. And it's a hell of a way to . . ." He was on his feet now, and Titus was right beside him. "Make a living? Are we making a living here?"

He dropped some money on the table, but Titus picked it up. "Not on coffee, we're not makin' a living. Coffee's free, and there's no tipping. It's called hospitality." He slapped the cash into Reese's palm. "You think this was bad? I saw a guy lose his whole calf check once."

"Christ." Reese felt guilty about shoving his money back in his jeans when he could still hear that woman sobbing.

"But I've seen guys spend their last quarter on a bottle of Thunderbird, and so have you. When you get down to it, it's the same damn thing."

"Beautiful."

"How do they handle it out where you are?"

"I don't know."

"Tell you one thing for sure, they don't give the money back."

Reese couldn't help glancing toward the office, meeting Helen's eyes for a moment. It was an odd look she gave him, as though she was trapped, too, and frantic and frightened. Frightened for the woman, maybe, or maybe *because* of the woman; could be she didn't want to be alone with her. He sure as hell wouldn't. It was a fleeting look, and maybe he'd read it all wrong.

And maybe he'd stick around a little while longer.

"That Helen is a born social worker," Carter said as he joined Reese and Titus. "Whatever kind of anonymous you want to be, she's got the phone number handy."

"She's a teacher," Reese said, as if that explained any and all resourcefulness.

"She *was*," Carter said. "She says she's looking to be again. Maybe she'll stick around this time."

"Is that part of her job, dealing with losers in distress?"

"Not really, but like I say, she's good at it. I could just tell Security to take the woman out, but that's the kind of scene that's bad for business." Carter shrugged. "Besides, she's local. We care about our local customers."

"She's not from here," Reese clarified, "from here" meaning Bad River, meaning Indian or part Indian or married to an Indian. He realized he was saying *She's not one of us*, and he hadn't thought in those terms in a long time.

"She and her husband have a ranch across the river. He's a big ol' ham-fisted redneck. I don't blame her for not wanting to go home." Carter glanced at Titus. "Hell, as much money as she dropped here in the last couple days, I'd probably want to kill her, too."

"Can't you just . . ." Reese knew this was going to sound very stupid, but what could it hurt? "Give her *some* of it back?"

Carter tapped Titus's shoulder. "We'd be out of business in a month if my brother ran this place."

"What if he does kill her?" Reese said.

"She's over twenty-one. Time to grow up. This is what you call adult entertainment. We're not playing for points. We're playing for cold cash. And it's about damn time we had some of that coming our way, right, Titus?"

Titus nodded. "We donate to Gamblers Anonymous and to a couple of treatment facilities."

"Most people just come here to have a little fun," Carter added. "They spend twenty, fifty, a hundred bucks, and they go home. Some of them go home with a nice jackpot. When that happens, their husbands or wives are damn glad to see them."

"I played ball with a guy who got himself into a lot of trouble."

"Sam Garrett, right?" Carter always had to supply the names, dates, and titles. Carter was a wellspring of information. "It's no secret. Everybody heard about him betting on point spreads and that kind of shit. That's crazy, dealing with bookies and sharks. You're taking your life in your hands, you start doing that."

"It ruined him." Reese remembered the way the media had delighted in taking a shredded man and holding the pieces up before the cameras.

"Excess will do that. You've got to know your limits," Carter said, and he nodded toward the alcove as the distraught gambler emerged. "There, see? We're all settled down, ready to face the ol' man. Helen's got a real knack for handling these people. It can be sticky sometimes. Women especially. They get to boo-hooing like that, you hate to throw them out into the parking lot."

"You're all heart, little brother." Reese turned his back on the woman, sidestepping as he did so, shielding her retreat with his body. "Better you than me."

"Better me than most people. I'm very good at what I'm doing. Ten Star put me right into management. I already had the background in business, so I slid right in." Carter illustrated the sinuous move with his hand. "We're doing great, aren't we, Titus?"

"The contract with Ten Star is up for review. Some people

say we should go with a different company," Titus said. "Your dad was kinda leading that charge."

"He was always looking for some kind of charge he could lead," Carter replied, but Reese was losing interest in the whole conversation. The unlucky gambler had beat a retreat to the nearest exit, and Helen was coming out of the office now, wearing a pair of dark glasses. He could feel the eyes behind those shades connecting with his. He could also feel that contact being ripped away, as though it had happened against her will, and the set of her mouth was so thin, so tight . . .

"I'll catch you guys later," Reese said.

"You got some charging of your own to do, big brother?"

"She's an old friend."

"Whatever you say." Carter grinned. "Might as well see if the old shoe still fits."

Reese ignored the crack as he walked away. "Can I buy you a cup of coffee?" he asked when he caught up to her.

"They give it away here," she told him with a tight smile.

"Buy you lunch, then. Or supper. What's your pleasure?" He just wanted to sit with her for a while. He wished he could see her eyes.

"I have to go. I want to make sure . . ."

"I saw what happened. Are you the troubleshooter for that kind of crisis?"

"Oh, no. I'm just a dealer." She adjusted her purse strap on her shoulder. "We're trained to handle people who get into trouble like that. We try to head it off if we can, but sometimes you don't spot it in time. I just hate to see it happen."

He could tell. "Let me take you somewhere else."

"She's afraid of what her husband will do."

"How much did she lose?"

"I can't say." Another quick, tight smile. "But it was a lot of money for her. A lot for most people."

"This is no place for you to be working. You're not . . ."

"I'm not what?" She was smiling at him still, and he had the feeling she was giving him one of her secret looks, like she knew things he didn't know. He'd hated it when she'd looked at him that way, back when all he'd known was his little corner of South Dakota. "It's a good job," she was saying. "The pay is very good. I'm not . . ."

Not what?

"I don't know what you think, Reese, but this job is not beneath me. I'm not doing anything illegal or dishonest or—"

"Hey, I don't think anything." He touched her arm. She stiffened a little, but she didn't move away, so he took hold. "That was a bad deal for that woman, whether she got herself into it or not. It shook you up. It shook *me* up, just as a bystander here." He smiled. "I'm only asking you if you want to go someplace and get something to eat."

"Thank you." She shook her head. "I don't. Not right now. But thank you." She put her hand on his in a comforting way, as though this whole incident was merely an extension of the bad stuff that had been happening lately. "It's good seeing you again, Reese, and I'm glad you're not . . . I'm glad to see that you're well."

She was glad to see that he was well? *Well?*

He wished he could see behind those damned sunglasses.

$\mathcal{T}$he noon sun beat hard on Reese's back as he lined his long fingers up with the rickrack imprint baked into the South Dakota clay. It still looked fresh. There had been no rain since investigators had taken impressions of the tire tracks and concluded that the vehicle that struck his father down was a three-quarter-ton, four-wheel-drive pickup. They knew what the wheel base was, the brand of its tires, the speed at which it was traveling. The main detail still missing was the name of the so-called individual who had fled the scene.

The medical examiner couldn't tell for sure whether the old man had died right away. Reese had asked. He wanted to know whether the chickenshit driver had killed his father by hitting him or by running away and leaving him to die at the side of the road.

Reese had been doing some running himself, and now that he'd stopped, the sweat ran more profusely, dripping off his chin and puddling in the depression beneath his hand. His heart pounded in his ears as the image of the old man lying there in the dark burned in his brain. He let it burn. He tortured himself with it. He listened to the wind and he thought he could hear the roar of a big engine, but no sound from his father's throat. No outrage, no cry of pain. The ditch grass rustled all around him while the cicadas made their racket in the shelter belt by the creek below, but at the center, thunderous and insistent, was his own heart pounding around the image of a dead man.

It was foolhardy, running in the heat. He usually ran early in the morning, but today he'd gotten a late start, and he'd needed to get away from his father's house and all those damn relics. He'd given up almost everything else, but he couldn't stop running. Everything he'd been had begun with his running. He'd been running all his life, and if he ran himself to death, so be it.

Why was it that he could never get away?

He had stuck with his old man through the lean times, through the mean times, waiting for his chance, his time to walk, cool and easy. No big deal, just "I'm gonna go for it now, Dad," and his old man had given him the nod. Just that, a simple nod. It wasn't approval so much as admission that he couldn't stop him.

His father had been deep into tribal politics by then, and Reese had done a hitch in the army before he'd tried it the old man's way, by going to college first. Get an education and play the game on the side. Basketball was just a game after all, a sport Roy himself had been good at in his day. *Taught the kid everything he knew.* All the skills a man needed—passing, pressing, faking. Reese was great at faking. Came in handy when his own turn for his own lean-and-mean came around.

He'd handled his early retirement in style. There were no press conferences, no talk-show appearances. He'd walked away quietly. His injuries had gotten plenty of press, and they were decent, respectable, manly injuries, incurred in the line of duty. He'd given it all for his team, no questions asked. No pathetic bleeding-heart explanations necessary.

Hardly anybody knew about his crazy running. He had run every inch of these hills when he was a kid. As a teenager, he'd run wild from one end of the rez to the other. He had run circles around every basketball team from every podunk South Dakota town in the league. He'd run and run until he didn't know when to quit. Or how to quit. He'd given up the game, but not the running.

Which maybe gave him something in common with the guy who had left these tracks. But at least this guy had to know *why* he was running. Wherever he was, he must have heard the news by now. He must know that he'd killed somebody, and he had to believe he was a dead man if Reese ever caught up with him.

He stood up now, laughing at himself. Oh, he was a big man, all right. If he happened to run into his father's killer, he would mow him down. But he knew damn well this was going to be another one of those shit-happens incidents. That pickup was long gone from Indian country, the driver home free the minute he crossed the river. The driver wasn't from Bad River. Reese knew that to be true, if for no other reason than because he didn't want him to be.

"I want you to have that much peace," he said aloud. "It wasn't one of your own people who did you in. It was some outsider, wasn't it?"

Had to be. In his later years Roy Blue Sky had become the man to talk to, the man to see. His spirit would never rest if he'd been killed by one of his own people. Internal strife was their downfall. Indians fighting Indians. If they could ever get together, the old man used to say, they'd be dangerous. Like at the Little Bighorn. The old man was an expert on the Battle of the Little Bighorn.

"If we ever got together, we'd be dangerous," Reese muttered into his shirttail as he wiped his face.

He was answered with a bark.

"Hey, Crybaby, where've you been?" The black-and-white shepherd scooted under the barbed-wire fence. He looked just like his father, Babe, who had been Reese's dog when he was a kid. "I thought we were going for a run together. How come you took off on me?" The dog answered with his habitual whine. "Damn. You smell like skunk. You ditched me for a skunk?"

I'm back now, the dog seemed to say as he bounced back and forth, challenging Reese to get going again, which was a good idea because he needed water. The plastic bottle in his holster was empty. He trotted back toward the house, trailed by a foul-smelling Crybaby, who ditched him again when a car turned in at the approach and nudged them from behind. Reese picked up a little speed, thinking he wasn't in the mood for company. It was purely stupid of him to be running in this heat, and he didn't like the way his heart was pounding because of it, and he didn't like having anybody around him when his body was acting stupid. His weakness was private.

Then he saw that the driver was Helen.

She parked her little blue VW in the shade of a cottonwood and emerged smiling. Her hair was pulled up and held by a clip, a few wisps brushing her long neck, untouched by the heat.

"Hi." She stopped short of greeting him in a physical way, but she came close. "I was on my way back from town and I thought I'd stop and, um . . ." Her nose bobbed like a rabbit's.

Reese laughed. "That's not me. I've worked up a sweat, but not that bad."

"Crybaby, did you have a fight with an old skunk?"

The dog's ears perked at the invitation, but Reese leaned down and grabbed his collar just in time. "Hold on, mutt. You'd be wise to keep your distance until we've both seen some soap and water."

"It so happens that I just came from the store. I'll show you soap." She ducked into the car, pushing the driver's seat forward so she could reach the grocery bags in the back. She produced a quart bottle, brandished it under his nose as though it were the answer to a prayer.

"Looks like tomato juice."

"I've never actually tried it, but I've heard it's the best cure in these situations." She took a closer look at the label. "I wonder how much it takes."

"To do us both? Probably more than you've got, so you'll have to choose. Which one of us do you think'll clean up better?" Better yet, he thought to ask, "Who did you come to see?"

"You."

Ah, she was smiling again. She had the prettiest of smiles.

He decided it was the smile that was making him feel a little light-headed.

"Do I get to shower before or after the tomato juice?"

"It's your call." She was letting the dog run his nose over the cap on the tomato juice bottle.

"His tail stays outside while I get my head under some water. Ten minutes?" She nodded. "Do you have anything that needs to go in the refrigerator?"

"Just some milk."

"Need help?"

She shooed him along with an amiable gesture.

"Just make yourself at home. Ten minutes."

He popped a pill, drank a good quart of water, and headed for the shower. When he emerged from the back room he was afraid she'd left. He felt profoundly let down until he discovered a couple of packages in the refrigerator, things like skim milk and cottage cheese that hadn't been there before. It was easy to tell, since he'd thrown out everything he'd found in there except for a few cans of pop. Then he heard her squeal, and the hissing below the sink told him that water was running somewhere. He looked out the front window, and there she was in the yard. Somehow she'd coaxed the dog into a metal tub, hosed him down, and now she was dousing him with tomato juice. And the big dummy was putting up with it.

She had summer legs. Long and lean, lightly tan, beautifully shaped for anything short, like the khaki shorts she was wearing now with that skimpy little tank top. It was a hot day and she was dressed just right, shaped just right. Damn, she had the sweetest little ass. Maybe it had broadened a bit, but in all the years that had passed, she'd remained the standard by which all women were compared. He'd begun to wonder whether his memory was playing tricks on him, whether it had embellished those perfect legs and that sweet, sweet ass and that—ah, there it was, that laugh that bubbled in her throat when she was enjoying herself. She had been a bittersweet gleam in his memory bank, a cherished throbbing in an ailing heart.

He was glad to see that her niche in his chest was still justified. How could she have changed so little in all these years? It was just like her to pitch right in and bathe the stinking dog. He laughed out loud when Crybaby stood up and gave a quick, all-over shake and doused her back. She couldn't hear him, but she laughed, too.

"How about some pop?" He'd brought two cans.

"Sure," she said, smiling over her shoulder. The dog seized the opportunity to stand up in the tub and shake himself again. Helen jerked back, but she kept hold of his collar. "Oh! You're asking for it, Crybaby. Do you have any idea what a favor I'm doing you? No appreciation."

The dog surely had no idea what a favor he was doing Reese by soaking her cotton shirt. "Need help?"

"Can I trust you to hold the hose?"

"What kind of a question is that?"

"A foolish one," she acknowledged as she unfurled herself in an effort to hold the dog, hand Reese the hose, and straddle a puddle all at once. The wide-legged stance was the funniest part. Her socks and shoes were thoroughly soaked.

"Exactly. The damage is already done."

"Exactly." She swung around to the far side of the tub, tethered to the dog like a Maypole dancer. "Try to aim at the dog. You're supposed to have a pretty good—"

"I do. All-star aim." He plugged the end of the hose with his thumb and aimed most of the spray at the dog.

"Reese! It's cold!"

"That's what *he* says."

The dog whined a little, but he didn't sound too miserable. Sure, hosed down this way, he looked scrawny and pitiful, but how miserable could a guy be with that little bit of a shirt plastered to those pretty breasts so close to his nose? She was wearing a bra—Reese could see the straps—but it wasn't much of one. It didn't do much to hide the beading of her nipples.

He took a long, slow, deep breath. "The tomato juice got rid of the skunk, but now you both smell like a pot of dog soup."

"Did you hear that, Crybaby?" She smoothed the dog's shiny black coat with her hands, trying to press the water out. "Yes, don't you worry. If he hasn't had dinner yet, I'll protect you. There. I think you're all done."

Crybaby shook himself again, and the water went flying. Helen shrieked, and Reese, since he was out of range, laughed. "*Now* he's all done." He grabbed a can off the front step and popped the top for her as he nodded toward the door. "Shower's free."

"Really?" She reached for the can. "You're not charging, huh?"

"Nope. I'll even see if I can find you a dry towel. Or maybe I should just hose you off out here."

She took a quick sip before she set the pop on the step, planted her fists on her hips, and offered an irresistible invitation. "Go ahead, hose me."

Grinning, he stuck his thumb over the end of the hose and doused her, avoiding her face in favor of her chest. She laughed and squealed, defending herself with outstretched hands as he stripped away the years and turned her into a dripping stringbean of a girl.

When he lowered the spray to the ground, she tipped her head back, laughing, and opened her arms to the heavens. "That felt good. Now I'll just stand here and become a sun-dried tomato."

He tossed the hose aside and turned off the spigot. "Now you get a real shower and some dry clothes. One of my shirts should cover you."

"Down to my ankles." She hopped up onto the step, toe-heeled her shoes off, and peeled away her socks. "But I don't want to get your floor wet."

"Why not? You can't hurt anything here. Come on." Crybaby was ready to follow them through the door. "Not you, dog, and don't you be crying about it. Wet woman and wet dog are two completely different matters."

"How so? A puddle's a puddle."

"Ain't talking about the runoff aspect," he quipped as he closed the door on the dog and the sunshine.

He turned to his guest, who stood sodden in the shadows, breasts tightly enfolded in her arms, eyes big, feet bare, shorts droopy. She looked every bit as forlorn and bedraggled as the dog he'd banned from their company. He felt a strong urge to do something for her, something both masterful and courteous, something like taking her clothes off, wrapping her in a soft blanket, rubbing her dry.

He cleared his throat, jerked his chin. "Through there. The towels are on the shelf."

"I know the way." She started toward the bathroom, then stopped. "That summer," she said quietly, pausing in the hallway to look back at him. Stripped of her usual dignity, she looked heartbreakingly young and utterly vulnerable. "You never brought me here, and I always wondered why."

He thought about saying *Look around,* but it occurred to him that looking around now wasn't the same thing. The colorless little place was pretty much the same, but he was seeing it differently. Maybe he was wearing a different head.

"Why didn't you take me home to meet *your* family?" he returned.

There in the shadows she smiled. It was, if he was not mistaken, a sad smile. "I guess we never got that far, did we?"

"Guess not." They'd gone pretty far, and he'd come pretty far since, but *courteous and masterful* he had not quite attained. "And I guess you *are* making a puddle."

He went to his old room—where he'd been sleeping as he had years ago, with his head jammed against the wall and his feet hanging off the bed—and found her some clothes. He decided a T-shirt would look too much like a nightgown, so he chose a long-sleeved dress shirt. It was too bad he hadn't switched to boxer shorts. She'd look good in those. His father's jeans would fit her better than his own, but the old man's room was closed off for now, and his clothes were not to be worn again.

He knocked on the door after the water stopped running. "I'll trade you my dry clothes for your wet ones," he said, and they made the exchange through the door. "I'll hang these out on the line."

She thanked him, and later when she joined him in the kitchen, she handed him his jeans. "I gave up on trying to keep these on. But this is enough, huh? I'm decent."

"Definitely decent. That shirt never looked that good on me." It hung down around her knees, and with the sleeves rolled up, it could have been a dress. "Put a belt on it, and we'll go out to lunch." He handed her the can of pop she'd left behind. "You turned me down yesterday, and I generally don't ask more than once, but here you are, and here it is lunchtime, and my cupboard's pretty bare."

"That's one of the reasons I stopped by, actually. To apologize. I didn't mean to be rude yesterday, but after dealing with . . ." Her gesture drifted with her words.

"Is that part of a dealer's job? Dealing with big-time losers?"

"No, not usually. I was handy. I have some experience with . . . counseling. You know, as a teacher." She was fiddling with his shirt's buttons. They were the ones she was wearing, but still they were his, and she was unbuttoning and rebuttoning that one in the middle of her chest. She could button up to her chin if she wanted to, but he'd still be thinking that her bra and panties were hanging out there on the clothesline. He'd put them there himself.

"Actually, *I* can offer *you* lunch," she said, the idea just occurring to her. "I put a few things in the refrigerator, and there's some other stuff in the car."

He wasn't hungry. "I'll go get it. What do you need?"

"Just bring both bags. Do you have any mayonnaise?"

"Nope."

"Mustard?"

He pointed to the small cupboard next to the refrigerator. "Check up there. You find anything that hasn't been opened, I guess we can use it."

He turned away from that funny little look she was giving him and headed out the back door. You didn't use the old man's personal stuff, like his clothes. Reese figured the food he'd been using qualified as personal. She'd probably call it superstition. When he returned to the Cities, he'd probably call it the same thing. But not here he wouldn't, and not now.

When he came back with the groceries, he asked her if she'd found anything, and she said she hadn't looked. "No need to disturb anything that was here," she said. "I brought plenty."

They made easy talk while they built sandwiches together. He suggested putting the cottage cheese with canned fruit, and she recalled that her mother had called that "heavenly hash," but she thought most people used whipped cream instead of cottage cheese. He couldn't remember her saying much about her mother before. She was right; they'd pretty much kept family out of it then. All they'd wanted was each other, the way he remembered it. Anything else had been too complicated. But now he found it easy to ask about her parents, and she told him they had been divorced for a long time and that her mother had moved to Ohio, where her sister lived. Didn't sound like Helen was too tight with any of them, and he wondered about that. But he didn't ask. Maybe she'd tell him sometime.

They held their paper plates in their laps while they ate. The kitchen table had been turned into a miniature Little Bighorn battlefield. Reese had walked around the thing and shaken his head for days, unable to believe his dad had been playing cowboys and Indians. He'd built the hills and draws of that haunted valley in southern Montana on a sheet of plywood, and he'd peopled the area with tiny plastic rivals. The terrain had been carefully molded out of plaster on some kind of base—chicken wire, Reese assumed. The care the old man had taken with the project was evident in the detail, and except for the little horsemen, it was all homemade.

He couldn't picture his father constructing this thing, and that bothered him. He'd had about three things to play with when he was a kid—one big round ball and two little ones—and his father had warned him not to mess with the little ones too much. Once when Ray was tanked, he'd made the comment in front of some of Reese's friends, telling them that was why they all had zits. Reese remembered how hot that flush of shame had felt. But this meticulously constructed plaything was not the work of a drunk. Maybe the old man had made it for his grandchildren, a visual aid for one of his favorite adventure stories. Reese wondered whether he would take up such a hobby when he got old. *If* he got old, which wasn't too likely. But if he did, he'd have no one to play with but himself.

Christ, what a thought. It actually made him laugh.

And then he realized that Helen was giving him that funny look again, like maybe it wasn't safe to be around him. She had just been telling him how Roy had given her a personal tour of his valley of the Little Bighorn the night he died, and she obviously didn't think that information was too funny.

"The Greasy Grass," she amended. "Not the Little Bighorn."

"That's more like it," Reese said, and he encouraged her to recount the old man's "blow-by-blow" description of the famous battle, even though he'd heard it before. Hell, he'd watched the video a time or two. Or twenty-two. He liked the way the old man regaled the "experts," had them hanging on every word, heads bobbing.

She pointed out some of the tiny figures to him—Crazy Horse, Gall, Sitting Bull, and Iron Necklace, who, she informed him, was his great-grandfather. He watched her slip into her teacher mode, heard the enthusiasm in her voice, saw it in her gestures, but the words were his father's. He knew them so well.

"He worked for the railroad years ago," Reese mused. "He admired the model-train setups you'd see on display at Christmas, but he wasn't one to spend money on toys. I don't know when he got into this little hobby."

"He told me he saw one of those models in a magazine. He said they had it all wrong, so he started making his own." She set a fallen horse back on its feet in Major Reno's entrenchment position near the river. "Sidney would love this."

"Sidney?"

She glanced up quickly, as though he'd jerked her back from somewhere else. She was entitled, he thought. He'd been elsewhere, too.

She covered with a shrug. "My son."

"He still likes toy soldiers?"

"He likes history. We never pass up a museum. He . . . he reads a lot."

"Sports and books," Reese said. He tried to imagine a ten-year-old-boy version of her pretty face. "Good combination. Bet he's a smart kid." And then, impulsively, he added, "You can have this thing if you can figure out a way to move it."

"Oh, you shouldn't part with this, Reese. Roy put so much

into it. Did you see that History Channel program where they interviewed him?"

"I did."

"I have it on tape. Would you like a copy?"

"Thanks. I have it, too." He tipped his chair back and tossed his half-full plate on the counter behind him. "He put the whole place in my name. I don't know what he thought I'd do with it. Carter lives close by, and he has kids. So does Rose. I don't know what the ol' man was thinking, leaving it to me."

"He must have had a reason."

"Perversity." Reese laughed. "Is that a reason, or just an old habit?"

Helen shook her head. Her fingers drifted over the tiny figures on what she'd described as Last Stand Hill. "I don't think your father's death was an accident."

The flat, spiritless way she said it chilled him. "What makes you say that?"

She sighed and straightened slowly, as though she was lifting a burden up to him. "He was very outspoken about a number of controversial issues around here, and lately he'd been rattling the cages of some pretty big gorillas."

"This is South Dakota. There isn't a gorilla in the whole state." *Believe that, and I'll meet you at the top of the Empire State Building.*

"The issues concerned the casinos."

"Oh, yeah. *Those* cages." Back to the government's latest new deal for Indian country. "The old man didn't have a problem with putting up the casinos."

"No, but he had some problems with the way they're being run, and he was vocal about what ought to be done. He was gaining a lot of support. Which means he was also making enemies."

Enemies. Reese dragged his gaze from the doomed plastics on the hill to the tiny tipis across the river. "Did he mention any enemies in particular?"

"No."

"Did you get the impression he was afraid?"

"No. He wasn't afraid. He said that a man his age could

afford to speak out because he'd lived his life. He didn't think he had a lot to lose."

"Speak out about . . ."

"Ten Star," she supplied. "The casino management company. Your father was opposed to renewing their contract."

"So you think they ran him down? Seems like a sloppy way to off somebody if you're in the business of offing people." He leaned forward in his chair, studying her now. "That's not what you're suggesting, is it? A hit man hit my old man?"

"No, I'm not suggesting that. I'm just saying—"

"You know what I thought when they called to tell me? First thought, first picture in my head, was an old drunk wandering around in the road and getting hit." It was her turn to be surprised by an off-the-wall suggestion. "I know. He quit drinking years ago," Reese admitted. "Why did I assume, even for an instant, that he'd fallen off the wagon?"

Helen shook her head, as though she couldn't imagine.

"And I didn't want you to know that about him or about me, so why am I laying it on you now?" He laughed, wagged his head as he glanced away from her, from his father's last big project, the one he ought to be giving him some kind of credit for. "Carter didn't know him then, either, and Rose mostly stayed with relatives. Back then, it was just me and the old man and his bottle. Jesus, he's *dead*, and here I am dragging that up." He stared at the back door, and he felt like a kid again, watching and waiting for that door to open, worrying over what kind of shape the man who opened it would be in. "That's not what I want to remember about him, but that was my first damn thought."

She laid her hand on his thigh, just above his knee. No big deal, just a little consolation between friends, but it drove him to his feet. He hated sympathy. He wanted her hands on him, but not in sympathy, and he was disgusted with himself for angling for it now.

"You want me to ship this thing to your son, I'll be glad to do it."

"What about Carter's children?"

"I offered. He said it would just be in the way at his

house." Reese leaned against the counter, feeling foolish about the rush her mere touch had just given him. "I told him he oughta keep some stuff for his kids, but I think he's pouting. I'm the one who ought to be pissed. It's nothing but a damn headache."

Helen stood, brushed crumbs from his shirt, put her plate on top of his. "So you'll be around for a while?"

"A couple of weeks at least." He smiled. "Maybe I'll take up blackjack."

"Just between you and me, it can become an expensive pastime. I don't recommend it."

"No? What do you recommend? Just between you and me."

"Riding. Your dad has two—*you* have two very nice horses."

"Two's good."

"In fact, one of them is named Blackjack."

"General Pershing." He could tell she was a little disappointed that he got the connection before she had a chance to enlighten him. "It wasn't just Custer and Crazy Horse. My dad was a soldier once, and he loved all kinds of war stories. What's the other one's name?"

"Jumpshot."

Now, that name did surprise him. There had been a time when basketball was the only good thing they'd shared, but later, when he'd taken the ball and run with it, run his own way, the old man had stepped back from him altogether, like a face in a B-movie, ominously fading to black.

"He was proud of you, Reese."

"Was he? Did he tell you stories about me?"

"He said you were busy and that he didn't get to see much of you. He said you always gave him tickets to your games and that he tried to go as often as he could."

"Which wasn't often."

"He said he didn't like to fly. But he loved watching you play. His face fairly lit up at the mention of it."

"Lit up?" He laughed. He'd seen him lit, but not the way she meant. "I don't think I ever saw that."

He hated the way these thoughts kept crowding into his

head, even as he tried to do these final things in a respectful way. Anger was useless and ugly. He wanted Helen's memories now, those good things, respectful things, the fondness he heard in her voice when she recounted them. "I haven't seen much of him since I retired. I guess I didn't want to see what that did to his face."

"I can tell you he worried about what it did to you," she said. "I wanted to ask him more about your retirement."

He glanced at her. She glanced away. It embarrassed her, his goddamn throwing-in of the towel. It embarrassed him.

"Do your injuries still give you problems?"

He said nothing.

"I remember reading about a back problem. Something about bone chips in your ankle, too. But I see you still run."

"I still run." He moved away from the counter and from her, but she followed. "I'm a physical player," he explained, falling back on the old defense. "I get in there and scrap. I have to make up for what I lack in size and speed with something else, and my something else is—*was* . . ." *I went down fighting.*

"Heart," she said. He stared at her, dumbfounded, and she smiled. "I remember one of the commentators saying you always put your whole heart into it, that you were fun to watch because you played every game like it was a final showdown."

"Did your face light up when you heard that? It lit up when you said it." And he felt incredibly relieved. It tickled him to see her blush, and tickled, he always smiled. "Yeah, that's a good way to put it. I played from the heart."

"Was it your back? Was that the final straw?"

"It was a combination of things. Nothing you want to hear about." *So chase her away, away from that heart shit.* He folded his arms, took a hip-shot stance, and gave her an utterly male snake-behind-the-back smile. "Sweaty, twisted, bloody, pus-filled things you don't want to hear about."

"You've just about convinced me."

"There's a whole list of other terms, but those are the ones I can pronounce. Now, can I offer you some more baloney?"

"This was turkey." Her smile was sweet. "You look . . . very healthy."

"So do you." He stepped closer. "Now what?"

"Now we catch up?"

He took that as an invitation to reach for her, but she foiled his intent.

"All caught up," she said quickly, busying herself with putting food away. "We're both healthy, your father is dead, and we're just sort of wondering why."

"He got in the way of a pickup," he said offhandedly. "You must've been hanging out with him a lot. Was he into blackjack?"

Reese was half kidding, but when Helen slid him a guarded glance, he lifted an eyebrow, his eyes demanding a reply.

She shook her head, her negative reply barely mouthed.

"So what was the attraction?"

"I, um . . ." There was something she wanted to tell him, but she was going to make him dig for it. "My job."

"What about your job?"

"He helped me get it." She tossed their paper plates into the trash bag under the sink. "Denver has become a difficult environment, at least where we live. I wanted to come back to Bad River. It's a smaller community, and I still have friends here." She closed the cabinet door and turned to face him. "But things have changed."

"What's changed? We've got ourselves a couple of flashy casinos, a little more money floating around, more people coming through, more cars, more—"

"Crime. More crime, Reese. More money means more crime. And your father might well have been—"

"Now wait a minute. I thought crime was supposed to go hand in hand with poverty. You're gonna try to tell me that all the money you see rolling through your casino is stirring up political trouble, corrupting the natives, and now they're turning on each other, running each other down out there on the highway?"

"It's not my casino," she said. "It's your casino. I just work there."

"Then you're getting more out of the place than I am. I

just came home to . . ." He shrugged. "I just came *back* to bury my father."

"You've done that."

"Seems there's more to it than putting him in the ground." He leaned against the counter again, thinking how fine it felt to hang around the kitchen after a meal and talk things over with a woman. This woman. They'd done the bedroom scene together before, but never this kitchen scene. He'd probably been too young for that. In those days he'd been a kitchen raider, not someone interested in kitchen palaver. "So you think I oughta play detective."

"I didn't say that." She handed him a knife she'd washed. "But I think that if Reese Blue Sky demands to know what happened to his father, and I mean in a public sort of way, there'll be some people scrambling to get him some answers. Other than just that your father got hit by a truck."

"They want to appoint me to fill out the rest of his term. It's tradition, they say. He's a fallen leader, and I'm his older son." He dropped the knife into a drawer.

"Really? You mean you'd be on the tribal council?"

"Until the election in November. They say if I'm willing, the chairman can't refuse to appoint me." He nudged the drawer closed with his thigh. "Apparently it's true that there are two factions, two groups turning on each other, just like you said."

"Like *you* said." She studied him, her arms wrapped around his billowy shirt. "What if he died because someone wanted him dead, Reese?"

He stared at her for a moment, wishing he could just crawl inside her head. For starters. "Why don't you just tell me what you know?"

"I know that he suspected some skimming, some scamming, some big-time siphoning off of casino profits."

It bothered him when she wouldn't look at him. She wasn't doing it out of politeness. She was holding out on him, pure and simple.

"He told you this?" Reese asked.

"In a manner of speaking."

"What manner of speaking? Like a whisper in your ear, or

a big announcement to anyone who cared to listen? You obviously cared to listen."

"I did. I liked him. I enjoyed listening to him. He wasn't afraid to speak out, Reese, and I think that may have been the death of him."

"Why didn't he just call in the Feds?"

"Security is handled by the management company," Helen replied. "They've uncovered a couple of penny-ante card scams lately."

"Yeah, but if big money is missing, it's probably an inside deal."

"It was no secret that your father believed the tribe was getting the worst end of the agreement with Ten Star, and lately he was very critical of their relationship with the tribal chairman. But . . ." She sighed. "Well, your brother has a good position with Ten Star."

"Wouldn't wanna jeopardize that." *Damn*, he thought, *was this jealousy he was feeling?*

"Your father was in a tight spot, you see. And yet he spoke out. He made waves."

"And he washed up in a ditch along the road." He was thinking maybe she cared more than anybody, and that hurt for some reason, because he was also thinking how he could get lost in her eyes himself, how he'd done it a time or two. Her eyes, her hair, her mouth, her . . . "How do you fit into all this, Helen?" She stared at him, her eyes glistening with secrets. "Helen?"

Her response was barely audible. "I was his friend."

He was sure there was more to it than that. "You'll be around for a while?"

"I will, yes."

"You're serious about a job here?"

"I'm serious about my job; yes, I'm very serious."

"I've been through Denver a hundred times in the last ten years. If you'd left me a number or an address . . ." He'd looked her up in the phone book a couple of times, just for the hell of it. He'd decided that even if she'd been there, she'd probably gotten married, changed her name. "What is your name now?"

"It's still Ketterling."

He smiled. "Liberated and independent, that's you."

"That's me."

"That's Helen."

He'd almost said *My Helen*, and, God, how moronic that would have sounded. Like a big, dumb kid who had followed her around until she'd let him kiss her and then touch her and finally crawl between her legs and worship her with his whole huge horny self. He wasn't sure whether he was reaching for her or remembering reaching for her, whispering her name or thinking it, touching his lips to hers or dreaming it, until the sweet honey taste on his tongue settled all doubt. This was really Helen. He was holding Helen in his arms.

She rose on her tiptoes. He lifted her off the floor so that she wouldn't get a stiff neck while he kissed her. Somebody moaned—he thought it was she—and he let her slide down the front of his body. He meant to let her go, but his tongue wasn't satisfied to quit completely, so his lips followed hers with small kisses, little kisses, don't-want-to-stop kisses.

"Oh, dear."

"Oh, dear, what?" He buried his nose in her hair. "Oh, dear, he still kisses good and he's not a big, dumb kid anymore?"

"You never . . ."

"Yeah, I was."

"Yeah, you do." She had her arms around him, he realized now. He ducked back just enough to look into her eyes, to see whether she meant to hold him or simply hang on for the ride. She smiled. "You kiss good. You always did."

"You, too."

"Better now, though."

"Better now," he agreed, and he started in for another kiss.

"Oh, dear," she said with a soft sigh, but then she stiffened, her head cocked like a wary animal. The pretty kind. "Oh, *dear*. Reese, someone's here."

He kept her tucked under his arm as he turned to look out the window that faced the driveway.

Damn. "It's my brother."

4

"*H*ey, Bro-gun!" Carter shouted. He'd gone to the front door.

"The man of a thousand nicknames," Helen whispered as she moved away from Reese, trying to recover the tempo of their exchange without letting him see that she'd missed more than a beat. Hard to believe, but there she was, getting caught in his arms again and feeling far too satisfied for a woman who'd always known better.

"Too bad 'Magic' ain't one of 'em." He slid her a flirtatious wink, and damn if it didn't make her feel giddy.

Carter continued to announce himself on his way through the living room. "Unless you're taking in laundry, I know that little outfit on the line out there doesn't—" He barged into the kitchen with a triumphant grin, as though he'd just found his way through a complicated maze. "I thought I recognized the car. Looks like old acquaintances ain't been forgot."

"Hello, Carter." Helen reached for the bread. "Would you like a sandwich? We've got plenty left." *When in doubt, offer food.*

"What I'd like is a couple dozen of your shirts, big brother.

I just might change the uniform for some of our dealers." He waved off the sandwich offer but lifted an appreciative brow. "Looks good on you, Helen."

Reese folded his arms and leaned against the counter, proclaiming his territory. "Not that any explanations are in order, but it all started with a skunk."

"Aw, jeez, I've been living in the outback too long, obviously missing out on the latest fun and games. All I can think of is . . ." Carter's gesture invited either of them to help him make the connection. "A black-and-white critter that stinks."

"You got it," Reese said. "Helen stopped in to pick up a raincheck on lunch and ended up giving the dog a bath."

"Hell of a host, isn't he, this man? I came by to check out a rumor." Carter turned from Helen to Reese. "About you getting appointed to finish out the old man's term on the council."

Reese lifted one shoulder. "I've been approached."

"Who approached you?"

"If what you mean is which side, I couldn't tell. I'm not up on who's in whose camp this week." But since Carter was still waiting for an answer, he added, "Marvin Grass."

"Are you thinking about it? I mean, is it a possibility?"

"Anything's possible. Retired athletes go into politics all the time. Bill Bradley, J.C. Watts, and now Jesse 'The Body' Ventura," Reese said, smiling. "I voted for Jesse myself. Figured Minnesota could use a governor who's trained to knock heads."

"Well, hey, don't forget The Gipper," Carter said. "You're right, there's some solid tradition here."

"Marvin was pitching me Indian tradition. The oldest son."

"Probably bullshitting you to get you to do it."

Reese shrugged.

"And I think you should."

Reese eyed his brother speculatively, waiting for a laugh, maybe.

"Hell, you've got it made in the shade, Reese. You can afford to do stuff like this. In a couple of months you could straighten that bunch out, have them living in the twentieth century by the time the twenty-first rolls around." Carter turned to Helen. "My brother's not only a hero, he's also a businessman. Those old guys, the ones that keep dragging their feet on the prospect of making any progress, hell, they'd listen to the Big Gun."

"About what?" Reese wanted to know.

"You name it." Carter tapped Reese's flat belly with the back of his hand. "You could spare a couple months, couldn't you? It would give you an excuse to stay around for a while, give us a chance to kinda get to know each other again."

"Again?"

"We both got cheated, the way we grew up." Carter smiled. "You probably don't know this, Helen, but I was adopted by a white family when I was just a little guy. I didn't even know who I was until I was about fourteen. The old man used the Indian Child Protection Act to claim me back."

"I think I might have heard something about that."

"Yeah, well . . ." He sniffed his hand. "Damn dog." He turned on the faucet, dribbled some dish soap into his smooth palm, kept talking while he lathered his hands. "I grew up out East. The folks who adopted me were good to me, I'll say that. I got a good education. I didn't appreciate being jerked out of school and coming here. But it all worked out. I went to Harvard on a full ride, got my MBA, and then Ten Star provided the training I needed to manage the casino. It all worked out."

He shut the water off and shook drops off his hands. "But all that time I had a brother I hardly knew. We lived together for a couple of years, then went our separate ways. Now that the old man is gone, it's time we made up for some of that lost time." Intent on Reese now, he accepted the dish towel Helen handed him without even looking at her. "Don't you agree, Blue?"

"Sure. I agree."

"And besides, there's all kinds of casino business coming before the council, and some of those guys, it just goes right over their heads. It's a new day for the Bad River people, and we need educated leadership. I hate to say it, but the old man was part of that old guard. He didn't understand the requirements of this business."

71

"He was concerned with the requirements of the people he represented," Helen put in.

"Well, yeah, his heart was in the right place, but not his head. The head gets past a certain age, it just can't be expected to do the job anymore. Use it or lose it, right, Bro-gun?"

Reese was using his. "There's no conflict of interest, a councilman's close relative being general manager of the casino?"

"Conflict of interest? This is Indian country, brother. Hell, you know Indian country better than I do, and that's just a fact of our lives." Carter laid his hand on Reese's shoulder, which stiffened visibly. "Relax, there's no conflict. I'm not a tribal employee. I work for Ten Star."

"Which the old man had some kind of conflict with," Reese added.

"Like I said, he didn't understand the business. He didn't understand how much money it takes to do business. But you do." Carter gestured with his thumb. "In and out. Couple of months. Not even enough time to dirty your hands. Plus, there's the matter of your inheritance."

Reese sighed. "I don't know why he did that, Carter."

"He wanted you back here, just like he wanted me back. That's all. Plain and simple. He left it to you to get you back here." He laughed. "Hell, these are the ties that bind."

Reese looked around. "Is that what these are?"

"Like I said, better you than me," Carter replied too easily. "But I really think you oughta hang out with us for a while, brother. Right, Helen? We'd like to get to know the big man again, wouldn't we?" His grin was stupid and suggestive and completely unwelcome.

"Speaking of hanging out, I'm sure my clothes must be dry."

"I'll get them," Reese offered, with a deferential glance at her bare feet. "The yard's full of sand burrs."

"I need to be going," Carter said, and they all started moving toward the back door. "I just wanted to let you know that, well, if you're considering that appointment, I'm behind you."

Helen stood on the steps, the dappled shade of a cottonwood playing over her as she watched the brothers exchange some private words while Reese unclipped her clothes from the line. It seemed such a personal service, performed surprisingly unself-consciously, as though he handled her bra every day. As though he handled laundry every day, which somehow seemed incongruous with his big hands and the distinctively masculine way he used them. She thought herself a fool for thinking how sweet he looked, saying his good-byes with her wind-stiffened clothes tucked under his arm.

From below the stoop he handed them up to her carefully, like an offering. "Are we missing anything?"

"I can't imagine what."

"Carter hasn't heard anything from the cops since their initial investigation. Have you said anything to him about your suspicions?"

"My suspicions don't mean much. Nothing but . . ." She shrugged, clutching her clothes to her chest, trying to suck herself into a small thing, an insignificant deception. "I'm just a concerned friend. A mouse in the corner. That's all."

"A mouse, Helen? The kind that roars?"

He chuckled, so enchanting her with his smile that his brother, like her small lie, was out of mind even before he was out of sight. The roar of his engine dissolved in their ears well before the car was gone. Reese's smile, with its hint of sadness, was just between them. And her lie was so small it didn't have to count right now. Her suspicions didn't point to anyone in particular, so they meant nothing, little more than a squeak. For the moment.

He took her hand, sat down on the bottom step, and drew her down beside him. "I hear him, loud and clear. Always have. No matter where I am, I can hear him. Even now."

"Your father?"

"You know what you have to do after somebody dies?" His eyes challenged her, as though he expected her to doubt the obligation or ridicule it before she even knew what it was.

She shook her head. His eyes reminded her of his father's and of her son's. She doubted nothing.

"You have to feed the spirits," he told her quietly as he stared off into the silent hills behind the pole barn. "You actually have to put food out for them so they'll leave you alone. Even without a recent death, there's always that spirit world that crosses ours in ways you don't have to see or touch or explain. At least he didn't."

"Do you?"

Without looking at her, he shook his head. "I guess I don't. I haven't thought about these things in a while. I've been busy with . . . with *this* life, the busy life. The elusive *good* life, which I can't see or touch or explain, either. I just know . . ." Absently he rubbed his long thighs, and she thought how soft his well-worn jeans looked beneath his swarthy hands. "When I was a kid, we used to hunt a lot, the old man and me. We'd kill a deer, he'd always cut off a piece of meat and leave it for the *wanagi*. You have to feed the spirits. It might look superstitious to do a thing like that, but what it really is . . ." He was turning it over in his mind, recollecting and rediscovering. "It's a show of respect, an acknowledgment." He looked at her now, surprised, maybe even glad to see her interest. "I did that today."

"Killed a deer?"

He shook his head. "I fed him chicken. I went to the grave-yard early this morning. It should have been *wasna*. You know, pemmican. But I didn't have any, so I took what I had. Chicken for two, marinated in some kind of mustard sauce, which is what I cooked last night." His face brightened with a slow smile. "Guess I must be a twentieth-century Indian, huh? I fed the spirits with chicken from the grocery store. I told them it tasted like rattlesnake."

She smiled, too.

"I don't know why I told you all that," he said. "Ten years ago I never would have told anybody from your world that."

"It's been—"

"Closer to thirteen years. I know." He reached for her hand again.

She let him take it, but she gave his a quick squeeze as she slid off the step, still holding her clothes to her chest. A friendly but dismissive squeeze.

He laughed. "Are you afraid of me, Helen?"

"Of course not," she said too quickly. Then she laughed, too. "Even though I am sort of underdressed at the moment, which makes me feel a little insecure. It's a woman thing, you know."

He nodded, amused, unconvinced.

"So I'd better put my clothes on."

"Probably a good idea."

She mounted the steps, stopped on the top and stood directly behind him. She wanted him to do something. She wasn't sure what, but something.

"If you don't want to hear any voices, you probably should turn down that appointment."

"Is that a dare?" He looked up at her, studied her until she feared what he might be reading in her eyes. "You think I'm afraid of him now? You think just because I toss a piece of meat on the ground that I'm . . ." He shook his head, and the sharp glint in his jet-black eyes softened. "Just in case, you know? What can it hurt?"

"Did it help?"

"Didn't change anything." He shrugged. "It's all a bunch of nothing, right? Nothing to do with you, nothing to do with ghosts, nothing to be afraid of." He gave a quick, humorless laugh as he stood. "Nothing but a random hit-and-run, nothing but a body and a box and a hole in the ground. Nothing but a friend. That's a hell of a lot of nothing, when you think about it." Their eyes met. His glittered. "And you're no mouse in the corner, Helen. That's for damn sure."

No mouse in the corner.

Okay, how about a wolf in sheepskin or a blackbird in the pie? She couldn't tell Reese what she was really doing here, couldn't tell anyone, and hinting at her suspicions about his father's death was a bad move, a foolish move. What was she trying to accomplish? Like everyone else, she was stupidly hoping he'd stay around a while. Was she as bad as everyone else who wanted to stand around in his shade, catch his quips, bask in his smile because he was who he was? Did he linger in everyone else's head the way he did in hers?

She was playing with fire and she knew it, and she also knew that the heat of that risk excited her. It was a risk she couldn't afford to take. She wasn't just some female in heat, damp from a hot shower and clothed in his shirt, the one she knew he'd worn because it carried his scent and his— Damn!

She was a mother. A *mother*, not just any female. She couldn't gamble with her son's security, and that was exactly what she was doing every time she got near Reese. *She could not permit herself to gamble.* It was a temptation to her, a challenge, an illusion that could ruin her. It very nearly had.

Challenging fate could become an addiction. Flying in the face of all the odds and seizing the chance to single-handedly turn the world on its ear had strong appeal. Unexpected appeal for Helen, who surely never thought of herself as a gambler. When she became one, she found ways to put Helen the Gambler into her own separate compartment. Most aspects of her life were sane and ordinary, and she was able to keep them that way for a while. The Helen who bet the rent money on the turn of a card was only an occasional Helen. The real Helen would replace the rent money somehow. The real Helen was sensible, hardworking, a good mother, a good friend, daughter, person. She had always been good at what she did.

But somehow never quite good enough, that real Helen. That plodding, ho-hum Helen. There was always a vague dissatisfaction, a feeling that she could do more, be more, make something more happen. *Take a risk.* She was afraid to lose, but sometimes Chance, that terrible tempter, would present himself in such an irresistible package that she would sneak a little taste of him. Just a taste. And sometimes—oh, that taste. Juicy, sugar-coated, slightly metallic. Her mouth watered as she drove up the wide stretch of faultless new asphalt toward Pair-a-Dice City's flashy marquee. At least her palms didn't get clammy anymore.

She remembered the first time she'd played blackjack at a casino in Colorado. She'd been with friends who were trying to fix her up with somebody's cousin from out of town, an association that was utterly forgettable. But the game was not. Although she'd long considered herself a good card player, she'd never been exposed to gambling. She was no gambler, but she didn't mind watching the others play. When one of the players moved on, Helen's date for the evening suggested that she sit down and give it a try. She remembered feeling unusually restless that night, impatient with the company she was keeping, eager to separate herself in some way. And somebody's cousin's suggestion had sounded patronizing, as though it might be amusing to watch her dabble in a man's game.

She had taken the dare. She'd played a prudent, unpretentious game, and she had gone away a hundred dollars richer. It was enough to buy Sidney the video game he'd been asking for, the one she could not afford. But this was a hundred-dollar windfall, and it was okay to blow a windfall on a faddish toy. She was a winner. Fortune had smiled on her, and a winner's fortune must be shared with those she loved.

Somebody's cousin would have been history much sooner had he not provided more casino dates. A few more social outings down the road, he was no longer needed. Blackjack was not a social function for a serious player. A *good* player. Helen was good at it, and she began to believe that she controlled the outcome. She acquired a whole new vocabulary. It was her destiny to be a winner. She had an inside track with Fate. A gilded tally sheet of winnings burned in her mind, and the debit column that had been there at the start began to grow faint, hard to read, easily forgettable, until she'd simply lost track of her losses.

The fixation had consumed her for nearly a year, and by the time she'd looked it square in the eye, she'd racked up some awful debt. She had lost her savings, her modest investments, her car, her computer, her good credit rating, her self-respect. Those things had proved less important than the need to play the game. Only one part of her life remained inviolate, one thing she would not throw on the table. It was the very real risk of losing her son that saved her.

But now that bleak winter of her weakness was over, and she had survived. She had been a fool, not a criminal—although but for the grace of God she might have gone there, too, and with a criminal record she would not be qualified for her present assignment. Like the recovering alcoholic who becomes a bartender, she had turned her obsession into a tool that she had learned to manage and put to good use with the

Bureau of Indian Affairs, her longtime employer. Her judgment might have been clouded, but never her loyalty.

She could have turned the Bad River assignment down, probably should have, but she had not, and she suspected that old demon Chance of working on her in a different guise. He wasn't blackjack this time. He was the way back to her son's roots, the light on Roy Blue Sky's front porch. He was both dangerous and dear. He was irresistible. For Sidney's sake, she embraced what for Sidney's sake she had avoided.

For your own sake, the old demon whispered on the warm prairie wind as she locked her car.

Not so, she insisted, but for the sake of greater knowledge. Sidney was asking more questions these days, and he wasn't satisfied with her vague tales of a man she'd loved and lost. She had a job assignment, and she had a mission. She wanted the kind of answers her child deserved. Truthful ones. She thought she could gather them for him the way the Indian women in the earth-tone mural in the casino lobby were shown gathering wild cherries and digging roots. She too was a digger of roots. She would store them for her son, give them to him for his eighteenth birthday. It wasn't much, but it was something.

She'd been dragging her feet since she'd left the Blue Sky place. She'd wanted to stay, and the wanting irked her. She had a job to do. Since Roy's death, she'd been feeling a new sense of urgency about getting it done, turning up the big shell game. She wasn't sure what that was yet, but she could smell it, and she would root it out. Oh, yes, she was deep into roots lately. But along with the scent came a new sense of uneasiness. She wasn't sure where this uneasiness was coming from, but it had taken root in her gut. Roots were supposed to be *stabilizing.* She had no business feeling queasy.

She couldn't afford to worry about who was shuffling the shells.

On her way to the blackjack pit she exchanged nods with Peter Jones, one of the other dealers. A passing smile went to the housekeeping supervisor, whose name escaped her. Housekeeping was not suspect. While she was friendly with everyone she worked with, she became friends with no one.

She had a knack for mentally separating herself and becoming an observer, even as she smiled and took part in the card players' patter. She appeared to be on autopilot, and a dealer on autopilot was just what cheaters looked for. But for Helen, there was no autopilot. There was self and second self. It was a skill she'd developed as a teacher and honed as a gambler. She was so good at it that rarely did she get that I'm-onto-you look from anyone. And when she did, she simply shifted her focus.

The pit boss supervised the shift change, and all seven of the seats at Helen's table were soon occupied. No one would have guessed that she was more interested in the game going on to her left than in her own. The dealer had just paid a player for a losing hand. A simple mistake, or a "push and pay" move? She would watch the pair to see whether it happened again. And if it did? Helen wasn't looking for penny cons. She was looking for patterns. She was looking for serious money.

When the pit boss told her to take a break, Carter was on hand with a cup of coffee, complete with cream and sugar, just how she liked it. Carter was good about things like that, and not just to her. He took a personal interest in the employees, noticed things about them, and remembered in a nice, easy way.

"Your favorite customer was in a little while ago," he told her with a grin. "You know, that cowboy from Nebraska. He said to tell you he'd be back later, and that you were in for a long night. Said he was on a roll and mighty cashy."

"Did you mention anything about a fool and his money?"

"I said, 'Miss Ketterling will be on the floor soon, and you're welcome to roll right up to her table whenever there's an open seat.' I have a feeling if my brother knew somebody was promising you a long night, he'd have him rolling in a different direction."

She gave him a doubting look, and he laughed. Then he glanced away.

The place was really jingling tonight. It never rocked or jumped or even hopped. The movement on a busy night was surprisingly sedate, with the exception of the occasional bells and whistles signaling a large payout on a slot machine. The sound of money pouring in was a soft, seductive sort of jingle, as soothing to casino buffs as elevator music.

"I have a feeling Reese might stay around a while," Carter said, slipping his suggestion into the mix like a clever angler. "What do you think?"

"I think he might finish out your father's term, if that's what's expected," Helen replied. It was her habit to hover near the pit during her break, chat with someone, grab a soft drink, observe, and the mention of Reese should not have made a difference in her habit.

"It has nothing to do with what's expected. You two lost touch altogether, did you?"

Helen said nothing.

"Well, he was flying pretty high there for a while, playing pro basketball," Carter went on. "It was like he moved to a different planet. Of course, we'd go watch him play, and in the off season maybe he'd come and see us for a day. Sometimes we'd get to the Cities and maybe do the town, go to a concert or something. He's a real jazz fan. Did you know that?"

"No, I didn't." He hadn't been a jazz fan when she'd known him, back when he was twenty-two years old and full of himself and his prowess.

"It's funny how that kind of success can isolate a person. And then he started having his problems."

"With injuries," she said. She'd seen one of them happen, watched the play on TV. Somebody had stepped on his hand during a tussle over a loose ball. He'd finished the game after the team doctor had popped his finger back into place and taped it up. The announcer had marveled at how tough Blue Sky was.

"Well, yeah. Is that what he told you?" Carter shrugged, then leaned against the low divider that separated the bar from the landing above the first tier of slot machines. "I mean, he sure had his share of injuries. The kind of stuff a man doesn't like to talk about much. Especially Roy Blue Sky's son. He doesn't want any crybabies."

"I suppose that isolated him, too. Not being able to talk about his . . ." Injuries. *Is that what he told you?* "Problems."

"With the kind of money he made, he wouldn't have any trouble paying somebody to listen."

Listen to what? Helen wanted to say, but she simply nodded. Injuries was what she'd heard, what she'd understood. What kind of problems couldn't he talk about?

"It'll be great if he gets on the council, even for a short time," Carter said. Helen was still dwelling on Reese's isolation and his need to talk with someone, but Carter was on to more pressing matters. "Our employer needs more supporters."

"You think Ten Star could count on Reese for support?"

"Reese has been around. He's a businessman now. He understands what it takes to make a profit in the real world. If he got on the council, I think he'd help us." Animated by the prospect, he pushed away from the wood-trimmed divider. "And if you stick around, Helen, you've got a bright future with us, too. I know you're a teacher, but I might be able to make it worth your while to switch horses here."

"It would have to be *very* worthwhile," she said. "Teaching is my first love."

He touched her shoulder. "You help me nudge Reese in the right direction, and I'll show you how I define *worthwhile*."

"I'm not sure how much help I could be."

"It'll be interesting to find out, though, won't it? Isn't that why you're really here?" A slow smile shimmered in Carter's dark eyes. "Isn't the big man the fish who got away?"

"Maybe *I'm* the one who got away."

"Well, sure." He nodded politely. "Who knew he'd actually do what he said he was going to do, huh?"

Anybody who knew him, she thought. She'd had no doubt that he was going to play basketball some way, somehow, somewhere. She'd known he was completely absorbed in the dream. She understood now that they had both gotten away. Parts of them had. For a time.

She watched the dealer she'd been observing make another unwarranted payoff to the same player. The dealer would probably be out of a job tomorrow. If he wasn't, Helen would find out why.

"Do you catch a lot of muckers when you view the tapes?" she asked.

"Muckers?" Carter laughed, as though the threat of a hand-mucker was pretty remote. A handmucker had to be able to palm cards, a rare skill. "We get some cheaters, but they're not usually very accomplished. We caught a dealer running a scam last winter."

"I remember you telling me about that one." She smiled innocently. "The tapes they showed when I took my dealers' classes were amazing. Some of the tricks people use would be hard to catch."

"You don't have to worry too much. The eye in the sky sees all." He nodded toward the nearest security camera.

"But the eye in the sky doesn't report it until someone views the tapes, and that someone would have to watch those tedious things pretty carefully."

He started ticking off the list of "someones" on his right hand. "You've got your tribal people, you've got Ten Star, you've got Security, you've got me and my assistants. You've always got somebody looking at those tapes." He paused. "Why? Did you spot something fishy?"

"No, but I'm watching. I'd love to see a good card cheat in action." She smiled. "I think it would be fun to catch one."

"You wanna land a big fish, Helen?" He gave the Blue Sky wink. "Go after the one that got away."

*R*eese wasn't sure how the ceremony was supposed to be done, so he decided to make it up as he went along, *the Indian way.*

The Indian Way could be a solemn way or a twinkle-in-the-eye way, depending on which Indian's way you were talking about. With Roy Blue Sky it was hard to tell sometimes, so Reese decided to improvise a little. If he did something wrong, he would feel it. The eyes in the night would see, and the hand in the night would turn him, the Indian Way. Or Roy Blue Sky's way, the way that haunted him now.

He made his bed for the night in the bower his father had built behind the house at least thirty years ago. It was a rough, round, open-sided structure that was restored and newly thatched with leafy cottonwood branches every spring. The derisive term "squaw cooler" had been ditched somewhere along the way—during the seventies, probably—in favor of calling the structure a shade during the day and a cooler at night. Sleeping in the cooler had been a summer treat, especially on hot nights.

Everybody had had one when Reese was a kid. Old people

loved to cool their heels there when the afternoons turned boxy houses into ovens. Kids loved to sleep there after the adults had gone inside for the night. And Reese was about to perform the final ceremony there. It felt right to do it this way, and so it must have been. The old way was to burn the lodge, and that was still done on rare occasions. But when he'd thought about torching the whole house, it felt wrong, and the feeling, right or wrong, was all he had to go by.

The feeling was right when he gathered the sage, made the fire pit, assembled his father's personal belongings, the black-and-white shepherd dogging his every step. He liked having someone there when he felt like saying something, and he liked how the dog cocked his head as though he was hanging on every little word. Saying "Let's go find some matches" had Crybaby's ears on high alert. Maybe he was confusing *matches* with *meat*. "You hang with me tonight, and I'll make it worth your while."

And the dog obliged, even though, unlike Reese of late, he had a night life to tend to. There were rustlings in the brush to be investigated, shifting shadows in the pasture to be checked, a springing toad to be nosed. Reese sat cross-legged on his pallet of canvas tarp, sleeping bags, and blankets, toying with the matches. He lit one just to watch it flare up, just to smell the sulfur. Fascinating. He'd accidentally started a prairie fire once because he'd been fascinated by the flash and the smell of matches. The volunteer firefighters had told his father about the matches they'd found. "Damn deer hunters," Roy had said. Reese remembered hiding behind the bedroom door, listening, terrified. When the men left, he'd emerged to face his father, who examined his small, sooty hands, touched his singed hair. All he said was, "You get caught setting fires, they'll take you away. Then you'll be eating squash soup and sleeping on a cold, hard floor somewhere."

Reese hated squash, always had, and he wasn't sure he could actually sleep on the ground anymore. But he was going to try. He watched the sun set behind the hill where his father had died.

"Roy Blue Sky's own Last Stand Hill," he told the dog. "Was that how it was, him taking the high ground up there?

It's picture-perfect this time of day, isn't it? I ought to come back more often, just to look at the sky."

The tall grass sketching its silhouette on the pink-and-blue sky reminded him of a tattered little storybook someone had read to him so long ago that his mind's ear could not identify the voice. Long before he'd set any fires, before he'd seen a basketball, before he'd known what squash was. But he remembered repeating the words "Great-Grandpa Bunny Bunny" after the reader and touching the beautiful Easter egg colors that streaked across the sky on the page. His father could not have been the reader. His father's stories were recited, not read from a book, and they never mentioned bunnies. Rabbits, maybe, and there were always grandmothers and grandfathers, but no *bunnies*.

"Where did Grandpa Bunny Bunny come from, then?" he asked aloud, and then he laughed. "Must have hopped in off the Bunny Trail and left those painted eggs in the church yard, huh? And the sky, did he paint this sky like the story said?" He half expected an answer, and when he didn't get one, he pressed further. "Or is that your job now? Western sunsets by Roy Blue Sky."

He heard deep, distant laughter on the wind. It made him smile.

"What? Not a fitting legacy, old man? How should I picture you, then?" The wind carried the laughter away. He waited for a new image, but nothing came to mind. "I want to know where you are. Do you wander the hills and draws at night looking for offerings left by the hunters? If I throw some meat out there, am I feeding you or the dog?"

Crybaby yawned noisily and stretched out on his side.

The first stars were beginning to appear in the evening sky. Pale spirits these were, maybe old searchers who had to get started early. Or maybe they were new to the heavens, the eager young souls running ahead of the pack. That was what Reese would be when he got there, one of the runners. No aimless wandering for the Big Gun. He'd be a streaker. A shooting star.

Run, then, Big Man. Run as far and as fast and as high as you can.

85

Ah, yes, the familiar dare.

"Yeah, I ran. I flew. Hell, I *soared*. Is that what you're doing now?" Whatever the old man was doing, he'd left something behind. Reese could feel it. "Am I keeping you? Do my thoughts trap you here? If I say your name, will that bring you near?"

I am as near as blood. Better than anyone, you have always known this, whether you name me, claim me, or blame me. I am your father. I live in you.

"Yeah, right," Reese muttered as he arranged the oak and dry cottonwood the way he'd been taught when he was a boy. *But by whom?* "None of the above."

He was simply doing his damn duty, and thinking about the old man felt like part of that. He didn't want to go overboard with any kind of seance. He wanted to know where his father had gone, was all, whether he was in a good place. He wanted him to be in a good place, not wandering around worrying about unfinished . . .

"What unfinished business?"

Damn, who was he talking to?

The dog had gotten bored and kicked back for a nap. Reese was keeping himself company now. Roy Blue Sky's Last Stand Hill was just a black slump on a purple horizon now, and soon even the tint would be gone. Soon he would light the fire.

"I tend to think that if you can't rest, it doesn't have anything to do with what happened on that hill," he said as he rubbed another wooden match between his thumb and forefinger. "There's only the question of who did this to you, and even if we find the answer, that won't change anything. We know that.

"And so I give away your pickup and your rifles and burn your shirts and pants, and then what? Then you leave me alone?" No answer. Nothing but the rattle of dry leaves on top of the bower behind him. "If it's done the way you want it done, then that's it. You let me go." He squatted, struck the match on his thumbnail, blinked at the flame. "And, yeah, then I'm left alone."

The dry tinder at the base of his sturdy tipi of firewood flashed and popped, like the camera his Auntie Lil was always dragging out on holidays. It had been a long time since he'd thought about that damn camera or all the coaxing it had taken to get him into the picture with his smaller, cuter cousins. "Bean Pole," they'd called him then, and Auntie Lil had told him not to scrunch down but to stand up tall, like his Uncle Silo, who had been his father's buddy long before they'd become brothers-in-law.

But Roy Blue Sky was the last guy Silo would have picked to marry his beautiful baby sister. Roy was too old for her, too wild, too poor, too damn ugly. He'd already been married once, and Bernadette was barely out of high school. Auntie Lil loved to tell the story about the time Roy had won himself a bride by losing a fight with Silo. She had given Reese the photograph that went with the story, the one she'd taken when Bernadette had disappeared for two days and come back married. " 'He looked so pitiful,' your mother said, 'all busted up and still swearing he'd keep on fighting until I said yes.' " That was the closest his parents had come to posing for a wedding picture—the tall, slender beauty with hair down to her waist and the triumphant groom nearly twice her age, standing beside her with a fat lip and a shiner.

Reese had missed seeing Auntie Lil at the funeral. He'd heard she was having some health problems, and he needed to check in on her while he was here. He hadn't been too good about such things recently, but going through the old man's belongings had stirred up some sentimental notions in him about being duty-bound.

How the hell could a guy get sentimental about *obligations*?

He hoped the fire pit was far enough from the cooler. The flames were licking the sides of the firewood tipi, and if the wind shifted, he could end up with more bonfire than he was bargaining for.

And then they'd take him away. Not to a cold floor, but to a cold, white, antiseptic room, where he'd lie on a table and listen to people talking about him in hushed tones. "No way should a guy in this condition be playing basketball for a living."

No way should he have given it up. If they hadn't taken him away that time, if they hadn't hooked him up to those machines and eavesdropped on the private, personal workings of his body, maybe he would have gone down again. Down and out in a blaze of glory. Or maybe not. It would have been a weighty gamble, the only kind worth taking.

He fed a pair of jeans to the flaming cone too quickly, creating an indignant cloud of smoke. *Break it down*, he thought. A step at a time, a piece at a time. The Indian way took time. Took it but did not measure it or begrudge its passing. He tossed a piece of sage into the flames. The pungent scent filled his passages, cleared his head. A pair of white boxers burst into flames, then another sprig of sage.

No rush, take your time; set it up, aim, and shoot.

"I remember this shirt."

He recognized the scrolling on the yoke and the small three-corner tear in the back tail. It was the Western shirt his father had made him wear to the spring dance he'd dreaded attending in the eighth grade. But he'd gone because there was a girl he'd wanted to please, and that afternoon he'd asked for something new and nice to wear.

He knew damn well there was no money for new clothes at the end of the month, the end of a long, hard winter, the end of what had turned out to be his father's very last binge. But he'd asked anyway, partly to make the old man sorry to have to turn him down.

His father had found the shirt in the back of a drawer, said he'd worn it only once or twice because he'd wanted to save it. Save it for what? Reese had wondered silently. It was an old-fashioned, ugly thing. But there was something about the way the old man had unfolded it and held it up for his inspection that kept him from saying anything. There was some rare, wistful thing in his father's eyes that made him put the damn shirt on and leave the house in it, even though the sleeves didn't quite reach his wrist bones.

He'd gotten a little wild himself that night. He'd been too shy to ask the girl to dance, which was probably a good thing, since he'd never learned any of those moves, so he'd claimed a seat at the top of the bleachers and watched his classmates fumble with this foolish, foreign courtship ritual. "White dancing," it was called, and the eighth-grade version was mostly girls dancing with girls, shaking their skinny hips for the guys in the bleachers. What a contrast, he thought now, with "Indian dancing," for which it was the men who wore the colorful plumage and strutted their stuff in the middle of the circle. In the old days the women had performed a more sedate step on the perimeter, the better to view and evaluate and select.

Maybe that was what the basketball court was for. But if that were the case, why hadn't he been selected? Hadn't he shone pretty damn bright in that arena, even without any plumage? He'd outdone them all, outdone himself on many occasions.

Outdid, outplayed, and outgrew, didn't you, Blue?

Not that night, as he recalled. The night of his eighth-grade spring dance, he'd ended up in a beat-up Chevy with a bunch of guys and a bottle of Everclear, altogether hell-bent on feeling good and doing bad. They'd smashed some glass just to hear the noise. They'd broken into an old storage shed behind the community center only because Reese had been tall enough to boost Titus Hawk through the only window. Later Reese had caught his father's shirt on some barbed wire while making his escape from the three-hundred-pound cop who'd nearly nabbed them.

The next day the old man had said nothing about Reese's all-too-apparent hangover. Without a word, Roy had accepted the torn shirt and disappeared into his room with it. Reese had never seen him wear it, figured he'd discarded it for the tear and maybe the shame when his son confessed to his part in what became known as the Spring Dance Rampage. It had taken Reese all summer to work off his share of the damages, and even then the old man had had to kick in with part of the money. And *even then,* he'd not said a word.

The shirt's garish colors had dwindled to ink and ash. Reese added more sage despite the way the pungent smoke burned his eyes. He wiped them with the back of his hand and piled on more sage. Then, one by one, he burned the personal pieces of his father's earthly life. The heat rolled over him, so intense that he took off his own shirt. A plaid wool coat smoldered and gave off a singed-hair smell. White smoke drifted toward the swaying tops of the cottonwood trees, into the darkness.

A song rose in the back of his throat, words of sorrow and contrition in a language his brain had let languish but his heart remembered. His poor, clumsy heart, which had all it could do to keep his big body going from day to day, would not divest itself of the old, useless, fugitive fragments. So the song found its way through his mouth, which gave it to the smoke, which took it into the night.

Tunkasila, hear me, for this spirit who comes to you was my father. See him coming alone, he who led our people, he ya he.

He felt strange to himself, his body wondrously small and oddly obscured by the huge sound of his voice and the echo that ricocheted from star to star. The night sky had taken his song. He was so completely absorbed that he did not hear anything but the crackle of the fire feeding on his father's clothes, nor did he see any light but fire and star.

A set of headlights bathed the road briefly before being extinguished. An engine rumbled, idled, then fell quiet. The dog leaped to his feet, but did not bark. A door opened and closed, softly. Respectfully. Reese marked none of this. He stood close to the fire, sweat flowing freely, cleansing every pore as he sang for the spirit of his father, sang his song through again and again, because the trail was long and the night was vast. One small soul might easily be lost without a strong-heart song to carry it to the other side, to make the announcement so that those who waited would know it was time to receive this one.

He comes. See where he comes. This brave man comes.

When he turned and saw Helen, there was no surprise in him. There was no displeasure, no self-consciousness, nothing to keep him from her. He was filled to overflowing, resonant with power and celebration, and he felt only delight in seeing her. He lifted his arms, turned his palms up in invitation.

She acknowledged the dog, but her eyes were on Reese. She started toward him slowly, picking up her pace as she got closer. When she reached him she was like a bird sailing into his arms. Without a word, he lifted her to his kiss. There was fire in his heart and at his back, and she felt airy and cool next to his sweat-slick body, her face above his, her lips kissing and kissing him. He drank her kisses like water, hadn't realized his thirst until this moment, and when she stopped the kissing to simply look and let him watch the fire dance in her eyes, he swallowed, swallowed, savored the taste she'd left in his mouth.

Cool hands came to his wet face, stroked his cheeks, and he thought her face appeared to be wet, too. But the water was in his eyes. In his mouth, in his eyes, from the fire, he thought. From the acrid smoke. She must have thought he was crying, which, of course, he couldn't be. There could be no tears on the face of Reese Blue Sky. But her fingers touched him so sweetly, stroked so gently, he would not protest.

He let her down slowly, a long, easy slide, and when her shoes touched his boots he bent to kiss her more. He could tell that his kisses were welcome by the way she clung to his shoulders and stroked his hair and answered him, kiss for kiss. He wanted to bury his face against her, and he found himself down on one knee, undoing the buttons on her white blouse, the hook between her breasts. She stroked his hair, watched him, said nothing until he laid his face in the valley between her breasts, and then what she said was not a word, but more than a word. It was a come-to-me sound. He was welcome. He was safe. He was where he belonged, at least for this moment. He kissed the swell of her breast, stroked its lower curve with his tongue. She hooked her fingers into his hair.

He closed his eyes and learned her shape all over again with his hands, the once-familiar curve of her bottom, the firm curve of her belly, the womanly curve of her hips. He wasn't looking for a zipper, but there it was at her hip, so he opened it, pushed her skirt off her hips, ran his hands over her silky slip.

He looked up at her, a thousand wishes whirling inside his head, yet they were not to be uttered, not even one. To wish out loud would break the spell. Instead he tightened his arms around her hips, lifted her, and carried her to the pallet of quilts he'd laid on the grass for his bed. He grabbed the top item from what was left of his father's things—a shirt of some kind—knelt on the pallet, and began mopping his torso. She took the cloth from him and did him this service, blotting first his face, then his neck, his shoulders, his chest, handling him carefully, as if she were cleaning some precious heirloom. He knelt there and permitted this ministering of hers, testing his forbearance in the face of his need to reciprocate.

The invitation came in her eyes, and he answered with a hungry kiss. Her mouth was succulent, moist, her tongue darting to meet his. He brushed the sides of her neck with solicitous fingertips, peeling her blouse away as he tracked tight muscle to her shoulders. Her blouse slid to the ground, freeing her arms to hold him while he kissed her and tasted the cool sweetness she'd brought him from the earthy side of the night. He unhooked her bra and pushed that away, too, so that her breasts might touch him and be harried by the feel of him while his hands skated unimpeded over her lovely, tapered back. Contact with his chest honed her nipples to fine, sweet points.

He kissed her again, let her taste his hunger as she slipped her hand between them, over his belly, into his pants. Yes, he wanted her, and yes, he was ready. He lifted his face to the blaze-warmed breeze, cleared his head with starlight.

"Reese . . ."

"Shhh." He held her close, trembling on the inside exactly the way she was trembling on the outside. Eyes closed, he filled his head with the scent of burning sage, the promise of heaven and Helen. "I'll go get what we need in a minute. Don't send me away yet."

Her fingers fluttered in his pants, and he groaned.

"I don't want you to go anywhere," she whispered. "Let me—"

"You want me to stay?" He smiled because he had to loosen his pants to extricate her. "Hit or stay. Those are your choices," he reminded her. "I'll stay and make you come, how's that?"

"You can't . . ."

"House rules," he whispered as he lowered her to his blankets. "My house, my odds, my . . ."

He worshipped her with his mouth, teasing, suckling her, flicking his tongue over sensitive places, steadily nudging her until her breath was trapped in tiny spasms and he could feel her teetering, topping off, echoing, "My . . . my," and then, tumbling back to him, "My oh my oh my . . ."

He held her, his body absorbing her delicate tremors, making them partly his. Not the time to get up and walk away, but he couldn't think of too many options. Too bad there hadn't been a box of condoms among the old man's personal effects. He'd never heard about any repercussions from the *wanagi* for using condoms they might have left behind, but he figured whatever he found could well be holey.

Damn, this was not time to bust out laughing, either.

"I could use some water. Can I bring you something?" Reluctantly he moved away. "You won't leave me, will you?"

"That wouldn't be very nice, would it?" She caught his hand. "Anyway, I still want a hit."

"Blackjack or bust?"

"Blackjack or . . ." She brushed her cheek over the back of his hand. "Or Blue Sky. Much rather have Blue Sky. I've missed you."

"Really," he said, doubtful, but thinking maybe she meant for it to be true, and that was enough. She wanted him now, and that, too, was enough.

He fastened his jeans and disappeared into the house after telling Helen she was to be the fire-tender until he returned. Huddled in a summer-thin quilt, not for warmth but for cover, she watched him go, feeling something akin to the rush she got when she'd won two or three hands in a row. She knew she was pushing her luck, and that was the best part. Foolish, foolish, foolish. She could lose everything. He could take everything. Why was she taking this terrible, terrible chance?

She sat up slowly. Close, so close to the flame. Reese was doing his duty to his father, and he had given her a piece of it. *Tend my fire.* She added a piece of dry cottonwood and a handful of sage. The fire leaped to consume her offering. She held the quilt open and scooped the white smoke inside, hoping it would purify white skin as well as brown. She had no idea what words to use. "Cleanse me," she whispered, adding, "For this one night. Wash everything else away and let me love him just for tonight."

Whom was she trying to fool? It was a selfish prayer, and

she knew it. It was a dumb thing for a woman in her position to utter, even in the dark with no one else around. But she'd come to him in fire and darkness, and the power that drew her there had little to do with past or future. It was truer than that, and the only way to deny it was to separate herself from it. But it was too late. She listened to the door close. She heard him speak to his dog. She watched him, a tall shadow striding across the yard, prairie grass swishing against his jeans.

He brought two bottles of spring water. "I ought to pour it over my head, but that would wake me up, and this is one dream I don't want to . . ." His knee cracked as he squatted next to her and handed her a bottle. "What made you come?"

She stared at him, he at her, and the laughter hit them both. She poured a little water in her hand and splashed his face with it. Grinning, he replied by pouring some in his hand and cooling her face with it, then her neck and chest.

"Feels good," she said.

"Fire-tending's hot work," he said as he stretched out beside her.

"I was on my way home from work. I saw the fire."

"This isn't on your way."

"No, but I don't think I would have stopped otherwise."

He studied her for a moment before tipping his head back for a long pull from the bottle. Through the clear plastic she could see the fire dancing in the water. He pressed his lips together, swallowed, gazed at the fire. "You would have come this way only to drive past?"

"But I saw the fire. I knew you must be . . ." She looked at the things left to be burned, waiting there like a diminished pile of laundry. "I didn't want you to do this alone. Maybe you're supposed to, but I . . ." She laughed and groaned and shook her head. "Oh, I came anyway."

"Okay, so I made you come, and I can do it again." He was smiling as he reached out to tuck her hair behind her ear. "Again and again, but you know that. You've known that since the beginning. I was born to please you, remember?"

"Whose line was that? Not mine, I hope." She nuzzled his palm and whispered, "I do have some protection in the car, in my purse."

"In my pocket," he said as he pulled her into his arms for a kiss. It was the kind of kiss a man gave to a woman he shared his days and nights and all of his secrets with.

She wanted the kiss without the rest. Oh, maybe a little of the rest, a hint of what it might have been like if she had wanted the rest, if he had wanted it, if they had taken the risk.

He withdrew from their kiss smiling, as though they were proving something to his satisfaction. "We're smarter than we used to be, huh?"

"Older and much wiser."

"Oh, I'm gettin' there," he assured her. "That was the problem you had with me, wasn't it? When we were alone, I was a man. When we were around other people, I was still a boy to you."

Around other people? She didn't remember them doing much socializing during their short, sweet season together. But his dark eyes informed against some memory that troubled him. She'd hurt him somehow, and the fact that she was unaware made it worse. She remembered feeling a little awkward about some of her colleagues having been his teachers. Maybe more than a little. What had she done to cover that up?

He could see her struggling to remember. His eyes twinkled in the firelight. "But I'm catching up, Maggie May."

She laughed. That damned Rod Stewart song he used to tease her with. If she'd embarrassed him, he'd gotten back at her with that. "I'll always be older," she insisted.

"Only if you're looking at calendars. I used to be too damn big for my age. Now I'm too damn broken-down for my age." He adjusted her wrap, brought his fists full of blanket together beneath her chin, and touched his forehead to hers. "Age means absolutely nothing to us now, and we both know it. That's one strike you can't hold against me anymore."

"I never held it against you."

"Don't lie to me, now. It's my turn to pitch, your turn to swing." There was a challenge in his smile. "So you wanna help me burn stuff?"

Don't lie to me, don't lie to me, don't lie to me. She swallowed hard. "Is help permitted?"

"It is if I permit you."

"You're not burning memories, are you?" She ducked a dry, drooping cottonwood branch as she followed him to the pile of clothes. "I mean, surely you want to keep the memories."

"Mostly I'm burning the things he wore." He poked at the glowing ashes with a stick. "I remember when we did this for my mother," he said as he rolled a log, reviving the flames. "It scared me. There was all this talk about ghosts, all the old stories, and I didn't want my mother to be a ghost. That was the worst. Bad enough that suddenly she wasn't alive, but if being dead meant she might be around in some other form and that she might turn on me . . ." His eyes met hers. "That was the worst."

Helen had been trying to adjust the quilt around her shoulders, but she stilled and stared. "Did you tell your father you were scared?"

"I cried. He told me to stop it."

"He was grieving, too, though."

"Yeah, but crying wasn't allowed. He never cried unless he was drunk, and that didn't count with him." Reese sighed, shook his head, chucked a bit of sage toward the fire. "Yeah, I want to burn some of those memories." He took over with the quilt, slipping it under her armpits, tucking it over her bosom to create a sarong. He'd freed her arms for his hands' quick caress. "Help me finish this."

She handed the remaining pieces to him one by one without looking at them until flames crackled around them. A cutting of sage burned with each item of clothing, filling the night with a heady scent.

"I remember this one," he said quietly, and she risked a glance. It was a white shirt. "He wore it the last time he came to a game."

"To watch you play. Maybe you should keep that one."

"That's not the way it's done."

"But it's a good memory," she insisted as the white shirt became a torch. "Let's acknowledge the good ones, then."

"This must be a new one," he said of the dark shirt Helen handed him. "I never saw it."

"I did." She took it back, stroked it as if it were a cherished piece of satin. "I came over to ride horseback, and he went with me. He showed me a place where you fell into the creek once."

"*I* fell into the creek?" Reese gave a brief, abrupt laugh. "I remember *him* falling in once. I must have been about eleven or twelve, had a hell of a time getting him out. Sobered him up pretty quick." His gaze drifted to a point beyond the fire, past the night. "We laughed about it, though. Both of us, flopped on our backs in the mud, we laughed so hard we got the hiccups. *Both* of us."

"But you never fell in the creek?"

He shrugged. "Yeah, I guess I did once. I was pretty little, but I remember it was spring, and the water was running real high. We were running the horses in. I was feeling real big, you know, because he'd let me go with him and help. He told me to follow him, cross the creek right where he crossed. Only I didn't listen. My horse balked a couple of times. Dad was already up at the top of the ridge, and I didn't want him to think I couldn't keep up, so I moved down a little way and whacked that mare's shoulders with the reins." He looked down at the shirt still in his hands, wagged his head. "It wasn't a good place to cross."

"Too deep?"

"Over both our heads, and my mount was the only one who could swim. I don't even know how the ol' man got me out. The current was pretty swift, and he wasn't much of a swimmer himself." Reese balled the shirt up and tossed it into the flames. "I swallowed a lot of water, I remember that. And I remember the look in his eyes. I thought he was gonna yell at me or hit me or something, but then I realized it wasn't that kind of a look. It was a look I'd never seen on him before." He laughed. "Like he'd seen a ghost."

"I know exactly how he felt. I saw Sidney get hit by a—" She caught herself, tried to downshift, but it was too late. "A car."

"Jesus," he breathed, all his soft delight evaporating. "Was it bad?"

"He was on his bike, shot out of the driveway into the street. The car—" Helen could see the red Honda, hear the squeal of the brakes, feel the icy horror as Sidney bounced off the seat and sailed over the hood. She swallowed, remembering that terrible taste in her mouth, that awful inability to connect with her legs, the pain deep in her stomach.

She shook her head, went a little hoarse. "We were lucky. The bike took the brunt of it. He broke his—" She clasped her forearm, grabbing for the right word, the right bone. *Take a breath and distance yourself. Give him the cold, anatomical details.*

"His left arm?" he supplied, eager to assist. She nodded. "Clean break? Did it heal up okay?"

She nodded again. His worried tone pinched her gullet, and she imagined him sharing that scene with her, seeing it through the window. She couldn't look at him.

"I broke the same one when I was a kid," he said, much too buoyantly. He pointed toward the dark hulk she knew to be a pole barn. "I fell off that roof over there. Must be awful for a parent, watching something like that happen to your kid." His arm became a crook, hooked around her neck to draw her against his side. "Worse than seeing a ghost, huh?"

"I've never seen a ghost."

"I've never had a kid," he said softly. The claim speared her in the chest. "As for ghosts, hell, ghosts don't scare me. I keep them well fed."

She drew a deep, shaky breath. He gave her a comforting squeeze, and they stood together and watched the remains of the shirt she had remembered for him melt away. Her eyes burned horribly. She hardly noticed his movements until he held a water bottle to her lips. She drank deeply, blinking back tears as he whispered, "Thirsty work, huh?"

She nodded. She told him about helping his father trim the horses' hooves that day. She wanted to know how he knew how much to take off. He didn't tell her; he showed her. He let her watch him, then gave her a chance to try it herself.

"He didn't like to explain himself," Reese recalled. "He'd try to get me to do something, and if I didn't catch on right away or didn't do it to suit him, he'd just do it himself. He was such a perfectionist sometimes, you know, every little detail. Like that miniature Little Bighorn in the house. I can just see him. Christ, he must have spent hours on that thing, but when I was growing up, the games weren't . . ." He glanced at her, quirked a little smile. "Kinda makes a guy wonder what kind of a father he'd make."

Oh, yes, she'd wondered, too. It usually started out with some sweet "what if" and turned into gut-gnawing speculation.

"You played basketball together. He had to raise the hoop because you wouldn't quit growing." The hoop, she remembered, was still attached to the side of the same barn he'd fallen from. "He told me about that, too."

"Told you how he taught me everything I know, did he?" Reese chuckled. "We used to play one-on-one, back when it was just me and him. He never played down to me, you know? He made me work for every shot. But when I got to be too much of a challenge, he quit playing me."

"He went to bat for you, though. He said there was a coach—"

"Sam Clark. That guy only knew one way to make a pass, and he preferred women, the younger the better. My old man got him canned."

"For . . ."

"For being a piss-poor coach."

"*And* for benching you for playing the game the way it was meant to be played."

"That's what he said?" Reese looked surprised.

"Exactly what he said."

"It's only a game." He got lost for a moment in fire-dreaming. Then, as though she doubted his filial devotion, he said, "I do want to know who hit him."

He bent to pick up a sprig of sage, came up with a little spring in his knees when he lobbed it onto the fire. "It won't change anything, but I still need to know what happened." A white tendril of smoke rose from the sage, his signal to inhale. "I love that smell. It's like frybread. It takes me home in a good way."

"I love that expression," she said. "*In a good way*. 'Nothing's good or bad but thinking makes it so.' Right? Or remembering, or allowing yourself to feel. Did we do this in a good way? I mean . . ."

"It's good that you're here. For balance. I went away from

him, and I never really came back. You saw him that night. You talked to him, and you knew what he was thinking these days." He tossed more sage onto the fire. "It's good that you're here to honor the man you knew."

"Maybe you weren't as distant from him as you think, Reese. I believe you know him in your heart, and that's why—"

"Remember that time we drove out to the Badlands?" he cut in, turning to her, taking her bare shoulders in his big, warm hands. "Remember how we built the campfire and made love and talked and made love while the stars gradually dissolved and the night faded, and there we were . . ."

"Stark naked in the sunlight." She laughed. She'd almost forgotten what it was like to be that bold, feel that free. But the feeling was back, just for tonight.

"Let's do that again." He bent his head to kiss and nuzzle and whisper, "It's just us, Helen. Just us."

It was an echo from the night he had recalled for her, a reminder of the words he'd said then. The sweetness, the innocence of that night spilled over into this one. She loosened her quilt wrap and let it slide to the ground. A deep sound of pure male delight issued from his throat as he lifted her straight up, heading for the stars.

Then down, down to his blankets they went, holding each other, kissing hungrily. The bower was like a fairy ring, a magic place where nothing could touch them. Wrapped in his long, powerful limbs, she felt shielded and safe. He treasured her with stirring hands and stimulating mouth, laid open her secret places, and adored her sacred places.

He bared himself for her, trembled when she touched him and stroked him, brought him to the brink of madness. He reveled in teetering close to the edge while he drew her to him, shaped her, made her his conduit, and turned her ordinary self into something strange and wondrous and soaring.

6

 $\mathcal{T}$he rustle of dry cottonwood leaves above her head brought Helen back to earth. Good earth. Welcoming and gracious earth, where the darkness was beginning to stretch and would soon pull away. The crisp crackle of the dying fire, the warmth of Reese's breath filling the hollow of her neck, the syncopated thumping of their hearts spoke of summer-sweet earth. The pure luxury of it all had surely lulled the man in her arms off to sleep. He lay still except for his breathing, his torso rising and falling in unison with hers. She cherished his nearness.

She remembered holding him in her arms long ago while he slept and how she'd struggled with the pleasure and the uncertainty. But now she knew better. She'd lived a little and learned a lot. Why struggle with a good moment? She thought about her son and how small he'd once been, how he'd grown so much lately, how he would one day be just as big a man as the one whose hand began to stir slowly over her bare hip.

He rolled onto his back, drawing her into the shelter of his shoulder. "Are you warm enough?" he asked. She responded with a contented sound. "I think I'll move in here," he mused.

"Really?" She lifted her head, balanced her chin on his chest. "Leave Minneap—"

"Shh. That's far away, outside this place. Don't name it and bring it here." He stroked her hair. "I mean *here*. I'll live in this homemade shelter, live the simple life, the one I took for granted. I had a cousin who spent a couple of summers with us. Him and me, we used to sleep out here a lot. It was like we had our own place, our own world. Nobody could touch us here."

Her fingertips tingled where they lay against his warm skin. "Don't you want to be touched?"

"You can touch all you want, but just you."

"Where to start?" she said, giving a girlish sigh as she slid her hand over his long, smooth torso, skated over his pelvic bone, and grabbed his firm backside. "I like this part most especially, this cute little—"

He laughed. "I ain't got nothin' little, sweetheart."

"Compared to the rest of you, *this is* quite compact. Why are you basketball players always slapping each other's butts?"

" 'Cause they're too hard to pinch."

She groaned.

"Hey, it's the football players who do most of the butt-smacking. Basketball players have their own hand jive. Besides, guys have a different set of standards on the playing field. You've got your own language, your own signals, your own—"

"Your own world?"

"I suppose." And then, quietly: "You don't think much of it, though, do you?"

"Basketball?" She was surprised to hear the tender bit of strain in his voice, as though it mattered to him what she thought of his game. "I think it's a wonderful sport. Much more fun to watch than football. Especially when you know someone, and that someone was someone . . ."

"Someone?"

"Like you. I mean, you played so well. It must have been hard to give it up." Then, gingerly, "Do you, um . . . do you work now?" She felt a tremor in her pillow, and she looked up to find him soundlessly laughing. "You probably don't have to, which is—"

"Ah, the myth of fame and fortune." He measured half an inch of air between his thumb and forefinger. "I'm this close to a college degree. Finally. You maybe wouldn't think it's work, but for me it is. I've had to work my ass off."

She reached around him, tried to take the same measurement on his rear. It was like trying to use scissors on a rock.

He laughed again. "See? Not much left."

"What's left is very nice piece of . . . you. What's your major? Phy-ed?"

"I have a double major. How do you like that?"

"I'm impressed."

"Well, I've been at it for so many years, I oughta have a quadruple. They practically gave me the phy-ed. The history major I did the hard way."

"History? How interesting." One of his father's passions. And yes, one of hers. She'd taught English and history.

"Yeah. It really is interesting." He pulled a quilt over her, effectively bundling her against his side, tucking as he continued talking. "I went back to school for something to do, something to keep me from going crazy, get my head out of my, uh . . . my own belly button. Now I'm almost an educated man. Otherwise I'm a partner in a couple of pretty good businesses."

"A silent partner?"

"I can make noise when I feel like it. You think I'm silent?"

"Quiet." She rolled a finger around the belly button he'd mentioned, tracing the circumference of the small hollow, and added, "Sometimes."

"I used to get tongue-tied around you, but I've gotten better, haven't I?"

"Decidedly looser with the tongue."

"You like that, huh?" He dipped his head for an exchange of tongues. "No more knots," he whispered between kisses.

"Smooth."

"Rich, too." He nibbled her bottom lip while she was still caressing his belly. "Do I taste rich?"

"You taste like game."

He laughed. "The man got game, honey. Made some good coin, got some good advice, made some good investments, and I do all right. Plus I do a little coaching. Kids your son's age."

Her fingers stilled on his belly.

"I had a basketball camp last month. I've been doing it for three years now, and it's gone really good. It's been . . ." His voice hushed on a wish. "I want to be a teacher, Helen. Maybe coach a little bit. I remember . . ." He paused, stroked her arm, stoking the fires of his recollection. "I stood outside your classroom door once, right after school started. You know, not long before I left for Minnesota. Anyway, I stood there in the hall, and I listened to you talk about the Constitution. Jesus, *the Constitution*. It hadn't been that long since I'd had to sit through that stuff myself, and all I could think about *then* was, if you don't get through this, you don't graduate. This is the required bullshit. But there I was back again, listening in, getting a hard-on over all that freedom you were—"

She smacked his hip, her giggle trailing off into a groan.

But he was serious. "And I was thinking, Damn, this is good. She's making this sound interesting, like it really has something do with these kids, with *us*, with Bad River. You were doing this 'free speech' exercise, and you really had some of those kids hooked." He pressed a kiss into her hair and whispered, "You had me hooked. I thought you were magic."

She closed her eyes, her scalp prickling from the breath of his kiss, and she imagined him standing alone in that long, dim hallway with its lustrous, newly waxed floor. Standing there, standing up, standing out no matter where he was. Outstanding, and he knew it. The outsider, even in his own hometown, because he always stood out.

That was the problem, wasn't it?

"You think I can make the grade?" he was asking her now.

Oh, yes, she'd always thought so, but had she ever told him? *I think you'll go far, too far for me.*

"I think you'll have them eating out of your hand."

"I just want to get them reading out of some books." He brushed her hair back from her face. "You're the one I want eating out of my hand. What would you have me feed you?"

"What's in your hand?" She turned her face into his palm,

inhaled his scent. "Mmm, the skin is my favorite part. Seasoned with sage and smoke." With a flick of her tongue she traced his long, deeply etched lifeline. "And with sex and a little salt. Tasty, tasty."

"Only an appetizer." He hoisted himself up, leaned over her, smiling. "Tongue is considered a true delicacy hereabouts. Care for a little more?"

"I would love . . ."

She would love. She *did* love. She loved his deep kiss and his probing tongue, and she knew how he loved making love in the early morning when the world was vaporous and fresh and new. Such a good time to go riding. They rode the pleasure horse until they'd played him out, then dozed in each other's arms on the lavender threshold of morning. But neither of them actually slept, for every move or shifting of limbs was answered with tender accommodation.

Soft gray light opened the herringbone cracks in their thatched roof. The air smelled of dew and ash. From the misty copse of cottonwoods by the creek came the doleful call of a dove. Its mate coo-coo-cooed in response. Beneath damp quilts, Helen cuddled against Reese's side, and she was immediately enfolded in his arms.

"Ready to let me feed you from my kitchen?"

"I should go soon. I hate to move, but if I do, it really should be toward the car."

"Don't move, then." He pulled his arm free of the quilts and checked the contents of the hand he'd had her eating from earlier. "Damn, I wish I could make bacon and eggs appear here. But as we've already established, my name ain't exactly Magic."

"Your name is Blue Sky, and I can't think of anything more magical." She planted a kiss in his empty palm, then one on his lips. But her pleasure was stolen suddenly by the thought that Blue Sky could be her son's name, that given the truth, given the choice . . .

She pulled away. "Mine should be Blue Moon, because I really have to disappear with the morning sun."

"Or because I only get to see you once every *tona* years," he said, using the Lakota word for "many" or "how many."

"Or because . . ." Oh, she had *tona* reasons. "I have to go to work."

"What time?"

"Well, I have things to do before I go to work." She wanted to call her son, for one thing. *Their* son; yes, in the misty morning light, looking up at him, she could not put the truth of it from her mind. She wanted him to know, wanted them both to know. So often she had imagined the telling of it, imagined forgiveness, imagined disaster. "Reese . . ."

"You still need a cup of coffee in the morning, don't you?" He was sitting them up. "I found some papers I want to show you. I'd like to hear your thoughts. Will you stay for coffee and have a look?"

"Your father's papers?"

"Yeah, some stuff about the casinos. Stuff you might understand better than I do. I figure I'd better take a closer look if I'm going to finish out my father's term."

"You've decided?"

"It feels like the right thing to do." He crawled out of the blankets and ducked under droopy branches, explaining as he retrieved his pants. "Right now, this morning, I'm sure it's the right thing to do, and not just because of us."

Because of us? Oh, God, she thought, don't spoil it, Reese. *Us* was a dangerous word. There could be no *us* without the truth. "Dangerous" didn't begin to describe it. "Fatal" was more like it. Where had she left her clothes?

"It's because it feels right," he was saying. "You know how you say, okay, I'm in this game, and you feel like it was meant to be? You own the ball, you own the court, you're the man with the power." He tossed her slip into her lap. "It feels like the right thing to do. You never felt like that?"

"I have. It's a deceptive feeling sometimes."

He stepped into his jeans. "You think I should stay out of it?"

"I didn't say that. You asked me . . ." She wrestled with satin straps. What else had she been wearing? There must have been other underwear, maybe a skirt. She needed something to clear the fog. "I could use some coffee, but as far as your father's papers are—"

"Did you know he requested an investigation? I found a copy of a letter he sent to the BIA area office."

She watched him zip his sleek, dark, intriguing nakedness into his jeans. The letter was less interesting. She'd seen the letter once, and once was enough for a letter. "Toast and coffee are all I ever have for breakfast."

"Yeah, you're right. You start poking around in a dead man's letters, you might stir up all kinds of ghosts." He handed her the damp wad of wrinkles her white blouse had become. "Better to stay out of it."

"I didn't say that. I'm just not sure your father's papers are any of *my* business, especially since . . ." She plunged into the blouse, one arm at a time. The morning light was stealing over her now, exposing her for a rumpled hustler. She didn't feel much like tap dancing, yet it was part of the act. "Well, I work at Pair-a-dice City."

"But you're new there. You weren't there when he asked for the place to be investigated, so you're in the clear." He took her hand and hauled her to her feet. She groaned, and so did he. "Sleeping on the ground ain't as easy as it used to be."

"Have we been sleeping?"

"We've been, uh . . . laying together?" He grinned. "Lying together? Which is it, Teach?"

His confidence had always been a pretty thing, the way it made his eyes shine. He put his arm around her to walk her to the house, and she leaned against him, tucked in her chin, closed her eyes. "Lying, I guess."

"For sure we got laid."

"For sure we did," she said, and for his gentle tone, she smiled.

He told her to jump in the shower while he made coffee. Her head was under the water when she felt the curtain slide. A large bare foot joined hers in the tub. She looked up, to find him filling every spare inch of space in the cubicle, giving her an impossibly sheepish wolf grin. Lord, he was big.

"Coffee's on," he said. "Thought I'd save us some time here."

"Are we in a hurry?"

"I'm not."

She had to laugh. He looked like Daddy visiting the play-house. It couldn't hurt to extend the magic a bit, allow it to enter this small place, too. She could contain it here in the tub, which was even smaller than the backyard bower. She could take the risk in this small, private place, harness it here, enjoy it a little longer. It would not have to spill out if she drew the curtain.

He washed her hair, and when she offered to return the favor, he knelt in the tub. She adjusted the spray, but still he got soap in his eyes, feigned blindness, and groped her. She laughed until he found her mons with his mouth, which was oddly startling. She tried to back away, but there was no room, no backing or escaping or denying the pleasure he would give and give and give, for he was also big in the giving depart-ment. He clamped an arm around her hips and sipped between her legs and stroked her with his tongue, and there was no such thing as a harness. There were no limits. Neither of them noticed immediately when the hot water ran out, and when they did, it felt good. Everything felt good.

Dressed only in jeans, he served her coffee. Dressed only in a slip, she served him poached eggs on toast. When he disappeared to turn on some music, she sneaked the dog into the house and fed him bacon. Reese caught them under the kitchen table and scolded her, using the words his father had obviously recorded in his brain. She'd heard them from Roy herself not long ago. "Dogs don't belong in the house. You start letting them in, they forget how to be dogs."

But to his father's line Reese added, "Don't they, you sneaky ol' coyote? What am I gonna do with you, huh? I got no place to . . ." He eyed Helen as he ruffled the dog's black-and-white ruff. "Does your son have a dog?"

"No." Her heartbeat tripped into high gear. Whenever he mentioned Sidney, her stupid heart raced so fast she felt light-headed. Crybaby was still licking bacon grease off her fingers. "We can't have dogs where we live."

"Every boy needs a dog," he professed, and she could hear her son saying, *Yeah, Mom.* "You guys need to move back here and give this mutt a home now that you've spoiled him so bad."

"I have not."

"Yeah, you have. Look at the way he's lookin' at you." He paused while Crybaby demonstrated soulfulness on cue. "How about your boy? Have you spoiled him?"

He was teasing her with that I-know-you look, and she wanted to warn him that he didn't, and she didn't know him. Not well enough, not the way knowing really counted. She wasn't sure what he'd do if he found out that his innocent look was misplaced on her. The only knowing he could claim was a physical thing, purely sensual, senseless and risky. But, ah, enjoyable beyond reason. The capricious realm where children came into play.

"Probably," she confessed as she stood, leaving him on the floor with the dog. She was exposing too much of herself. "I can't believe I'm wandering around here half dressed," she said, heading for the bathroom in search of her blouse. She felt like a wilted flower, losing pieces of herself every time somebody barely breathed on her. "Did I bring my skirt in, or did I abandon it in the grass?"

"*I* abandoned it in the grass," he called after her, "but then I retrieved it, put it in the bedroom with your shoes and stuff."

She followed his directions and the music to the end of the hallway. She'd never seen the bedrooms. One of the doors stood open to what had once been a boy's room, now being visited by a man. A man's pair of shoes lay beneath a boy's desk. A man's classical jazz played on a boy's boom box. A man's black leather suitcase stood next to a boy's chest of drawers, and a woman's skirt and shoes lay at the foot of a bed that had to be too small to accommodate the man who had stripped it down to its sheets and taken every blanket in the house outside. Something he had probably done as a boy. Something her own boy had done many times. Her boy, *her* son, as long as she could get all her pieces back into place exactly the way they'd been. No cracks, no leaks, nothing left behind in this enchanting and chancy territory.

"See? I didn't burn everything."

Reese had sneaked up behind her. She stiffened, but she

refused to let him startle her. She felt him invade her space without quite touching, so close she could feel the warm shower dew.

He lifted her damp hair off the back of her neck and kissed her nape. "Personally, I like the way you're dressed," he said, his voice low, near to whispering. "You're elegant no matter what you're wearing or not wearing. Classic. The first time I saw you, you were wearing a plain dress, pale yellow, but it just sort of skimmed over you." His fingertips skittered over her shoulder. "It flowed with you when you moved, and all I could think of was lemon sherbet. You made my mouth water."

She stepped into the room, turned, looked up at him in wonder. He remembered what she'd been wearing that day? He remembered the color?

"You know what else I like? I like the way you forget yourself sometimes. Like you did with me last night and then"—he nodded over his shoulder, but his eyes held her gaze—"then crouched under the table with the dog."

"No similarity whatsoever." She smiled, teasing. She would take charge here.

"You're such a surprise sometimes, the kind that takes a guy's breath away." With a long arm he easily bridged the distance she'd put between them, touching her shoulder again. He slipped two fingers under her satin strap. "But sooner or later you always remember again."

"Remember what?"

"I don't know. Something better, maybe. Someplace else you're supposed to be, something you're supposed to be doing." He shrugged. "Somebody you're supposed to be with."

"I forget myself," she echoed deliberately, examining the notion. It was a nice way to put it, nearly absolving her of all responsibility. To forget and do the natural thing. It sounded wonderfully harmless. "There's no one else I'd rather be with, Reese. Believe me."

"I didn't say *rather*."

She saw his kiss coming, and she lifted her chin to meet

it. Point well taken. But still she whispered, "I should be going soon."

"You're hung up on *should*."

"No, I'm not, but I shouldn't be . . ."

"And the flip side is *should not*." He kissed her again, sliding his hands over her shoulders and down her arms. So disarming a gesture, so appealing his smile. "I have things to show you, things I want to talk with you about." He squeezed her hand. "So don't be in such a hurry to remember whatever it is that pulls you away. Forget yourself a while longer."

But she did pull away. "Was this your room?"

"Mine until Carter moved in. Guess he got it all to himself when I left, but this is pretty much the way it's always been, except there used to be posters on the walls and clothes on the floor."

"You and Carter shared this bed?" She plunked herself down, bounced as though testing the mattress. The springs chirped.

"When he came home we got a pair of those damn twin beds, which is probably what did my back in. My father gave those away and got this one back out when I left for the army after my first attempt at college." He sat beside her, then flopped back on the bed. The springs screeched. "Damn, this thing is shot. A new one's being delivered next week, which is going to take up the whole room, wall to wall. But, then, so do I. Meanwhile, I'm better off on the ground, sleepin' out. Does your kid like to sleep out?"

"He's—well, summer camp, he—"

He laughed, pulled her down beside him, and cuddled her. "We don't need to be talking about kids or brothers or any of that stuff right now, huh? It's just us. Let's do things, just us."

Her nose was pressed against his smooth skin, and his tangy male scent went straight to the weak side of her brain. A smooth clarinet carried the mood along.

"What kind of things?"

"The kind we've been doing. Man-and-woman things." He pushed a strap off her shoulder, touched the tip of his tongue where the satin had been. "I'll do some more man things. You do more woman things."

"Speaking of hang-ups, that sounds pretty sex—" Something was crawling up her flank. She reached back and discovered another tongue, this one lapping out of a fuzzy face. "Uh-oh."

"Is that what I think it is?"

She giggled. "Crybaby, we agreed you were going to be quiet and inconspicuous, remember?" The dog answered with a solicitous whimper, his front paws gaining ground. "Now what are you trying to do?"

"He's trying to compete." Reese sat up and peered over her. "You can't. You're not a man. You're supposed to stay outside and be a dog."

"He misses your father, too."

"My father would be the first to tell you that no good could come of this. To prove it, he'd spin you a really long, kinda tangled-up, little bit off-color Coyote tale."

She flipped over so she could give the dog a proper ear-scratching. "He's just lonesome, aren't you, sweetie?"

"It's an act he puts on. Coyote's a sneaky sonuvabitch," Reese said, and she scolded him with an over-the-shoulder glance. He shrugged. "He sleeps around. You know that, don't you?"

"Only because you won't let him in, poor thing."

"Seduces softhearted women, turns them away from their men."

"He just wants to be with us. Oooh, he's such a good boy."

"Yeah, well, so am I. I'm the master now, and the master wants to do man things with his woman. So the dog gets DOWN." The paws hit the floor. Reese stabbed a finger in the direction of the door. "And goes OUT."

The dog was thinking about it, backing up, sucking what sympathy he could get from Helen.

"Don't look at her, you big crybaby. You're ruined now, aren't you?"

"He just wants somebody to play with."

"I can identify with that." To the dog he said, "Go find your own." And to Helen: "What do you want to play? A little one-on-one?"

Crybaby got as far as the door, and then he sat, watching, waiting for the games to begin.

They played the morning away. "I should go," she would say, and he would remind her of the papers he was going to show her. She really should look at those papers. But first they grained the horses, which led to playing ball with the dog. Going back inside for another cup of coffee led to playing war on his father's battlefield. He lined up his soldiers against her Indians, and they hurled insults at each other. For every good insult, a plastic man keeled over.

"I'd shoot you, but you're too ugly for carrion." *Ping!*

"I'd drag you behind my horse, but you're so fat I'd need a damn Clydesdale." *Zap!*

Over a second cup of coffee and a painted field full of plastic corpses, Reese allowed that Helen talked trash pretty well for an amateur. Admittedly he wasn't one of the best trash-talkers in the NBA, but he'd learned to hold his own, he told her as he finally served up the papers. He dealt the pages out to her at the edge of the battlefield, summarizing facts and figures with each exhibit. Here, from his father's perspective, was the history of his people's foray into the casino business. Roy Blue Sky had done his research and concluded that there should have been more profit showing somewhere.

"Is it a lot of money?"

"Yeah, the way he had it figured." Hovering over her with his cache, Reese produced copies of Roy's whistle-blowing letters. "It looks like we're paying through the nose to lease the slot machines. He's saying the tribe would own them by now if they'd bought instead of leased."

"That's what they agreed to, though."

"Yeah, but look." He plunked a budget analysis in front of her while he recited from one of the letters, saying, "And he's right. The management company has an answer for everything except the bottom line. Where's the money? That's what he keeps asking here. See, Ten Star takes the leases off the top, plus operations costs, plus, plus, plus. They keep revising their projections. Like he says here, whenever he tried to pin them down, they gave him a lot of 'puff words,' he says, 'meaning nothing, explaining nothing, just nonsense on top of more nonsense. But underneath it all, there's money being made by somebody, and it's not the Bad River Sioux Tribe.' "

He glanced at the miniature encampment on the far side of a convoluted ribbon of blue paint. "Or Lakota Nation," he amended. "Why did he say Sioux? He's probably the one who got them to change the damn sign. He's the expert now. *Was* the expert."

"Who's that letter to?"

"Some white guy," he said absently, then caught himself and cast her an apologetic smile. "I mean, some bureaucrat."

"I'm not a guy," she said with an easy shrug as she scanned the papers. "It looks as though he wrote a lot of letters." A typical Roy Blue Sky phrase caught her eye, and she smiled. "They're wonderful. So straightforward, just the way he talked."

"Yeah, he was a straight shooter, all right. I've been looking this stuff over pretty carefully, and I think he was onto something. If his information is right, the figures don't add up."

"His information comes from . . . ?"

"Some of it comes from Ten Star. Some from tribal accounts, some from the gaming commission, some from . . ." The next words, spoken carefully, clearly troubled him. "My brother."

"Well, Carter's the general manager."

"The ol' man calls him Mr. Marshall." He handed her another letter, but he peered over her shoulder and read aloud. "He says, 'Mr. Marshall claims that surveillance tapes are closely scrutinized, and there's been no significant cheating. If that's true, then there's something else going on.' And here's the reply." Helen recognized the government letterhead on the paper Reese tossed atop the pile. "They promised to investigate."

"Then . . . they will."

He spun a kitchen chair on one leg, straddled it, folded his arms over the backrest, getting into Helen's face now. "How would they go about it?"

"There's nothing in the letter?"

"Something about sending someone in . . ." His smile was disarming. He knew, she realized now, just as Roy had known.

". . . undercover. Sounds funny, doesn't it? An undercover agent in Bad River, South Dakota."

"It's probably just . . ."

"Just what?"

She returned his smile with a little sauce of his own making. "Some white guy."

"Be pretty hard for a white guy to go *undercover* here. They're kind of conspicuous." He waited for a comeback, but she shook her head, gave a small shrug. "Did they send someone, Helen?" The head shaking stopped. "Did my father know it was you?"

She bolted from her chair. It didn't matter what he knew as long as he kept it to himself. "I can't talk about this, Reese."

"How in the hell did you get into—"

She turned the corner into the sparsely furnished brown-and-white living room. The front door stood open. Cool morning air wafted through the screen.

Reese pressed her from behind. "Who do you work for, Helen?"

"I've worked for the government ever since you first met me."

"You were a BIA teacher."

"My GS rating is a little higher now, but . . ." She'd retreated to the open door, drawn to the fresh air and the view of purple coneflowers, golden brown-eyed Susans, and gray-green sage scattered throughout the tall grass. "Everything I've told you is basically true, Reese. I hope to get back into teaching full-time very soon. I'm working as a blackjack dealer right now. I really can't say any more, and if you tell anyone what you've surmised, then I'll probably lose my job. No one will trust me." She turned back to him.

"Who's no one? The Bad River Sioux Tribe? You think they trust you now?" He was looking at her differently, trying out a new concept, one that had apparently just occurred to him. "They don't really know you, do they?"

"Not really," she admitted, meeting his gaze, if not on an equal level, at least with equal challenge. "Not any better than they know Reese Blue Sky anymore, but they're willing to let him serve on the council, no questions asked."

"I'm still—"

"One of them? Still Roy's son? Still Lakota?" She could tell she'd hit a nerve by the quick spark in his eyes, and she regretted her cynical tone. She wanted no battle line drawn between them. She laid a hand on his warm, bare chest. "Trust is such a fragile thing. Such a risky proposition."

"Tell me, did my father know what you were doing here? Did you . . ." He lifted one eyebrow. "Did you level with him?"

"We didn't discuss it, other than . . ." She let her hand slide away. "He said if I wanted my old job back at the school, he'd put in a good word for me."

"I guess filling in for him means making good on some of his promises." He hooked his arm around the back of her neck and pulled her close. "You need a Blue Sky, you come to me. I got all kinds of good words for you."

"All I really want is for you to be careful. I really don't know why those figures don't add up, but I think it might have something to do with why your father's dead." She looked up at him, and she saw three generations. "I don't want anything like that to happen to you."

"Seriously?"

He was almost smiling, and she knew it had nothing to do with what had happened to his father. He could see how serious she was about his life being important to her. She was lost in the splendor of his eyes, and for the moment, she couldn't worry about what he might know or what he might discover. For the moment, she could think of nothing but the kiss he was about to give her.

*R*eese wasn't sure what to think about who Helen really was. If she really was working undercover—there was that bizarre word again—then she had an interesting side to her that he hadn't imagined.

So interesting, she had him flying down the road thinking like some kind of a detective. He figured he'd hook up with Titus Hawk, and maybe they'd pay Dozer Bobcat a call. If Helen could do the undercover thing, hell, he could do some snooping around in plain daylight. He had a friend or two on the police force. Well, he was pretty sure they were still friends, even though Reese hadn't been around for a while. They'd played ball together. Once a team, always a team.

Once a lover . . .

Maybe he'd never learn all there was to know about Helen, but he was willing to take the time to discover each facet one by one. And he was willing to wait if she couldn't talk about it right now. Far be it from him to blow his own side's cover. And if there was one thing he knew for sure, it was that somehow, some way, they were both working for the same side.

Which meant he was into some kind of a game. That was

fine by him. He'd been on the damned disabled list long enough. He was ready for a game, ready to take on all comers, but he needed more than one other team member. He needed Dozer Bobcat and Titus Hawk. He and Dozer had joined the army together—the kind of a move it took two guys to spur each other into after they'd quit college the first time out, knocked around for a few weeks, looked at each other bleary-eyed and said, *Now what? Go home, or what?* Uncle Sam was always *or what.* Dozer had been a cop in the army and a cop when he got out. Reese had been a basketball player, and no matter what uniform he'd ever worn, they'd always put the ball in his hands.

He found Titus at home in his 1970s vintage trailer at Riverside Trailer Park. Somebody had written "Tornado Target" above the words "Trailer Park" after homes had been rolled by three twisters in one season. Reese remembered that year—he'd been a freshman in high school—but it didn't surprise him that the graffiti was still there. Change was not a hot ticket in Bad River. Surprisingly, he found himself taking comfort in that.

They got another cop to track Dozer down, and they met him at Big Nell's Café. Reese laid his cards on the table along with a round of burgers.

"I'll be taking that seat on the council for a couple of months, so I decided to study up a little, and the way it looks to me is . . ." He braced his forearms on the edge of the table and used his hands to set up the play. "There are two sides on the casino-contract issue. You're either with Ten Star or you're suspect. So if I'm going to be open to alternatives, I'll need some backup."

Titus was nodding already. Dozer was working on his fries, dunking five at a time into a pool of ketchup.

"I want to know who ran my father down, Dozer. Is anybody making an effort to answer that question?"

"They're going through the motions," Dozer said around a mouthful of fries. He'd always been beefy, and Reese figured he'd added at least fifty pounds since high school. But they were friendly pounds. "I wasn't on duty, but I know it was tribal cops on the scene first. Whatever they found, they already turned it over to the FBI."

"And then what?"

"And then we probably won't hear any more about it unless we come up with something ourselves. And then, you know, we'd have to turn it over because it's federal. Funny thing is, first I heard they'd found a piece of a headlight. Then I heard they didn't find nothing but tire tracks."

"You heard *who* found . . . ?"

"It was Gene Brown and I think Earl Sweeney who got to the scene first, but all I heard was *they*. They found a broken part that they thought came off the vehicle, but then no, they said, that was bullshit."

"Earl Sweeney? Preston's brother?"

Titus chuckled. "At least once a day Earl likes to mention his brother is the tribal chairman."

"Gene's talked to me a couple of times since it happened," Reese said. "The first time he was all condolences and cop questions, but he acted a little skittish the last visit." He thought about it for a moment, then tapped a finger on the table. "I need you to find out about that evidence, Dozer. Anything, *anything* anybody picked up or anything *you* can pick up. Even if it's pieces that don't quite fit."

"You think somebody ran him down deliberately?"

"What do you think?"

Dozer sucked his teeth, pulling his thoughts together. "I've been thinkin', why him? We know he was home earlier that night, and everything was fine and normal. What was he doing out on the road? There was no stock loose, no gates reported open, nothing. No reason he should be wandering around in the road."

"Where was the dog?"

"Right beside him. That's how they found him, you know. The dog was standing guard. And the other thing was, the body was found on the left side of the road, but the vehicle was headed north. You can tell from the tire tracks." Quietly, Dozer added, "So looks like to me the driver had to bulldoze him across the southbound lane, which sounds pretty damn deliberate to me."

"Or else the driver was wasted," Titus put in.

"If he'da been that drunk, he'da never got away clean."

"Never?" Reese couldn't buy that word. Too many crimes went unsolved on the reservation.

"I told you, Blue, I keep comin' back to the same question. Why him?" Dozer sighed as he tossed a limp French fry toward the edge of his plate. "He'da run for chairman, I'da voted for him. I told Earl that, too. Just yesterday, I told him."

"I, uh . . ." Reese sighed, too. Dozer's considerable loyalty struck deep. "It's been a while since I talked to him about anything besides your basic health and weather. We'd kinda lost . . ."

Titus laid a hand on his shoulder. "Seems like he had the bad days behind him, Blue. Seems like losing him, we all lost a father. That's how it feels to me."

Reese nodded stiffly. "Let's find out what happened to him. Somebody must know something."

"You come around to the high school gym on Law and Order night," Dozer suggested. "You could shoot some hoops with us."

"That's right, Blue. Infiltrate."

"Eez, that guy. Infiltrate? Where'd you get . . ." A word like that? Reese chuckled. Cloak-and-dagger was exactly what he was asking for. But it sounded as outrageous as *undercover*. "How am I supposed to *infiltrate*?"

"Hell, he's *Reese Blue Sky*," Dozer rhapsodized. "He can hardly just blend in with the rest of us on the court."

"Why can't I? I played with you guys before. That gym, it's my home court."

Titus and Dozer looked at each other.

"But *infiltrate*? That sounds like something out of a book."

Titus and Dozer grinned at each other.

"Or some damn . . ." Reese looked from one to the other, then fell right in. The grins were contagious. "Game."

He hadn't expected that Carter would give him his first infiltration opportunity. When he ushered Helen past the huge Two Gray Hills rug on the wall in the foyer of Carter's sprawling house overlooking Rapid City, he was expecting the family dinner he'd been promised. He figured the new pickup and the Beamer in the driveway were his brother's latest acquisitions. Carter was a collector. You name it, he collected it. Especially if it had a hefty price tag. His adoptive family had trained him for good taste, and he had it in spades. The house was done up in all the good stuff. Rich textures, ripe colors, Southwestern style. It reminded Reese of his own condo, but there was more space here, more stuff, more money tied up in it. If he wasn't mistaken, the geometric-style painting hanging above the pine staircase was an original Oscar Howe. He'd almost bought one himself, but decided it was a little too spendy for his blood.

"Guess who's here," Carter said after he had closed the front door. His eyes sparkled. "Preston Sweeney." He turned to Helen. "You know our tribal chairman, don't you?"

"I've met him." She glanced at Reese. *What's going on?*

"And Bill Darnell. He's the manager over at Little Pair-a-Dice, the original bingo hall, used to be called B-Four, remember? Now it's our smaller casino operation. Bill trained me there. He's—"

Reese pulled his brother up short. "I thought this was going to be family."

"Preston has something for you, and I wanted you to meet Bill."

"I think I already met him at the funeral."

"There were so many people. I wanted you to . . ." Carter lowered his voice. "They probably won't stay long. Sarah doesn't think much of Bill, and you know how she is. She doesn't like somebody, it shows."

"Uncle!"

A bundle of nine-year-old energy careened into Reese's legs like a bowling ball picking off a spare. Reese laughed as he ruffled his nephew's water-slicked hair. In his crisply ironed white shirt and khaki slacks, Derek had clearly been dressed up for show.

"Dad says we get to have a basketball game later, and I've got three friends coming over, just three. Dad said not too many because they'll be hangin' all over you, but we need a little bit of players, don't we? For a game?"

"Can't play without a little bit of players."

Another small whirlwind came charging down the stairs. "I wanna play! I wanna play!"

"Well, sure, you get to play, Alicia." Reese swung the child up in his arms. "Man, you're getting big. You're gonna catch up to your brother one of these days. Do you have friends, too?"

Derek groaned.

"I didn't ask any friends," she said. "Just me. But I have to be on Daddy's side."

"You can be on Daddy's side, but we're not going to play right away, so just cool it." Carter unloaded his daughter from Reese's arms. Reese felt as though he'd picked up one of the collectibles and was subtly being told he wasn't handling it quite right.

"They've been bragging about you to the whole neighborhood," Carter said as he led them toward the living room. "I ain't kiddin', they're going to be lined up around the fence. Sarah, they're here," he called out.

Two men stood near the huge fieldstone fireplace—a beefy, balding white man and a small but paunchy Indian, to whom Carter deferred first. "Here's the chief."

Reese offered his former classmate a handshake.

"Hey, Blue. Glad to have you on board. This makes it official." Preston produced a letter headed with the Bad River Lakota Nation emblem and finished off with his ornate signature. Reese noted his own name and the proclamation of his appointment to the tribal council. "We've got a meeting tomorrow. You have to take an oath, pass a test, sign your name in blood, relinquish all your worldly possessions."

Reese laughed. "You're just after my limos, Sweeney."

"Did I mention the vow of chastity?"

"Yeah, you first."

"Hey, I'm the chairman. I'm exempt." On the heels of polite laughter, Sweeney added, "I'm glad you could do this. Your father had a very loyal constituency, especially the older folks. They're already pleased with you for staying around, for showing this respect for your father. You'll be a real asset to us, Blue."

"It's only for what, three months?"

"We've got a lot of business to do in that time."

"I'm anxious for my brother to learn more about our gaming operations," Carter said. "He's been a team player, so he knows—"

Sarah Marshall appeared in the doorway with a nervous smile and a tray laden with mugs of coffee, which she unloaded on the coffee table. Carter's wife was a tiny, strikingly beautiful woman from the Yakima Nation. She reminded Reese of a small, shy bird, but she was tough when she had to be. She'd thrown his brother out of her life more than once. But she loved him, and she was a hopeful woman. She'd also forgiven more than once, and Reese figured she would again. He could tell by the tender glances she kept stealing Carter's way. She thought she was keeping that tenderness a secret, but her eyes gave her away. She said she had to get back to the kitchen because she had food in the works. Helen popped out of her chair immediately with an offer to help.

Reese would have liked nothing better than to follow the women. He'd come for family, not for business. He'd been used a time or two, and he knew damn well he was looking across the coffee table at two smiling opportunists. Dripping with touristy jewelry and bureaucratic lingo, Preston Sweeney had become quite the politician. Reese already had Darnell pegged for one of those guys who put in his two cents, then sat back and kept score. But Carter had set up this little meeting for some reason, and Reese figured he was required to stay for more happy talk. Even though he generally rebelled against requirements, he told himself to think *rules*. Every game had its rules. These guys didn't offer to lay them out, so you had to read them between the lines. Which meant you had to wade around in their bullshit.

"Roy, Carter, and now, finally, we have Reese Blue Sky back," Preston was saying. "You'll be amazed at what you can do for your people in just a few short months. When you see how we're organized now, the kind of support we're getting from Ten Star in bringing our Indian people on board—"

"Like you and your brother," Darnell put in. "Right up there in first class, where the decisions are being made."

Is that some favor you're doing us? Whose ship is this, anyway?
Reese smiled. He was glad he was wearing boots.

"Carter says you and Reese used to go together."

Sarah had given Helen the usual guest's task. She had the
olive section of the platter filled, and she was working on carrots and celery when the opening came. "For a short time, just
before he went to Minnesota," Helen said. "One summer. Part
of one summer."

"They didn't grow up together," Sarah said, and she nodded toward the kitchen door and beyond. "They're not close,
the way brothers should be."

Helen welcomed the opening. She was wary of the territory
it was bound to lead to, but recently she had thought of little
else, and Sarah's husband could have been the poster child for
the Indian Child Protection Act.

"It must have been difficult for Carter, growing up with
one family and then having his father take him back."

"Carter generally prevails," Sarah said. And that was it.
The opening disappeared. Sarah wanted to go elsewhere.
"What kind of a boss is he?" she wondered as she turned
from the refrigerator with two plastic bowls in hand. "Hard
to work for?"

"No. He's a good manager."

"He's spoken of you often lately. I wondered." She glanced
away quickly, and Helen realized her own eyes had widened
at the suggestion. "I was glad to hear that you were with
Reese. I thought you might have been someone my husband
wanted for himself, the way he talks about you."

Sarah set the bowls on the counter, started to peel back a
lid, replaced it, finally permitted Helen a glimpse of the embarrassment in her eyes, her brief, tight smile. "But that's just
him," she said. Table utensils jangled in the drawer she yanked
open. "Not you. Nothing to do with you, probably."

"I don't know what to say. I'm not . . ."

"I'm sorry. I'm not accusing you." Sarah gave a quick
laugh and shook her head, her profusion of soft black hair
gleaming under the white fluorescent light. "I'm not very good
at this. We don't have a lot of company."

"You have a lovely home. Beautiful children. And I'm not . . ."

They exchanged looks. Not what? Not willing to exchange such telling details? Sarah was uneasy with her, but she was ready to give her a chance.

"I have a son about Derek's age," Helen heard herself say while she noticed children through the window above the sink. Sidney was a little older, of course, but the resemblance was unmistakable. *He must favor his father*, people would say, angling for entertaining details. "He's in summer camp."

Sarah's interest perked up. "Derek's taking swimming lessons and playing Little League baseball. Summer camp, where?"

"In Colorado." And since Sarah hadn't asked, Helen said, "His father and I aren't together."

"I know how that is. We were split up for a while, too. Even got divorced and remarried again, to each other. He was married to someone else for a little while in between. We can go through tribal court, so it's not like . . ." She waved a serving spoon. "But it's not easy. It's sure hard on the kids."

"And their mother."

"I'm pretty tough. Carter's such a smart man, maybe too smart. Sometimes he outsmarts himself." She covered her smile with a quick hand, but her eyes were dancing. "I shouldn't talk. He's your boss."

Helen smiled, too. She'd seen Carter outsmart himself a time or two when he'd supplied answers no one had asked for or instructions nobody needed. "How did you two meet?"

"In college, back East. I felt pretty far away from home. I'm from Yakima. Washington State. Carter more or less had two homes, and one was back East, so he did great there. I was only starting out when we met, and he was almost done. I never finished. I got pregnant."

"That does change things, doesn't it?"

"You, too?"

Helen turned back to her carrot peeling. "My son is the best thing that ever happened to me."

"Same here." Sarah thought about that for a moment. "No, Carter's the best. And the worst. Without him there wouldn't be any kids. I tried it without him, and I missed him. He missed us, I know he did, but it's like he's got this empty place inside him that he can't fill. I don't know what he wants." She jammed two spoons into the salads in her plastic bowls. "All I know is, he's really smart about some things, but when he wants something to be a certain way, there's no telling him any different. He trusts nobody for a while, and then he trusts the wrong people."

"You mean business people, or personal people?"

"All I know is, he owes too much money." She said it as though everyone knew, and then she got her hands into the act to help her elaborate. "I kick his ass out, and then I see him again and I want him back, even with all his moods and his secrets."

"You kick him out, and he just leaves?"

"It's a good excuse for him to stay at the casino hotel. He lives for that casino. As long as he knows we're sitting here in his pumpkin shell, just waiting for him . . ." She shrugged. "I could take the kids and go home, you know? Just pack up and go. I've done it before." She lowered her voice, as though this were the extraordinary part. "He came looking for us, came right to the house and told me he couldn't stand to be without us, said it right in front of my mother. He said we were all he had." She was studying the coleslaw now. "I know that's true. That's the thing. But we can't make him happy."

"You don't have to. He has to stop trying to outsmart himself and realize that his happiness is here for the . . ." *For the taking.* "Are the kids enrolled with your tribe or with his?"

"They're Bad River Lakota."

Tread lightly, Helen told herself. "Could he use that to take the kids away?"

"He's never tried." But Sarah thought about it, which stirred up some spit and vinegar. "He'd never dare. He knows he'd have a fight on his hands."

Helen nodded, wondering whether it would be Sarah's tribe against Carter's. Maybe the tribes would neutralize each other. Then it would be little Sarah against big Carter. Carter would surely outsmart himself, but not Sarah. Helen could see the fight in the woman's eyes, the kind of fight a man had no answer for, the kind that was fueled by high-octane estrogen. Helen herself had a full tank.

Still, she wished she had a tribe of her own for backup.

"I think Reese feels kind of bad about Roy leaving the place to him instead of Carter," Helen volunteered. Sarah had her head in the refrigerator again. "Because of the children."

"Roy had his reasons, you can be sure of that." Sarah joined her at the sink with a load of broccoli and cauliflower. "It'll be good if they can become true brothers now. Carter's all happy about Reese sticking around to finish out the term on the council. I haven't seen him this excited about anything in a long time."

"When did he decide to ask these other guys over?"

"I didn't know they were coming. We'll need a few more of those carrots, but that's enough celery. This green stuff's probably a waste of time."

Helen emptied the bag of carrots into the white enamel sink. "Roy and Chairman Sweeney were sort of at odds lately, weren't they?"

Sarah turned the cold water on with one hand, waved the rivalry away with the other. "I don't pay attention to the politics around here. Carter says Reese and Preston were in school together. As for Bill Darnell, he's like this wallpaper, that one. He's just always around."

"He trained Carter, didn't he?"

"I guess he did." As she spoke she went to work on the broccoli with a carving knife. "Part of the deal with Ten Star was that they had to hire Bad River enrollees, but for a long time it was just entry-level jobs. People started complaining. Then they hired Carter, and the complaining died down, even though some people still grumbled."

"Because his father was on the council?"

"That wasn't it so much. Some people don't really accept Carter. For one thing, he never changed his name back to Blue Sky. Plus he never really stayed here much after his father got him back, so he doesn't have those friends from school days the way Reese has. People are all the time telling him they're his cousins. He doesn't know." Sarah shrugged. "Besides, his father had to get off the gaming committee on the council when Carter went to work for the casino."

"So Roy didn't have anything to do with getting him that job?"

"Carter's well qualified for the job. He didn't need any help."

"But there's the appearance," Helen suggested carefully as she split the last of the carrots.

"I don't care what it looks like. Carter got the job on his own."

"I'm sure he did," Helen said, and truly, she thought, Carter had all the right credentials. "Have you heard him say anything about the hit-and-run? About anybody who might have had it in for his father?"

"No." Sarah shut the water off. They could hear the men's voices, deep and distant, punctuated by the occasional laugh. "He took it hard. You can't always tell from what Carter says. It's what he doesn't say. When he doesn't say anything, that's when you know he's taking it hard." She looked up at Helen. "It's good for him to be with his brother now."

"Reese burned Roy's personal things, his clothes."

"That's good. That's the way it should be done. Carter doesn't understand traditional ways. Maybe Reese can help him with that while he's here."

They finished mounding the vegetables on the platter. Sarah brought out a carton of store-bought vegetable dip, saying she didn't know how to make it from scratch, but she always put it in a bowl and hid the carton, and nobody ever complained. Helen suggested adding a few ingredients, including a dash of hot-pepper sauce. Sarah tasted the result and declared the hot sauce to be the magic ingredient.

"How long are you staying?" Sarah asked.

"I don't know. Right now, all I have here is a summer job."

"Your son might not like it here. It's hard to move kids when they get a little older."

Helen nodded.

"But I don't think a summer job is all you have here."

*   *   *

Bill Darnell said he appreciated the invitation to stay for dinner, but he had to be somewhere else. Preston Sweeney knew better than to refuse food in an Indian home. He shared in the meal but excused himself soon after it was over, when Reese asked him to join Carter and himself under the hoop in the backyard. Preston had been one of the few boys in Reese's class who had not played basketball, not in the school yard, not in the gym, not even during physical education class. Not ever. Preston was totally uncoordinated. Clumsiness with a football or a baseball was generally tolerated on the reservation, but not with a basketball. Either you played a decent game or you got out of the way. Preston enjoyed a certain level of respect—he had twice been class president, served two terms as a councilman, and now was chairman—which was why, when it came to basketball, he got out of the way.

Not so with Carter, who suddenly seemed almost as eager to play as the children were. It was hard to believe that he was Reese Blue Sky's brother. Carter was shorter, slighter, finer featured, finer boned, yet he moved like the heavier man. His feet were heavier than the new cement slab court he'd had built for his son. He was a player, but he was not an athlete.

Reese was still the man. With a basketball in play he became a big cat, his every move fluid and effortless, but he did nothing for show. It was all for joy, the pure delight of making his body and the ball do what pleased him. He pleased the children, too. Derek had three young friends to impress, and they were intimidated at first. All they wanted to do was watch. But Reese was ready to play. Where there was a ball and a hoop, he was home. He was the benevolent master. He owned the game, and it was his to give. On the court he was more than a player. He was host, entertainer, and teacher. It pleased him to feed the ball to small hands and help them find joy in their own moves, delight in seeing the ball drop through the net at their direction.

Helen and Sarah sat at the round glass table on the multi-level deck—"the owners' seats," Reese said—and cheered for everybody.

There wasn't much trash talk on the backyard court, but the boys were soon convinced that Derek's uncle was, indeed, the hero their friend had bragged about. Like most nine-year-olds, they were full of questions and fully capable of playing—or playing *at*—a game of pickup ball and conducting a running interview at the same time.

"Did you play on the Dream Team?" a tanned, towheaded boy named James asked, wide-eyed and worshipful after watching Reese's shot kiss the backboard and slide through the net.

"Nope."

"Make the All-Stars?"

"Twice."

"Get any endorsements?"

"Do you eat rice?" Reese passed the ball to James, who took a shot and missed.

"Huh?"

"I was on a rice box."

"Riiice . . ."

"It's good stuff. I eat it myself."

"Did you ever play against Michael Jordan?"

"Sure did."

"Did you ever beat him?"

"Nobody can beat Michael Jordan," said a chunky redhead called Bigger, whose freckles overran his perfectly round face.

"Uncle Reese did," Derek claimed. "Didn't you, Uncle?"

"Once or twice, but it was more like the Mavericks beating the Bulls. It's a team sport. You've gotta pass the ball." He passed the ball to Bigger. "Now what do you do?"

The boy twitched his nose like a rabbit, glanced at Derek, his teammate, then up, up, up at Reese. "Pass?"

"Do you have a shot?"

"I can't shoot. I'm terrible." But the boy hoisted the ball two-handed, positioning it over his right shoulder for a shot.

"It didn't look that heavy a minute ago," Reese said. "There must be something wrong here. Do you have a shot?"

"I think I'm too far away."

"If you think so, you're probably right."

"I should pass the ball." And he heaved it to Reese, taking him by surprise.

"Whoa, hot potato here—" Bounce, bounce, quick signal to

Bigger to keep moving while Carter danced around him. "Get it while it's hot. No, you're not rid of it yet. While I'm doing the tango with their big man here, you cut to the basket, fast. Their defense is asleep, right?"

"They're watching you."

"They're watching me, that's right, because I'm in position."

But so was Bigger, enraptured now with the attention and eager to please. A bounce pass completed the give-and-go play, and Bigger shot the ball. It ricocheted off the backboard into Reese's hands.

"Instant replay," Reese announced with another bounce pass. "Take the shot again, only this time, visualize. See it in your mind. Look up there, now. It's a big hoop. Two balls can fit through there at once. The ball you've got in your hands is going to go through that hoop. Imagine it dropping through." The second shot dropped through, and Reese whipped a high five on the small, triumphant hand. "Nothing but net."

"Can you stuff the basket?"

"Do a windmill tomahawk," James pleaded.

Reese obliged with a flashy overhand dunk. His delight in the soprano cheers was written all over his face.

"Don't be hanging on my hoop, Bro-gun," Carter grumbled as he grabbed the rebound. But he fell against the backboard support and lost the ball to Reese.

"You need to pad that pole," Reese said, chuckling. "Somebody's liable to separate a shoulder. Hey, where's my team? Who's guarding me?"

"Dad is! C'mon, Dad!"

"You wanna keep me from shooting, you trap me." Reese positioned two opponents toe-to-toe with him behind the basket. All four of their feet would have fit into one of his Nikes with room to spare. "You get on me like flies on watermelon juice. I try to move, you're there. You trap me at the edge of the floor, I'm out of bounds."

"We can't trap you!"

"Yeah, you're too big!"

"If I run over you, somebody calls me for charging. Helen!

Sarah!" Reese motioned to the women to come on down. "You're the refs."

Helen laughed. "What if I don't know the rules?"

"You just call 'em like you see 'em," he told her as he in-bounded the ball.

And within moments she stuck two fingers in her mouth and blew her whistle. "No fair!"

Each player turned, looked, scowled, scanned the perimeter of the court for culprits.

"That means foul," Helen explained as she sashayed across the lawn to the court, carrying herself with new authority. "Alicia gets some free throws."

"Free throws!" James protested. "You don't have free throws in pickup ball."

Reese hoisted Alicia onto his shoulders and motioned for the ball. "How many?"

"As many as it takes." Helen stood behind the basket, folded her arms, staked her claim. "That's how I see it."

Reese grinned as he lifted the ball to Alicia on the tips of his fingers.

"Nice whistle."

Their eyes danced with each other.

"Nice too-hard-to-pinch."

The game continued until everyone had shot and scored, passed the ball seven ways from Sunday, switched teams, and tried again. After several games, Carter's team finally reached the magic eleven points first, and Reese flopped on the grass and called time. He tossed the ball to Bigger. "You guys give a good workout."

Carter bent over him, hands braced on knees, sweat dripping off his face in great dollops. "You okay?"

"Yeah."

"You sure?"

"I'm fine." Reese sat up, stretching. He'd barely broken a sweat. The boys were still bouncing the ball on the court. "Hey, I'm fine. No problem."

"You look a little flushed. Alicia, get your uncle some water."

"Don't." The quiet order was for Carter. "I run every day,

Carter. *Every day*." The hard edge dropped from his voice for his niece. "You'd better get your dad some water, honey. He's the one who's huffin' and puffin' here." He tapped his brother's small belly roll with the back of his hand. "Look at you."

"Yeah, well, I've got a club membership, but I haven't been using it much." He gave Reese a pointed look. "But I don't have any kind of—"

Reese raised a warning hand. "Don't crowd me, Carter."

"Hey . . ." Carter's hands went up, too, in defense. "Just a little brotherly concern."

"I'm feeling crowded. Your friends had me . . ." He rolled his shoulders as though he was trying to stretch his space. "Trying to box me in right away is what it felt like."

"Preston was your friend." Reese's scowl forced Carter to amend, "Classmate, then, and he's a good man. He looks ahead. He . . ." The sales pitch was obviously missing its mark. "Your buddies were the jocks, right? Most of them are lucky to get a job parking cars."

Reese waved the vague insult-by-association away. "What's with this Darnell?"

"What do you mean?"

"He reminds me of a turkey buzzard, the way he sort of looks at a guy like he's dead meat. I was glad he didn't stay for dinner."

Sarah laughed as she exchanged glances with Helen.

"He's okay," Carter insisted. "He's sharp, really sharp. Knows the gaming business. He's worked for Ten Star for a long time, in different places."

"Indian gaming?" Reese asked.

"Gaming is gaming."

"And vultures are vultures. What did the old man have to say about these guys?"

Carter shrugged. "He was talking about running against Preston next time around. No way could he beat Preston, no way in hell. Dad was living in the nineteenth century, fighting all those old battles that nobody cares about anymore."

"What about Darnell? What did Dad have to say about him?"

"What difference does it make, Reese? Dad didn't get it.

He didn't understand that gaming is a business. It takes a businessman to run a business, and Bill Darnell is a businessman. I've learned a lot from him. All of us have."

"I didn't much like the way he talked to you, but maybe that's just his way, huh?"

"It's just his way." Carter reached for his wife's iced tea. "You've got your way, he's got his."

"What, you don't like the way I talk to you?" Reese reached over and punched Carter's shoulder. "I'm your older brother. You got those other guys to call you 'sir.' It's up to me to keep you from getting a big head."

Carter looked surprised at first. For a moment he cast about for a comeback, and Helen thought he'd taken offense, but then the smile came, the blush, the basking in his brother's ribbing, in the big man's claim on him.

"So who gets to keep *you* in line?" Carter took a swipe at Reese's hair. "You must be up to a size fifteen here. Where do you get hats that size?"

"Same place I get my shoes, boy. A big man has his stuff tailor-made."

"See what I'm stuck with?" Carter said to Helen. "You were smart to get out while he was still buying hats off the rack." And to Reese, "But you're just friends now, right? Helen's your token friend who's not a jock."

"Leave them alone, Carter," Sarah said. "Let them be friends if they want to be friends. Maybe we can see how it's done."

"Ah, she wounds me. I married her. Twice, just to show her I really meant it. Still, she wounds me." He handed Sarah the iced-tea glass he'd drained. "Friends don't do that, honey. Only wives do that."

Sarah got up from her chair.

"Hey, I'm just kidding." He reached for her arm, but she stepped away. He gave a pitiful excuse for a smile. "Just kidding."

She nodded. All eyes were lowered. The children were still playing noisily while in silence all four adults tried to wish the joke away. The basketball hit the backboard, the rim, the slab, slab, slab.

"I was just going to make more tea."

"Actually," Reese remarked as he uncoiled himself from the grass and rose to his feet, "I promised Helen a drive through the Hills before the sun sets, then a visit to Deadwood."

"Deadwood?" Helen didn't remember any such promise, but it sounded like relief.

"I haven't been there in years, and I hear it's quite a gambling town again. Thought I'd take a look at the competition. I've become something of a businessman myself since I hung up my . . ." Reese smiled. "Jock gear."

"That was fun, wasn't it?" he said, slipping Helen an apologetic smile as he turned in the driver's seat to back down the driveway. "Now, how do we get to I-Ninety north from here?"

"We're really going to Deadwood?"

"We're really going to have some kind of fun on your day off."

Deadwood was not Helen's idea of fun. As a gambling mecca, it was small, but it predated Las Vegas, and gambling wasn't fun. It was work. "It was fun watching you play basketball with the kids," she said. "I'll bet your basketball camps are well attended."

"I have a waiting list of kids who want to come, especially at the junior high level. We give what we call scholarships, although it has nothing to do with being scholarly. It has to do with having the will but no way. For kids who have money, seems like the more we charge, the better their parents like it. It works out fine. And thanks for doing this with me."

She looked back at Carter's showplace as they pulled away. "I enjoyed it. I've never met Sarah. She's very nice, and very . . ." A light went on in what was probably a bedroom window, and she wondered where Reese's brother would spend the night. Pair-a-Dice City, probably. "She's frustrated, but I think she's also worried about Carter. She said something about him owing a lot of money. Have they mentioned that to you?"

"No. You mean, like credit cards?"

"She didn't say. And she didn't say *we*. She said *he* owes too much money, and she said he trusts the wrong people. Wonder what she meant by that."

Reese snorted. "I wouldn't trust Darnell with my weekly garbage."

"Darnell is Ten Star's man. He trained Carter. I think it was a show of tremendous confidence when they put Carter in at Pair-a-Dice City rather than Little Pair-a-Dice."

"Does he do a good job?" He lifted his hands from the steering wheel, cut off her too-quick affirmative. "Forget that he's my brother. Do you think he's good at his job?"

She weighed her answer. "I think he's very well qualified."

"You don't think he got the job just because his father was on the council?"

"I don't know about that. Sarah became very defensive when I suggested that maybe people assumed he might have had just the slightest edge. She pointed out that he has plenty of qualifications, and she's right."

"He's got a good education," Reese allowed. "That boy's smart. Ambitious, too."

"He's also very good with people, with planning, with organizing, with—"

"I hear you. What is it that he's *not* good with?"

"He hasn't had a lot of experience."

"And?"

"And he needs time to develop that sixth sense for trouble. In the casino business, trouble is spelled with a capital T. Which rhymes with C, and that stands for crime."

He looked at her. "The organized kind?"

"Sometimes."

"So who's protecting us from crime with a capital C? Us meaning the tribe. Us Indians." He chuckled. "Who's protecting the savages from the mob?"

"I didn't say there *was* any criminal element involved, other than the usual card cheats and scam artists. They sort of come with the territory."

"How bad are they?"

"Bad enough. Where there's money to be made . . ."

"It's funny, isn't it? You go to a reservation, you see what you see, what most people see—poor land, poor housing, poor

136

people—you think, Hell, there's no money here. But there's always been money to be made by the enterprising, the . . . entrepreneur."

"The white guy?"

"Which you're not," he was quick to admit. "Hey, crooks come in all colors."

"So do entrepreneurs." She smiled. "You're an excellent example."

"Are you grading me? Based on what? A limo ride? A visit to one of the stores?" He did a mock double take. "Don't tell me you had your son in my basketball camp."

She shook her head again, this time with a soft "No."

"There was a time when I'd've taken the benefit of the doubt or any other break you were willing to give me, but nowadays I like to earn my E's. The ones for *effort* ain't worth much."

What effort? she wanted to say. What they'd had since the beginning had surely been effortless. Great sex wasn't work. But it was surely a gamble.

"How's your back?" she asked.

"My back?"

"I noticed—I *thought* I noticed an oh-my-aching-back look when you were showing off for the kids."

"Showing off!" He laughed and wagged his head. "Damn. I'll take that benefit of the doubt now, Miz Ketterling."

"And I also noticed your brother's concern. It was a back injury that forced your early retirement, wasn't it?"

He looked at her as though there was more to tell, as though he might be sizing her up as a potential confidante. Wordlessly he turned his attention back to the road.

There *was* more to it. The possibilities started popping up in her head like the road signs—there, gone, there again, a little bigger this time. Maybe great sex was more of a gamble than she thought. Or maybe he was . . . "What was it, Reese?"

He shrugged, tossed off a flippant "A broken heart." And then a refrain: "You broke my heart, 'cause I was . . ." He scowled. "Too young? I can't remember the words."

"Was it . . . something else?"

"You mean like sex? Drugs? Alcohol?"

"I didn't mean . . ."

"Was the big man from Bad River a bad boy when he went to the big city?"

"*Are you all right?*" She realized she'd turned in her seat, which was the closest she could get to jumping out in front of him and saying, *Cut the comedy and look me in the eye and tell me you're all right.* "I'm asking the same thing your brother was asking. How are you now? Are you—"

"I'm okay now." He added softly, "Honest."

Jhey took the long way around, through Sturgis and Spearfish, because Needles Highway with its towering granite spires was a glorious sight when sunset streaked the sky in pink and gold. And because there was another big casino going up in the area. Reese wanted to get a feel for its reputed grandeur and its proximity to the gaming operation that until recently was of little concern to him. Suddenly Pair-a-Dice City and its smaller sister were major concerns, personal concerns. They were important to everyone who was important—did he dare form the thought? _Important to him._ Hell, what else was there? His picture on a box of rice? A fleet of limousines and a bunch of stores that sold overpriced sneakers?

He saw for himself that the new resort was in fact under construction. Hotel, golf course, swimming pools, family amusements surrounding the flashy jewel that would become the largest casino in the Dakotas, close to the Hills, an easy drive from the Rapid City airport. "Jewel" was the right word. In travel brochures the Black Hills were billed as the Jewel of South Dakota, complete with the largest gold mine in the country. To the Lakota, _Paha Sapa_ was the heart of the earth. In the beginning, the people had emerged from the earth through an opening in the crotch of these hills, they said.

"Your father said?"

"My father?" He had spoken his thoughts aloud, spoken as he had been taught, with "they say" affixed to the end. He smiled at Helen, his father's friend. "No doubt. He told me a lot of stories, and I always figured whoever *they* were, they were still saying through him."

"Now it's your turn."

"Already?" He laughed. "Jeez, that's for old men. I'm still a warrior."

"You've made your mark as a warrior. Now you get to sit on the council wearing all your feathers."

He groaned. He didn't have any feathers. Carter had all the feathers. The first thing their father had done when he'd gotten his younger son back was make him a beautiful dance costume, which Carter had never worn. But he'd kept it. Reese had noticed the bustle hanging on the wall in Carter's den.

"Your All-Star ring, then," she said, obviously reading his mind, because he knew he hadn't said anything this time. He was no pouter, no crybaby. "Do you get rings for that?"

"You do. Big, fat, gold mothers." He pounded the steering wheel with an open palm as he watched the construction site slide past the window. "Jesus, what am I thinking? *Politics*, for God's sake. I'm no politician."

"You don't have to be. You didn't even have to run for office. You were appointed. *Anointed.* You don't owe anyone. You're your own man, which is powerful medicine, if you ask me." She glanced away. "Which you didn't."

"I did. I asked you about my brother, which shows how much I trust you. I'm feeling my way along in the shadows here, and yours is a hand I know and trust. Yours and maybe a few others. The ones I played ball with, some of them. And I've got more family. I've got . . ."

He peered into the bright path ahead. There were more Bad River people he needed to talk to, people who had been there forever and would always be there, casinos or no casinos. Sweeney had made a reference to playing ball that had rubbed him wrong. His gut was telling him it wasn't his kind of ball.

He was expected to fulfill his obligation quietly, nod when they elbowed him. A silent partner. Like he'd told Helen, he just wasn't as quiet as he used to be.

"I've noticed," she said, and she was smiling at him. He'd spoken his thoughts aloud again. He was used to being alone, and he talked to himself sometimes. Talking to Helen seemed to come just as easily.

The evening had turned to purple velvet, which dressed Deadwood up considerably, if only for a moment. The once-infamous little town still appeared to tumble headlong over steep mountainsides toward the trough that was Main Street, where gambling had become king. Where once the false fronts had housed saloon after saloon with the occasional brothel for variety, now every sign boasted of slot machines and blackjack tables. With the lay of the land being mainly vertical, floor space had become a valuable commodity. There was no such thing as a simple store or restaurant. Every establishment, be it candy store or clothier, had its slots.

A busman's holiday for Helen, probably, but it was getting so the bus was the only way to fly in these parts. And Reese was thinking they'd fly Deadwood style tonight and head back to Bad River in the morning. This was a date. He'd never had an actual date with Helen.

It pleased him when a couple of tourists recognized him and asked for his autograph. There was some part of him that wanted her to see this, to know that complete strangers occasionally remembered who he was. He laughed when they asked if he was in town for an old-timers' game. They said they had seen Rick Marino at the Cousin Jacks Pub.

"You see how quickly a retired athlete becomes an old-timer?" he told Helen as he held the rough pine door to the Cousin Jacks open for her. Steel-guitar music greeted them first. "Might as well say I passed you up in age a long time ago."

"So how old is this Marino? Any good years left in him?"

"Hell, no. Over the hill and ugly to boot, that guy. I've got nothing to worry about there."

Marino was older than Reese, but he had retired only a couple of years ago. A "small forward," Rick had learned to play ball in the Brooklyn school yards, and he was a scrapper on and off the court. A white man with some jump in him, he had been a Maverick when Reese was drafted for the team, and he had helped Reese adjust to the strange fishbowl existence of a professional athlete. But he hadn't come into his own until after he was traded to Seattle, when he'd become Reese's best rival.

When Rick saw Reese at Cousin Jacks, he immediately ditched his entourage.

"Drinks are on you, Bad Man; you owe me for that last playoff series," he told Reese after they commandeered a table in a pine-paneled corner. Reese barely got Helen's name out before Rick was reliving a game, drawing her in with one hand while he tapped Reese's chest with the other. "Four times this guy fouls me. Four times, and he doesn't get called for it. Magoo for a ref that night. And then he draws a foul off me. A minute and a half to go, I've got five personals, I barely touch this guy, and Magoo's suddenly got his eyesight back. So I'm out, and him and his damn Minne-apple Mules take the series away from us. And that was supposed to be our year. I mean, we were—" He brandished a fist. "I was ready to take you on right there, man. Right in front of God and the rest of the fans."

"I know you were," Reese said, laughing, remembering what a night it had been. Win or lose, he'd always been pretty collected. That night the fans had gone wild. The team had gone crazy. It was the only time he'd ever leaped into another man's arms. "I nearly got a technical out of you to boot."

"Yeah, it would've been worth it." Rick leaned back in the booth while the jeans-clad waitress served his beer, Helen's white wine, and Reese's bottled water. "This is the cagiest damn Indian ever walked this earth, I ain't lyin'. You watch yourself, Helen."

"Even if I'm not playing basketball?"

"I wouldn't play with him at all if I was you. No, ma'am. He's, like, no holds barred, this man, and I can tell just by looking, you're the kind of woman who oughta be held properly."

"Which is why she's with me," Reese said, slipping Helen

a cool wink. "Not Blue Sky the jock, but Blue Sky the cool-headed businessman. Real dull. Tight-ass dull." He was grinning at Rick, but it was really for that cute little choke that came out of Helen.

"So, Helen, if you're not into basketball, what *do* you play?" Rick asked her.

"She's hell on wheels at blackjack."

"Is that a fact?"

"No, not . . ." She slipped Reese a look with a message in it. "It's just that Reese isn't."

He wasn't sure how to read the message. It sounded like *dumb ass*, but that wasn't what he saw in her eyes. Didn't she like it when he bragged her up? "Hell, I'm just an amateur. Helen's a dealer at Pair-a-Dice City."

"Hey." Rick cocked a long finger in Helen's direction. "Have I got a deal for you. You, too, Blue, as long as I don't have to worry about taking an elbow in the gut anymore. I need another partner."

Reese drew back, pulling his bottled water toward the edge of the table. Rick was in on the Spearfish monstrosity, along with some movie star and a Texas cattleman. "From what I hear, you've got plenty of deep pockets in on your deal, and one of them holds a few state legislators."

"You're right. I'm beginning to think I've got too many chiefs on board. And no Indians."

"The Indians are bound to get screwed," Reese muttered over the mouth of the water bottle.

"No, Blue, no. That's not what we're about. Casinos, they're like . . ." Rick sipped his drink, then gestured with the glass. "Well, they're like bookstores."

"*Book*stores!" Reese laughed. *Good places to meet women*, Rick had once told him when they were both tired of being on the road, seeing the same faces, the same places with different names. They'd actually gone into a bookstore looking for romance. Rick had left with a foxy coed. Reese had added to his Lakota history collection.

"Yeah. You know how they're putting up those huge bookstores all over the place? Everywhere you go, they put one up on one corner, you look across the street, up goes the competitor. You think one's gotta knock the other off, but they both hang in there, and you know why? Certain people like books, and those people are gonna cruise both stores because they're both right there. You know, you only got so many people who like books."

Reese looked at Helen. "So far, this makes some sense," she said.

"Sure it does," Rick said, a little too warmly appreciative of her support. "And it's not just the snobby places. You go looking for a bottle of booze, you're gonna find the bars and the package stores kinda collected together at the low end of Main Street. It makes complete sense." He leaned in, arcing his long torso like a goose-neck lamp. "What I'm saying is, the more casinos we put up in this area, the better all our business is going to be. People who like to gamble will come here in packs because we'll have plenty of gambling for them to choose from. And this is Deadwood, man. This is the real thing, the original Wild Bill Hickok country."

"Some of us think of this as the original Indian country," Reese said.

"And you're the real thing. And that is so cool."

"You know what, Rick?" Reese smiled. "My elbows are starting to twitch."

"No, here's all I'm saying. If you were to throw in with us, your people would see that we're not a threat. I mean, they'd know this was a good thing for everybody."

"How would they know that?"

"Because you'd show them, you'd tell them. We could go to the statehouse together and get them to raise those betting limits."

"You already got that."

"No, hell, that was a pitiful compromise. That wasn't half what we wanted." Rick peered at Reese, winding up for the punch. "You could be a very rich man, Blue. You know what I'm sayin'? We could all be . . ." Rick's expansive gesture signaled no limits.

"I don't know about you, Rick, but I've got more money than I can spend right now." Reese laughed at Rick's get-outta-here grimace. "Seriously."

Rick turned to Helen. "What do you wanna bet this guy's still got the first dollar he made, plus a ton of interest? He doesn't know how to spend money. He'll give it away, but he won't spend it."

"Give it to . . . ?" she said.

"This and that," Rick replied with a shrug. He wagged a finger at Reese. "Hey, I'm not against Indian gaming laws. Some of those Atlantic City boys, they'll cry foul the minute their little toe gets stepped on. I thought about investing with them since that's where I hang out most of the time, but, hell, that's big money and some of those guys play some pretty nasty hardball. They cry around in the press about injustice, but they'll stab a guy in the back for a buck and twist the knife around for a little added fun." He poked Reese on the shoulder. "I'm saying we could open things up in this state even more with somebody like you on our team. A homeboy, know what I mean?"

"Yeah, I do." But Reese wasn't interested in hearing about opening anything up from Rick, who had no understanding of the difference between being home in South Dakota and being home on the reservation. He pushed back from the table. "I know how to lose money at blackjack. Let's go play a few hands. I need to get the hang of this game."

"I don't think so," Helen interjected, then added, "I don't think you need to."

He reached for her hand. "If I'm going to be surrounded by this gaming business, I want to understand the ins and outs of the damned game." *Her* game, and he figured that offering to play was as close as he'd get to asking her to dance.

"The money is in the slots. A lot of it goes in; sometimes a little comes back out," Helen said quickly, demonstrating with her free hand. "Those are the important ins and outs. All you need to know, really."

Reese smiled. He liked the way she talked fast whenever she was trying to resist something she really wanted. She wasn't one to jump at the chance to show off. Why should she? She had such quiet beauty, such rich polish. He could watch that elegant hand all night. With his thumb he caressed the back of the hand he held beneath the table.

"Sometimes a lot of it comes back out," Rick said. "Yeah, let's play. Better yet, let's bet on the pro here. Us pros should stick together."

"I don't play." She looked to Reese for support. "I deal forty hours a week. It's not play. It's work."

"Helen's really a teacher."

"Then teach us, Helen." Rick was out of his chair, ready for some fun. "You play, and we'll place the bets."

"It's a simple game. If you can add, you can—"

"I can add, but you can play cards," Reese countered. "It's fun to watch you because you're somebody who knows her game. I know that confidence when I see it." He drew Helen to her feet, following Rick's lead.

"Nah, she's right, Blue." Rick slid him a devilish look. "There's no real skill involved with blackjack."

"I didn't say that." Helen bristled, taking the bait, tossing it back at them. "I said it was a simple game, much like basketball." She shrugged. "Well, you toss the ball through the hoop, right? But it's possible to be very good at it."

"So show us," Rick said. "Can you count cards? Now that's a real skill, and there's real talent in being able to do it without anybody recognizing it." He craned his neck like a pop-up toy, looked around the bar full of cowboys and tourists, and lowered his voice. "Because if they catch you, they'll show you the door. I mean, the pit boss will see that you don't have lunch in this town again. But if you can do it, and you're shrewd about it . . ." He tapped his temple, challenged Helen with a look, then a quick shrug. "Not many people can do it, from what I've been told."

"It's quite possible to . . ." She edged closer to Reese, hung onto his arm, as though she wanted him to shield her from something. "Maybe if we set a limit. Say five hands. No matter what, five hands is the limit."

"That's just getting started," Rick said. "Let's see you do your stuff."

"A limit," she insisted, and she was moving toward the blackjack pit, which was a step down from the bar. "Because we have to get back to Bad River. A few hands can't hurt, I guess, but no more than that."

She looked up at Reese, something fragile and troublesome in her eyes. She was scared. She was standing at the edge of the pit, and she was eager to jump in, but she was also terrified. Her nails were digging into his palm.

He squeezed her hand. "You don't want to do it, we won't do it."

"I *do*." She heard herself, startled herself, shuddered oddly, and shook her head. "I do, but I can't, and that's, um . . ."

"It's a long drive back, and you're tired," Reese murmured as he tucked her under his arm. He felt her draw a deep breath and release it so heavily that it deflated her completely and left her leaning against him for support.

"I didn't mean to butt in," Rick said. Another table, another face, had caught his interest. He signaled that he would be there in a minute. "But let's speak about this again, Blue. You could really diversify with this."

"I've got my hands full right now. My father left me with some responsibilities."

Rick questioned the last word with a comic mug.

"*Responsibilities*. Things I have to take care of, you know what I'm saying?"

"Cool." Rick leaned in close to Helen. "Did you know this guy was the only All-Star player in the history of the NBA to retire without a press conference?"

She looked for truth in the charming man's big blue eyes. Rick gave an umpire's "Safe" signal. Done, clean, settled, no discussion. That part was true.

"That's gotta be bullshit. Who would keep track of how many guys retired without . . ." Reese laughed. "You're so full of it, Marino. You're the one for the record books. Me, I got better things to do."

"I hear you, man. We'll talk."

"See you on the road."

Helen wanted to walk. It was a cool night, typical of the Black Hills, where there were no mosquitoes to detract from the pleasures of pine-scented air, the distant fiddles, and the throng of glittering stars that seemed almost close enough to touch.

She'd had a close call with temptation, and she'd warmed to it, tipped, leaned, nearly reached out and touched it the way she wanted to touch the stars. But she had pulled back, escaped, and now this big man made her feel cosseted and cared for, safe enough to let him in on just this one secret.

"I didn't mean to get you in trouble with that suggestion," Reese said as he grabbed his denim jacket from the car he'd left parked on the street. The parking meter required his change. "Is there some rule against you playing blackjack in another establishment?"

"I have my own rules."

"What's counting cards? I mean, I've heard of it, but I don't know how it's done. You've got four decks in the shoe, right? I don't see how anybody could keep track of that many cards."

She raised a coy eyebrow as he draped his voluminous jacket over her shoulders.

"They can?" Towering over her, he sounded absurdly innocent.

"They can. There are at least fifty different ways to do it. One system is called High-Low."

He was waiting.

She was walking. Tinkling piano music escaped briefly through a door behind them. Helen slipped her arm through Reese's as they strolled past Carry Nation's Temperance Saloon and Gaming Hall. She thought maybe Carry would want to hear her disclosure, too, but they turned the corner into a quieter street. A sign advertised a tour of Old Deadwood's opium dens.

Walking gave her the momentum for launching her answer.

"High cards, ten and up, count as minus one," she said, choosing the instructional approach to the hazard. "Low cards are plus one. Seven, eight, and nine are neutral, so they're zero. As the cards are played, you keep a tally using that point system. When the count is on the plus side, you figure more high cards remain to be played, so it's a favorable deck for the player. With a minus count, the house has the advantage. People watch the tables for what's called a rich deck. You get into a rich deck game, and then the key is careful betting."

They were crossing the street now, she chattering away, he with his head bowed, intent on every word. A car stopped and let them pass through the flood of its headlights.

"That's the key and the killer," Helen continued. "A gambler loves the risk. It's hard to resist the urge to push your luck. That's how you get caught. That's also how you lose, big-time. You have to be able to stay in the game for a while to make it pay, so you have to be cool and manage your bankroll intelligently. If you have two hundred dollars, you can't make twenty-five-dollar bets. It's easy to lose eight hands in a matter of—" She snapped her fingers, shook her head. "You blink and it's gone, which is why you keep your eyes wide open and your head on straight. But sometimes, when you feel like you're on top of the world and you can't lose, intelligence doesn't figure in."

"You can do this? This card counting?"

"Oh, yeah."

"So this is what dealers—"

"No."

"No," he echoed. "Then why would you waste your time as a dealer if you had that kind of skill?"

They'd put enough distance between Main Street and the kind of action they were discussing that she was able to breathe easier. Because she was without her uniform, without a job to do, the thought of sitting opposite a dealer who was undoubtedly less skilled than she had made her heart pound a little harder. Now it was back to a sane, steady pace.

They'd reached a secluded side street that was lined with the cars of the latecomers, those who had had to park and walk. A bench near the entrance of a dentist's office was flanked by split whiskey casks overflowing with white petunias. They stopped there, and he laid his hand over the arm she had linked through his. When she looked up, he asked, "Who do you work for, Helen?"

Her silence was her answer.

"I keep trying, don't I?" He chuckled. "They say you can't blame a guy just for trying. Tell me this, then. How did you get into it?"

She sat down, and he took a seat beside her. She watched

the cars glide past for a moment. She'd gone over and over it during the treatment program she'd been referred to, the one that had saved her life. Her counselor had taken her back to the days when she and her sister had spent the school year with Mom, summers and weekends with Dad.

"My father taught me how to play cards. We'd play hearts or whist or even blackjack—twenty-one, he preferred to call it—and afterward, if I was his partner and we lost, he'd say, 'You knew there was an ace still out,' or 'You knew how many clubs had been played.' He expected me to know, and I felt stupid if I didn't, so I worked at it. He was a good card player, and I wanted his respect. I became a good card player."

"Was he a gambler?"

"No, he wasn't. He was a dreamer, but he always played it safe. Which is smart, I think—playing it safe."

"What about his dreams?"

"They were just dreams. People don't do the kinds of things he talked about doing, like building a boat, going to Africa, being a professional—" She looked at him and smiled. Fill in the blank, she thought, but he only smiled a little and waited on the edge of his seat. "Golfer. He's a golfer. Still pretty good at it, too."

"Some people do," he said, his smile broadening slightly, his dark eyes trapping moonbeams. "Get to Africa."

"Some people go off to the big city and become heroes of mythical proportion, too," she said, "*if* they have the skill and the drive."

"And a whole hell of a lot of luck. Some people thought it was a damn fool shot for a kid from nowhere to be taking, going pro when I did."

"But it was right for you."

"Maybe." He slid back on the bench, dropped folded hands between spraddled legs. "Who's to say what would have happened if I had stayed in school then? Maybe I would have had a broader perspective. Maybe . . ." He shrugged. "But college wasn't for me back then. I'd stuck it out in the army because all they wanted me to do was play ball, which was all *I* wanted to do. Not too many guys get noticed that way, but I did. I took my shot when I took it, and I don't regret that. There's no such thing as what-might-have-been. It didn't happen, doesn't exist."

He looked at her suddenly and grinned. "We were talking about you. Damn, you're good at getting turnovers. How'd you do that?"

"I mentioned the word 'heroes,' " she said with a smile, "of 'mythical proportion.' And you stepped right up to the line."

"Somebody call my name?" he aped, then laughed. "So your dad taught you to play cards. Now, my question was, how did you get into this?"

"Get into what? Dealing blackjack? It's just a job." There were no streetlights close by. Moonlight made the white petunias luminescent, and their perfume sweetened her sigh. "Sort of like bartending for the recovering alcoholic," she confessed. "I became compulsive."

"About gambling?" he asked, and she nodded. A silent moment passed. "How bad?"

"Bad. When you can't walk away, it's bad."

They sat there for what seemed an interminable length of time, side by side but separate, and Helen thought, *He didn't need to know*. She should have kept this from him or glossed over it. She could have said it was nothing. She could have *said* nothing. He didn't need to know that part of her, and now that he did, he would think, How wretched, how . . .

He slipped his arm around her, firmly but gently, as though there might be some fragility to her, and he kissed the close curve of her forehead. "I thought you were like an angel with that woman who lost all her money on the slots."

"Angels don't hang out in casinos." She closed her eyes and let her head rest against his lips. "A gambler might think there's an angel on her shoulder, but it's an illusion."

His lips moved again, another soft kiss. "I'm sorry about tonight."

"Don't be." She swallowed hard. "I'm sorry I disappointed you."

"When?" He leaned back, tipped her chin up with a gentle forefinger. "When did you disappoint me?"

"When I didn't turn out to be a true champion."

"Aw, Helen," he crooned as he enveloped her in his arms,

half laughing, half groaning. "Don't you ever think that. I was trying to show you off, which is a jackass jock kind of a thing to do. You set me straight, honey. You said no."

"Right now, what-might-have-been is very real for me, Reese. I can still feel the rush it gave me just *thinking* about it tonight. And I was going to show you how good I am, how I can defy the odds and the gods. I was all set to please you, amaze you, astound you with my dubious skill. It's very real, because it has been and it could be again, anytime I choose."

She drew back, looked him in the eye. "Yes, I can count cards, and I'm good at it, but I'm also compulsive. Now say it: *You, Helen? You always seemed like you were in complete control.*"

"Not always."

"No?"

He shook his head, pushed his fingers through her hair.

"When didn't I?" she asked.

"When you got involved with me even though you didn't want to."

"But I did want to. I knew I shouldn't, but I did."

"So you're not always in complete control." He smiled. "Is the casino job a test for you?"

"It's a job. It's a way to put what I've learned to some use. It's a way to pay a debt." She nodded; *Yes, Reese, yes, this is me.* "I had many debts. Now I have one, and I'm paying it."

"Did you get into—" He broke off when she gave him a look that pleaded for a reprieve. He sighed, stretched his arms out along the back of the bench. "Okay, but don't try to tell me I can't find angels in casinos. I know what I saw in Pair-a-Dice, and you were an angel."

She groaned, laughed a little, shook her head at his stubbornness.

"You don't have to be one every day, but *that* day, with that pitiful woman . . ."

"I've had a good deal of counseling. Training." *Pitiful woman no more.*

"But that's not your real job, either." He drew a deep breath and glanced across the quiet street, away from her face. "Is my brother being investigated?"

"Reese . . ."

"I know. You can't talk about it."

Oh, Lord. She wanted to tell him that she was only a small player and that she was on his side, a silent partner. She had been his father's ally, and she was not out to get anyone but the bad guys, the liars, cheaters, and thieves.

Bad guys. Now *there* was an in-the-eye-of-the-beholder concept.

"What do you think of your friend's proposition?" she asked.

"Ah, this is *my* test." He considered his answer for a moment. "I'm interested in what's going on here, but I'm not interested in getting into the casino business. I don't even like cards. Maybe because I don't like losing, huh? But suddenly I'm up to my neck in this gaming business—my father, my brother, the council . . ." He touched her temple with the backs of his fingers, drew them slowly along the side of her face to her neck, whispered, "You."

"Not me. You're not up to your—"

"My neck doesn't begin to describe what I'm up to in you, and you know what's different about it this time?" He smiled. "I don't mind telling you."

"Well, as far as the anatomy of it goes, you don't have to tell me. I was there."

"That's what I thought. You were with me." He leaned down to touch her lips with a butterfly kiss. "In a good way. Right?"

Her lips tingled. "In a good way."

"And you're with me now in a good way. We did the family-dinner thing, which we've both noted we didn't take the time to do before." He chuckled. "Hell, we barely took the time to get our clothes off before."

Before, before, she thought. For him, it was the *time* before. It was the summer of a brief affair, the new-green summer, the summer before blooming. For her, it was before Sidney.

Tell him.

An honest woman would tell him, no matter what, because he was obviously a decent man, and he deserved to know. An angel? An angel would have told him long ago. Helen—less-than-honest and far-from-angelic Helen—wanted to tell him, and she would have if the gamble had been hers and hers alone.

I don't mind telling you.

Why should he? He was up to his neck in—little did he know what he was up to his neck in—but at least it was his own neck. Just his, and not his child's.

His child's neck. Reese's child. She had worried about the claims that might be made on Sidney's life, his security, his well-being, but she had not allowed herself to personalize those claims, to think of him as *Reese's* child. Reese was too big. He was Touch The Clouds, the Big Man, the hero of mythical proportion. The man who was—

". . . glad you were there today." He'd claimed her hand, absently lacing their fingers together, splaying hers wide to accommodate his. "It's hard, you know. I—I have a brother, and it's about time I got to know him better, but it's hard to know where to start. Like, I want to tell him to give his family their due, but that's not my place. Not to start with, anyway."

"Maybe you could find a way to ask him about those debts Sarah mentioned."

"Yeah, right, like that's not butting into his business." He sighed. "They've got nice kids. I hate to see kids caught in the middle of a mess made by their parents. Kids deserve their kidhood, you know? Parents owe them that." He squeezed her hand as he lifted and lowered one big shoulder. "I can say stuff like that real easy, not being a parent myself."

"You're good with them." She squeezed, too, a poor excuse for encouragement and she knew it. She was going to have to tell him about his son sooner or later. She knew that, too. She'd planned on later, but she had not planned on nights like this, honesty like this. "The first time I saw you, you were surrounded by children," she recalled.

"And you thought I was one of them. An overgrown kid." He shook his head when she started to object. "But I wasn't. I only got to be a kid when I played ball."

"You still do. Today you were—"

"It's a game, the old man would say, just a game. But it was *my* game. He said the sports gurus were using me, but nobody used me the way he did. I was his keeper. He'd go on a binge, and I'd be looking after myself, looking after the place, looking out for him. I was never a kid then. And by the time he quit drinking, it was like he didn't have any use for me anymore. He got Carter back. He had a brand-new son, a kid somebody had been keeping on ice for him. Fresh, smart. Damn, that kid was smart. My father was so proud of how much Carter knew, the way he talked, his fine manners, all that was so—"

"He was very proud of you, too, Reese," Helen interjected.

"He never said it. He was always coming at me with more advice."

"So you stayed away?"

"Not completely. You know how it is when you go your own way. You look at the phone bill, and you think, Damn, how long has it been?" He wagged his head sadly. "People came to me with this council thing, and it wasn't me they were looking for. They were saying it was about tradition, but the way they were talking about him, I knew they really wanted Roy Blue Sky back."

"How do you feel about that?"

"Maybe that's why I agreed." He gave half a laugh. "Let him use me one more time."

"For what?"

"Haven't quite figured that out yet. Tell you one thing, though. If Darnell is Ten Star's man—" He snapped his fingers, a parallel complete. "He reminds me of my first agent. Smiles at you while he's telling you what a moron he thinks you are. 'You just let me do the thinking, son,' he says. I didn't renew *his* contract, either."

"Darnell isn't Ten Star. He just works for them."

"He's their eyes and ears, according to something I read in my father's papers. But if that's the case, I gotta wonder what part of the body my brother's supposed to be. Who writes his paycheck? And yours, is it . . . ?" She warned him off with a look, and he threw up his hands. "Hey, I'm not asking how much it's for."

"Mine comes from the casino."

"From the tribe?"

"I think you need to be careful, Reese. Tread lightly."

"Yeah, right." He jacked up one long leg. "Have you noticed the size of my feet?"

"I just want you to be careful. Don't talk about not renewing contracts until you have a better feel for the players here."

"You mean I don't get to see a roster?" He leaned back, held her hand on his knee. "I grew up here. I know the Indians pretty well. It's the hairy-faced cowboys I can't always figure. And I still like to keep my thoughts to myself pretty much."

"You used to," she allowed. "I think you should try to resurrect a little more of the old reticence while you get your bearings."

"Yeah, well, I did. Preston was telling me what was coming up at the next council meeting and how it would be okay if I abstained to begin with, since I haven't gotten my feet wet yet, but if a committee recommends passage, I oughta know it's probably worthy of my approval. I just listened. What I really want to know right now is . . ." He paused, peered at her in the moonlight, weighing the old reticence, setting it aside. "Am I safe with you?"

She looked down at their clasped hands.

He gave a quick squeeze. She didn't have to answer that one if she wasn't ready. "How about my brother? Is he safe with you?"

"I'm not out to get anybody, Reese. I'm trained to spot card scams." He lifted one eyebrow. "Like *all* dealers are. Please, let's leave it at that, at least for now."

"Sounds all right to me." He dragged her to her feet. "I've got my first council meeting tomorrow, but the Bad River Celebration is this week. I'd like to take you out for a hunk of frybread and a forty-nine. When are you free?"

"We're going *dancing*?"

"The only dancing I ever learned."

"I didn't know you danced at all."

"I didn't tell you I was a dancer?" He put his arm around her shoulders, walking her down the side street toward the main drag. "Well, that was back in my reticent days. I quit dancing when they started talking about using me as the tree. The center pole."

"You were sensitive about your height? How old were you?"

"Probably thirteen, twelve, something like that; and, you know, at that age certain words really set you off."

" 'Pole,' I suppose."

" 'Pole' ? What kind of a mind have you got in here, anyway, woman?" Reese laughed, hooked his arm around her neck and dropped a quick kiss on the top of her head as they strolled toward the car. "It was 'center.' The word terrified me. I had to stop growing, I thought, please, God. All I ever wanted to be was a point guard."

9

*H*elen had dealer Peter Jones's number. His two agents, an older man and a short, heavy woman who played Jones's table regularly, were about as inconspicuous as hounds in the henhouse. They ran their scams either solo or as a team. Jones's sniffing signal was ridiculously transparent. His nose ran only when his agents were around. Helen had half a notion to ask him whether he had an allergy to their Oklahoma drawls. And there were times when the dealer's push-through shuffles were so obvious that Helen seriously longed to call a time-out, march over to his table, and show him an artful false shuffle. What she didn't understand was why the cameras weren't exposing Jones's shifty moves. Hanging out in the security office on her supper break was a way to get a handle on how the security tapes were being viewed. And what she was seeing was gaping holes.

A dealer would not usually view security tapes, but Carter took no exception to her interest. "You oughta be in pictures," he was crooning to her as they watched her shift from a week ago. "You look good on TV, Helen. You should be a news-caster or something. Look at you."

"But . . . are the cameras positioned right? You can't see . . ." She tapped a fingernail on the monitor screen. "Look, all you're getting is the top of Peter's head here, and over here . . ."

"The number four eye needs adjusting, looks like to me." He made a note on a pad, tossed the pencil on the desk, and swiveled the big leather chair to face her with a bright smile. "Hey, did I tell you I had a visit with your son over the phone?"

She stiffened. "Sidney called here?"

"He'd been trying to get you at home but wasn't having any luck. Said you usually call on Sundays."

"I tried early Sunday, before we went to your place, and then later." Why would he call? It was always she who tried three or four times before she managed to get hold of him. He was too busy, having too much fun to call. "He's okay, isn't he? Did he say—"

Carter waved her worries away. "I think he was just feeling lonesome. We talked a little bit. Guy stuff. I told him I had a son about his age, or a little younger, told him Derek was nine. He sure set me straight on his age quick." He caught her eye with a steady look. "They grow up fast, don't they?"

She lifted her chin, squared her shoulders. "They do."

"I thought for sure you told me he was, like, nine or ten. He's got that dreaded voice change going on."

"I guess I'd better try to—"

"You won't reach him now." He tipped his chair back and clasped his fingers behind his head. "We've got a three-day wilderness expedition going on. He didn't know he was going, but he got picked."

"You really did have a chat, didn't you?"

He eyed her steadily. "You've got a real nice kid there, Helen."

"Yes, I do."

"Sounds like that camp in the mountains is a great program. I'll have to look into it for Derek." The chair squeaked when he jackknifed, sitting forward. "Oh, I hope I didn't blow anything when I asked him how he thought he'd like living in South Dakota. He didn't know anything about any plans to move."

"Thanks a lot." She injected enough sarcasm into her tone to cover her relief. Better topic. Easier to hedge. "I haven't told him."

"Jeez, I'm sorry. Timing is everything with these little bombshells, isn't it?" He grabbed the remote control, thumbed a button, and tossed the device aside. The monitor went black.

He pushed himself out of the chair with a heavy sigh, shoved his hands in his pants pockets, studied the floor. "I tend to think honesty really is the best policy. Not that I'm the best at practicing it lately, but . . ." He looked to her for agreement, the usual cool charm missing from his eyes. "Kids are just like anybody else. The longer you keep something from them, the harder it gets to come clean, and when you do . . ." His voice dropped, quavered slightly as he sat on the edge of the desk. "It's not the secret itself that cuts deep, but the fact that you kept it from them."

"Children have to be protected. Something like this . . ." She shook her head quickly. It *was* the secret itself, not the keeping of it. The keeping was necessary. The keeping prevented the taking, the losing, the cutting in two. "There was no reason for him to worry about it unless and until it happened."

"You think it's going to happen?"

She stared at him, her mind spinning around the startling notion that Sidney had spoken to this man, his boy-man voice cracking over the phone. The delicate shell containing her secrets had been cracked as well. A hairline crack. She could see it in Carter's eyes.

"Maybe you'd rather move out to Minnesota," he suggested. "Or maybe your sights are set on an office in—"

Bill Darnell's insistent single rap on the door brought Carter up short. He scooted off the desk and squared his shoulders, much as Helen had done under siege a moment ago, as though he expected to be charged with something. A hard chill came over the office. Sparing a disinterested "How're you" with a dismissive nod for Helen, Darnell told Carter they needed to talk.

Helen was only too glad to move along, but not without

stealing a glance over her shoulder at Carter. Sights set on an office *where*? He was onto something, *in*to something, but what? Was it Sidney, her investigation, what?

She had to get hold of her son. She ducked into the crying room, which was generally nice and private when there were no big losers in the house.

Darn that boy, he *knew* better than to call her at the casino. *You don't want to blow Mom's cover.* He loved that. He knew how sensitive her job was. He'd been a mature kid at every stage, and she had been honest with him, almost religiously. Almost.

He knew about her gambling problem. Not the worst details, but the gist of it. Yes, Mom was a good card player, but she was a lousy gambler. He knew that she had worked hard to recover her sanity, and he was proud of her. He'd told her so. He liked to brag about his mother being a dealer, especially if he could get people to wonder what kind of a dealer. And when she took these undercover assignments, he thought it was cool. But he wasn't supposed to talk about it or contact her at the casino unless it was an emergency.

The camp counselor assured her that he knew of no emergency and that Sidney's group had, indeed, set off on a three-day hike.

Carter felt a little silly tossing off a casual greeting after Helen left the office. He knew damn well he was looking down the barrel of a loaded cannon, but still he played the battlefield tourist.

"What's up, Bill?"

"I just got word that the council tabled the gaming committee's recommendation."

Bill Darnell never raised his voice. He didn't have to. People could read the consequences of not hearing him in his cold gray eyes. Especially people who owed, and Carter's debt was massive. He'd fallen into it with silky ease, beginning with the Ten Star perks—the entertainment, the trips, the vehicles, the line of credit. This was the way business was done, they said, and why not? Why shouldn't he benefit from a few dividends? He was entitled. He had paid his dues in two worlds, and he had a right to enjoy the best of both. The best thing Indian country had going for it right now was the gaming business, and Carter was a key player.

He pushed his tailored navy blazer out of the way, shoved his hands into the pockets of the custom slacks he'd bought on a trip to the East Coast, and stood his ground. He knew what was coming.

"You know who made the motion to table? Your brother." Darnell paused to let the news sink in. Reese had moved to table. Carter was supposed to be contrite over this, but he felt like laughing. When had Reese gotten into parliamentary procedure? His first meeting and he single-handedly put the whole issue on hold? Damn, Carter wanted to laugh. But he kept his face as straight as Darnell's.

"Sweeney thought he had the votes to eliminate the other bidders so that when we make our presentation it's a done deal," Darnell said. "They can't seriously think they're going to bring anybody else in to manage this operation. Ten Star *built* this place."

"That's true, but it does belong to—"

"You know better." Darnell snatched the small yellow tablet with Carter's videotape notes off the desk. "What's on paper is not necessarily what *is*. Ten Star put this place up, and Ten Star can take it down. You and me, Carter, we're the front line, the facilitators. We maintain. Now, we figured your brother would go with the flow. "He's just passing through, right?"

"Well, yeah, this is just a formality."

"And you were supposed to talk to him."

"I *did* talk to him. He was . . ." Carter drew a deep breath. He hadn't talked to him, not really, other than during the little session they'd all had in his living room when Reese hadn't said much. He'd taken that as a nod. "He was completely agreeable, I thought," he told Darnell.

"And Sweeney was thinking it would be good to start moving things through right away, before they regrouped, before every John Doeskin creeps out of the bush and starts bending your brother's ear."

"He's not going to listen to every—" Carter shook his head.

He would have Reese's ear now. They were brothers, after all. "Reese lives in the real world. He's going to be reasonable."

"Well, he'd better be reasonable, Carter. You need to see that he's going to be reasonable. Because you do know what Ten Star *does* own, don't you?" Darnell waited until he had Carter's full attention, full apprehension, eyes on eyes. "That's right, Mr. Marshall. Your red ass."

Reese pulled Helen off the floor early that evening. The last time he had been to a powwow, the celebration committee had made a big deal over his first year as a pro basketball player, asked him to carry a staff and lead the grand entry, had him present the beaded crown to the new Miss Bad River, gifted him with a special quilt and an honor song. He'd donated generously to every drum in the bowery and to the fund for the next celebration, but he'd felt like a fraud. His rookie year had been unremarkable. It wasn't enough for him to wear the uniform. He wouldn't deserve the attention until he was a starter, until he was making a difference in every game, until he'd lasted a while. By the time that happened, he'd found it too easy to put off going home, especially in the summer.

Now he couldn't remember what else he'd had to do that was better than watching beautiful young people parade around the powwow grounds dressed in brightly colored dance costumes trimmed with fans of feathers and shocks of satin ribbon. He'd seen a troupe of Irish dancers on stage in Minneapolis, had marveled at the staccato clicking of their metal taps on polished floors, but here the floor was prairie sod and the feet were marvelously stealthy. And here, as the sun dipped low in a vermilion sky, he could feel the heart of the earth singing along with the resolute beat of the drum.

Helen greeted almost as many friends as Reese did while they walked the courting path outside the circular bowery—the shelter for spectators surrounding the grassy arena, open to the sky, where the dancing took place. People knew her from the casino. Some remembered her from her teaching days. She didn't have to be reminded which ones had been her students. They were the ones who received the warmest greetings and made her blue eyes shine so that Reese's heart swelled, simply because he was the one who walked by her side.

She made him get her a grape snow cone, and when he told her there was no way he was getting on any itinerant carny Ferris wheel, she cracked him up by sticking her purple tongue out at him. He was going to be able to tease her good and proper when she spilled the purple stuff on the long, light blue dress that flowed around her legs like spring water when she walked, but that didn't happen.

Her eyes glistened as they watched the little boys' fancy-dance competition. He remembered dancing himself when he was that age, before sprouting up to become the lone willow in the alfalfa patch had made him shun dancing. But Helen's eyes shone for memories of a different little boy, one Reese wondered about more and more, tried to imagine, sometimes even spoke to in his head. "How about a game of one-on-one?" he would say to this blond, blue-eyed boy, fair like his mom, but sweaty and dirt-necklaced and skinned at the knees, like a boy. And he would play him for fun, for the pure joy of sharing the wonder of the big round ball and what they could make it do. Helen might join in or she might not, but her eyes would shine, the way they did now as the lights came on over the bowery where the children danced.

Daylight lingered forever on a Dakota summer's evening, and it was still twilight when they strolled over to the campground. A voice drew Reese's attention to three tents pitched in the shelter of a large cottonwood tree. A tall man with brown leather skin and long gray braids waved a cowboy hat and shouted again. "*Hopo! Tonska!*"

Reese waved, then dropped his hand to the back of Helen's neck and steered her toward the dusky green and light tan tents. "More family," he said. The old man stood as straight as a tent pole and nearly as tall as the man who introduced him. "Uncle Silo, my mother's brother, the one they say I favor."

"Sylvester," Reese's uncle said as he extended his hand to Helen. "Silo is the name they hung on me long time ago." To Reese he said, "The old women are waiting to see you. You know how they are. You got to go to them."

He took them to a grassy pocket behind the tent where he'd been laying a fire in a pit. There a barrel-shaped woman was planted deep in a folding lawn chair, her foot in a cast and propped on a canvas camp stool, her diamond willow cane close at hand. "Here's Auntie Lil," Silo said. "Still my little round grain bin, but now she's kinda tipsy on her feet."

"Eee, that one." Auntie Lil waved a weathered hand at her husband and squinted at her nephew. "Come down here, my boy. This far away, I could mistake you for your old uncle."

Reese glanced at Helen, delight jigging in his dark eyes. "I'd better be careful, then. I might get my ears boxed."

He kissed her cheek first, then hunkered down beside the old woman's chair to let her peer into his face by the light of the kerosene lamp hanging on a pole behind her.

"Oh, now I see. You're much prettier than that old thing." She mopped her neck and chest with a blue bandanna. "Eee, it's been hot and dusty out here today," she complained as she patted Reese's arm. "Summer's been hard on us old people. I couldn't get up to the funeral, my boy. They had me in the hospital with this bad foot I've got."

Reese introduced Helen, who asked how Auntie Lil had hurt her foot.

The old woman leaned forward, turned the walking cast to one side as if to show off the damage. "I broke it last winter, and they can't get it to heal right. Three times they've cut into it now. Old bones don't wanna mend, I guess."

"You remember Gramma Mary from the funeral," Reese told Helen as a gray-haired woman ducked through the opening in one of the tents. She seemed taller than she actually was, regal in the way she carried herself in her buckskin dance costume. "My father's sister."

"I thought I might see you again. I saw that look in your eye." The fringe on Gramma Mary's sleeve swished with her proffered handshake. Reese chuckled behind her back, but she turned her gentle charge on him. "You, too, Sonny, I saw you looking at her. You think with these glasses I don't pick up on these things, but I don't miss much. Glasses like this, they're sensitive to heat." She shoved her thick lenses to the bridge of her nose with one hand while she fluttered the other. "Those

166

heat waves, they make the air kinda shimmery-like. These glasses pick that up right away." She glanced at him and laughed. "Ehhh, that's the look, all right."

Reese laughed, too, but his face felt hot. He couldn't believe he was blushing. "I'm not bringing any more women around you guys."

"This is the first one you've brought home." Auntie Lil caught the surprise in Helen's eyes and wagged a finger. "Saaay, look at the smile on her."

"They have no mercy." Reese hooked one arm around Helen's neck and playfully drew her to his side, a confessional claim. "Helen used to teach history at the high school in Bad River."

"She told me that when we were working in the kitchen. Said she knew you then, before you went to the city," Gramma Mary said. "You're getting to know each other again, looks like. What do you think of our boy being on the council?"

Helen nodded her approval. "I'm sure he'll do a fine job."

"If they don't do a fine job on him first," Auntie Lil said. "Look what they did to his dad."

Reese stiffened. Beneath his arm he could feel Helen's parallel reaction. "What do you mean?" he asked. "Have you heard something?"

"He was speaking his mind about that casino business." Uncle Silo was unfolding web-strap chairs for his guests. "Puts me in mind of that BIA cattle program. You remember that program, my boy? That time I had cattle for a while?"

"No, Uncle, I don't think I was around then."

"I almost got my head blown off that time."

"Seriously?" With a gesture Reese invited Helen to take the chair while he squatted next to his uncle at the edge of the fire pit. "What happened?"

"Well, see, they were buying these cows with program money, got a few Indian operators going, and then they were supposed to start up a tribal herd. We ranchers paid on our loans with our heifers, see. We could sell our steers, but our heifers were supposed to go into that new tribal herd. I delivered my heifers out to the tribe's herd that one time, then fixed a flat tire on my pickup and went off down the road. But in a little while I came back. I forgot my tire iron. Really caught them cowboys by surprise. I seen what they was doing, too, kinda rearranging the brands a little bit. So I tried to tell the superintendent. He told me that my eyes were deceiving me."

Reese scowled in disbelief.

Silo laughed as he withdrew a book of matches from his shirt pocket. "That's exactly what he said. 'Your eyes must be deceiving you, Silo. That's not what those boys were doing.' " He waved the outrage away. "Shee-it, I know my own brand. I know the Bad River Sioux Tribe brand. What they were putting on those heifers was a whole lotta somethin' else. So the superintendent—it was that Mosely then, remember that one?"

Reese shook his head as he rolled some newspaper in anticipation of his uncle's need for tinder. The reservation superintendent was an employee of the Bureau of Indian Affairs, and Bad River, like all reservations, had had its share of the good, the bad, and the ugly, going all the way back to the days when they had been called Indian agents.

"Well, he was a slick one," Silo said. "He told me to just forget about it. Like that picture we saw about the gangsters, remember that?" He looked up at his wife for affirmation as he imitated some actor's delivery. "Fer-get about it."

"But you didn't," Reese said with a smile.

"Hell, no. I tried to tell a couple of guys, and they said, 'Silo, you damn sure better forget about it. Hell, you can't do nothin', and you might just get hurt.' And then somebody went and shot a hole in the door of my pickup—damn near killed me, except it went into the seat." Again he looked at Auntie Lil. She pressed her lips together tightly, remembering. "This one says I'd better shut up, so I shut up."

"Didn't forget about it, though."

"Well, I for sure shut up. But I guess I didn't forget about it." Slipping into his gangster voice, Silo grinned as he struck a match. "Fer-get about it."

Chuckling, Reese touched the newspaper to Silo's flame and watched it flare. "What do you think happened to Dad?"

"He wouldn't shut up. That's all I know."

Reese shoved his torch into the kindling in the fire pit.

Sounded like Roy Blue Sky, all right, he thought. Never could shut up.

So now what?

"You guys said you wanted me to do this," Reese said as he watched the flame climb the carefully arranged ladder of firewood.

"Well, yeah, you're his son. It's a good thing, you finishing out his term. That's the way it's supposed to be. But you don't have to be sticking your neck out the way your father did. You don't even have to say much. You just go to the meetings, and you sit right in front of their faces, and you make them remember."

Reese looked his uncle in the eye. "I thought you said I was supposed to finish the job he started."

"Finish his *term*. Just go to the meetings and silently remind them. That's our way, you know, us big Indians. They like to see them silent tears." Silo sat back on his haunches. "Hell, you don't know nothin' about politics."

"Just shut up and go to the meetings," Reese said.

"That's the best way. You just watch the council at work. You got the talkers and the ones that sit there and nod."

"Nod off, you mean," Auntie Lil put in.

"Well, you got those, too," Silo said. "But you play it smart and be one of the nodders."

"Nod and approve, or nod and vote my conscience? Or Dad's conscience? Tell you one thing, this is one big Indian won't be showing any tears." Reese draped his forearm over his upraised knee and eyed his uncle. "What do you want from these casinos, Uncle?"

Silo shrugged. "I want to win that Jeep they got sittin' in the lobby there."

Reese chuckled. "Which do you play, cards or slots?"

"I don't play either one," Silo claimed, stealing a quick look at his wife. She laughed and shook her head. "No, hey, I hardly go in there. Maybe the nickel machines sometimes, but I don't get much out of it. It's kinda boring, you want the truth." He tossed a handful of gray-green sage on the fire, sending up a flurry of sparks. "But I wouldn't mind having that Jeep. I could have some fun with that."

"What do you expect the casinos to do for us? If we ever make a profit, what're we going to do with it?"

"It's jobs," Silo said. "That's one good thing. Those *Dah-kotas* out there where you're staying now, do those guys really get half a million dollars apiece every year off Mystic Lake?"

"You mean our rich cousins?" Reese smiled at the emphasis his uncle gave to the name for the eastern Sioux. "They get big money, Uncle. They only have maybe a couple hundred tribal members, and they're situated near a big city, just like that little tribe in Connecticut. Most Indian casinos will never pay out like that."

"I wasn't expecting it to. I guess what I expect is the usual. Program lasts a couple of years, some outsiders get rich off it, then they go away and we've got another building to argue over."

"This isn't a program. It's a business."

"If we start making money off it, I think we ought to create more business."

"Like what?"

"I don't know. They start up these plants on the rez, we always make something for the army. You know, like camouflage net or something. We oughta make something people need. Something they'll always need and they can only get from us."

Reese laughed. "Talk to Bill Gates about hanging onto that kind of a deal."

"I want the *jobs*," Silo repeated, tossing another sprig of sage into the flames. Reese filled his lungs with the pungent scent as he took in the old man's answers. "I want our children to have a future, you know? Here, where we live, where we've always lived."

"You wouldn't put the money into schools or roads or health care?" Helen asked. "Those things could stand some improvement, too. And housing."

"I want us to be in charge of all those things for ourselves," Silo said. "To build them for ourselves the way we want. Not the way the government says we want."

"And you think I should just sit there and nod," Reese said, glancing from his uncle to his invalid aunt, who sat behind him in the deepening shadows. They'd said it was the smart way, not the good way. And they hadn't used the word "should."

"What can you do in three months, my boy?" Silo asked. "Tell you what, you keep your head down and you ride out your dad's term, shoulders square."

"Head down, shoulders square," Reese echoed. "And my horse, does he hang his head in this picture, too? Even with my head down, I'm still a pretty big target."

Silo laughed. It was a familiar image of the defeated Indian, and no one much liked it anymore. "Me, too. I sure found that out."

"I've already been to 'the end of the trail,' Uncle. I looked over that cliff. Nothing down there. You either stand there forever hangin' your head over the abyss, or you jump that sucker."

"Well, you always had a hell of a stretch, Blue. I remember that time you took State in the broad jump."

"There you go, that's an example. Once you take off, you gotta go with it, lean forward and fly as far as the wind will take you. No time to nod off."

Like his Auntie Lil was doing now. He smiled when he noticed her chin resting on her chest, his gaze shifting easily to Helen, sitting between the two old women who had taken their turns mothering him whenever he'd allowed any mothering. It was his turn to do for them and to care for Helen if she would let him. And he would make her let him. Seeing her sandwiched between those dear old women, between the bookends of their experience, he made up his mind to help her see the perfect fit that he was looking at now. He wasn't going to lose her again. He felt as though he'd finally awakened, and he wasn't going to nod off.

He turned to his uncle again and to the crackling fire they'd started together. "You think somebody murdered him?" he asked quietly.

"I don't think we'll ever know. They could film *Unsolved Mysteries* in Indian country every week."

"We'll know," Reese said. "One way or another, we're going to get some answers on this particular mystery. If I pick up where he left off, we'll know soon enough who his friends and enemies were."

"Be careful, Blue. Don't be letting your dad's tall tales and war stories go to your head. You don't wanna be the bait for any—"

Reese laughed. "Do I look like a worm to you? Even if somebody had it in for the ol' man, they're not about to go after me. That'd be too good of a news story. I'm still famous, right?"

"Right."

"Right. That would be a spectacle, going after me." He tossed more sage into the fire. Cleansing sage, purging smoke. "We'll know the truth, Uncle Silo."

Gramma Mary piped up. "The *wanagi* won't be satisfied until we do. Three nights now they woke me up, makin' noise outside, scarin' the dogs."

Both men turned, surprised by her contribution. She was looking at Reese, firelight and shadow flickering over her face. "You, too?" she asked.

"It's not like that with me, Gramma. Nothing that dramatic. It's just a . . ." He glanced at Helen. "A feeling."

"That's what I said. You don't have to see what it was that made that noise. You feel it when it isn't natural." Gramma Mary settled back in her chair, deeper into the shadows. "You get to be my age, you don't care what other people think. You know what you know."

"Get to be your age, you're already halfway there," Silo said. "Pretty soon you'll be talking to them out loud. We'll be sayin', Don't mind her, she's just trying to sweet-talk the gatekeeper."

"There's no gate," Gramma Mary reported. "There's no gate and no big bird wings. I know what I know."

"Did he say anything to you about any particular worries he might be having?" Helen asked, her voice coming as the surprise this time. They all looked at her, wondering who was lost here. "Roy, I mean. Before he died."

"Was he afraid of anybody?" Gramma Mary asked for clarification, then shook her head. "Not so's you'd notice. Not lately. My brother used to be Mr. Nicey Nice, you know, always doing people favors, but that was long time ago."

"When he was drinking," Silo said. "Man, he could suck up the sauce. Remember that, sonny?"

"Yeah, I remember."

"But that was years ago. He told me not too long ago he'd been sober nearly twenty years. That's a long time."

Reese nodded. The number was truly sobering to him. Hell of a long wagon ride, he had to admit. The truth was . . .

Jesus, the terrible truth was that he'd known his father better as a drunk. Maybe that was the only way he'd really known him at all. Maybe he'd never really accepted his father any other way, never believed his sobriety to be anything but temporary. Never dared. He pushed the words "Long time" out on the tail of a weary sigh.

Silo laid a hand on his shoulder, squeezed, rocked him a little, and launched into a remembrance.

"Marvin Grass put on a sweat not too long ago, and your dad and me went in, along with a few other guys. Old friends, you know, and a couple of young guys. We try to bring the young ones in, and they're coming. Slow but sure. This is a strange road we're on. Some guys, guys like your dad, there comes a time in their lives when they don't want to be Indian. So maybe they give up the old ways, or maybe they just go off somewhere. Just *fer-get about it*. And then they seem to lose their way. You know, they get to boozin', a lot of them, and they go blind. That's how I see it. They just go blind. You see their eyes?" He waved a hand in front of his own unwavering, unblinking gaze to demonstrate. "Nothin' there."

"But some recover their sight somehow, and they come back," Gramma Mary put in.

Silo nodded. "Your dad came back. He started going to sweats with us again. It was still hard for him to talk about how he felt."

"He always had to be the *man*," Gramma Mary said. "But, oh, could that boy tell stories. When he was in school, he was so smart, that one. Smart as a fox."

"Smart as a damn bee bite on the ass," Silo said with a chuckle.

"But he had to quit school," Mary recalled. "He got into it with the priest at the mission school, and he said he wasn't going back."

Reese hadn't heard this story. "They didn't make him go back?"

"He got through the eighth grade," Mary said. "That was pretty good back then, to get that far. And my dad said it was up to him, so he went to work for some white ranchers. He always worked, you know."

Reese was having trouble fitting these new pieces into the puzzle of his father's past. "I thought he played high school basketball."

"He did, but he wasn't exactly enrolled in school." The firelight was dancing in Gramma Mary's eyes as she smiled. "Oh, he could wangle his way in and out so easy. He was a fox, that one."

"He was a fox, all right," Reese agreed.

"This last time we were passing the pipe, and he was praying for you boys, like he always did—" Silo caught the surprise in Reese's eyes. "Oh, yes, my boy. He always prayed for you. Anyway, he got real emotional. It was like he knew something was up. Not like he was scared, but like there were some things he wanted to say or try to make right or something. He was never one for talking about his feelings. Instead, he told stories." He nodded toward Reese as he spoke to Helen. "He was always tellin' stories about this one here."

Helen smiled. "He told me a few."

"He was proud of you, my boy. He said he never had to worry about you because you're a real fighter."

"I guess he can take some credit there. But this council thing, it's my last duty to him." Reese looked intently at his uncle. "I want to do it right."

"Whatever you do, you're still the big man from Bad River."

"Damn, you sure know how to lay it on thick, Uncle."

"Are you camping?" Silo asked.

Reese and Helen gave simultaneous noes. "Just came for the—"

"Dancing," she finished, and he pointed at her and said, "Food," and they shared a warm look, a small laugh.

Silo elbowed his nephew, leaned over, and whispered, "We got an extra tent."

Family dinner at a powwow meant that the elders were served first, followed by small children, and then everyone else lined up. There was always soup—tripe for the traditional palate, jerked or boiled meat, maybe some buffalo with wild turnip, parched corn, sandwiches, and frybread with *wojapi*, a thickened fruit soup. Reese and Helen helped Auntie Lil get situated, served their elders, then waited in line for their supper. Waiting was part of the tradition, as was sharing news and jokes along with the food.

But Reese's new status as a councilman brought him a new round of attention, a new level of respect, wordless handshakes from people he didn't really know. "Your father's path," they said. "Your ol' man's footsteps," words both pleasing and troubling for Reese, but he kept telling people he'd do his best and that he was open to their suggestions. "Just don't sell us out," one old man said, and Reese promised not to.

Now all he had to do was figure out what that meant.

"I'm having such a good time that I hate to look at my watch," Helen said later as they strolled back from the rodeo grounds, where they'd cheered for Titus Hawk, who had entered the wild-horse race and gotten dumped on his ass.

"Didn't you check your watch at the gate? Watches aren't allowed. We're on Indian time." He hooked his arm around her and drew her to his side. "Which is amazing to me, because you know what? It feels right."

"As though you'd never left?"

"If I'd never left, I might not feel the rightness of it." He pulled her off the well-worn path between rodeo and powwow grounds to let three coltish kids race past them in the dark. They hit the wooden footbridge over the creek and clattered across. Helen moved to start up again, but Reese held her in front of him. "Let's stay here tonight in Uncle Silo's extra tent." Another kid galloped past them, and Reese lowered his head close to her ear. "I want to make love to you while the drums are playing."

She leaned back against him. "I love the drums. I love the way they do funny little things to your heartbeat."

"How funny?"

"I don't know. Speed it up, slow it down. Like the original pacemaker."

"That *is* funny. You're a funny lady. Stay here with me tonight, and I'll tell you just how funny you are." He took her hand and drew her around, pressing her palm over his heart. "I'll even show you my own funny side, and we'll see what funny things the drums do to us."

"I should get back," she said with a sigh.

"To what? An empty place? I've got one of those, too. Hot and quiet and empty." Probably emptier than hers. She was torn because she had thoughts of her son. He could see what those thoughts did to her when she watched other children and heard their voices, and she thought she should go and be alone and be a proper mother.

But there was nothing improper in what he felt for her. "Stay here with me tonight," he implored, still pressing her hand to his chest, risking his secret. "That drumbeat's really working on me. My heart's racing." She shivered, and he wondered whether she sensed something unnatural, like Gramma Mary's *wanagi*, or like his heart skipping a beat. "Cold?"

"South Dakota nights," she said, and he could feel another shiver shimmy through her.

"There's a place I want to show you, Helen, if I can still find it. I'll show you the night like you've never seen it before." He kissed her temple and whispered, "The Lakota night."

He drove her out one gate and back through another one, into community pasture. He was counting on the tire-track road still trailing through the pasture where tribal members were allowed to run a mare or a gelding if they had no place else to keep a horse. If they'd started running bulls there or buffalo, he'd be in big trouble.

But the fence hadn't been built up any, and the gates were the same post-and-wire ones he remembered. He'd never come out here except on horseback, and every clay rut that scraped the undercarriage of the Lincoln told him there was a good reason God made horses and Ford made pickups. He was driving the right vehicle for impressing a pretty woman in a pretty dress, but he was headed the wrong way. He ought to be taking her to a show at the Ordway in Minneapolis instead of to the top of a hill in the middle of the South Dakota prairie.

But the Ordway had no spotlights to compare with a full August moon. He'd been to the top of this hill during pow-wow before, and if memory served, it was the best seat on the planet. *Someday I'll bring a girl up here,* he'd promised himself. He'd been feeling sorry for himself that night for some reason or other—probably for being a lonely teenager—and he'd vowed to find himself a girl who didn't care if a guy didn't have his own car.

"Would you have come with me if I didn't have a car?"

Helen turned, laughing, adjusting her skirt as she cocked one knee toward him. "I was just thinking we probably needed a pickup for this excursion."

"Or a horse," he said.

"Oh, yes, a horse."

"One horse between us," he said as he arced the steering wheel, gunning the Lincoln off the track and into uncharted territory. "What if that was all we had?"

She peered at the grass ahead. The headlights exposed the mist gathering in the draws. "One horse sounds good."

"One old gray nag, what if that was all I had?"

"Maybe we'd have to walk," she said, "but if there's good grass up there, we'd take her on a lead."

Grinning in the dark, he parked the car at the foot of the hill. This was as far as his buggy would take them. "What about your dress?"

She fussed with the skirt again. "One old blue dress, what if that was all I had to wear? Would you still take me to your special place?"

"On my back, pretty lady." He got out of the car, grabbed the blankets he'd thrown into the backseat, and came around to her door just as she was emerging. "I'm not kidding. I can carry you from here."

"I believe you," she said, and she drew his head down to her lips for a kiss to thank him for the offer. "But I can also walk." She reached down, pulled the back of her skirt between her legs by the hem, and clutched it to her tummy, improvising pants. "Lead on."

Just looking at her in the moonlight, her hair wispy around her luminous face and tumbling around her shoulders, the look in her eyes that said she'd follow him anywhere tonight—just looking at her made his heart double in size. Which couldn't hurt him, not tonight. He was with Helen, and Helen was magic.

The drumbeat set the pace as they hiked up the hillside,

leaving the car and the mist and the chirping insects below. She was a little winded when they reached the windswept tabletop, and he renewed his offer to give her a lift because he fully believed he could carry her to the top of the world tonight. "Aren't we there yet?" she puffed, and he laughed, took her by the hand, and led her to the promontory, where she dragged back on him when she first glimpsed the view of the powwow grounds below. "Oh, yes, we are," she whispered. "Oh, Reese."

The lights from the little traveling carnival glittered off to the side. The bowery was a bright circle filled with the dancers' flouncing colors, and its outskirts were dotted with campfires. "The best seat is over here," he told her, and she hesitated, because from where they stood, it looked like the edge of a cliff. But he coaxed her, and she trusted him; and sure enough, there was a natural observation deck, a grassy place at the base of a tall rock, a place carved into a hilltop to accommodate two lovers and their blankets.

"I could live here," he said as he put down the thicker one, made of dense wool, and spread it close to the guardian rock. He dropped the folded star quilt on top of it, took his boots off, and sat down with his back to the rock. Then he drew her down between his thighs, positioning himself as her backrest, her cloak, and her shelter.

"If you were a bird," she said as she settled into him.

"Maybe I am. Or maybe my spirit guide is a bird. I never went out and searched for one, so I can't say for sure, but I'm pretty light on my feet for a man my size." He draped his arms loosely around her. "At least, that's what they say."

"The storytellers and the balladeers?"

"Those who know me well." He seriously wanted her to be one of them. He rubbed his cheek against hers, relishing the view below and the moon above, the smell of her hair and way she filled his substantial hollow.

"I'm getting to know you pretty well," she said, and he sensed wonder in her, as though she hadn't expected this or hadn't intended it. Probably because she'd left him so far behind, too. "And I think you're looking for more than just a place to light." She hooked her hands over his forearm, as though she were chinning herself. "What do you think of these lights?"

"I've seen brighter."

"Have you seen better?" She pointed toward the north end. "Would that be your uncle's fire, somewhere in that vicinity? And I'll bet Titus's is over there. And who else? That darling little boy who won the fancy-dance contest? I'll bet he's sleeping near one of those fires right there," she said, sliding her outstretched finger southward.

"You're right, these are fine and friendly lights, and they warm my heart."

"As if your heart needed warming," she said, turning in his arms to lay her hand on his chest. "I thought guys who made it big in sports were supposed to get unbearably self-centered, but not you."

"What's your definition of making it big? I've known guys to get permanently bent out of shape over a hole in one."

She lifted her head. "You play golf?"

"Try to. I'm sure your dad's a lot better than I am. Since it's not my game, I don't have to prove much." He rubbed her shoulder. "Just good exercise. Good for the heart."

Her fingers patted him gently. "*Ta-tum, ta-tum*, it's keeping time with the drum."

"Can you hear it?" he asked, and she slid down, put her ear to his chest. "I meant from where you were. But don't move again. Stay where you are." He rested his head against the rock, looked up at the stars, stroked her hair. "Sometimes you can hear the thing a mile off."

"A strong man needs a strong heart," she said simply, easily.

"Like I said, you're a funny lady." Funny and sweet and smart, and he wanted nothing more than to be strong for her. "The truth is, Helen, I have a weak heart."

It took her a moment, but just as he expected, she did draw back, straighten up, give him that look. He couldn't see it—he was looking at stars—but he could feel it. He'd used the wrong word. "Strong" was what she wanted, too, and it was what she expected when she looked at him, what anyone would expect.

"What do you mean?" she asked finally.

He shrugged. "That's why I had to quit playing pro basketball. It wasn't my back or any of the other stuff you heard about. Those injuries were a nuisance, but the doctors have pretty much repaired them. They can't really fix the heart problem."

"What heart problem? What's going on with—"

"Funny little things. It's built a little weird, thicker than it should be in places, so it doesn't always beat strong and clear, like the drum. You know how you've got your four chambers that work perfectly together, valves opening and closing, *ta-tum, ta-tum*, blood moving along through the chambers in an orderly way?" She nodded. "Mine are messed up because I've got this thickness that can be what they call obstructive. And it's sneaky. Latent, they say. But my heart does make these funny noises, which helped the doctors to diagnose the problem."

"Funny noises?" She said "funny" like the word was becoming a touchy thing.

And it was, but he liked "funny" better than "sick." Easier to say, so he liked to make it sound a little funny. That way he could keep right on smiling.

"I think of it like I've got these four brothers on my drum, and two of them could keep up whatever pace I asked them to for another fifty, sixty years if the other two would just lay off the sauce. But you can tell when somebody's been nipping because he throws everybody's timing off."

"But you don't drink."

"No, but . . ." She was sitting there staring at him, as wide-eyed as a shock victim. "You've gotta work with me now, woman. It's a good story, isn't it?"

"Not if it means you're going to have a heart attack. Reese?" Her hand closed around a fistful of his shirt, then hammered on his chest three times, punctuating her reprimand. "This is nothing to joke about, mister."

"Honey, I'm dead serious."

"Don't!" She pounded him again.

He grabbed her fist and pressed it to his lips. "We're gonna save this for emergency use only."

"What do you mean, thicker than it should be?"

"The wall down the middle, the septum, toward the bottom it's too thick, so it interferes with the blood flow a little bit. Sometimes. It's not a big problem most of the time for me. For some people it's really bad, but you notice I'm still kickin'."

She was still staring. She hadn't moved one damn bit, and it made him feel wretched, pitiful. Obviously he hadn't been funny enough.

He rubbed her arms, hoping to get her to let down some while he explained. "The clinical term is hypertrophic cardiomyopathy, and what it means is that life insurance companies don't particularly want to take my money."

The little sound she made shook him inside, where he'd been carrying this condition long enough so that it had its own place, and it rode with him quietly.

"Not many people know this, Helen, because I don't want them to. I didn't want any public discussion over it. I'm telling you because . . ." God, she was tense. He slid his hands around to her back and rubbed up and down. "Because I'm kinda gettin' attached to you again, and I just thought you oughta know. In case you're getting at all attached to me."

"Attached? How . . ." Her first try drained away. "How serious . . ."

"Pretty serious. It can be a killer. It doesn't have to be, but it can. You hear about it sometimes. Basketball players and runners, especially, dropping dead on the—"

"Reese! My God, you were running that day I came—"

"Mine isn't the worst kind, Helen, so just calm down. They found mine because I was in the right place at the right time with the right doctor, and they found it." He took her face in his hands. "You see why I don't tell people? They get all panicky around me and start asking me if I'm okay every time I break a sweat. I have to run. I have to play ball. I'm an athlete. I can't live without sports."

"But they might *kill* you."

"A lot of things might kill me. A truck might kill me, or a snakebite, or some weird bacteria off a piece of fruit." She was making that little hurt sound again, like this was all bullshit, like he still wasn't being serious enough. But he was. Living, breathing, surviving serious when he looked at her and said, "Inactivity might kill me, but you know what really kills me?"

"What?"

"Being treated like some kind of freak. I start thinking maybe I *am* a freak. Hell, I'm taller than most people, darker-skinned than most people, quieter, clumsier, homelier . . ."

"What are you talking about? You are *not*—"

"Prouder, meaner, more arrogant, hell, yeah! At the top of my game I am." He had her shoulders in his hands now, trying to find the right way to hold her through all this shit. "You know what happens when you find out you've got a problem like this? You get all wrapped up in it, and if you're not careful, it takes over your life. I've been there, and I don't want to live like that. I could just possibly live to be a very old man, and the last thing I want to do is spend all those years worrying about whether I'm gonna die tomorrow."

Yet again there was that little sound. He wanted to shake her, but he shook his head instead. "And I really don't want to see that in other people's eyes when they look at me. Especially not yours. You know what I want to see in yours?"

"What?"

He made his hands relax, made his voice go softer for her. "I want to see, 'Kiss me, Reese.'"

Her lips parted. He couldn't see much in her eyes, but he heard a quick breath. He smiled, and he thought, Pick it up, honey. That shiny thing, that's what you want from me. Pick it up.

"The very first time I saw you, that's what your eyes were saying to me. The very first—"

"Oh, that's not true," she protested. "I didn't think about kissing you the first time I laid eyes on you, for heaven's sake."

He laughed, relieved. Back to the good stuff. "Liar."

"There were a bunch of little kids around, and you were . . . I thought you were . . ."

"A little overgrown but still a kid. I know. And I fooled you, didn't I? Turned out to be more man than you thought."

She slid her arms around him and buried her face against his neck.

He smiled in the dark and whispered, "In some ways, huh?"

"You turned out . . . I always thought you were quite a man. But young." And then she added quickly, "Compared to me."

"Am I old enough for you now? Tell you what, I've aged a whole lot more than you have. You've gotten more beautiful, is all."

She rewarded him with a small laugh as she turned in his arms. He helped her get situated so she could see what he'd brought her up there to see, and he figured he'd better keep talking, since it seemed to be working. He loved it when she laughed, even a little.

"They say women become more beautiful when they become mothers, and you're sure proof of that."

She groaned. "Quite a man and then some."

"Well, I've been polishing up my act. You were obviously underwhelmed the first time around, the way you took off without even leaving me a note. You're supposed to leave a guy a note, a phone number, some way to find you."

"You could have found me," she said quietly.

"Sure, if I felt like hiring a detective." Okay, this wasn't the good stuff, but it was easier. It was past. "I thought about doing just that, and I came close, but then I thought, what was the point? It was pretty clear to me that you didn't want to see me again."

She was silent for a moment, and he almost regretted opening the valve on this particular chamber, but then she said, "I'm seeing you again now."

"That's right. You hang tough, the parts left hanging kinda heal up a little bit, and along comes another chance. Life's funny that way, see?" He was looking for that small laugh again, and he got it this time by touching her sides, her ticklish spot, the one he'd discovered thirteen years ago and rediscovered on the first try.

"No fair! It won't be funny when we're tumbling down the hill."

"That'll be the funniest of all. Can't you just see us, somersaulting into the middle of an Intertribal round?" They both laughed as he drew it out for them in the air. "*Hopo*, new step, they'll all be saying, and pretty soon everybody's rolling down the hill."

Ah, they laughed. With the lights twinkling below them and the velvet night taking heart from the steady beat of the drum, this was the spirit, he thought, the willingness to reach for the shiny thing. How could he show her more of the same?

"When do I get to meet your son?"

"My son?"

Damn, she'd gone tense again. He had his arms crossed around the front of her, hands on her arms, suddenly gone stiff on him. He started rubbing again.

"I figure I could make more points with you through your son. Kids really like me, especially kids who like basketball. You did say he plays basketball."

"Yes, he does. Well, he's only . . . he's young yet. Still has a long way to go."

"Of course he does—at what, ten? Nearly eleven, huh? He's pretty young to be away from his mom all summer."

"He's very mature. He's always been pretty independent, eager to explore the minute he found out what feet were for."

"He's not tied to your apron strings?"

"My apron strings were never long enough for him."

"Does he look like you?" Oh, yeah, she'd like this. "Show me a picture when we get back to the car. You must have one in your billfold." Women loved to show their kids' pictures.

"I usually do, but I just switched to a new one, and we had new pictures taken, so I was changing wallets, changing pictures." It all came out in a gush, as though she felt guilty for not having the pictures right on her. Then, in a small voice, she said, "I guess I'm between pictures."

"Not even a baby picture?"

"Not—not with me."

He heard sadness. He shifted, surrounding her a little better, cuddling her a little more. "You get too lonesome for him when you look at his picture?"

"It's not that. It's . . ." She sighed. "I do miss him. I don't like being away from him at all, so this has been difficult."

"We could pay him a visit at camp. It's what, little more than a day's drive? You think he'd like that?"

"I think he would, but . . ."

She would, too; he could feel it. She wanted to see her kid, but there was some kind of catch, some doubt about somebody in this equation. Probably the kid. Kids were funny about their moms getting interested in guys.

"It's kind of a special camp," she said. "The idea is to develop confidence and self-sufficiency. They do a lot with survival, wilderness experiences, that sort of thing."

"They don't let them have any visitors?"

"They don't encourage it."

"That's not the way I run my camp," he said proudly. "If I have it next summer, he's welcome to come. As my guest."

"Thank you. That's—I know he'd enjoy that."

"I require parent involvement, though." He lowered his head, tucking his nose into her hair, muttering, "Lots of parent involvement. Private consultations." He slid his hand beneath her breast. The bra was a true inconvenience. "How did you feed him when he was a baby? Did you—"

"Yes, I think we should consult right now, Reese."

He nibbled her ear. "Excellent idea."

"About your heart."

"Treat it gently," he warned, hooking his thumb over the neckline of her dress. "You run off on me again, you're liable to break it so it can't be mended."

"Is there no cure?"

"No cure." He kissed the curve where her neck met her shoulder and wondered whether the curve had a name. "But like I said, there's treatment."

"Surgery?"

"Not right now, thanks."

"Is this hereditary?"

"Could be," he said, settling back against the rock. "My mother died of heart failure not long after she had Carter. She was only thirty-one. Nobody knows of anyone else in her family having a problem, but there were other people who died young. With Indians, dying young is not unusual. The doctors wanted a family history, and that's it. She died young."

"Is that why you haven't gotten married?"

"I haven't had time to get married. I haven't been able to find the right woman. Or the right detective agency."

"But your heart wouldn't prevent you from getting married," she concluded. "Or discourage you from . . ."

"We'd have to have this consultation." With his thumb he stroked that curve he'd kissed, and he thought how absurd for his heart—always, *always* tripping over itself when she was around—to keep him from her now. His pride, maybe, but never his poor heart. "She'd have to know that I'm not the best risk. On the other hand, I think she could do worse."

"What about children?"

"Now, there's the risk," he admitted. "I don't think I'll ever have children of my own. But I wouldn't have a problem being a father to somebody else's. Adopting or being a stepfather." *Show me his picture, Helen. Let me put a face to the name you've given me, and I swear . . .* "Do you want more children?"

"I'm too old."

"You're barely thirty-nine."

She turned her head toward him. "How do you know? You don't remember—you couldn't even remember how long it had been since you'd last seen me."

"I remember your age by counting up from mine." He yelped when she reached around and pinched him high on the thigh, and then he laughed. "Aw, Helen, I remember only because it was such a big deal for you that I was a few years younger."

"It wasn't for you?"

"I guess it scared me," he admitted, now that he thought about it. "You were educated and I wasn't. Sophisticated, and I wasn't. I was *going* to be, once I got off the rez; at least that's what I had planned. But I wasn't yet. I was just . . . plain damn cocky. That's all I had going for me."

"You were going to become a big star, and that scared me."

"You believed me?"

"*You* believed you, and that was what mattered."

"My dad wanted me to finish school. But I had a chance then, a chance I thought might not come around again. I'd had a heart thing when I was a kid. Nothing serious, just some palpitation, a little fluttering. I didn't tell anybody. My dad knew, but I wouldn't let him tell anybody. It never bothered me. I passed every physical. I passed the army physical. And I had to play basketball. I *had* to. What good does it do to be this tall, this gawky, when you're a kid? You've gotta be able to turn it into some kind of an asset, you know?"

"So this is a genetic, um . . ."

"Weakness? They tell me it could be. Carter and Rose had some tests done, and they seem okay. So far, their kids are okay. But if I had kids . . ." He hadn't thought about it a lot, this kids-of-his-own thing, so talking about it—going at it all serious, the way she wanted to—well, he was feeling *his* way along. "Put it like this, if you had a horse like me, you wouldn't put him out to stud. Kind of a shame, 'cause I'm a damn good specimen, you know, in some ways."

"I believe we've established that," she allowed, serious as hell. "What kind of tests did your brother and sister have done?"

"Blood workups, looking for something genetic. It's a problem that kinda sneaks up on a person, usually a teenager or young adult. You can have it without even feeling any symptoms."

"And then one day . . . ?" she prodded gently.

"One day you feel a little dizzy after a workout. Next thing, you think you've got a kettle drum in your chest. Then this seven-foot center lands on your chest, cracks a couple of ribs, one damn specialist leads to another, and they're talking diagnosis and prognosis, and all you know for sure is you're out of the game."

"Was it your choice?"

"I would have taken the risk and kept on playing if it had been up to me," he told her. "They still don't have all the answers about this condition, which turns out to be a lot of variations on a condition, and the ones you hear about are the guys who drop dead on the court. But people live with it, too. Anyway, it was my choice not to disclose my whole damn medical history. I was out for the rest of the season with the ribs, and then I retired."

"So now . . . you seem fine. Is the risk . . . are the chances . . ."

He had to laugh. He couldn't help it. His compulsive gambler was trying to assess the odds. He felt like telling her, *Hey, it's six for one, half dozen for the other, sudden-death game.* But he had to remember that she was new to this game, and her sense of humor wasn't quite the same as his. So he just laughed.

And she turned and hammered him on the shoulder. "I don't want anything to happen to you!"

"You don't?" He slanted his mouth over hers like the kid in the school yard, repaying her cuff with a kiss. "I do," he whispered, taking the hand from his shoulder and sliding it over his chest. "I want *you* to happen to me. Make my heart skip a beat."

"Is that what it does?"

"What it does is pump blood, almost like your heart and everybody else's." He pushed her hand down, pressing her fingers to him, over the ribs long since healed, over the belt he would soon unfasten, over the zipper that held his jeans together where he wanted them apart. "Right now, it's pumping most of it right here. See? You're happening to me already."

She massaged him through his pants. "What about your head?"

"Coming along just fine." He found the zipper on the back of her dress. She flipped his belt buckle open, and he laughed, not because he was being terrifically clever, but because he was happy. "Oh, you mean the ugly one? Light as a feather. Headin' for the stars."

"I'll make you touch them," she said, and he shifted his hips to assist her in his unzipping.

Her dress slipped down her shoulders, and he saw the soft white pillows he would more than gladly touch, and he told her so as he unhooked her bra.

"No, the clouds," she said as she slipped her hand inside his jeans. "Touch the clouds, my beautiful man, while I touch this heavenly Blue Sky."

$\mathcal{T}$he drum tenderly pummeled the night from below. The stars cheerfully jigged in their places on high. Helen felt small but abundantly significant, bundled in her lover's arms. Perched high on a hill where nothing could see her but the silent rock, where no one could touch her but the man she loved, she felt utterly secure, otherworldly safe. Red flags fluttered in the back of her mind the way they always did, yet she intended to ignore them right now. She knew the moment couldn't last, but she could surely live it as though it would.

She didn't want to think too much about what he had told her, only about what he had given her, what she had tried to give him. Pure bliss. Sensational oblivion. She had stroked him and nursed him, straddled him, taken him into her body and milked him until he had given over, given in, and given her his seed. If she said such a thing aloud, she would feel foolish about it, but there was no self-consciousness under the stars. The black sky was too vast, and the drum was too elemental, and self dissolved into the beauty of it all. In that ageless, timeless context, seed was a beautiful thing.

Reese's seed most particularly.

Particularly. Back to particulars, back to self, back to consciousness, back to Reese's particular seed, which felt powerful and tasted like the salt of the earth and made life. Her lofty thoughts turned to self, returned to a consciousness of her own petty fears as she pressed her ear to his chest, thinking, How are you, my love? Are you feeling all right now?

Su-per, su-per, su-per.

His heart beat strong and sound, and she couldn't imagine it faltering, no matter what he'd told about thickened muscle, about demands for more oxygen, about pain when the demands could not be met. He could not die from it. He was such a big man. His powerful arm cradled her against a long and lovely bed of muscle, and muscle was invincible. He was a tower. He was a wall. His hip and thigh buttressed her fully, keeping her off the ground, caring for her comfort. He felt solid, a sure winner.

But what about her son?

This was not a selfish question. It was not a petty fear. Sidney was still a boy. He had his father's eyes and nose and feet. He even had his father's smile, and yesterday she would have said what a good thing it would be if he had his father's big heart. Not his mother's, forever protecting itself, forever in hiding.

But that was yesterday. Tonight she loved his father more than ever, and tonight she prayed that her son was not like him in the heart. An awful wish, another of her narrowly focused prayers. Don't take my son away, don't make him weak, don't make him sick, don't let him know what I've done, don't let him hate me for it, don't don't don't . . .

Don't ever go away from me. Somehow I'll fix this if you give me a chance.

She didn't realize how fast she was holding him, hanging on for dear life, until Reese shifted so that he could look into her eyes. "So what was that about? Not sympathy, I hope."

"No." She made a conscious effort to relax. "I'm pretty sure it was about sex."

"I could have sworn there was more to it," he said as he finger-combed her hair, separated a piece, and carefully wrapped it around his finger. "Some kind of urgency, like time might be a little short, so you're gonna make sure I get to come once more."

"You wanted me to happen to you."

"That's what I get for trying to be clever with words." His finger was bound in her hair, with a tassel of it left to be used as a paintbrush for her lips. "I want us to happen to each other."

"I didn't do it right, did I?" She'd only meant to give him pleasure, though she wasn't exactly practiced in the art.

"You did it just right, but you wouldn't let me have a turn. I don't want you to be afraid to let me love you for all I'm worth. I promise you, it won't kill me."

"I should hope not." She followed his lead, adding lightly, "Imagine a story like that getting out."

He used her hair to play-write a headline across her forehead. " 'Retired Basketball Player Goes Out Coming.' "

"Oh, no, Reese, it would be a terrible scandal. You're in politics now. I'd be—"

"You could name your price. They'd be beating down your door for an interview, wanting to know every intimate detail."

"Even if it's just between us?"

"You, me, the coroner, the Internet."

She sighed dramatically. "What's this world coming to?"

"Jeez, then guys would be beating down your door looking for the ultimate orgasm, and I couldn't do a damn thing about it. I'd be dead."

"You'd be a spirit."

"That's riiight, e'en it?" The prospect had him grinning in the dark. "There I'd be, looming in the doorway. Pretty soon they'd all be freakin' out and streakin' back to where they came from." He was using her hair brush on his own full, luscious lower lip now. "You think big people get to be big spirits? Big and scary?"

"I hope so. Especially if the tribal chairman can appoint a special prosecutor." She raised her right hand. "It was an accident. That wasn't what I meant by 'touch the clouds,' sir, I swear."

"Then what did you mean?"

"Well . . . do you ever fantasize when you're making love?

When you go deep inside me and you close your eyes, what do you see?"

"I try not to close my eyes. I might miss something."

"So you don't imagine that I'm, say, Julia Roberts?"

"I imagined that she was you."

"Julia Roberts?"

"She's a real basketball fan," he said, deadpan. She couldn't tell in the dark, couldn't see the light in his eyes, wasn't quite sure until he said, "Kidding." And then she laughed, though there was an unwelcome image in her mind, one she couldn't hold a candle to.

But he passed her a torch.

"I make love to you," he told her, tickling her nose with her hair. "It's all pleasure. Looking at you, touching you, being inside you. Making you fantasize whatever you want to fantasize. I enjoy the whole trip."

"You were telling the kids to visualize before they shot the ball. To imagine—"

"That's different. When I want to make something happen, I visualize execution, completion. But this was complete every step of the way. It was all pleasure."

"It was about mending." The tickling stopped. He waited for her to explain. "I saw us mending you," she whispered.

"With sex?"

"Good sex is powerful."

"It brings us together, but I don't know if it fixes anything. I mean . . ." He cursed a sharp stone beneath the blanket as he shifted his hips. "Do you think we can be fixed, Helen?"

"You mean . . . ?"

"You and me, can we be fixed? If we're gonna do any mending, let's work on *us*, not me. Let's fix *us*."

The red flags in the back of her mind moved forward.

"Reese . . ."

"Maybe there wasn't anything to start with, huh? Nothing breakable. I don't think sex is breakable, do you? By itself it's—" He snapped his fingers. "Here and gone. You can't break anything that fleeting."

"It isn't that fleeting, not for me." She drew a deep breath. *Well enough* was an illusion, and she knew it couldn't, *shouldn't*, be left alone much longer. "There are things I should—things I wish I could tell you. I want to tell you. I *will* tell you, but I want you to promise . . ."

Unfair, the red flags warned. *You can't expect to extract promises before you roll out the moment of truth, you idiot.*

"About why you're here?" he demanded gently. "You think I can't put two and two together? Hell, you work for some three-letter government agency, and you're under more covers than just mine. And you're not supposed to be fraternizing with any Blue Skys because they're on the prime-suspect list."

He lifted his unencumbered shoulder, and he went on, unruffled. "Or maybe fraternizing is actually part of your job, but the boss draws the line at sleeping with the suspects. So now that you've crossed the line, you might as well tell me—" He shifted gears, gently turning serious. "Tell me just how much trouble you think my brother is in."

"He's not in any trouble with me," she said, grateful for a temporary reprieve from the hook.

"Or the people you work for?"

"Or the people I work for. It's the people *he* works for whom he probably needs to watch, and so do you."

"Ten Star?"

"I don't have much on them yet, but I know they're powerful, and I believe they can be dangerous." She turned her head for a better view of the lights below. Okay, so this was a diversion, but it was a better topic right now, wasn't it? She hadn't divulged anything that he hadn't figured out himself, and there was clear danger to be considered. Danger that didn't involve her child. "I want to know who's holding Carter's marker," she said.

"You think he's gambling?"

"I think we're all gambling. But I think he's doing it with borrowed money." She looked up at the stars. "I've been there, Reese, and I know how a perfectly intelligent person can get sucked in. This is all I want, you say to yourself. Just this much. When I have this much, I'll be happy, and we'll be all set. I know what I'm doing, and it'll only take a little bit more.

One more good game. One more shot. I'll only risk what I can afford to lose, right?

"Before you know it, all you're paying is the interest, and then you can't pay that, so you get desperate, and you dig a deeper hole for yourself, and your whole life becomes the perfect model of the vicious circle." Turning to him with a humorless laugh, she said, "It sounds stupid, doesn't it? Total insanity?"

He flexed the arm that held her, effecting a small hug. "Sure it sounds crazy, but so does a car wreck. So does getting into deep water and being washed downstream. You can't talk about a thing like that and make it sound like something that could happen to anybody. It's too wild. Nobody thinks it could happen to them."

"Do you?"

"Sure," he said, with the ease of innocence. "Anybody can get carried away."

"Can you see yourself as a compulsive gambler?" When he stammered a little, she came to his rescue. "You're not just anybody, Reese. But I am, and so is Carter. We're the anybodies who get caught up in these whirlwinds that—"

"Jesus, Helen!" He sighed. "I can't seem to say the right thing around you. I'm trying to tell you that I don't think you're stupid or crazy. No matter what you've done or what you're up to, you're still . . ." He was holding her tighter now, unwilling to be separated from her by what she was and what he was not. "You're still Helen. You still make me crazy. One look and I'm high on you again. High as a damn bird, I swear."

"Touch The Clouds," she whispered to the winking stars. "Whenever I fly, I look out the window, and I think of the clouds as a cushion. If anything happened up there, they would catch you. If I walked out on the wings, I could jump down on a cloud, walk on them, see if they feel as soft as they look. Everybody wants to touch clouds." She buried her face in the pocket of his shoulder and kissed his smooth, musk-scented skin. "You do that for us, you know, for all of us. Sometimes you even lift us up and give us a moment up there with you. The first time I saw you, you were doing just that."

"I had only one thing going for me back then, and I knew that wasn't enough for somebody like you. I had a lot to learn, a lot to prove. A lot of boasts to make good on." He kissed the top of her head, then tipped her face up with his free hand. "You like gambling, Helen? Good. That's good, because that's just what I need. I need a gambler. I need somebody to take a chance on me, help me beat the odds." Lovingly he stroked her hair. "You want to touch the clouds? I'll carry you on my shoulders. I'll give you the ride of your life. What I don't know is—"

"So much has happened."

"So what? There's more to come. You're worried about this job you're doing and how it might affect us if my brother's caught up in something—"

"No, Reese, don't. Your calculations are going to be a little off. It's more than just two plus two."

"I'm missing some numbers, huh? The value of X?" He gave a dry chuckle. "Damn. I'm pretty good at arithmetic, but I hate algebra. I guess you just do what you have to do."

"You're like your father in some ways," she said, and he groaned. "No, you are, and in *good* ways. I saw you in him, and now I'm hearing . . . certain principles of his." That drew a disgusted snort. "Well, you *are* his son," she insisted. "He was afraid of what Carter's involvement might be, too, but he did what he thought was right when he asked for an investigation."

And the words "you are his son" stung her ears. She should not have been the one to come to Bad River. She should have turned this assignment down. But when it was offered, she could no more have refused it than to have denied her next breath. Especially when she'd seen Roy Blue Sky's name in the report.

"Yeah, well, I'm not that high-minded," Reese said. "I didn't ask for any of it. Carter's job is his business. Your job is your business. The way I feel about you has nothing to do with any of this intrigue."

Ah, but it will, she thought. God help us, it will.

"But I'll play it by the rules," he vowed, "whatever the

hell they are. It's your deal. Just be straight with me, okay? Don't deal me any sympathy cards. I don't need that."

She held her breath, yet the red flags were all aflutter again.

"Do you?" he asked, his low voice exquisitely gentle. "You want me to feel sorry for you because you had a problem with gambling?"

"No, I don't, but the word is 'have.' I *have* a problem with it."

"You've licked it," he said. "Looks to me like you wrestled that monkey to the ground and made him say uncle."

She swallowed hard. "How *do* you feel about me?" she asked quietly.

"Crazy, but it's a pleasant kind of crazy." He traced her cheek and neck and throat with caring fingertips. "Crazy in a good way."

"You don't look crazy," she whispered, but her eyes were closed, her chin lifted to abet his touching. "You don't sound crazy."

"You asked me how I *feel*." His hand slid over her breast. "You're a dangerous woman. You get me going, you might have me acting as crazy as I feel, and then what? You go off and leave me stewing in my own hot juices, and that's not a pleasant kind of crazy." Fingertips crept around the fullness of her breast, outside, underneath, between . . . "Not a pleasant sight, either, a big guy like me. I hate to look like a fool."

She would not argue that it was he who had left. It was a poor argument. He hadn't "gone off" and left her. He had simply gone elsewhere. He'd gone on, and so had she. On and on, round and round. Round and round could drive you crazy. Yes, and his fingers moved round and round, very slowly round and round. He was driving her crazy. The closer he came to her nipple, the crazier she felt. Crazier in a good way. She wanted it to go on forever.

She had no arguments. There were no arguments. *How do you feel about me?* meant so much more than she dared explain. Every minute she spent with this man was a risky minute, a minute stolen from the safe place where she guarded her life with her son. Every moment was at once a tiny golden treasure and a troubling white lie, and she was shamelessly stealing all she could grab. Questions like *Do you love me?* and *Can you forgive me?* were perilous enough, and they were only the beginning.

Tell him, don't tell him, tell him, don't tell him. The monkey chased the weasel.

What would he do? If he knew about Sidney, what would he do?

How could she say, *Can I trust you with something far more precious than you and me and our frail egos?*

"I feel a little crazy, too," she said. "And for me, it's scary."

"So's a roller coaster."

"My favorite ride." Better than the merry-go-round.

"Front seat, right? You get to the top of the first hill and you reach for the sky, don't you?"

Finally he taunted her nipple with his thumb and made her smile crazily at the stars. No more thinking, only feeling.

"Climb on my shoulders, darlin'," he whispered. "Anytime you need a boost."

When the night sky began to fade, they made their way down the hill, hand in hand like two joyous children. Dewy grass brushed Helen's bare legs. A bat startled Reese when they reached the car, but Helen credited the creature with clearing the mosquitoes out for them. "I don't think I got any bites at all," she exclaimed when he slid behind the wheel. He apologized for the oversight and asked her where she'd like one.

A truck stop provided bathrooms, then coffee and doughnuts, which they enjoyed while they sat on the hood of the car and watched the sun rise.

"Remember when we did this before?" she asked. "The way we ditched the people we were with—"

"*You* were with."

"*I* was with. And then we . . ."

"I remember everything."

His beautiful smiling lips were dusted with powdered sugar, just as she remembered from the time before. She drew his head down to kiss and lick and love the sweetness of his mouth. A passing semi saluted them with a happy honk, and they laughed as they slid off the hood without spilling a drop of coffee.

He didn't ask her about going to his place, but that was where they were headed. She didn't ask any questions, either. The answer was that she would stay with him as long as she could on this most beautiful of mornings. A white haze hovered over the lush fields of August. The clouds they'd spoken of touching billowed high overhead, casting racing shadows on an alfalfa patch that was ripe for a second cutting. Fence posts flitted past the window. A profusion of sunflowers filled the next field. The right-of-way had been cut and windrowed, but one clump of sunflowers, missed by the mower, stood tall in a shaft of sunlight. Golden frills anchored to solid brown hearts swayed in the morning breeze.

Beautiful morning. Sweet contentment. Comfortable silence. No questions, no need for answers. Being together was enough for now. Being together was a precious thing.

Reese was thinking about taking her horseback riding if he could find something for her to wear. She looked heartbreakingly beautiful in those long dresses of hers that hugged her sweet breasts and fell in loose folds around her lovely calves, but what could a guy do with a woman in a dress? He didn't dance, and she didn't run or play ball. He had to make love to her. That was all there was to it.

Eyes on the road ahead, he was smiling a little to himself when she suddenly unbuckled her seat belt and scooted close to him. He put his arm around her, not too surprised that she'd read his mind considering how smart she was. But then she put her hand on his chest, right over his heart, and he knew what was on her mind again. Well, she was just going to have to get over it.

"I think I made some waves at my first council meeting," he told her. He figured politics was as good a distraction from matters of the heart as any.

"Already?"

"The gaming committee made a recommendation, and I moved to table it. I said I didn't think we ought to be eliminating options just yet, and I got enough people to agree with me that, well, the thing actually got tabled." He laughed. "Kinda surprised me, you wanna know the truth."

"So you just walked right in and started making plays, huh?"

"Yeah." He grinned. "That's what I did. I set it up and took a shot. I did get a little pre-meeting tip from my buddy who's on the gaming commission, which is different from the gaming *committee*, which was hand-picked by Sweeney, and I don't trust Sweeney. Titus—you know Titus Hawk?"

He was buoyant with his achievement, and she was smiling with him now. Okay, a little sadly, but he would put her blues on the run soon enough now that he had her smiling, acknowledging that she knew who his friend was, that she knew the commissioners were the tribe's watchdogs, operating independently of the council, and that he could tell her again, tell her more, tell her anything about his first day as a councilman. She was with him now, and she was smiling.

"A presentation from Ten Star is next on the agenda," he told her. "I've been looking over my old man's papers, and I've got some questions I want answered. I don't know any other way but to ask straight out. I don't have time for much fishing around, and I figure if I ask, they have to explain. Hell, I'm on the *council*."

"Yes, you are."

"And I—" He saw a white pickup top the rise in the road ahead. "Honey, I've got a feeling there might be a tribal cop or two who wouldn't hesitate to haul me in on a seat-belt charge."

"Oh, I'm sorry."

He was, too, but he was a little suspicious of pickup drivers now, and he'd be a hell of a lot sorrier if she went flying through the windshield. "A regrettable precaution," he said. "Anyway, do you know we could have bought the slots we're leasing from Ten Star three times over by now? My first question is whose piss-poor plan that was and how they plan to compensate for it."

"The council agreed to it. After the Indian Gaming Regulatory Act was passed, a lot of tribes agreed to whatever terms they could get when outfits like Ten Star appeared on the doorstep with the money and the experience in the gambling business to help them get started."

"Well, it's time to change the terms. The debt's almost paid off, and we've got experience now. For one, we've got Carter."

"He works for Ten Star."

"The way I see it, we hired *them*. That means they all work for us." He lifted one shoulder. "Carter belongs to the tribe. He's Bad River Lakota."

"So is Preston Sweeney."

"Yeah, but Sweeney's always been a damn suck-up. In grade school he used to get in good with the nuns by selling the rest of us out."

"That was a long time ago."

"Once a suck-up, always a suck-up."

"You don't know what your brother was like in grade school."

"No, I don't. But somebody's been selling us out, Helen, and it looks to me like my father died trying to stand in their way." He glanced at her as he slowed to make the turn to his place. "That somebody wasn't my brother, no matter what other kind of trouble he might be in."

It surprised Reese, hearing himself get defensive over a suggestion nobody had made. Surprised Helen, too, from the look she was giving him.

Then a wail went up from the house. Crybaby came bounding down the driveway, howling as though Reese had a particular scolding coming for being out all night. He was about to laugh before he noticed that the dog was favoring his left hind leg.

"Hey, buster, did you tangle with a bear or something?" Reese slammed the car door and knelt in the gravel to greet the dog, who was so happy to see him he spelled it out in piss, all over Reese's boot and down his pants leg.

Helen was right there with a bundle of baby talk. "What's wrong, sweetie?"

"Hold his collar," Reese said, trying to get a look at the leg while the dog whined and wagged and peed. The black hair of Crybaby's hindquarter was matted and sticky, and when Reese touched him, the shepherd yelped and jerked away from Helen, nipping at the cause of his pain.

"Easy," Reese said. "I won't hurt you, boy. Just let me have a—"

With a snarl this time, Crybaby warned him away.

"There's blood, but that's all I can tell. How far do we have to go to get to a vet? Is it still . . . ?" Damn, he couldn't remember ever calling a vet. There had never been many cattle on the place, but as a small-time rancher, his father had always given the shots, stitched, birthed, medicated, put down . . .

"The Yellow Pages? We could call a neighbor for a recommendation," Helen suggested.

The local phone book was a mere pamphlet.

"I recommend Indian Health," he said as he lifted the protesting animal in his arms. "It's the closest, and I know how to get there."

She opened the door to the backseat of the car. "Do they treat dogs?"

"They'll treat this one."

They didn't want to. The young nurse who met them at the emergency door told them in no uncertain terms that dogs were not allowed. But Reese soon found an ally in one of the ambulance drivers.

"Hey, Blue, what's up?"

"Hey, Dexter," Reese greeted the small, wiry man. He couldn't shake his hand with his arms full of whimpering dog. "Tell this lady to find me someone who can give my friend here a little Novocain or sodium pentothal or whatever you've got in the medicine cabinet so we can fix his back leg up. We might need to X-ray him, too."

"Jeez, I don't know, Blue." Dexter squinted at Helen. "She don't look Indian."

"Helen, this is Dexter White Mountain," Reese supplied, and she offered a handshake. "The *dog*, Dex."

"We don't—"

"Full-blooded Lakota shepherd."

Dexter grinned. "Good try, Blue, but it's against—"

"Dex, Crybaby was my father's dog."

"Oh." The little man nodded solemnly. "How bad is it?"

"That's *my* question!" Reese barked. The dog whined.

Dexter nodded vigorously. "I'll see what I can do for you, Blue."

The nurse sounded like a chipmunk, chattering to Dexter's back as she marched behind him to the double doors. "Do you know who that is?" Dexter said. "That's Reese Blue Sky."

She was busy discrediting the importance of the name as the doors swung closed behind them.

Dr. Eugenia Flynn introduced herself as a temp, which meant that she was a volunteer who had come out of retirement to help alleviate the shortage of medical doctors in Indian country. And it meant that she was a busy woman. Reese assured her that he didn't mean to distract her from any human patients, but didn't know where else to go.

"I wouldn't even be talking to you except that my shift is over and I'm going to bed," the wizened woman told him as she approached the dog. Crybaby growled. "If he bites me, you're all getting the boot."

Helen helped Reese control the animal while Dr. Flynn irrigated the wound so she could assess the damage. "It looks like a bullet grazed him. Laid him open along the flank right down to the bone. I'd say he's one lucky dog. A little to the right, and some coyote hunter would be trying to convince you it was an honest mistake."

"The hunters who come around our place lately don't stick around to explain."

"It's hard to understand that kind of cowardice, isn't it?" She turned the water back on and washed her hands in the sink. "He'll need stitches, which I can't do here or I'd be in a heap of trouble."

Reese offered a charming grin. "Heap plenty trouble, huh?"

"When troubles come, they come not in dribbles, but in heaps," the woman said as she mopped her hands with a paper towel.

"Well, I've had my share recently, Doctor, and I'd really like to spare this mutt."

"I knew your father," she told Reese. She turned to include Helen. "He was a wonderful man."

"Crybaby was with him when he died." Reese knew he had her when Dr. Flynn questioned the reference with a funny look. "That's his name. Crybaby."

"Ah, Roy," she said with a wistful chuckle. "Crybaby, indeed. There's one painkiller we have here that can be used for dogs. That would be lidocaine. We'll take him over to my place. My kitchen table never gets much use, anyway."

Helen was late for work that afternoon, but no one said anything to her. She wondered if the word was out that she was Carter's brother's girlfriend. If so, she didn't have much time to get her job done and file some kind of a report. People would be too careful around her if they thought she had those kinds of connections.

She knocked on the door to Carter's office and stuck her head in when he responded. "Do you have a minute?" she asked.

"Take all the time you want. I'm staying at the hotel. Sarah and I need to get out of each other's hair for a while, if you know what I mean." He stood up behind his desk and greeted her with an easy smile. "She likes you a lot, by the way. She told me she thought you had a nice, uh"—he gave a rolling gesture—"way about you, and you were easy to talk to, which apparently she did, and I'm sure you got an earful about me."

"I wouldn't say that."

"No, of course you wouldn't, because you watch and you listen and you take it all in and you figure us all out." He folded his arms and tipped his head to one side. "You got Reese figured out yet?"

Backlit by the afternoon light from the office window, Carter looked a lot like Reese. It was a stronger resemblance than she'd ever noticed before, and she felt it tug at her heartstrings. He was just a man who'd gotten in over his head. She truly hoped he hadn't sold his soul as a consequence.

"I know about his heart condition," she said.

"Well, that just about makes you family. One thing about Indians, you know, they're good about keeping each other's secrets." He drew a deep breath and nodded as he blew it out slowly. "The main thing is, he has to take care of himself. He's not immortal. He's not a god, like everybody thought. He has to take medication. He has a close relationship with a cardiologist. He can't be . . ."

"Can't be what?" Upset? He'd been pretty upset over Crybaby, but the dog was going to be fine, and Reese was fine. "What are you worried about?"

"I don't know if I should have encouraged him to get on the council. I thought it would just be something he'd sit in on for a few meetings, just ride out the rest of the term, not get too serious about it. I mean, you start getting too serious about it, that's major stress."

"Which isn't good."

"Not for Reese."

"Not for any of us." Including Carter, she thought. Good men had been known to do foolish things under stress. "I was wondering if we could watch some surveillance tapes together."

"You wanna watch movies with me?" He laughed. "You could get me in trouble, Helen. Sarah thinks I'm cheating on her as it is, but she wouldn't want to hear that we've been . . ." He sat on the edge of his desk and peered up at her. "Or, you could save me a lot of trouble."

"How?"

"Forget the tapes and just worry about Reese. Worry about him getting himself all worked up over something he knows nothing about. Help me persuade him to let it go. Let Ten Star have the contract."

Intentionally or not, he was giving her a peek at his hand. Helen's pulse tripped into higher gear. "Why?"

"Because they built this place. Switching horses in midstream is dangerous. You lose your momentum, for one thing." He lifted one shoulder. "And people get hurt."

"People like your father?"

He shook his head. His eyes cooled. "My father got hit by a truck. He wasn't switching horses."

"He was talking about it, recommending it loud and clear."

"Reese doesn't need to be rabble-rousing over the management contract. Ten Star's not perfect, but we could do worse. They got this place up and running. They've been as fair with us as—as anybody else would be. It's business." His voice dropped to a gentler register. "So, for the sake of his health, Helen, I think we need to persuade Reese to back off and just go with the flow."

"Jones is cheating the house," she said. "Did you know that?"

"You're sure?"

"Absolutely. Aren't you seeing it on the tapes?"

"I've seen him pay a loser, and I've called him on it. He wasn't paying attention."

"It's more than that." The looks they exchanged said they both knew he realized it. She looked down at the floor and said quietly, "I just thought I should report it."

"I appreciate that," he said, and when she looked up again, he asked, "What about Reese?"

"You have more influence over Peter Jones than I have over Reese."

"I don't believe that for a minute." An openhanded gesture said that he was asking for a personal favor. "You don't even have to push, Helen. All you have to do is give him something else to think about. That's all he needs. Not a cause to sacrifice himself for, but something good and promising to think about."

"Is it really Reese you're worried about?"

"Yes," he insisted. "Yes, it is. He'll tell you his condition is no big deal. He tells me it's none of my business. Which could almost be true, if you consider how little contact we've had in recent years. But it *is* a big deal, and it *is* our business. Because we care about him."

He looked her in the eye, and she saw that he meant it. His brother was important to him. She wasn't sure about his father, or his father's dog, or his father's people, but his brother mattered to him.

"Don't we?" he asked.

"We do."

12

"Somebody shot my dog," Reese told the two men who were waiting for him on the playground. He bounced the orange ball once before firing it across the court to Titus. "Parted his hair down one side," he said, turning to assist the wounded shepherd emerging like an elder from the backseat of the car.

"Hell, it ain't time to be hunting coyotes." Decked out in blue sweats with a Law and Order emblem, Dozer strode across the blacktop. "Not if they're looking for pelts."

"My guess is they were hunting for something less hairy, and I'm not sure what. A window screen was cut, but it didn't look like they got in. Crybaby must be a better watchdog than anybody gave him credit for."

"So who's watching the place now?" Dozer braced hands on thighs as he straightened, knees cracking, after take a cop's look at the victim.

"Nobody. They can take whatever they want. But Crybaby and me are onto them, and we're keeping an eye out for each other."

He'd called his friends the night before and told them he needed to shoot some hoops, preferably early in the morning, before the courts were overrun with kids. Sunup, he'd said, and the sun had just appeared on the purple horizon. Both men had beaten him to the playground.

"You think they might be after you?" Titus tested his aim. The ball kissed the backboard and dropped through the hoop.

"No." Reese caught Titus's chest pass and injected more conviction when he got rid of the ball. "Hell, no. Who'd be cutting on a screen to come after me?"

"Somebody carrying a gun," Dozer pointed out as he caught Reese's pass and returned it directly.

"Somebody who's a piss-poor shot, hoss," Reese said, crouching now, dribbling close to the ground, challenging Dozer with a sly grin. "Somebody who cuts and runs without too much threat. Whatever he was after, he couldn't have wanted it too bad. What's your best shot now, Doze? The game is Horse."

"Maybe breaking and entering isn't normally on his schedule," Dozer suggested, thinking like a cop. "Anyway, what would they want from you, Blue? Besides an off-hand J?"

"A better question is, who's *they*? Nothin' but net on an off-hand J," Reese said, calling his shot. If he made it, the game of Horse required the other players to duplicate it. His jump shot was legendary. He took a left-handed twenty-five-foot shot, releasing the ball from the top of his jump, which made him nearly unblockable. The swisher dropped into Titus's hands. Reese grinned. "I got no off hand."

"You can call the shots, but don't change the question, Blue. That's my game. What have you got in that house?"

"Nothing of any value." Reese caught Titus's pass and turned the ball over to Dozer. "To most people."

"We're not dealing with most people." Dozer took Reese's wing spot, following his lead to the letter to duplicate the shot.

"His papers?" Reese watched Dozer's shot hit the rim. "My father's papers. Letters, notes, mostly stuff that has to do with the council. And the casinos. And you've got H, Doze."

"Just gettin' warmed up. These papers, are you talkin' stuff that every other councilman would have in the drawer?"

"No, not necessarily," Reese said. Both Titus and Dozer were looking at him now, and Titus had the ball. Reese shrugged. "At the council meeting the other day, I did say that I'd been reading through my father's papers and I had some concerns about Ten Star's management, mainly about where all the money was going. Said I was in no big hurry to sign on with them again."

"Draggin' your big Blue heels?" Titus said, grinning. Titus was no fan of Ten Star's.

"Gotta use them for something."

"Who investigated the attempted break-in?" Dozer wanted to know. "You should've called me. Did they check the dog for—"

"I didn't report it. I didn't see the screen until I got back from getting Crybaby fixed up, when I went to open up the windows in the house. So nobody else knows about the break-in part, and I'd just as soon keep it that way for now."

"How about your woman?"

"Helen was with me when we found the dog, but she doesn't know about the rest. I don't want to give her any more to worry about."

"Yeah, that's cool." Dozer hooked hands on hips and studied the ground. "Listen," he said, but barely audibly, "I've been kinda nosin' around Law and Order, trying to figure out who knows what about the hit-and-run, and the best I'm coming up with is that some guys don't know much about it and they're frustrated about it. They feel like we do, like somebody's gotta catch this guy. But others, a couple guys, you say anything to them, they set you straight right now. They don't know a damn thing, and they don't wanna know."

"They're scared?"

"Looks like."

"Not just Gene and Earl."

Dozer squinted into the rising sun. "You think about who your dad was up against, Blue. He was Preston Sweeney's main opposition."

"Over the Ten Star contract."

"And the chairmanship. Hell, your father was gonna beat him out for chairman. So what it looks like to me is, if you're a cop and you want to stay a cop, in this case you're better off not knowing. You let the FBI do their work, you stay out of their way. It's an Indian victim, and how many do they solve, right?"

"He was a councilman," Reese said, suddenly realizing what that had meant to him whenever he'd spoken of his father. Too damn little. *He's on the tribal council. It's sort of like a governing committee.*

"And that's our business. Bad River Sioux Tribe."

"He was my father." Too little, too late.

"That's our business." Dozer laid a hand on Reese's shoulder. "Bad River Lakota."

"It's got to do with Ten Star."

"I believe you're right about that. And I'm thinking they're bad news."

"Hell, I've known that for two years," Titus crowed.

"I never heard you say it," Dozer chided.

"I've been thinking it." Titus bounced the ball. "Now I'm thinking about my famous behind-the-head bank shot from the top of the key."

Helen sat on the front step of the furnished garden apartment she had sublet, waiting in the long shade of early evening, watching the end of the quiet street where Reese's car would soon appear around the corner. He had called her and asked if he could stop by, said he would bring supper and that he had some news. She didn't mind that he was late. She was eager to see him, but she had something on her mind, too.

Some*one*, the one who could never be far from her thoughts. Those thoughts had been growing heavier each day, just as her son had when she'd carried him in her body and then in her arms. Now she could no longer carry him at all, and that thought—*that* thought—weighed a ton. He was growing up fast, and his needs were changing.

Children's voices drifted from the riverbank on a soft summer breeze, their chatter punctuated by the occasional pop of a bottle rocket left over from the month past. If Sidney were here he would beg to go down there with them, promise to be careful, swear he'd just hang back and watch. Within five minutes he'd be setting up for the next blast, that boy of hers. He had to try things.

Tonight she would say something. She wasn't sure what she was going to say exactly, but it wasn't fair or right to spend another hour with Reese without—

Oh, God, without *telling him*.

She was such a coward she could hardly form the thought. It was too chancy, and there was no way to hedge her bets. She'd called the attorney she had consulted in the past and asked her to go over it all one more time. Once Sidney's paternity was established, Reese could—could he still?—yes, he could get custody, and he could do it through the tribal court. The federal court would back the tribe, and the state court would probably cooperate. There were plenty of precedents. In this case there would be plenty of sympathy and an abundance of money on the father's side, not to mention his whole tribe. She had no reason to think he'd do such a thing, other than the fact that Sidney might be the only child he'd ever have. No reason to think they couldn't work things out amicably, other than the fact that she had kept his son from him all these years. If he didn't resent that, he wasn't human.

But he *was* human. He was a good man, decent, distinguished, distinctive, and distinctly mortal. Suddenly there was more at stake than the risk of losing her child. She had long wrestled with guilt over denying her son a father, but now she was responsible for denying a good man his only child. She could no longer suppose that Reese was too young to be a father, or too busy with his career, or too rich, or too arrogant, or too self-absorbed, or any of the other probabilities she had used as donkey tails and tried to pin on his larger-than-life image. She had done it now, killed all assumptions. She had risked everything on this time they'd shared.

Whatever made her think she could seal this interlude off from the rest of their lives?

It wasn't a question of thinking. She was acting on anything but reason. He'd stayed too long, and she loved that he had. She'd gone too far, and she'd loved even that. Selfish woman that she knew full well she was, she didn't want to lose him. She didn't want to lose her son, either. Right now, in this shaky moment, she had them both. Her footing was unsteady. Soon, when the balance tipped, she would fall. But for right now, she had love on both sides.

She stood when the big white Lincoln appeared at the top of the hill. She brushed off the seat of her shorts and pushed open the gate to greet him when he unfolded himself from the car. He kissed her and held her as though their coming together revitalized him, and she wondered what his news was. Was it more pressing than hers?

Hers had kept for over twelve years. It would keep for a few more minutes.

Reese let Crybaby out of the backseat, and Helen dropped to her knees in the grass to greet her friend, let him lick her face even as she tried to get a look at his wound.

"He hasn't started chewing yet, but if he does, I'll have to go looking for one of those collars," Reese told her. "Are you hungry?" She looked up, and he produced a paper sack. "You're working that weird shift again, and I'll bet you haven't eaten all day, so I've got that covered. Big Nell's Indian tacos to go."

"Actually, that weird shift is going to put me in bed early tonight."

"I can cover you there, too."

"I have Diet Coke and water." She peeked in the sack. Paper plates, napkins, plastic utensils. Nell packed a nearly complete picnic.

"Two waters for me and my pal, ma'am. One tall glass and one bowl."

"Let's go out back," Helen said, leading the way around the side of the plain white building that truly did resemble a Saltine box. "It's too hot inside."

"We should go to my place. I just put in a couple of air conditioners. They were delivered with my new bed."

"You really are settling in." She smiled. Her sandals flapped against her heels. Crybaby stuck nearly as close to Reese's heels.

"I may keep the place for a while. No reason to be as stubborn about comfort as ol' Roy Blue Sky. I offered to do some fixing up for him, or have it done, but he liked things the way they were, he said."

"It's an efficiency house. Feels very male." She set the bag on the picnic table that was shaded by two rustling cotton-woods in the backyard. "Your father struck me as a man who had learned to live comfortably in his own skin."

"Old, worn leather." He looked down at his own hands, braced on the tabletop as he climbed over the bench. "I used to like watching him use a hammer. A couple of good whacks and he could bury a nail in a fence post. I'd still be pounding away. He had the touch."

"That's exactly what he said about you," she told him, and he questioned her with a look. "We were talking about fathers and sons and how it feels to lose yourself and find yourself in your child, and he was saying that he thought you had inherited his stubbornness."

She watched him remove the plates from the bag, then the napkins, dealing them out on top of the plates. Incredibly long hands, larger versions of Sidney's. She remembered the OB nurse remarking about the length of Sidney's hands and feet. "Well, who knows whether you can inherit such a thing, huh? But some things . . . Reese . . ."

He looked up from the job he'd assigned himself.

"Water," she said quickly. "I'll get it."

She went to the house for ice water—glasses for them and a big bowl for Crybaby—put it all on a tray, and started toward the door. Then she stopped, set the tray down, and opened the kitchen drawer. There was Sidney smiling up at her, all washed and combed for last year's school photographer. He was wearing a Denver Nuggets T-shirt. What would his father think of that? She'd taken the picture out and put it back in the drawer a dozen times at least. Now she tucked it into the pocket of her shorts, snatched up the tray, and backed out through the screen door.

The backyard overlooked the Bad River, which glistened as it rushed past the cutbank in the bright summer sun. Reese had several Styrofoam cartons lined up on the table. Flat slabs of frybread filled the two paper plates, and he was adding the taco meat and beans.

"I think you were right about Dad's death," he told her as she set the water down for the dog.

"Right about what?"

"Dozer says there was a piece off a headlight housing found at the scene. The cop who found it is sure that's what it was. Later, it disappeared."

"Evidence disappeared?" She climbed over the seat across from him.

"The guy who found it kinda got persuaded he hadn't found what he thought he'd found. He hasn't been on the force long. He's unsure of himself and procedures and all that, but he told Dozer, just between them—which, of course, includes me—that he had no doubt about that piece of metal. This is a guy who worked on cars all his life."

"So who's covering up?"

"We're not ready to place any bets, but . . ." He slid a plate toward her and handed her the salad container. "Helen, do you think this Darnell has any kind of criminal connections, like mob connections, like . . ." He took a deep breath and expelled it on a demand. "You need to bow out of this, Helen. Call in reinforcements from the BIA or the FBI or whatever. I don't like the idea of you—"

"What idea? You have no idea what you're talking about." She smiled, so he'd know she wasn't trying to be mean, and then she forked lettuce onto her taco meat. "I'm trained to spot card scams. Okay? No big deal. You're the one who needs to be careful."

"Were you working with my father? If somebody ran him down—" He stayed her hand with his. A chunk of tomato fell on the table. Crybaby lapped at his water. Reese's eyes were suddenly full of fire. "If somebody ran him down, Helen, and if you're the one who was working with him—because I know he asked for an investigation, and if you're . . . They kill people, Helen. You don't have to do this. I don't want you to. You're fired, okay? You're done."

He was serious. He was sweet and fiery-eyed, and he seriously thought he could tell her what to do. She laughed.

"Who do you think you are, Reese Blue Sky? One council meeting and suddenly you're hiring and firing?"

"I'm—hell, I'm—we've been together a lot lately, Helen. We've even been lying together. *Have lain* together."

"Very good," she said, still smiling. "But just because you've got *that* right doesn't give you the right to—"

"Loving you gives me the right." He said it so forcefully, he looked as though he'd scared himself. He lowered his voice, but not his gaze. Dappled light and shade played over his beautiful face. "If I have the right to love you, I have the right to care what happens to you."

Her throat felt tight. The river rushed in her ears. She wasn't sure where her next breath was coming from as she stared across the table. "That . . . rolled out fairly trippingly."

"Trippingly?" He came up with a lopsided smile. "Is that, like, tripping over it? I didn't trip over it. I've been hanging onto it." And then, softly, "I would've told you a long time ago, but I was scared shitless."

"*You* were scared?"

"You said it yourself. I was a big, dumb, shy—"

"I never said that. I never thought . . ." She shook her head. Deep breaths, deep breaths. "*Quiet*. You were quiet, and you were young, and you were determined to try things." The forgotten fork fell from her hand. "I couldn't be sure. Reese, I've kept things, too, because I was scared. I'm *still* scared. The risks . . ."

"It's always been risky, you and me. Even before I turned pro, even without the heart thing, it was crazy for me to go chasing after you that time I saw you at the rodeo. Remember? But there was something that passed between us every time we saw each other, and I had to take a shot, even though . . ." He caressed the back of her hand with his thumb as he spoke. "Even though I fully expected to get shot down."

"I don't know why. What passed between us was obviously crazy on both sides." She was smiling now, laughing a little. "But there's always more excitement in the long shot than the sure thing."

"If you have a shot at the goal, you take it. That's the only way you can hope to win." He shoved plates and lettuce and plastic forks aside. "Helen, what you give me whenever we make love feels like more than a one-shot deal, more than a great rush. It feels like a beginning, even now, like there's more to come. If we want it."

"Do you know what love is, Reese? Do you know what it takes to—"

"Jesus Christ, will you stop talking to me like you think I'm a child?" He closed his eyes and nodded. "Yes, I do. I know it's me not wanting you to get hurt. I know it's me telling you I'm not going to let them do to you what they did to my father. I know it's me keeping you." He clutched her hand. "I'm about to dive over this stupid table, Helen, me keeping you safe and making you happy. It's me *keeping you*. It's me not ever letting you out of my life again."

"That sounds like something I'd say. Keeping you."

"Then say it. Say you want to keep me."

"Saying it and wanting it doesn't make it possible." But the truth might, and the truth was in her pocket. All she had to do was take it out and trust him with it. "I want what you have. I want the right to love you."

"The right?" He scowled. "Don't you have that? I mean, okay, maybe you need to tell me what you know about love that you think I'm too dumb to—"

"Stop that!" She smacked the table with her free hand. It smarted, and she immediately felt stupid. "That's not what I think. I've never . . ." She sighed. "Oh, I underestimated you, all right, but not your intelligence. I never thought—"

"Well, here you are!"

They were there, indeed, nose to nose and a table apart. And there was Carter, standing next to the corner of the house with a big, silly grin on his face.

"Mind if we interrupt?"

They didn't see anyone else.

"I brought a surprise. You ready?" Carter looked over his shoulder, gestured. "Hey, Surprise? Where'd you go? Come on, they're in the backyard." Turning back to Reese and Helen, he shoved his hands in the pockets of his khaki slacks and took a few steps closer. "Listen, when I picked him up at the airport, I realized I probably should have checked with you first, but he said he had . . ."

Helen went numb as she extricated herself from the picnic table. Her heart hopped into her throat, jammed it up, jack-hammered in her ears. Sidney ambled around the corner of the house trying to look cool and easy, but, oh, the mischief danced in his kohl-brown eyes. He was full of himself and the accomplishment of surprising her, and he hardly spared a glance at anyone else because he was more than a little glad to see his mom. It had been a while since he'd taken part in such an unrestrained hug with her right out in front of people.

And it felt so good to hold him in her arms again.

Helen leaned back to look at him. His dark hair fell into his eyes. She couldn't resist trying to brush it back, which he permitted briefly before he turned his head away from the gesture. By now he was grinning triumphantly, and, oh, he was beautiful. The sun had turned his skin deep chestnut, dewy with exuberant man-child sweat, glowing with good health and newfound independence and reunion.

But her first question was automatic. "Is everything all right?"

"Everything's great." He gripped her shoulders, playfully rocking her back and forth. The motion on top of the shock made her dizzy. "Surprised you, huh?"

"Oh, yes. How did you—"

"Mr. Marshall got me a plane ticket. We have a break between sessions, and I want to stay for the second session, but Mr. Marshall said it would be cool to surprise you, so I said okay. He said the casino has a special fund for family emergencies. Or, not exactly emergencies, but like . . ." He looked to Carter for help.

"Special contingencies," Carter said, offering Sidney an encouraging smile. "General manager's discretionary fund. I haven't given it a name yet. This is one terrific young man you've got here, Helen. He said he'd never been to South Dakota, and I thought it was about time we remedied that."

"Well, he's been through South Dakota, but we haven't . . ." It was so good to see him. She couldn't take her eyes off him, couldn't stop delighting in the familiar look and sound of him, couldn't stop noticing new details. "My gosh, what are they feeding you at camp? You've grown an inch, I swear!"

"A lot of mystery meat, but I think they lace it with the stuff they give calves, you know? That . . ."

219

"Ralgrow?"

Reese's voice reverberated on the single word, supplied to complete Sidney's quip. One word, one meaningless word, a slapping reminder. Helen turned from her son to meet his father's gaze.

Carter came to the rescue. "This is my famous brother, Reese Blue Sky, the guy you said you'd heard about."

"Yeah, we've got some All-Star basketball videos, and you're on some of them." Sidney's eyes lit up in the presence of the hero rising from the picnic bench. "Mom told me she knew you in person from, like, before you turned pro."

"My son, Sidney," Helen said. The chips were about to fall, and she was shaking inside.

Reese offered his hand. "Hey, Sid, how's it going?"

"Great. Jeez." Gleefully Sidney pumped the hand of a champion. "You played for the Mavericks, right? Point guard."

"Right. It was . . ." Like Helen, Reese was finding it difficult to take his eyes off Sidney, but she couldn't tell how he felt. He was completely composed. He even managed to smile. "It was a few years back."

"Yeah." After the handshake, Sidney stuck his hands in the back pockets of his hiker's shorts. "Yeah, they really suck now."

"They need a point guard," Reese said. "Your mother's told me a lot about you, Sidney. I hear you play all kinds of sports."

"Yeah, but basketball's my best. I'm a lot bigger than most guys my age."

"You sure are." Reese speared Helen with a pointed glance. "You just had a birthday, didn't you?"

"June eighth. I turned twelve." He grinned. "You know what, Mom? These Nikes are getting too small already."

"We'll get you some new ones this weekend."

"I've got four days. Aw, man, you should see . . ." Sidney always got his hands into the act when he told a story. This one involved heights. "We went on a three-day hike, you know? Up in these mountains? They're called the San Juans, and we were up at about twelve or thirteen thousand feet, which is, like, thin-air city. And we had to rope up 'cause we were scaling rocks, man. It was so cool. And you know what we saw?"

"Do your hiking boots still fit? You weren't wearing—"

"No, we got those bigger, Mom, remember?"

Reese was interested in only one voice right now. "What did you see, Sid?"

"Petroglyphs. You know, those really old, old paintings, like stick figures only better, because they're like . . . You're Sioux, right?"

"Lakota."

"Yeah, me, too, from my dad. He died."

Deafening silence greeted this news. Helen stared at the ground. Her face blazed.

"I'm sorry to hear that," Reese said.

"I never knew him." Sidney shrugged. "Anyway, these petroglyphs are probably Anasazi, ancestors of the Pueblo people. Probably. Some scientists question that, but not the Pueblo people, and I figure they should know. It's their tradition. Scientists end up theorizing a lot, but traditional people, they know what they know. At camp they bring in speakers, or we go on day trips. Do you live here?"

"I grew up here," Reese said. "I'm from here, and I'm here now. Carter maybe told you, our father just died."

"Jeez. Was he pretty old?"

"Pretty old, yeah, but . . ." Reese laughed. It was a joyous sound, an unbridled response to Sidney's enthusiasm. "I don't think he knew the Anasazi personally, but I bet he knew a lot about them."

"Did he teach you how to play basketball?"

"He started me out. He, uh—" Reese looked at Carter as if to say, Did you know? Carter kept grinning as though he'd just played Santa Claus and everybody had gotten the gifts of a lifetime.

"You're still trying to get used to him being dead, aren't you?" Sidney asked, honest sympathy delivered in a child's guileless tone. "My friend's grandma died last year, and he said that was hard because she lived with them. But after a while it gets easier, he said. Hey, pup." He greeted Crybaby with a pat on the head, got his hand sniffed and licked in return.

"That's Crybaby," Helen heard herself say. She felt as though she'd stepped outside herself. The real Helen was watching and listening to the actor Helen carry on in some crazy dream. She might have been a character in one of Roy's shape-shifter stories. Whirlwind Woman, maybe, the Arapaho caterpillar, always spinning in circles and throwing dirt in people's faces. And these were the people she loved, would never hurt, never.

But such was her power, Roy would say.

"Did he cry when he got hurt?" Sidney was asking.

"I wasn't there, but it looked to me like he stood his ground. Maybe he deserves a new name."

"Who named him?"

"My father."

"Hey, Crybaby." Sidney ruffled the dog's fur and laughed when Crybaby whimpered and wagged his butt happily. "He doesn't seem to mind it as long as you're scratching his ears when you say it."

"You know what?" Carter said. "Sidney and I haven't eaten anything, and you guys obviously just ate, so I'm going to take Sid over to Big Nell's for a quick burger. Give you time to whip up some dessert here. Maybe some coffee?"

"Is that okay with you, honey?" Helen asked her son.

"Sure." A quick, bony-shouldered shrug, a boyish grin. "What've you got for dessert? Strawberry shortcake, maybe?"

"If you don't mind frozen strawberries." She reached for him, but he'd already skipped away, so she called his name. He turned, gave her a one-eyed squint, waiting. "I'm really glad to see you."

He grinned. "But you were totally surprised."

"Totally."

She stood staring at the space after her son and his uncle had left it. She heard Carter's car start. Funny, she hadn't heard it before. No, not funny. Before, she'd been totally engrossed. A moment ago Reese had loved her, so maybe it wouldn't hurt so much to turn and look at him now. Maybe.

"Aren't you going to say anything?"

She tried to swallow, but her mouth was dry. All dried up, she faced him. "Only that he's the most important thing in my life, and I have to protect him."

"Protect him? Who's threatening him?" He shook his head, the shock he'd been able to mask now plainly written on his face. "God damn. I feel like I've been punched in the gut. Can't catch my breath." He, too, glanced toward the side of the house, where they'd watched Sidney go. "Did it show?"

"No, and I appreciate that. Reese, I . . ."

"God *damn*." An echo, softer; as though, looking into her eyes, he had only one wish for her. "You know, I thought . . . maybe. I mean, I wondered why you up and left." The snap of his fingers startled her, jerked her to attention. "Just like that, quit your job and, *pfffft*, gone."

"I left between semesters. I was able to transfer because they were phasing out the—"

"Shit." Again he shook his head, staring at her as though she'd suddenly transformed and he was trying to figure out the trick. "You know, I really don't give a damn how you were able to transfer or what the goddamn BIA was phasing out, so forget the technical details. What I want to know is—" He spun away. "Shit."

Oh, God, he was leaving.

"Where are you going? Reese!" She went after him, grabbed his arm, made him look at her again. "What are you going to do?"

"I'm going back to—I'm going *home*." He shook her off, but the word reverberated. "Home," he repeated softly, almost reverently, as though this, at least, was something that made sense. "I need to . . ." She was still reaching for him. He put his hands up, putting new distance between them. "I need to think about all this."

"Think about what? Obviously you're his . . . a-and obviously I could have and maybe I *should* have tried to contact you." Her dry throat had been assaulted suddenly by a thousand needles. "A-at some point."

"It wouldn't have been too hard."

"I know. I know that."

"Jesus, why did you tell him his father was *dead*?"

"It was the least complicated explanation. At the time."
She swallowed, and swallowed again. "I thought it would hurt
the least."

"Really?" He snorted, his eyes ablaze. "Yeah, that makes
sense. Dying's painless." He flung an arm out toward the table,
the shady place where he'd all but taken his battered heart
from his chest and laid it in her hand. "What kind of a game
was this, Helen? What was this all about?"

"I wanted to tell you, but after all this time, I couldn't
just . . ." She took a deep breath. "I was trying to find a
good way."

"You didn't—"

"I didn't know he was coming."

"Did Carter—"

"I don't think so. He knew I had a son. That's all I told
him. That's all I ever tell anyone. That's the one truth I know,
the one that keeps me going. I have a son."

"But every time you look at him, there's gotta be another
truth staring you in the face. God, for me it's like looking in
a mirror."

"No, it isn't, Reese. He's not you. He doesn't know you,
and it would be—" She panicked when he turned on his heel.
"What are you going to do?"

"I told you. I'm going home, turn the damn air conditioner
up full blast. I need to think. I need to not be looking at you
right now."

She felt cold, a full blast in the heat of the day. He was
going, and with him went power. All kinds of power, power
she didn't even know about, and it all had to do with who he
was and where he was from. It scared the life out of her and
left her cold.

"Don't try to take my son, Reese."

He turned, retraced two of his angry steps, eyeing her as
if she'd just exposed something he hadn't seen before. "Why
would you think I'd do that?"

"Because . . ." Her eyes burned. Weakness. Damn it, she
would not cry. "You might think you can."

"Can and will are two different words. Isn't that what you
teach in school?"

"Can and may," she said, instructing out of habit. Tiresome habit.

"You mean, like, *Mother, may I?*" he sneered, his face stony. "I never really had a mother myself, used to think maybe I was missing something. But I don't know anything about *may I*. Either you do or you don't."

"I won't let you, so don't even think—"

"Don't tell me what to think, Helen." He drove splayed fingers through his long, thick hair, then tapped his temple with impatient fingertips. "I've gotta clear everything out of here and start from scratch, and I don't need you . . ." The words hung in the air while he drilled her with a chilling look. "To tell me what to think."

*H*elen made the shortcake partly to keep her hands busy, but mainly because Sidney had asked for it, and she was his mom. She wanted him to know that he could depend on her, no matter what anyone else said or did, simply because she was his mother. She would have the dessert ready soon, and then she would shore up her grit and go over to Big Nell's for her son. She and Sidney had weathered some big storms, and together they would get through this one.

"Helen? We're back." It was Carter's voice, coming through the front door. "Mmm, this smells a lot better that Big Nell's."

Helen met them in the living room. "Honey, you can put your stuff in that little room to the right. There's not much in there, but I made up the bed for you."

Sidney headed for the hallway off the living room with his duffel bag.

"He's gone, huh?" Carter asked, craning his neck for a peek in the kitchen. "I take it he didn't know."

Helen shook her head.

"Obviously I didn't, either. Weren't you going to . . ."

"Not like this. Not taking everybody by surprise."

Sidney came back on the last word. "The surprise was my idea, Mom. Don't blame Mr. Marshall."

"Carter," came his uncle's correction. "You can start calling me Carter since we're co-conspirators." He shifted his feet, offered a sheepish smile. "I hope I didn't cause you too much trouble, Helen. I'm sure you had your reasons. It'll be okay. You'll see."

She had nothing to say to that. No predictions. She returned a vacant look.

"And I think I'd better get my meddling nose pointed west, huh?" Carter answered his own question with a nod. "You gotta meet my kids, Sid. Derek's a little younger than you, as it turns out, so I think he'll end up dogging your heels like a puppy."

"Yeah, that'll be cool." Sidney was on the move, checking out his mother's temporary digs, following his nose to the kitchen.

"He's right. It'll be cool, Helen. Once everybody gets over the shock, and around here, that takes no time at all. You'll see. It's all in the family. Listen, I'm taking you off the schedule for the next few days. You need the time."

Sidney stuck his head around the corner, his mouth already full. "You don't want any strawberry shortcake, Mr.—Carter?"

"Thanks, Sid, but if you look at my belt, you'll see that I've had to give up two notches since we put in the bottomless dessert bar at Pair-a-Dice City. I've about bottomed out."

"Just get a new belt," Sidney said, catching a crumb as it fell from his lip and popping it back in his mouth. "Go shopping with us this weekend. What have you outgrown, Mom?"

Carter forced a laugh on his way out the door.

Sidney chattered about his flight, how he had to change planes and that the Rapid City airport wasn't very big, but Carter had said that Rapid City was closer than Pierre because of the Interstate, even though, on the map, Bad River looked like a little pinpoint maybe halfway in between.

Helen could tell he was uneasy. He'd taken a major step without consulting her. Lately he'd been hotfooting it between childhood and adolescence, the barefoot boy on asphalt. He was Mom's good boy one minute, his own boss the next, and he wasn't completely comfortable with either role. So he chattered. Some days he got sullen. Chattering was better.

She put her arm around his shoulders as he heaped the Cool Whip on the strawberries. "I'm so glad to see you."

He grinned. "Looked like you were mad for a minute."

"Surprised."

"It wasn't like I was taking a ride *with* somebody, even though I didn't know him exactly, but you do. And he said, you know, you work there and they do this for employees, and I thought—"

"It's all right, hon. I'm just glad to see you."

She sat across the table from him, much the way she had been sitting with his father little more than an hour ago. It was good simply to watch him eat, the primal satisfaction of feeding her child. His father's food had gone to waste. Her fault. Her secret revealed, her shortcoming. It was good to watch her son eat, but she felt sick to her stomach.

Ah, but she hid it well.

"How's the shortcake?"

"I like it better when the strawberries are fresh, but it's still twice as good as anything they make at camp." He looked up and gave her a juicy red smile. "I can't wait to tell Jordan and Scott that I met an NBA basketball player. They're my bunkmates. Jordan shoots pretty good, but I'm way better than Scott."

"I guess Jordan's got a name to live up to."

"Jordan's his *first* name."

"What did you think of Reese Blue Sky?"

"I think he's *big*." Sidney puzzled over a spoonful of whipped cream. "If him and Carter are brothers, how come they don't have the same last name?"

"Their mother died shortly after Carter was born, and their father—his name was Roy . . ."

Sidney had asked about last names several times before. When there was no father in the house, people generally didn't ask about names. But kids and their friends did, and the fact that Sidney's name was the same as Helen's father's had come up. Helen didn't go by Sidney's father's name because she'd kept her name. Besides, he'd died a long time ago.

Acceptance without question was becoming more the exception than the rule. Dead wasn't so painless. No lie ever was.

"He's the one who just died," Sidney supplied.

"Yes, Roy just died. He was killed in a hit-and-run . . . accident."

"That's the funeral you told me about, where they did that cool Indian stuff."

She nodded. He should have been there. He should have been allowed to stand beside his father and receive condolences on the death of his grandfather. But for his mother's cowardice, he would have. She sighed. There was never going to be a good time to tell him.

"Anyway, Roy didn't think he could take proper care of a new baby after his wife died, so he gave Carter up for adoption. Carter has his adoptive family's last name. He came back to live with Roy and Reese when he was your age, maybe a little older."

"Was the other family mean to him?"

"No, they were good to him. But there's a law, a federal law . . ."

The Indian Child Protection Act. A well-intentioned law, the response to a long history of non-Indians taking Indian children, legally, "for their own good." It was part of a terrible history between the two races that had, the more he'd learned about it, prompted Sidney to look at his mother and ask why, as though she would know.

She would know because she was his mom, and she was smart. He'd once trusted her for answers. But then he'd begun to understand that he looked like "something else."

Was his father foreign? Did you adopt? Is he . . .

He was hers. That was all anybody needed to know. Anybody except Sidney. And when he had started thinking of himself as an American Indian and trying to find out for himself what that meant, all she was able to give him were the books and the history. When he asked her why things were the way they were, why people behaved the way they did, it wasn't because she was his mom that he thought she should know.

It was because, for the first time, he'd realized that he was an American Indian and she was not. She was white. And that was different.

And the laws were different.

"There was a change in the law that made it possible for Roy to take Carter back. It's all very complicated, but Carter kept the name he'd grown up with, and I think he kept in contact with the family, and it all worked out okay." She offered a tight smile. "I think."

"Sounds like a big mess to me. Carter doesn't play basketball. He says he's more the bookish type." He shoveled a forkful of strawberries and whipped cream into his mouth, then captured a stray bit out of one corner with a quick tongue. "I'm both, huh?"

"You're both." And she wasn't. But she was, first, last, and always, his mom. She loved him, desperately sometimes. "There's something I have to tell you, honey, and I'm . . ." She folded her hands primly on the table. Desperation was a terrifying thing. "Frankly, I'm a little scared."

"What did you do?" His fork hand stilled. He stared. "Mom, you're not gambling again, are you?"

"No." His worst fear, that his mother would lose control again. His mother with the prim hands who loved him so much. She had learned to be up front with him on this issue. "No, but I did come close at a casino in Deadwood. I wanted to show off a little. It wouldn't have been our money, it would have been . . ."

"A bad mistake, right?"

"Right." She smiled. "I knew that."

"We're doing fine, Mom. The credit cards are almost all paid off, right?"

"I shouldn't say I came close," she added quickly. "I was a little bit tempted, but I handled it very well, I think. I kept my considerable wits about me."

She shook her head. She remembered when the gambling thing had been nearly impossible to talk about. Now it was almost a welcome distraction.

"That's not what's weighing on me right now at all. I need to talk about something else." She unfolded her hands, stacked them instead. "There's something I've kept from you, kept it to tell you when you were older. But now I can't keep it anymore."

"Keep what?"

"Keep him. Keep your father." She looked her son in the eye. "He's not dead, Sidney."

"He's not?" His eyes widened. This made no sense to him. "You said . . ."

"I know I did. I said it because I was afraid I'd lose you to . . ." That wasn't the part he needed to know. "Reese Blue Sky. He's your father."

Not a flicker in his eyes. No sense. Nonsense.

"Sidney, I haven't seen him—except on television—since before you were born. He came back here for his father's funeral, and I was . . . and that's the first time. I didn't think I'd ever see him again."

"Aw, Mom." His dark eyes turned sweet and soft, as did his high-low voice. "Didn't he want to marry you?"

That tingling was back in her throat. She pressed her lips together to keep them from trembling. She didn't deserve this dear child.

"We never talked about it."

"Was it like . . . he didn't want a kid or something?"

"He didn't know about you." She glanced away from the little furrow beginning to form between his straight, jet-black eyebrows. "He was on his way to Minnesota. I always thought about it like he was going off to war, you know?"

Sidney shook his head slowly, staring. "The NBA isn't the same as war, Mom."

"Well, I know that." He doesn't need your rationalizations, she told herself. He needs facts. "I didn't know I was pregnant when he left. When I found out, I . . . I didn't tell him. I moved back to Denver, I had you, and I never saw him again until now."

"You were scared to tell him?" he asked gently. "Is he mean? He doesn't seem—"

"No, no, he's very nice. He's a very good man, Sidney."

He thought about that for a moment, working on it the

way she'd seen him tackle his homework, trying to add it all up.

"Are you gonna tell him?" he asked.

"I don't have to. He saw you. He knew I had a son, but he didn't know you were *his* son. When he saw you—"

"What?" His fork clattered on the plate. He leaned forward, challenging her. "I don't look like him. I don't look like anybody but myself."

She reached across the little table to comfort, to touch only his hair, but he drew back, and it wasn't the usual adolescent boy avoiding the grooming hand. He didn't want to be touched, not now, not by her.

She gave a tight-lipped, respectful smile as she stacked her hands close to the edge of the table, her left hand restraining the offending right. "You're incredibly handsome, all right."

"So he could tell?" he asked reluctantly. She nodded. "What did he say?"

"He was just as surprised as you are, just as confused. It's all my fault, sweetie. I've handled this very badly."

He stared at the remains of his dessert as though it disgusted him. What was left of the cake was bloated with pink juice. His lips were pink with it, too. Parted slightly. Unmoving. She remembered the time he had gorged himself on Halloween candy and she'd found him sitting on the floor beside the toilet. He'd said he felt like throwing up and he wished he could get it over with. She'd wished she could do it for him.

Finally he sat back and folded his arms. "Yeah, well, I don't need a father."

"No," she said, too quickly. "No, no, no. Now, honey, he's not—"

"What do you mean, *no, no, no*? I'm not a kid, Mom!" His hot scowl wounded the mother in her as the budding man in him pointed out, "I'm not messing stuff up or talking dirty."

"I know. I just don't want you to make any hasty—"

"I don't care what you want." He pushed his chair back and reached for his plate. "I don't care about any of this, and I don't wanna hear it. I don't need a father."

"Most of what he said was about—"

"I don't care, Mom." His voice was far less troubled than

the look in his eyes. "I guess surprises aren't always the best, huh? But I don't have to stay the whole four days. Matter of fact, I think I'll go back tomorrow. I don't even wanna stay the whole four days."

"Sidney . . ." She followed him to the sink. She knew she ought to leave him alone now, but she couldn't help herself. She couldn't shut up, not even with the red flags waving wildly in her head.

"I didn't want to share you. It sounds selfish, I know, but my parents were divorced, and my sister and I had to—"

"I don't care!" He tossed the plate, shattering it in the stainless-steel sink as he whirled to face her. "I don't care, Mom. There's nothing to be confused about. My father was killed in the war, okay? I like that better than just, he died." He mocked her with a theatrical frown. "What war was it?"

"Please don't."

"Don't what? I'm not doin' anything." He shrugged. "Except I'm going back tomorrow. Will they change my ticket?"

"I don't know. It might cost a lot of money."

"I'll take it out of my savings."

"Not without my signature."

"You're gonna try to keep me here?"

"Now that you're here, and now that the truth is out, I think we should try to deal with it in a—in a good way."

"In a *good way*? What's that about?" he quipped as he turned back to the sink. He started to pick up the broken pieces of pottery, and when she reached in to take over, he pushed her hand away. "I'll do it myself, goddamn it!"

Oh, God, she thought, fighting hard against the tears. She couldn't permit herself to cry. Her son wasn't crying.

Hands full of shards, he looked up, allowing her to see a hint of his needs, one small hint couched in the need for her to show him where to go next. She pointed to the door beneath the sink, and he stepped aside. She opened, he tossed.

"In a thousand years someone might find these," she said, "and say that we must have been at least somewhat civilized."

He stared, needs growing.

She tried to smile. "Practical, if not very artistic."

He nodded once, but no smile would come. No smile, no

tears. But he did touch her arm. "Listen, Mom, let's just put the truth back where it was. Okay? Wherever you were keeping it before."

She bit her lower lip.

He moved away before she could return his touch, grabbed a plastic lid off the counter, and snapped it on the Cool Whip container. "This is my favorite dessert, and you're the only one who can make it right." He handed her the container. "And I'm really tired right now."

She nodded. "Unpack your pj's and I'll get some fresh towels."

"I don't wear *pj's*," he told her, putting a hostile spin on the word he clearly considered childish. "I want more boxers, by the way. That's all anybody wears anymore."

"Right." Another tight nod. "I knew that."

Sidney's plane ticket could not be changed. He asked Helen to call the next morning, and she did. All the flights were booked. He was stuck with her for four days, and he seemed determined to say as little as possible. He said he didn't care about seeing the sights in the Black Hills, didn't care about getting out of the apartment, did not—*did not*—care to meet any kids his age. But he wouldn't mind getting a new pair of Nikes.

They came to a truce with a tacit agreement to avoid any mention of his father. She expected Reese to call, but she didn't want Sidney reading her mind. If he was expecting anything besides new Nikes, he wasn't letting it show. She suggested a visit to Wall Drug, which, coincidentally, required them to drive past the Blue Sky place. Roy's name was still on the mailbox. Sidney noticed it, looked at the house, said nothing. Helen saw Reese's car, but all she said was, "All roads lead to Wall Drug. Have you heard of it?"

"Why would I?"

"It's famous," she said. "They have signs everywhere."

But the next billboard they passed advertised Pair-a-Dice City: COLLECT COMMEMORATIVE WILDLIFE COINS. PLAY TOURNA-MENT SLOTS.

"There's no skill involved in playing the slots, right?" he asked.

"Right."

"So what's the point of holding a tournament?"

"Profit," she said, pleased to be asked, to be his answer machine again. "Profit is the whole point."

He watched another billboard fly by, this one declaring the distance to Wall Drug.

"How many miles did it say?"

"I didn't notice," he told her. "Billboards are insulting to the environment *and* to our intelligence. We know where we want to go." He slid her a glance. "At least I do."

They couldn't find the right-style sneakers at Wall Drug, even though the sprawling tourist stop on the edge of the Badlands carried a sampling of everything else imaginable. Helen wanted to buy her son every toy and souvenir in sight to make up for all her failings. She knew the folly of such thinking, and so did Sidney. But he'd lost his Barlow knife, and he thought a rubber snake might come in handy at camp. Not the cheap kind, but the pricey one that looked and felt like the real thing. He decided he needed a cap when he saw a green one bearing the Seattle SuperSonics emblem. Helen mentioned that Rick Marino was a friend of Reese's, that she'd met the former Seattle player recently.

Sidney traded the green cap for Denver's dark blue.

On the way home they saw another advertisement for the casino, and Helen offered to show him where she worked. "Sure," he said with a shrug. "Casinos always have good restaurants."

The lunch buffet didn't interest him. He wanted barbecued ribs. "We have a chow line at camp, and it's all plain stuff. I've had enough macaroni and cheese to last me—" He nodded, and Helen turned to find Carter approaching their table.

Sidney greeted his newfound friend cheerfully enough, and Carter offered a handshake. There was a little chitchat about Wall Drug and what Sidney had in mind for his new snake. Then Sidney said he wanted to use the rest room before the food came.

As soon as he left the table, Carter asked the burning question. "Have you seen him at all?"

"You mean Reese? No, we haven't."

"Damn, I was hoping you were all together and everything was hunky-dory." He paused to thank the server for the iced tea he'd ordered. Then he leaned closer. "Because I've been calling out to the place and getting no answer."

"The car's still there. Well, we did drive past on our way to—" The look in Carter's eyes said no explanation was necessary.

"Do you think he's okay?" she asked.

"What I think is that he shouldn't be running in this heat, and that's what he does. He's like this hot thoroughbred who can't race anymore, you know? He gets stressed, he's gotta get out and run it off."

"What about his heart?"

"Well, that's what I'm saying. His doctors have told him, yeah, you can run, you can play ball, but take it easy, don't do it when it's hot, and don't do it alone." He glanced at Sidney's empty chair. "They haven't talked to each other, then."

"Sidney wanted to go back to Colorado, but I couldn't change his ticket." Carter was giving her a sympathetic look, and she jumped on it. "Carter, *you* understand, don't you? That thing about taking custody of Indian children. I couldn't risk losing my son."

"So why are you here?"

She glanced away. "Curiosity, maybe."

"What about this plan to get a teaching job here?"

"I didn't really think . . ." Well, yes, she had. She had a plan, and she thought looking for a teaching job fit very well into the plan. She still had a job to do. "I was thinking about sending Sidney to a private school or something. I wouldn't have—"

"You weren't serious about coming back here to teach. You were just testing the waters."

"Something like that."

"You've gotta go out there and talk to Reese. You two have to work this out somehow," he said, and she quickly warned him away from her personal life with a look. He lifted a hand in surrender. "All right, I'm sorry I butted in and caused this mess, but now I'm worried about my brother. And there's nothing I can say or do right now. It's up to you."

"Sidney won't—"

"No, don't take him with you. This might be the kind of conversation you don't want a kid to hear. He can spend the rest of the day with his uncle."

"You'd do well to stay away from that topic."

"Would you mind if he met his cousin? Sarah's coming over anyway. I'll call and have her bring Derek." He touched her arm. "Kids have their ways, Helen. No matter how badly we screw up their world, kids have their ways."

*R*eese didn't wear a watch when he ran, so he didn't know how long he'd been out. He gauged everything by the way he felt. He wasn't pushing too hard, and he was drinking plenty of water. The sun had been hidden beneath blustery gray-white clouds more than it had been out, but it didn't feel like rain. Good day for a run.

Once the endorphins had kicked in, his mind had stopped spinning around the love he'd declared for Helen and the bomb she'd dropped on him as a follow-up. He felt good now, like he could set his sights on the horizon and keep going until he reached it. But when he saw that crazy black shepherd waiting for him up ahead, he figured it was time to head for home. He slowed to a trot, then a walk, sipped some water, gave a nod to his father's horses grazing near the fence as he approached Roy's Last Stand Hill. His heart responded with a reminder of his own vulnerability.

PAY-at-TEN-tion, PAY-at-TEN-tion.

Pay attention? Usually it said, Slow DOWN, slow DOWN, slow DOWN. Was the old man messing with his mind again? Pay attention to what?

"Hey. What do you think of the air-conditioning? Cool, huh?"

Thump THUMP thump THUMP. *What do you think of the air you're breathing now? Fresh, huh?*

It was the old man, all right.

"Did you know I had a son?"

He looked back at Crybaby, tagging along at his heels. Trotting with his mouth open, the dog looked like he was smiling, giving him the lovin'est look. Reese didn't have the heart to say *Not you.*

"I don't think she would have told you, either," he told whatever he was talking to. "She'd be crazy if she trusted you and not me. You're the one to worry about, you and all your history."

Do it, then. Worry about me. Watch OUT watch OUT.

"I'm talking about *her* worrying, not me. I ain't worried about you. Hell, your worries are over."

They're yours now. Watch OUT watch OUT.

"Watch out for what?"

Mind how you go. Watch where you go. Go easy. EA-sy EA-sy EA-sy.

"Do you haunt Carter like this, or is it just me? Just my wild imagination." He shortened his stride a little, slowed his pace, watched his step. "All right, I'm easy. See? I'm minding, I'm—"

It might have been his imagination, but the spiky blue grama and buffalo grasses seemed greener on the side of the road where his father's body had been found. And it was in that strip of greener grass that a glint of metal caught his minding-where-he-was-going eye.

Helen knocked on the back door. Crybaby answered first, one cavorting bark, then his characteristic whimper before the door swung open. Dressed only in jeans, Reese was clearly fresh from the shower, but that was all that was clear. No inkling of welcome or go-to-hell crossed his face. She wasn't even sure he recognized her.

"Do you mind if I come in?"

He pushed the door open for her, stepped back, and gestured casually. She exchanged affectionate greetings with the dog, noticed his fresh bandage, his silky coat. "Somebody cleaned you up and combed your hair," she cooed. She looked up. And up. Folded arms, stony face. Chiseled brown stone. "He gets to be in the house now?"

"Call it a change of heart. Cooling off helps, plus I've got a bigger bed."

"So you're more—"

"Did you tell him yet?"

"Yes, I did." She gave Crybaby one last good head-scratching before she faced his master. "I told him that you knew nothing about him, and I tried to explain why I never told you."

"And now you're going to explain that to me," Reese inferred as he opened the cupboard for a drinking glass and a bottle with a pharmacy label.

"There's not much to it, really. What's that?" Okay, it was rude, but she had to ask. She wanted details, just as he did.

"This? A pill. I'm popping a pill. Sort of an antidote to bullshit." He scooped the white caplet off his palm with his bottom lip, then washed it down with a full glass of water. She was still watching when he set the glass on the counter, so he offered the bottle. "You want one? Have a seat, have a pill, and let's exchange bullshit."

"I'm not going to do that anymore. I was just wondering what . . . kind of drugs you have to use."

"I use *aaall* kinds of drugs, honey. You name it, I've got it. What's your pleasure? You want a little Valium?" He set the bottle back on the shelf, slid others back and forth with a long forefinger. "Everybody knows jocks know their drugs. Ask my new best friend. He ain't got nothin' to cry about now. He is feelin' no pain." More bottles pushed aside. She recognized the aspirin. "Maybe you need some speed," Reese said, turning to her with a sardonic smile. "Fast or slow, how do you wanna get through this?"

"Speed? But you have a heart—"

"I have a heart, yes. I have a heart. Do you?"

She allowed herself to look into his eyes briefly, yet even briefly was a mistake, for the hurt was there now, in those two words and in the dark sheen in his eyes. But emotion spurred emotion, and she wanted to hold onto hers, too. She bit her lip, shut her eyes, and her tears came.

She hated it, not because she didn't deserve to cry, but because he didn't deserve to see it. She had no right to play on his sympathy, and she didn't intend to. But she couldn't stop the tears except by taking a quick swipe at them with unsteady hands, breathing deeply, talking through it.

"I had to protect my son," she said, sinking slowly, perching on a kitchen chair. "You could have taken him. I didn't know whether you would, but I knew you could, and you wouldn't have to do it when he was a baby. You could have decided any time . . . if you knew . . . and so I couldn't take that . . . gamble."

"But gambling is your profession."

"Dealing blackjack is my profession. Gambling is my weakness. I'm a terrible, terrible . . ." Deep breath, nearly dry eyes, shoulders square. She looked up at him. He was so tall that when he leaned against the edge of the sink, he was actually sitting on it. "But I gambled with money, not with my son's security."

He didn't move. He was, it seemed, unmoved.

"That's good, most of it. The part about being concerned for the boy's security—I understand that. You know all about the laws where Indian children are concerned, and you know what happened with my brother, and you didn't want anything like that to happen with . . . Sidney." He said the name carefully, as though it was hard to pronounce and he wanted to say it perfectly. "I can almost understand that part. I mean, if you didn't want . . ."

There was a question in his eyes. Her lips parted for an answer, but her throat wouldn't give it up.

"Or if you weren't sure, or whatever," he finished, directing his gaze above her head now, a considerate reprieve. "And you must have figured that I had some money. But even when you were having all those financial problems with your gambling that you told me about, you never came to me. No way would you ever stoop to a shakedown of any kind. Sometimes people will use a kid that way, but not you, and I gotta respect that, Helen."

"I didn't want—"

He held up a halting hand. "Don't tell me what you didn't want, not yet. I'm not ready for that yet."

"It had nothing to do with—"

The hand was still up. "Just bear with me now, because I've been thinking, you know? Like I said I was gonna do? I've been thinking about nothing else, and I'd almost believe you wouldn't risk his—security, was it? Except for one thing." His eyes met hers again, and he spoke as though he'd discovered a marvel. "You came back here. You took a job in the casino my brother manages and started hanging around my father. What kind of sense does that make, Helen?"

"M-my son has begun to feel—t-to ask about his Indian heritage."

"Just lately?" He drew his head back in disbelief. "You have no mirrors in your house?"

"When they're little, they're satisfied with . . ." She helped herself to a steadying breath. She was about to play her face card. "With a mother's love, I guess. You explain in the simplest terms you can get away with. One time, one of his friends asked him if he was Mexican or Hispanic. Apparently there had been some kind of discussion around his friend's dinner table, either about those specific words or about Sidney. I told him that he was half American Indian, and we began to read and talk and see movies and . . ."

"Study up on where he came from?"

"I tried to approach it almost academically, I guess. I'm most comfortable with a kind of intellectual approach. Because it's really not—I mean, it doesn't make any difference to me what color his skin is. He's my son, my child, my baby. He came from my body."

"But it makes a difference to him."

"It's beginning to. People say things that he's beginning to hear and to take personally. Things like, I don't know . . ."

"I do."

She nodded, avoiding his eyes, feeling the same pain she

felt when she talked about these hurtful incidents with Sidney. "Most of the time I don't think it's meant to be, to sound . . ."

"Racist?"

She nodded again.

"You wouldn't think so, Helen."

"But I'm not prejudiced."

"Maybe not, but you're white."

"I'm not excusing anyone," she assured him, bristling now as though he'd called her something abominable. "I'm the mother of an Indian child. I know what it feels like to have people see him and think, *brown skin*, and then make some stupid judgment about him that affects him, his choices, his opportunities, his *feelings*." Nothing worse than tears clotting her throat at a time when she wanted to be most eloquent, but this theme did it to her whenever her son was at the heart of it. "To have them . . . hurt him . . ."

"Here." He snatched two tissues from a box on the counter and handed them to her, his reach so long that the gesture brought them no closer. "You're still white, Helen. You'll always be white. He's half white, but he looks like me." Brown arm still extended, he turned it, palm up, palm down. "He's walking around in skin like mine."

"I know." She wiped her nose. "I know. That's why I came here. That's why."

"You had to scout it out for him, huh? We've got white scouts now?"

She glanced up from drying her embarrassing tears.

He shrugged. "Thanks to the casinos, the times sure are a-changin'."

"The casino job has nothing—"

"That was a joke. A little Indian humor. It comes out at odd times."

"I've noticed. It's good, though, because . . . maybe it means you're not so angry with me."

"Oh, I wouldn't count on that," he warned. "But a little humor helps. And the tears do a number on me, too."

"I'm sorry." Deep breaths would stop them. Firm wiping. One more breath. "I hate it when I lose control."

"I know you do. So the question is, are these controlled?"

She closed her eyes, but the damn tears kept rolling because she'd made such a mess, and a mess was what she was.

She heard him move, denim brushing denim, his hand on the back of her chair. Her eyes flew open, chest quivering as they met his.

Swish. Nothing but love.

He knelt beside her, caught a tear on the side of his finger, and touched it to his lower lip, which he quickly tucked in and sucked, then told her, "It wouldn't matter. They'd work just as well either way."

He gave a small nod, and she hugged his neck and buried her face against his shoulder and wept for joy and loss. He held her. The harder she cried, the closer he held her. He was a human scaffold, the support she had sworn many times she did not need. It was wrong to cry all over him now, but she did. Not for long—a torrent like hers ran dry quickly—but for real, and when it was over and the tissues came out again, she felt cleansed.

"So much for control," he said with a wry smile. "Truth is, I don't seem to have much either these days, which is why I had to get away from you for a while and sort things out in my head. Now, here's what I've come up with." He rubbed her thigh, covered by cotton slacks, the way he'd been rubbing her back a moment ago. "I'm not going to take him away from you. I've thought about it, and that's not something I'd do unless . . . unless I was unsure of you. Unless I thought you . . ." He searched her eyes, more for her understanding of him than for something harmful in her. "But that's a terrible judgment to make without cause."

"It is."

"And you made that judgment about me. You keep calling him *your* child, and he is your child, because that's the way you raised him. You judged me unfit. You were determined to protect him from me."

"Not from you, Reese—from that law and from what happened with Carter and from . . . uncertainty. Yes, I *was* unsure."

"You were sure of who his father was."

"Yes."

"You knew I was his father."

"Yes."

He took her face in his hands. "I am your son's father."

"Yes, you are."

"Look at me," he demanded, and she opened her eyes, thinking she hadn't meant to close them. "I am *our* son's father."

"Ye—"

"*Say it.*"

"You are Sidney's father. He's your son."

He swallowed, once, twice, the muscles in his jaw flexing as he closed his eyes, and she felt a jab of fear, the fleeting notion that he might be struggling with some terrible anger. But he drew her face to his and touched his lips to one damp eyelid, then the other, before looking at her again.

"He's *our* son," she said fervently.

He nodded. "You didn't say it before. You just looked at me like I was your worst enemy." He raised his eyebrows, tilted his head to one side. "I missed that, the you-have-a-son part."

"I'm sorry." She touched two trembling fingers to his lips. "He's our son, and I love him more than anything, more than my life, and I don't want to lose him."

"I'm not going to take him from you," he said. She drew a sharp breath, and he squeezed her shoulders as though he was taking pity on her and pinning her spineless body to the chair. "I'm not going to take him from you. I just want to be—"

"I didn't know what you would do. You had a right to know, and I've always known that, but at the same time . . ." She shook her head. "We never talked about marriage or family. It was a beautiful, fragile, fleeting time we had together. You were off to become . . . Reese Blue Sky."

"And you had no idea what that was going to be."

"Oh, but I did. I didn't know much about basketball, but I had a pretty good idea that you were the best thing to come out of South Dakota since Crazy Horse."

A smile warmed his eyes. "He'da made a good point guard, according to my father."

"You were a great point guard."

"I was pretty damn good. I really was." He slid his hands down her arms until they reached her hands, resting in her lap. "You know, Helen, when I found out that you'd quit your job all of a sudden, that you'd left Bad River, it occurred to me that maybe you were pregnant."

"It did?"

"I was young and foolish, but I wasn't completely stupid. We got pretty wild sometimes, and we didn't exactly take all the right precautions." He was opening her hands, plucking a soggy tissue from each one. "And there were a couple of times right after I left when I called you, and we talked a little, and I knew something was different. Then you were gone, and I told myself, Well, so much for that. She's got better things to do."

"But you thought about the possibility of a child?"

"Yeah, I thought about it. But I wasn't gonna ask. I mean . . ." He'd tossed the tissues on the mock battlefield, taken each of her hands in his. "My first season was tough, you know, I was so green. If things hadn't started clicking for me by spring, it might have been my only season." His eyes sought hers. "I missed you."

"I missed you, too. I did watch you on TV."

He nodded. "I missed you, but I didn't want a kid then. I mean, when I thought about it, what I thought was . . ." He was looking down at their clasped hands, guarding what his eyes would surely have given away. Then he looked up, directly overhead. " 'God, I hope she's not pregnant.' "

Her throat burned again. "One of the reasons I didn't tell you . . ." More tears coming. More truth. She moved his hands from her lap to her belly. "I was going to get an abortion."

"You were?"

Tears streamed down her cheeks as she arranged his big hands over the small place where she'd carried the child they'd made, small and flat as it had been then, and she remembered how unlikely a child had seemed at first,

"I made arrangements with a clinic. And then I missed the first appointment. I missed the second one, too." Helen caressed the backs of the beautiful hands covering her middle, one at her waist, the other spanning her pelvic bones. "I felt him move. I was too far along."

Reese adjusted his hands, as though searching for the movement. "You're so small," he whispered.

"You should see how big I can get." Before he could wish he had, she said, "You might have thought I had stolen your basketball."

He touched his forehead to hers, laughing, and she joined in through her tears. He kissed her, and he told her, "I would have driven you crazy trying to play with it." They laughed until he kissed her again. She held his face between her breasts, and he told her she had a lovely heartbeat. "I hope you passed that on," he said. He put his arms around her hips and laid his head in her lap, ear to her belly, nose between her thighs. "I hope to God you did."

"I do, too. I like to think he took something from me. On the outside he's all yours."

"What does he think of that?"

"He thinks he looks like himself."

Reese chuckled. She stroked his cool, damp hair, leaned over him, and apologized. For what, he wanted to know, and she couldn't begin to tell him. She had made one choice and then another, an illusion of control. They had made sense at the time, her choices—not emotional sense, but practical sense—reasonable choices for a woman who didn't really believe in long shots. And the reasonable choice for the plans she'd made was not to have a baby.

"But now I don't even like to think about it, because I can't imagine not having him, and I came so close."

"No, you didn't. You only think you did." He turned his head in her lap, glanced up at her, smiled at her stomach. "The way I see it, if he wasn't going to be born, he wouldn't have been."

"If I'd had an abortion, he wouldn't have been born."

"But you didn't, and 'close' doesn't count." He lifted his head. "My sister, Rose, had an abortion. For, um, for health reasons, I guess."

"It's a hard choice to be faced with. A personal choice, different for every woman. For me . . ." Helen smiled wistfully.

He was caressing her belly again. "My head told me that it was the sensible thing to do in my circumstances. But something else spoke to my heart, and in the end, Sidney was born. So that time, for us, for Sidney and me, that was the way it was supposed to be."

"Roy Blue Sky himself couldn't have said it better. Did he know?"

"I didn't tell him. I wish Sidney had known him. Oh, they would have been . . ."

He came up from her lap, putting his face close to hers. "Didn't you ever want him to know me, Helen?"

"Oh, yes. I always have. I do now." She touched his face, his hair, wishing she could erase all the regrets. "But he wants to go back to Colorado—he says the sooner the better."

"Without . . ."

"He's scared, too."

"Jesus, when did I grow horns?" The question had Reese scowling. She rubbed her thumb over his lower lip, then her fingertips over his forehead, pressing the scowl away. "All right, if he doesn't want to see me right away, fine. I'll wait. A day or two."

"If you want to see him, I think the sooner the better. Lay your fears to rest, along with his."

"That just leaves yours."

Helen nodded toward the cabinet. "You still haven't told me what kind of pill that was."

"I take beta blockers. They help with the heart thing."

"I want to know more than that."

"Like what?" He reached for the other chair and deftly slid it under his butt as he pushed off the floor, muttering, "My foot's going to sleep here."

"Circulation?"

"You wanna trade places? Put your head in my lap?" He maneuvered the chair so that he faced her, his long thighs bracketing her legs. "I'll tell you whatever you wanna know."

"I want to know everything," she said. "I want to know what kind of precautions you're supposed to be taking, like with running. You shouldn't be doing that alone out here.

Should you? I mean . . ." He was grinning. "Well, it wouldn't be fair to Sidney for you to drop dead now."

"That's right, e'en it? I'll be sure and hold off for a while."

"A very *long* while," she demanded, pounding his thigh with her fist. "Which means you shouldn't go running alone."

"If it's gonna happen, it's not gonna matter whether I'm alone or I've got a crowd around me. I could rent a room at the Mayo Clinic and still drop dead on the john. I wanna be fair to Sidney and all, but some things I can't control. And neither can you."

"This is something I have to know about. Sidney's never had any problem that I know of, but he could, couldn't he?"

"He could. There's some DNA testing we need to have done. One good thing about money, it buys you the best doctors." He put his hand over hers when she glanced away. "Hey, chances are he's fine."

"I didn't mean to be so flip. Sidney's not the only one I'm worried about."

"Well, it's good for you to worry. You worry yourself into some hypertension, and then we can share pills."

"Oh, super." She turned her palm to his. "He doesn't know what to think, Reese. And I've gone back and forth. What if you rejected him? What if you wanted him? What if, what if. Either way, wasn't it better for him . . ." She held on tight. "And I know you could still take him."

"You're right. I could." He shrugged. "And I could drop dead tomorrow."

"So." She laid her hand on his smooth cheek. She blessed today, and she blessed his impish smile. "Nothing I can do, huh?"

"I think the expression is . . ." He planted a kiss in the hollow of her palm. "Live with it."

"Live with it." She nodded. "Do you want to see him now?"

"Damn right, if he's willing. Where is he?"

"He's with Carter."

"Good ol' Carter. What was he trying to achieve? Some kind of Geraldo reunion?"

"Sidney called me at the casino, and I wasn't there, and

they got to talking, and I suppose this was Carter's favor to me. He certainly couldn't have known . . ."

"Told you I'm not supposed to run without a partner, didn't he?" Reese leaned in close, both hands on her thighs. "My doctor says there's something else I should never do on my own."

"Have sex?"

He laughed. "Damn, you're getting the hang of that Indian humor."

15

$\mathcal{S}$idney ignored the message on the small screen. The machine wanted more quarters, but he was getting tired of hacking up goblins and orcs. Pair-a-Dice City's video games were really old stuff. He'd been the same age as Derek Marshall the last time he played Dungeons and Dragons.

"Aw, maaan. They killed me off again." Derek pounded the sides of the "X-Men" machine. He stuck his hand out. "Quick, gimme two more."

Sidney shoved his hand in his pocket and came up with four coins, which he dropped into the kid's palm. The money had come from Derek's father, so as far as Sidney was concerned, the kid could have it all. But Derek returned two of the quarters and went back to his game.

This wasn't the first time Sidney had played video games in a casino, but it had been a while. He'd pretty much given up the machines lately, preferring more live action. He loved to run and climb and explore. And he loved to play ball. But what he didn't love was baby-sitting, which was exactly what he was stuck doing. His brand-new uncle—first one he'd ever had except for Aunt Linda's husband, whom he called John, not Uncle—had told him he'd be "getting to know your cousin," but what it amounted to was being put in charge of two rolls of quarters.

Uncle Carter. Man, this was weird. Cousins, uncles, fathers, these were all alien beings. Sidney had no experience with such creatures and hadn't come to South Dakota looking for any. He'd come to see his mom, who was generally pretty cool. He could have stayed at camp during the break between sessions—some of the guys were—but he'd gotten to thinking about his mom a lot, and he was really starting to miss her. He liked the idea of bopping in and surprising her.

He didn't know what to think about all these new relatives, so he decided not to think anything. Goblins and orcs. He figured he'd hang loose until he could get on that plane, and then he'd be outta here. His mom would get her investigation wrapped up in a few more weeks, and they'd be back to normal.

Arms braced on the machine, Sidney took a couple of steps back and dropped his chin to his chest, "Aren't you sick of this yet?"

"Are you? What do you wanna do?"

The kid was ready to be his tail. Of course, he was only nine. Sidney glanced around the game room. The attendant, an Indian woman, was reading a paperback book. Two skinny girls and one fat one were just leaving the place, going to get something to drink, they said. Sidney was past the *getting* stage of bored.

"What else is there?"

"My dad says there's gonna be a pool next year if they add onto the hotel. Olympic-size, maybe. I'm taking swimming lessons now."

"I don't need any more lessons. Where'd your mom go? When she takes you home, I wanna go back."

"Back where? To my house? You can come to my house."

The kid was talking to his back, following close behind him. As long as he could hear his voice, Sidney was doing his job. Outside the game room there were benches, bathrooms, and signs with arrows pointing in three different directions. Sidney didn't like any of the choices.

"I got a basketball court at home," Derek was saying.

"I wanna go back to where my mom's staying so I can sleep."

"Sleep? What do you wanna sleep for?"

Kids never liked to sleep during the day. Sidney remembered what that was like, before you find out how cool it is to stay up at night. Getting up early was the only bad part about camp. Staying up after lights-out could be great if three or four guys were in on it together, even if it was just to play Zombie or tell stories. It was cool that everybody at camp was about the same age. No nine-year-olds who didn't get it. Sidney was the youngest guy there, but not too many others realized that he was only twelve. He was way bigger than a lot of thirteen- and fourteen-year-olds.

And now he knew why. His mom had told him his father— his *dead* father—was a big man. But not *that* big.

"If we go to my house we can play basketball." Derek, standing at his elbow, was rattling on. "My dad says you're going to a camp for Indian kids where they play basketball and stuff. He says you'll probably be as good as my uncle Reese someday. Is he really your dad?"

"So they say." Sidney shoved his hands in his pockets, just casual. But he was thinking, That's cool, Carter saying a thing like that about me.

Four curly-haired old ladies strolled past with their plastic change buckets. One of them looked at Sidney like his fly was open or something. When he caught himself checking, he decided he was getting out of this place, starting with the stupid hallway.

"You want some pop or something?" he asked.

"It's free here. But we can't go in the part where slot machines and stuff are. Kids can't go in there. But we can go—" They'd reached the archway that separated the gamblers from the regular people. Derek grabbed the back of Sidney's shirt. "Hey, we can't go in there. Adults only."

With a lofty glance, Sidney let the kid know that he'd overstepped. They weren't going through; they were going around. They had started out in Carter's office, and Sidney figured he could find his way back without consulting a nine-year-old.

He was permitting the kid to follow. He remembered having seen the gift store with the leather jackets in the window, so he knew they were on the right track.

"Kids aren't allowed where there's booze and gambling," Derek muttered, dutifully tagging behind.

"We can go to your dad's office, can't we? I'm getting tired of hanging out here. I hate these places."

"What places? Casinos, you mean? I don't get to come here very much anymore, but my dad . . ."

Sidney had found the little hallway he was looking for. He turned his knuckles to knock, but his hand froze when he heard yelling behind the door.

"I was just trying to help out, for crissake! Will you back off!" It was Carter's voice.

"You didn't need to get your nose into it," Sarah said. "You've always got to be throwing money around and being the big Mr. Take Over. Even if you didn't know whose kid he was, looks like you would have asked her first, before you went off and suggested this whole thing to the boy. If she wanted her son here, she would have—"

"She didn't have the money."

"And you do? You know, you've got your own kids and your own . . ."

The rest of her words were lost on Sidney.

"Jeez." His hand fell to his side. "Is she mad about me?"

"She's mad about bills."

Sidney turned his back on the door marked "General Manager." Derek was pasted to the wall, as far from the door as he could get, staring at the floor. "She's always mad about bills," the kid said. "She says my dad owes too much money."

"It's a bitch to owe a lot of money," Sidney said. Derek looked smaller now than he had in the video-game room. Too small to be much of a pest. "I'm never going to have any credit cards. They're too much trouble."

"My uncle Reese is rich. So you're lucky."

"Why?"

"Well, if he's your dad, that means you're rich. That car he's driving, that's not his real car."

"It looks like an okay car."

"He's got way better cars. He's got all kinds of stuff, I bet. I've never been to his house in Minneapolis, have you?"

"No." Sidney shrugged. He didn't know anything about a house in Minneapolis. "I thought he was dead."

"Oh, no, he ain't dead. He just can't play in the pros anymore." The little boy's eyes widened at the sound of more threats shouted behind the closed door. "She's gonna kick him out again."

"Does he gamble or what?"

"Gamble?"

"Never mind. Money's the root of all evil. Have you ever heard that?"

"No, but my dad's not evil. He doesn't drink hardly ever, for one thing, and he's gonna get us a different boat pretty soon. We've got one, but it's small if you wanna take friends, like if we go up to Lake Oahe." More shouts behind the door quashed Derek's enthusiasm. "I hate it when she kicks him out," he whispered. "We hardly get to see him then."

Sidney jerked his head toward the door. "You don't wanna listen to *that*, do you?"

"Better than never seeing him."

"Come on." For the first time since they'd met, Sidney laid a friendly hand on the kid's little shoulder. "We'll find something else to do."

But the end of the hallway was blocked by a big, bald-headed guy, standing there like a cork in a bottle. "What are you boys doing back here? Are you with your parents?"

"My dad's the general manager," Derek quietly informed the man, whose sweet smell—some kind of shaving lotion—made Sidney feel claustrophobic. That and the way he blocked the light, standing there at the end of the hallway.

"You're Carter's boy? Who's this, your brother?"

"He's my cousin. His dad's my uncle Reese."

"You're Reese Blue Sky's kid? Hey, I'm Bill Darnell." The man stuck his hand out. "I met your dad just recently."

"Yeah, me, too."

"Really." Darnell chuckled, folded his arms, and just stood there like a teacher on hall duty. "Well, when I met your dad, he was with a pretty, uh . . . Come to think of it, she's one of our dealers. Guess she must not be your—"

"That's my mom."

"Really."

If he'd been a little younger, a little less cool, Sidney would have taken off and squeezed past this guy. He was looking at Sidney like people too often did, trying to figure out where he belonged and with whom. But Sidney had just told him. For the first time in his life, he had two living, breathing reference points. The guy knew who his mother was, knew who his father was. So there it was, the explanation. He didn't look much like his mother, no, but he did look like his father. A little bit.

"You guys hungry?" Darnell asked.

The boys shook their heads in unison, as though they'd been hangin' together long enough to be thinking alike.

"You try out the video games?" The man fished a handful of change out of his pocket. "Here, I've got a bunch of quarters for you, and I'll tell your father—" He looked up. "Or your *fathers*—are they both here? I'll let them know we've got two guys out here who are getting a little restless, huh?"

Sidney shrugged. He didn't feel like explaining anymore.

"You hang tough now, and I'll—" Darnell nodded toward the closed office door. "I'll take care of it."

Sidney's mom came to pick him up when he and Derek were about to hit the make-your-own-ice-cream-sundae bar for the third time. The offer of food hadn't sounded too appealing coming from Bill Darnell, but it was okay when Carter suggested it, especially when he and Sarah agreed to sit down with them. That made Derek happy, and Sidney was feeling pretty sorry for the kid by then. He decided maybe he was lucky he had to live with only one parent, if having two meant that you had to listen to them yelling at each other all the time.

It seemed like a long way from the casino to the little town of Bad River, but his mother said it was only about five miles. It probably seemed like more because there was so much nothing in between. He'd been to a few Indian reservations before, but this one looked more desolate, scenery-wise. The Black Hills, the part of South Dakota he'd seen coming in on the plane, they looked nice. He mentioned that later, when he was helping her carry some groceries into the kitchen. She started in on seeing the sights again, and she seemed a whole lot more chipper than she had been when she'd left him at the casino. He didn't think the prospect of seeing Mount Rushmore had a lot to do with it.

"I'm not interested in seeing a bunch of rock heads, Mom. I spent today baby-sitting some kid who's supposed to be my cousin, and it felt weird. I mean, with his parents, I felt like I was in the way. It's all too weird." He set the bags on the kitchen counter next to the refrigerator. "I'll probably just sleep tomorrow."

"On my day off?"

Today was her day off, too, and he'd spent half of it with people he didn't know, so what was that about? He opened the refrigerator door so she could put the milk in.

"Why don't you go back to work and get this investigation over with so you can come back home?"

"I'll be finishing that up soon. I just thought maybe the three of us could take in some of the sights tomorrow."

"The three of us? I only see two." But he knew exactly what she was getting at. "I don't want you asking him, Mom. And I don't want . . ."

He felt a little bad about the funny look on her face, like she had strawberry shortcake in the refrigerator and he'd turned it down. "You know it'll just be a big mess, even if he *wants* me to be his kid, which he probably doesn't. So can we just forget it?" He shrugged. "It's embarrassing, is what it is."

It wasn't too surprising that she had no answer for that. He felt a little bad about that, too. She'd always been a pretty cool mom, never embarrassed him by yelling at him in front of his friends, or running around the yard in her bathrobe like Karl Pringle's mother, or wearing too-tight clothes. She went out of her way to be there when he needed her, and she knew better than to be too obvious about it.

But telling him he didn't have a father and then coming up with one, and the guy didn't know anything about him, *and the guy was a big-time basketball player* . . . jeez, not *too* embarrassing. The sooner he got back to Colorado, the sooner his "father" could go back to being dead.

Which was what Sidney was thinking when he answered the door and there stood his new father, very tall, very dark, and very much alive.

"Hi, Sid."

He stepped back to let the man in. Talk about embarrassment! It felt too weird now to look him in the face, so he didn't. He looked over his shoulder for help. "Mom's in the kitchen."

"It's always good to see your mom, but I came mostly to see you."

"Yeah, well, here I am." God, this guy was tall. Barely fit through the door. Was *he* going to grow that much? "I guess I'm stuck here for a couple more days."

"Surprising your mother with a visit, man, that's . . ." The guy was making himself right at home, sitting on the end of the flowered sofa. He looked up at Sidney like he expected him to do something next. "That's a very thoughtful thing to do."

"It was Carter's idea."

"Sounds to me like you hatched it together."

"Yeah, well . . ." Sidney lifted one shoulder. "I'm sorry about it now."

"I'm not." Reese smiled. It looked like an honest smile, like he wasn't just smiling because he had something to sell. There was some shine to his eyes, and it was aimed right at Sidney, made him feel like he'd done something right. "Everybody's a little shook up right now, but that's what surprises are all about."

"You're not mad?"

The big man shook his head.

"Why not? Because you don't believe it, either? I mean, how can you be sure I'm really your kid?"

"I'm sure."

"Okay, then, how can I be sure you're my father?"

"Well . . ." Reese hopped up from the sofa, laid his hand at the base of Sidney's neck, and steered him toward the big mirror above the buffet. Sidney was keenly aware of the warmth and the size of that hand and how light it felt, how easy it rode on his back. Was it really his father's hand?

And could he still dunk a basketball, or had he gotten too old?

"What do you think?"

"Huh?" Sidney blinked and focused on the mirror. The big man had to squat some to get his face into it. Jeez, *what did he think?* Little guy, big guy. Young, old. Zits, no zits. Neither one had much beard. Sidney shrugged. "I think we've both got almost the same color hair."

"That's just for starters. You wear contacts, don't you?"

"Yeah. You?"

"Nearsighted."

"Me, too. Mom doesn't wear glasses." So what does that prove? Sidney wondered. "You're darker than I am."

"I'm more Indian than you are, have more pigment. But you're definitely Indian. Your mother's a beautiful woman, but I don't think there's much doubt about who's got the dominant genes."

"Who's got—"

"You know, the—"

"I know what genes are." Sidney pulled away. "I got an A in life science." Nobody was going to prove anything by looking in a mirror. Mirrors were tricky. This guy could disappear from the picture as fast as he'd shown up.

"Your mom says you do very well in school."

Sidney put a chair between them, looked the guy right in the eye, and said, very quietly, "Yeah, well, I also know that just because you fucked my mother doesn't make you my father, and that's not something I learned in school."

The man didn't flinch. They stood there looking at each other for a long moment, with Sidney holding onto the back of the chair, thinking, Your move. Just try to tell me how to talk. *Just try.*

"Fair enough," the man finally said, equally quietly. "It's probably too soon to ask you where you did learn it."

"You can ask. I don't have to tell you."

"That's right, you don't." It was the man's turn to lift a shoulder. "What *would* make me your father?"

"How am I supposed to know?"

"Well, so far, you're the expert. I'm still in the discovery phase, kinda feeling my way in the shadows."

"Discovery? What discovery? I've been here all along. Other people have fathers they have to worry about—you know, like, I have to ask my dad, my dad says no, my dad says yes, my dad says this and that. *My* father's been dead. That's what *I* know." He was getting a little excited, waving first one hand around, then the other, and his voice had gone squeaky on him. His heart was pounding like a bass speaker. He tried for quiet again. "So now what?"

"Now I'm not dead."

"Maybe *you* aren't, but . . ." Sidney gestured wildly toward the mirror and shook his head. "Just because you think I look like you? Maybe I look like your brother, too."

"Nah, he's—"

"Maybe I do. Maybe she was fuckin' around with him, too."

The guy's eyes went stony, but the tone of his voice stayed low-key. "I gotta tell you right now, Sid, I want us to be honest with each other, but I care a lot about your mother. Any guy who bad-mouths your mother is looking for serious trouble." He nodded once. "Just so you know."

"What kind of trouble?"

"Depends on how big the guy is." The man squared his shoulders and drew a deep breath, which made him seem even taller. "I've got a feeling if it's you and me, we can probably come to an understanding just talking about it. Because I think we both feel the same way about your mom."

Sidney started to take exception to that claim, but the big man backed off quickly. "Okay, maybe not quite the same. She's your mom, and that's . . ." He paused, then shook his head, looking puzzled. "You know, I don't know what that's like, because my mother died when I was very young. *Really* died. You've had your mom with you all your life, so that's something special, the love you have for each other. It's not the same as what I feel for her, and there's no way I'm going to disrespect that." He took a step closer. "And I don't think you mean to disrespect it, either, do you?"

Sidney shook his head. He was still hanging onto the back of that chair.

"There are blood tests we can have done, if that's what you need, Sid. I'm willing, but it isn't necessary. And it isn't just because we look alike." He was there by Sidney's side now with that big, warm hand on his shoulder, looking him in the eye and telling him earnestly, "I know your mother. I knew her thirteen years ago, and I . . ." He nodded solemnly. "We both know her, and we both know that what she's telling us is true."

"But she never told you about me," Sidney protested.

"She was afraid to."

"Why? What would you do?"

"I might have . . . I *could* have done a lot of things."

"What's that supposed to mean?" Sidney had gone this far, now he wanted explanations. "All this time. All this time you didn't know about me?" His father pressed his lips together and shook his head slowly. "What would you have done?"

"I'm not trying to give you any runaround here, Sid. There's no way I can answer that now. Don't ask me to come up with some bullshit that can't do anything but cause us more trouble."

"Would you have married her?"

"I want to tell you something." The hand slid to Sidney's other shoulder, making it like they were buddies. "I don't know if you've, uh, gone out with any girls yet . . ."

"No."

"Good, so there's a first I haven't missed."

"This has something to do with marrying my mom?"

"When I first met your mother, I thought she was way, way beyond my reach. I couldn't even believe she'd talk to me, or sit beside me, or go out with me. I mean, she was that beautiful and smart and classy and . . ." He squeezed Sidney's shoulder and rocked him a little. "Hell, she still is; you know that. She's the most beautiful woman you've ever seen, right?"

"Well, pretty much."

"And at the time, I was a little younger than she was. I'm not anymore, though. We're even up now."

Suddenly there was a loud clattering of pans coming from the kitchen. Sidney glanced in that direction.

His father was smiling at him again, going on a little louder with his point. " 'Cause men are kinda slow getting started, but once that aging thing kicks in, man . . ." He urged Sidney to walk with him, pointed toward the kitchen, kept right on talking. "Do I look younger than she does? Not at all. Never did. Can't remember when I wasn't looking around at the tops of heads and feeling like everybody's papa, you know?"

Sidney knew.

The big man grinned, signaling toward the kitchen with his eyes. "But she's not that much smarter than me anymore, either."

His mom was laughing now.

"See, I knew that would get her," Reese said. "Does she usually spend this much time in the kitchen?"

"Not usually. She's probably trying not to listen. But she can't help it."

"Tell you what, Sid. I wasn't too sure whether I could come up with the right things to say, but I figure I must be doing all right because she's not gonna let anyone say or do anything to hurt you."

"What do you mean, the right things to say?"

"To get you to give me a chance."

"A chance to what?"

"To play on your team even though I missed the tip-off."

Sidney laughed as they walked into the kitchen together. "You missed a little more than that."

"We can't get that back, so we have to let it go. Right, Mom? Hey . . ."

She was laughing, sort of, but she had big tears rolling down her face at the same time. It was Sidney who moved to put his arms around her first, because one thing that really shook him up was seeing his mother cry. She hugged Sidney, but then he lost one of her arms to Reese, and pretty soon the longest arms Sidney had ever had such a close encounter with were there for both of them. But not too close. Just a hand on his back and an arm around his mother, which felt okay.

"I was so wrong," she was blubbering into Reese's shirt.

"Maybe." Reese was kinda messing his chin in her hair. "Maybe not. We don't know, and it doesn't matter. You did what you thought was right for Sid."

"But he needed—"

"Shh. Whatever he needs now." She looked up, smiling the best she could with all the sniveling, and Reese said, "Whatever he needs, whatever you need."

Sidney had to back out of this now. A little hugging went a long way. Pretty soon you started feeling cramped and noticing things like nose hair and skin pores that looked like craters, and you had to get untangled and stretch out a little.

"What's for supper?" He knew it was going to be chicken—he'd already seen his mother fooling around with it—but he wanted her to stop crying, and chicken wasn't something she was likely to cry over.

He was right. She cheerfully described the stuff she had going in the oven while she mopped her face with a bunch of Kleenex.

Then she pulled a drawer open. "Do you want to see pictures?"

Oh, man, Sidney moaned mentally. Baby pictures!

"I've got a few here." She whipped out one of her little albums. "I've got a lot more at home."

Reese gave him a knowing look. He held the small blue book of plastic sleeves in his hands like something valuable and delicate, something he maybe wanted to keep for later. "I'll have to get out there and see them, won't I?" he said, and Sidney wasn't sure, but it seemed like he was looking for *his* permission.

"Plan to stay a while," Sidney said. "She's got videos, too."

"That's cool." Reese grinned. Pictures were okay, but it seemed like he was more interested in the kid standing in front of him right now, which was what was *really* cool. "I hear you play a little round ball."

Sidney suddenly remembered Reese on video.

"I'm not really that good yet. You might want to hold off before you claim me."

"All right, back to the mirror again," Reese said, laughing.

And he made Sidney stand with him again in front of that mirror.

"Your mother made a few improvements," Reese said, squatting behind his son's shoulder this time, a little closer, a little more contact with both hands on his shoulders. It was okay, Sidney realized. He was cool with it. Both guys in the mirror were smiling, and maybe it was almost the same kind of smile.

"You've got that nice forehead of hers," Reese pointed out, "and I don't think your nose is gonna be quite as big as mine, but you've sure got Roy Blue Sky's ears, man." He tugged on one, just a little.

"Yeah, well, then so do you, man," Sidney said, tugging Reese's ear back.

"You've got to come out to the place so I can show you this thing he made, this miniature battlefield. You ever been to the Little Bighorn?" Reese asked, getting kind of excited about it, and Sidney had to shake his head. "Aw, we gotta go out there," Reese said with that quick little shoulder squeeze of his. "You gotta see where we whooped Custer's ass, and I'll show you a tape. They interviewed your grandfather on the History Channel. He knew all about that stuff, and he could sure set those big college professors straight on the Indian point of view."

"I think I saw that. But I didn't know who he was."

"Well, we'll watch it together, and I'll tell you who he was. I'm just beginning to understand who he was myself."

They shared their first supper together, looked at a few pictures, traded more than a few stories. Helen sat back and pushed the pesky worries and might-have-beens aside as she listened to them talk basketball. They liked each other already, and why wouldn't they? They were cut from the same cloth. They kept stealing looks at each other and at her, looks loaded with *Hey, this feels good.*

After Sidney went to bed, Helen and Reese cuddled on the sofa together, pictures on top of the side table, large boots and small sandals shoved underneath, National Public Radio playing late-night jazz. They were both thinking they'd waited a long time for a moment like this, and by rights it should not have to end.

He said it first.

"I've got another council meeting tomorrow. It would be kinda nice if Sid's dad could spend the night with his mom."

She looked up, smiled regretfully. It would be *very* nice, but it wasn't in the cards. The ice was still much too thin.

"Damn, I want to take you to bed *so bad*, and here we've got a kid in the house." He drew her closer, as close as two people could get without merging into one. "You think he's asleep?"

"Maybe."

"Maybe not. He had a little trouble with the birds-and-bees part of our conversation, so I guess we don't wanna push. He'd probably come after me with a bat."

She nodded. She kept her mouth shut, because if she said anything, it might be another "maybe," as in "Maybe if we were quiet." Lord, she loved this man.

"I remember hearing a noise across the hall one time, and I got up and . . ." He glanced at the pictures on the table and chuckled. "Hell, I thought the dog had gotten into the old man's room and was howling to get out. I opened the door and, whoa! Not exactly the same as opening up a centerfold, if you know what I mean. Man, I couldn't shut that door fast enough. The next day I tried to tell him I thought it was the dog I heard. Well, he never let the dog in the house, so he figured I was being a smart-ass."

"What did he do?"

"Nothing. He froze me out."

She sat up a little, shocked, picturing little Reese shivering on the doorstep. "Outside?"

"Jeez, not that bad," he assured her with an affectionate squeeze. "No, he just didn't talk to me for about a week. Not a word."

"Maybe he was embarrassed."

"Maybe. He never remarried, but he had girlfriends from time to time. We didn't talk about any of that, but sometimes I wish we had. I wonder if he missed my mother. I wonder if—" He smiled, gave a diffident shrug. "He used to tell me

stories. There was one about ol' Coyote making a fool of himself over a younger woman when it was really the woman
he'd lost that he wanted back. I used to think, Is he just making
this shit up?"

"He showed me a shirt your mother had made for him. It
was a Western shirt, hand-embroidered with colorful flowers.
We were talking about the people around here who did the
best beadwork, the best quilts—" She smiled too, remembering
the old man's animated delivery. "And yes, he was telling me
one of his stories about these two women who'd made a bet
on who could bead the best shirt. He brought that shirt out.
It wasn't beaded, but he was so proud of it, he handled it like
an egg. It was almost new, except that it was torn—"

"On the sleeve." He was listening more intently than she'd
realized, amazement growing in his eyes. "I didn't know she'd
made that for him. He never told me."

"Did you burn it?"

He nodded, but the look in his eyes said maybe he would
have saved that one, if he had known. "We just couldn't . . ."
He drew a deep breath as he glanced toward the hallway
where the two bedrooms were, where his son slept. ". . . talk
easily, you know? Maybe that's why he had to get Carter back.
Maybe he needed to start over clean."

"Carter didn't replace you. I think your father was trying
to do what he thought was right for Carter." And that was
what had scared her the most, that everybody had his own
idea of what was right for a child, and that maybe nobody
was completely right. Or completely wrong.

"Yeah, why not?" He shrugged. "Sure, why not? I'd better
not be too quick to judge, now that it's my turn to take a crack
at it. It's probably not fair to . . ."

He shifted his hips as he plunged his hand into the pocket
of his jeans. "Almost forgot. I found something interesting."
He produced a small round metal object, which he'd wrapped
in a bit of cloth. "Found it in the ditch, near where they killed
my dad."

She examined it. It looked like a small cap to something,
some part of a vehicle.

"I think it's out of a headlight," he told her. "I've got another piece, too, a little bigger, plus a little glass. I've gone over that ground a hundred times, and it was right there in plain sight. It's funny how the prairie holds onto something for a while, and then one day she gives it up."

She nodded. "Like a mother?"

"Like a mother." He pocketed his find.

"What will you do with it?"

"I'm not sure yet. Show it to Dozer and see what he thinks." He put his arm around her again. "Now, tell me what it was like when he was born."

She was still staring at his pocket. "Do you think they can tell anything from that?"

"We're sure gonna find out," he promised. "Now, tell me about—"

"You mean your ears weren't burning?" She smiled. "I do believe I heaped a few curses on your head during that final stage of labor."

"I'm sure I was in the gym feeling some kind of a strain. It was a hard year, but nothing like . . ." He shifted toward her, sliding his hand over her belly. "I should have been with you that day. Did you have anybody?"

"A friend. Another teacher who'd had three babies and knew the ropes. I hadn't even known her very long. I was very . . ." She put her hand over his, pressed it to her. "I wasn't planning on a C-section, so it was a little scary when they started talking about operating. I wanted everything to go smoothly and naturally, and when it didn't, I really wanted someone . . ."

She'd wanted *him*. She'd been angry and scared and suffering pain worse than any she'd imagined, and she'd wanted him there. She remember thinking he should have known. He should have appeared at her bedside. He was the baby's father, and he should have had a gut feeling, because she sure did, and they should have been in it together.

But they weren't. It had been she and her baby who shared the experience. She smiled. "The moment Sidney was born, I wasn't alone anymore."

"There's a scar here, isn't there?" He opened her slacks, asking permission with his eyes as he unbuttoned, slowly unzipped. "I noticed it before, but I stayed away from it because it bothered me a little that it didn't have anything to do with me." His warm hand covered her skin, his thumb tracing the scar. "Now it does."

"It does."

"How did you choose his name?"

"It's my father's middle name. Sidney's middle name is Roy. I think those connections give a sense of identity." Her choice of Reese's father's name clearly surprised him. "I always intended to tell him about you when he was older," she explained. "And to tell you about him."

He took her at her word with a quick nod. "That one picture in the hospital, he looks so little."

She laughed. "He weighed in at nine pounds, six ounces."

"Is that big?"

"You try walking around with over nine pounds of baby sitting right on your bladder."

"That's big," he said with a smile, his hand still warming her belly. "Did he cry much? When did he start talking and walking and all that good stuff?"

"His first word was *no*, and he ran before he walked, and he was into everything, and he strongly objected to being weaned, which was fine with me because when I nursed him, I got to hold him. Otherwise he wanted to be exploring."

She laid her head on his shoulder, put her hand on his chest, holding him as he held her while she remembered for him.

"He didn't exactly cry when he was hungry, but he let me know it was time. Once, we were parked in the shade at the edge of a parking lot. A friend had gone into the store, but I had to feed Sidney, so I stayed in the car. I had the windows down, and I was nursing him when I felt someone standing over us. Usually I would cover up, but it was summer, and I just opened my blouse a little . . ."

"Was it a guy?"

"It was an old woman. She had tears streaming down both cheeks. When I looked up, she smiled, apologized for staring." She looked up, smiling wistfully, almost the way the old woman had, feeling more akin to her now than she had then.

"She said she'd nursed ten babies, and the youngest was probably my age. 'Seeing you, I could feel the little mouth tugging and the surge of the milk,' she said. 'It feels good to be needed, doesn't it?' And I thought, yes, it does feel good, but to be needed so much, so completely . . .'" She paused, putting it all together in a new way. "I guess I was always afraid of that. Sidney taught me that I could handle it."

He nodded, swallowed hard. "I'm glad it wasn't some guy."

"Me, too. I haven't had much time for guys."

"Me neither." He smiled as his hand sneaked a little higher. "Not since the Mavericks."

"But I don't think I've spoiled him. He's not a mama's boy."

"No, but I can see his point. I'd strongly object to being weaned from these, too." He loosened the hook between her breasts as he whispered, "Let's go out in the car. I'll bet we could bring tears to some old lady's eyes."

"Are you calling me an old lady?"

"I already brought tears to your eyes, didn't I? I'm calling you *my* lady." He grinned and tried again with a pause in the middle. "I'm calling you, my lady."

She laughed until he started teasing her nipple, which made her stop laughing, made her tingle and ache for him and lift her face to his. He kissed her, his tongue demanding intercourse with hers, and they both came away breathless, speaking in heated whispers.

"Come on, lady, let's go out in the car." He withdrew his hand. "Before we get caught in the living room."

"Getting caught in the car wouldn't be good, either."

"We'll go somewhere," he said. "Crybaby's out in the yard. He can babysit."

"You have a meeting tomorrow?"

"Nine o'clock Indian time."

"You can sleep here."

"Mmmm . . ."

"But it'll have to be on the sofa."

16

$\mathcal{R}$eese met Dozer and Titus below the basketball hoop at sunup.

He had left his child, his woman, and his dog asleep in a place that belonged to none of them. Those facts—that he belonged with them, but not in that apartment—had struck him as he'd stumbled around in the stingy gray light, picking his way among borrowed furniture. He'd made countless early-morning exits from rented rooms, but this one felt remarkably different. This time he moved carefully, mindful of new ties, fragile cords he did not wish to trip over and break.

Be quiet, let them sleep, they are yours to care for.

So strange, gloriously strange. He'd come home alone, and he'd found these three who were part of him. Wonderfully strange, this feeling of not wanting to leave them, even for a few hours. But he had work to do. And that fact struck him, too. He had come home to say good-bye to his father, to give respect and finally take his leave of Bad River. But Bad River wasn't finished with him, and he had found more needs to tend to.

Reese arrived first this time. He took the basketball and his favorite court shoes out of the trunk and sat on a bench whose legs were anchored in asphalt. His buddies were there before he had his shoes tied.

The three longtime friends jump-started the morning with a three-man game of Around the World, which loosened muscles and thoughts. Reese had two things on his mind now— the council meeting and the evidence he'd found in the roadside grass. He handed the scrap of metal to Dozer, then slugged down some bottled water as he watched his friend put on his cop face.

"This looks like a piece of the weapon, all right. Headlamp." Dozer used his stretched-out T-shirt sleeve to wipe the sweat from his eyes. "I say we go to the Feds with this directly."

"What if it gets lost in their red tape?" Reese challenged, even though he knew Dozer was right.

"No choice, that's a chance we have to take." Dozer gave Titus a look at Reese's find, but he wasn't going to give it up. "We need to go outside with it, Blue. Listen, they've got Gene Brown convinced he didn't find anything, wasn't even hardly at the scene, like maybe he dreamed it. I know damn well he found something, and I know it got buried. Thing is, a broken headlamp like this, there should have been more pieces. Hit-and-run drivers generally don't stop to pick up evidence. I tell you, man, this thing's screwy as hell."

"Maybe I should talk to Gene myself." The early-morning sun glinted off the shred of evidence. Reese watched it pass between two trusted hands. He didn't feel much trust for the FBI. One of his cousins had been beaten to death a few years back, and the Feds had never found the killer.

"Gene's doing his damnedest not to cross anybody right now," Titus said.

"You don't think he'd trust me? We used to be pretty tight, all of us, remember?"

"Yeah, but Gene's been on suspension a couple of times," Dozer explained, "so he's on a pretty short leash."

"Suspension for what?"

"Procedural stuff. He can get a little hot sometimes."

Reese chuckled. Gene was the kind of a guy who'd give a

friend his last dime, but he had a habit of opening his mouth at the wrong time, regularly getting himself into trouble. Suspension had always been par for his course.

Dozer laughed. "Hell, you don't want to get arrested by Gene on days when his ol' lady's locked him out of the bedroom the night before."

"Or on nights when he don't know where she is," Titus said.

"Ain't love grand?" Dozer exchanged looks with Titus.

Reese glanced away smiling, thinking these guys knew exactly where his mind was. "Grand" was an understatement. At the same time, he was trying to imagine putting a scare into big Gene, who never used to worry about who he crossed. Except the feisty little woman who had become his wife.

"How long have you been married now, Dozer?" Reese asked.

"Eleven years, goin' on forever."

"You think forever's possible?"

"I can't think of it any other way. We've been through a lot, Genny and me." Dozer studied the piece of metal, spoke quietly as he turned it over in his palm. "We lost a baby a couple years back. We've got three kids, but that was hard, losing that little baby. Genny's a lot stronger than I am." He looked up, one eye squinting against the sun. "She's strong enough to make forever possible."

Reese nodded. Helen was like that, too. Strong enough to raise their son alone, which was a good thing. But it made him feel extraneous, so he put the thought behind him.

Strong enough to make forever possible. He liked that better.

"I think Gene would tell me what he found out there." He eyed his friends, looking for encouragement. "You know, if I just asked him."

"You're not the team captain anymore, Blue. It's been a long time, and you've been a lot of places guys like us will never see. This is all we've got, this little island in the middle of South Dakota, these badges, these . . ." Dozer jerked his chin in Titus's direction. ". . . these jobs with this casino that could shut down next year. You go by past history, that's the way it figures to work out."

"Blue don't go by past history," Titus said proudly. "Indian ballplayers don't make the pros. Hell, when we took the state tournament, we all talked about how we could be playing pro ball, but the rest of us were just blowing smoke. It's fun to blow smoke. For most people, that's all they really want to do. You turn that dream into a reality, man, then it's not the easy dream anymore."

Dozer nodded. "That's right. Most of us are satisfied just to watch. You can't blow the shot at the free-throw line when you're watching TV." He whacked Reese's chest with the back of the hand still holding the scrap of headlamp. "So you're our hero, man. You took the shot."

"What did I have to lose?" Besides his life? The love of his life? His . . .

"The dream," Titus said. "You put the dream on the line, Blue."

"Yeah, you could've blown it, man. Then you'd be sayin'—" Dozer did a passable Brando, droopy lip, sad eyes. " 'I coulda been a contendah.' "

"Well, guess what. I ain't done dreamin'." Reese tapped a finger on the piece of metal in Dozer's hand. "You find out what this came off of and who was driving it."

"That's a tall order."

"Blue's a tall man," Titus said. "I got one for you, too. One of the dealers over at Pair-a-Dice City just up and quit. He's only been here a few months, pops up out of nowhere, claims to be part Indian. They hire him, he stays a couple of months, then he airs out."

"Don't they do some kind of background check?"

"Yeah, but the paperwork jams up, so they hire on as temps," Titus said. "So I'm saying, hey, you guys haven't hired any of our own people as dealers in a while. Let's train more of our people. I mean, the last six, eight dealers we've hired, including your lady—no offense, Blue, but you gotta admit— where the hell are these people coming from? We've got people here who can do these jobs."

"The tribal gaming commission has to approve the applicants, right? That's you, Titus."

"Well, yeah," Titus agreed. "They'll give us a big list of

people, and there'll be some Indians and some non-Indians, and they'll tell us the people we approve will be placed according to their skills and qualifications. But see, the deal was—"

"Titus, can you get hold of this dealer's personnel file before it disappears, too?" Reese was gaining new respect for records. On the hunch that whoever shot Crybaby was after his father's papers, he'd stashed the boxes in the trunk of the car he had put on a lease contract. Like the dog, the papers were staying with him.

Titus grinned. "I'm already a step ahead of you there, man."

"Damn, why am I not surprised?" He planned to ask Helen about the dealer, and he thought the file might be helpful. "Could we manage the casinos ourselves?"

"You mean *now*?"

"When the contract is up with Ten Star. They're talking about expanding and taking on more debt, but the way I see it, we don't need that right now. We need to get control."

"They own the machines. We lease from them."

"That's our first mistake." Reese hiked his foot up on the bench and rested a hand on his knee. "I've got a meeting to go to, and I haven't figured out exactly what I'm gonna say yet when the gaming committee recommends that we act on Ten Star's proposal for another contract with them."

Titus laughed. "It's pretty obvious it ain't gonna be an affirmative."

"Tell you what, these two casinos are definitely making money," Reese said. "It's just that we're not seeing it. The trail to the bank is too long. We're so used to the money leaking away before it gets to us that we think that's the way it works. Well, it isn't. It's not supposed to be. I haven't yet determined how or who, but I know what, and so do you. We're getting screwed."

"That's what your father said, pretty much, and people were starting to believe him," Titus said.

Reese wagged a finger. "Listen, if Rick Marino and his partners can come out here and put up a casino and manage it themselves—hell, we're way ahead of them. We were here. We've *been* here."

"Their location is better."

"Yeah? By rights that whole . . ." Reese reined in his sweeping gesture toward the west, where, just down the road, the pale silhouette of the Black Hills appeared like a mirage. *By rights* didn't mean by law. "We've gotta go with what we've got."

"That's what they're saying about Ten Star."

"They *who*?"

"Sweeney and them."

"Titus, we haven't *got* Ten Star. Ten Star's got us. By the balls." Reese glanced at Dozer. "Unless the last of the Bad River balls got lopped off in that hit-and-run."

"No way," Titus said.

"I know I'm feeling a definite pinch, and I don't like it. I'm real fussy about who grabs me there." Reese grinned slowly. "And I just figured out what I'm gonna say."

Titus looked at Dozer. "We got women on the council. You think that argument's gonna go over with them?"

"Oh, yeah." Dozer bounced the headlight fragment in his palm. "In a big way."

The council chambers consisted of a large meeting room by Bad River standards. It was large enough to house the big meeting table, which was really several tables, and to provide seating for tribal members who wanted to listen in on the proceedings. The meeting started when everyone who was expected was there. Darius Three Legs announced that Ada Yellow Earring wouldn't be coming because she had to go out to Minneapolis with her mother-in-law, who was having that kidney trouble again.

Reese was sorry to hear about Ada's mother-in-law, but even sorrier to hear about Ada. She'd backed him at the last meeting when he'd asked for more time to look at competitive bids on the management contract. Or maybe he was the one backing her. She'd been on the council for several years. He had to stop thinking of himself as the play maker. He was changing a few minds, maybe taking advantage of the novelty factor, but the others around the table had been at this for a long time. *The ones who decide,* his father had called the council, a traditional name.

Reese had never considered himself to be a speaker, not like his dad was, but he decided he wasn't half bad after listening to Bill Darnell's presentation. Darnell's menacing delivery made a guy feel like punching him in the mouth and getting it over with. He claimed that Bad River had two fine casinos because Ten Star had come in and taken all the risks. Ten Star was a proven winner. As promised, they were training Bad River people to come into the business. Carter was sitting at Darnell's side as a prime example of Indian management. The council should be happy. Most management companies brought in their own general managers. Someday, Darnell said, the business would be Bad River-owned, Bad River-managed, but until that day came, Pair-a-Dice City and its smaller sister needed Ten Star.

When it was Reese's turn to question the speaker, he quoted his father's letter to the area superintendent of the BIA that complained about Ten Star's lease rate on the slot machines. Reese asked about buying out the machines. Darnell said they weren't for sale. Reese said he'd find some that were. Darnell kept glancing at Chairman Sweeney each time he repeated his refrain "That would not be a wise move."

Reese declared that approving Ten Star's proposal for a new five-year contract would be even less wise, a phrase that made him chuckle. "I hate to think we're down to picking the best of the least unwise. Leastwise, that's too damn many negatives for my blood."

Preston Sweeney announced a break. "An hour for dinner."

Carter stared at his brother, who was standing across the room like a mighty oak, being perched upon by his friend Titus Hawk and Councilwoman Hazel Red Bird, probably all atwitter over his clever shot. Who'd have thought the Big Gun would ever score with words?

"Let's go have a smoke."

Carter turned. Darnell was already smoking, out his ears,

but his eyes were as cold as ever. Carter had hoped to disappear after the presentation and let Darnell dig his own grave before the council. He might have saved the deal by agreeing to sell the slot machines. In all fairness, there should have been a buyout option on the lease, but when he'd pointed that out to Darnell and suggested giving the tribe a deal on them, Darnell had laughed and reminded him that this was not a charity operation.

They headed for Darnell's car, which was parked on the street under a shedding cottonwood. Darnell lit a cigarette, then stared at the front door of the tribal building as he spat smoke and measured out his fury.

"What the hell does he think he's doing? He's gonna flush this whole operation right down the toilet. Does he know that?"

"I don't know what he thinks or what he knows. I was surprised to see him at the meeting. I thought sure he'd . . ."

"He'd what?"

Carter shrugged. He'd seen Reese's car at Helen's this morning when he'd passed, on his way to the meeting. Scoring with more than words, was his big brother. Which was why he thought surely the man would . . . "Lose interest. I couldn't believe him, beating my father's old drum about the damn slot machines."

"I thought you said he burned your father's personal effects out of respect."

"Clothes and stuff. I didn't know what he burned. I didn't know what was over there besides ancient history."

"Every time your brother refers to his father's papers, it comes off sounding like pretty recent history. The leases on the slot machines, the percentage Ten Star has coming off the top."

"Nothing that hasn't been explained to them before."

"And agreed to by both sides so you people could get something going here. Your father caused us some problems, but your brother is a much bigger threat to us than an old man living in the past. Your brother's a big fuckin' hero."

Carter blew a long sigh. "I'll talk to him again." Nothing else he could say, but nobody was listening to him anyway. Not Reese, not Darnell. Not even Sarah.

"You'd better find something that works on him better than talk." Darnell stepped closer. "Look here, Ten Star has been taking good care of you all along."

"I know that."

"We've looked after you, Carter. We've looked after Sweeney, Sweeney's brother, Sweeney's secretary, who's also his cousin. We understand family values. Hell, we tried to help your father out, too, but we just couldn't find any way to please him."

Carter stared hard at those blue doors. He wasn't going to ask. He refused to think about that hit-and-run as anything but a hit-and-run. The bastard got away. Not a damn thing anybody was going to do about it. He didn't need to look Darnell in the eye when it was mentioned. He was scared enough already.

"You know you're all going to be in deep shit if Ten Star isn't here to take care of you anymore. What would you do without us?" Darnell took a deep pull on his cigarette. He didn't expect an answer. "I don't suppose you could think of a way we could please your brother?"

"I said I'd talk to him again," Carter said, and Darnell snorted. "You're not gonna bribe him, Bill, you know that."

"Bribe? Who said anything about bribing anyone?"

"I can maybe appeal to his—"

"Good business sense obviously won't cut it. He doesn't understand our business. Reason? Is he a reasonable man? Better yet, how about his personal life? I hear he's got a kid nobody knew about."

Carter stared at Darnell, surprised.

"Yeah, the kid told me. Said he'd just met his father, who appears to be back with the kid's mother, from what I saw when I met him at your house. This must have been quite a trip home for your brother."

"Women have been throwing themselves at Reese's feet for years. He's probably got a kid in every town that has an NBA franchise."

Darnell's mouth turned down as his brow went up. "Whatever. He's got kids, you've got kids. Hey, I've got *grand*kids.

You do what you gotta do to take care of your own. You understand what I'm saying?"

"Is 'threat' another word you're not saying?"

"I don't make threats, Carter, you know that. The people I work with know better than to approach that stage with me. I don't have to deliver an actual threat. It never comes to that." Darnell laid a heavy hand on Carter's shoulder. "You make your brother understand that as long as there's money in it, the management of this operation will be handled by Ten Star."

"I've got nothing over him."

"You'd better find something quick, because I've got plenty."

Carter wasn't sure what Darnell's notion of "plenty" was. He inspired plenty of fear in Carter because Carter had tasted the bait and climbed right into Darnell's ass pocket, thinking he was following the smell of money. Money for himself, for his family, for the tribe. It was big money, but he had a big job, and he was good at it. He deserved big money.

As the job had gradually taken on new dimensions, he'd adjusted. He'd had to, because he owed. Oh, how he owed. Now, suddenly, the smell was making him sick. Stink was what it was. But what could he expect, hanging around in some fat guy's ass pocket?

It was necessary to maintain the status quo. The casinos were doing well. Sooner or later the tribe would see more profit. Ten Star was part of some nebulous consulting business, and Carter knew it was connected. He wasn't sure how or to whom, but he knew Ten Star was a small piece of some larger picture. He knew Darnell wasn't making idle threats. And he knew he didn't want to die. He didn't want his family harmed. Sarah and the kids were on their way to Yakima by now. There was no way Darnell could touch them. Now all Carter had to do was talk some sense into Reese before he got himself or someone else killed.

He felt a little like a cat, pouncing on his brother when he came through the blue doors. "Wanna grab a sandwich with me?" he asked as he fell into step on the way to the graveled parking lot across the street. "I need to talk to you."

"Talk away," Reese said. He checked his watch. "I wanted to stop by Helen's and let her know—"

"You've gotta back off on this attack on Ten Star, Bro-gun."

"I'm not attacking Ten Star. I'm defending our right to . . ." They'd reached his car. "To mind our own business. Simple as that." Reese laid a hand on Carter's shoulder. "And you'd have to play a big part in that, Carter. You've got the education, the experience. The way I see it, you're our ace in the hole. One of them, at least."

"We're not ready to do this on our own."

"I'm not saying we don't need to hire people. What I don't like about Ten Star is that they don't seem to understand that they work for us. Their contract is up."

"They made a new bid."

"They're proposing to do business the same way they've been doing it in the past, and I'm saying it's time to look at new ways. *Better* ways, better for Bad River."

"Reese . . ." Carter had wedged himself between the big man and his car, and he felt trapped. He felt small. He tried not to sound desperate admitting, "I owe these guys."

"Owe them what?" Reese glanced away for a moment. The answer was obvious, and he obviously didn't want to hear it. But then he pinned Carter to the car with a look. "How much?"

"I don't even know anymore," Carter said honestly, and Reese rolled his eyes. "No, it's—it's not like that. It's more like a debt of conscience, you know? They've done a lot for me, given me . . . taught me; they've taught me a lot." He grabbed his brother's arm before Reese could step back in disgust. "And the thing about them is that, as long as we're all working together, we couldn't have better protection than Ten Star."

"Protection?"

"You know, from competing interests."

"Who else owes them besides you?"

"We all do. They got us started, and we gotta respect that." The remark drew a grunt of disagreement from Reese, who had pulled away now, folded his arms, taken an inaccessible stance.

Carter pressed him further. "You know, back when this

whole Indian gaming business got started, nobody expected us to build casinos. Most Indian reservations are out in the middle of nowhere. Bingo parlors, that's pretty much what people were thinking. But now we're big business. We've gotta do business the way this business is done." He tried to smile. "We're swimming with the sharks now, Bro-gun."

"Sharks in Bad River? Don't they need salt water?" Reese jeered, amusing himself enough to clap a hand on his brother's shoulder, friendly again. "We come from a landlocked country, little brother. What the hell would we be doing with sharks? Did we import them in a tank? Is that what those casinos are?"

"Seriously, Reese—"

"Maybe they smelled blood, huh? Or blood money. The old man used to say that Black Hills gold is pink because it's blood money. You believe that?"

"I believe we're doing business with guys who'll joke about blood before they'll joke about money."

"Man, they sure came to the wrong place, didn't they? Don't sit 'em at the table with the Indians, you'll have jokes"— Reese's big hands demonstrated ships passing—"sailing right past each other's ears, you know? Clinkers littering the floor, faces all granite." He was actually trying to get Carter to laugh, and Carter actually wished he could. "Sharks aren't gonna do well in our river, little brother."

"Right," Carter said with a sigh.

"If you owe these guys money, you come to me."

"You don't understand."

"It sounds to me like you're letting them play their game on your court."

"This is no game, Reese. That's what I'm trying to tell you, but you're just like the ol' man. I can't talk to you, can't . . ." Carter shook his head. Mistake to mention their father. Big mistake. "These guys don't play around."

Reese's eyes hardened. "What happened to Dad?"

"He got in the way of a truck." Carter took a step back, feeling as cold as the look his brother was giving him. "And I'm trying to drag you off the fucking road, Big Man."

* * *

Reese couldn't ask Carter who'd driven the truck. He didn't want the answer to come from Carter. He didn't want Carter to know. But Reese needed to know, and he understood that the answer wasn't going to come from the Bad River Tribal Police, not with guys like Gene Brown running scared.

Fortunately, Dozer Bobcat wasn't running. He was headed for a meeting with an FBI agent from Aberdeen. Reese would have gone with him if it hadn't been for the council meeting. He'd asked his friend to stick his neck out by taking Reese's find over the tribal police captain's head. "Drop my name if it'll help any," Reese had said with a laugh.

Dozer had told him it was no joke. He'd made Reese promise to meet him at the gym for Law and Order Hoops Night. "And bring your boy."

Reese liked that part. Bring *his* boy. He didn't have much time for lunch after Carter had pitched him Darnell's line, but he stopped in to ask Sid if he wanted to play basketball after supper. The boy did. And Helen offered Reese supper. Reese glanced at the little table and grinned. Family supper. He went back to the council meeting feeling like he was on top of the world. And he got enough votes to table the gaming committee's recommendation to award the management contract to Ten Star. All the doors were still open.

He told Helen and Sid about the meeting while they ate their spaghetti and the bread she had made from scratch. He left out the part about Carter and asked instead whether they'd spent the whole day cooking. They took turns recalling for him the things they had done: the visit to the school to see Helen's old classroom, the stop at the powwow grounds, deserted now that the celebration was over. At the mention of the powwow, Helen and Reese exchanged looks that were loaded with sweet memories.

"Mom said you guys went to the powwow," Sidney told Reese. "She said she got to meet some of your—some relatives."

"You will, too," Reese promised as he slid Helen a wink. "Tonight, probably be some cousins there. Here at Bad River, they're all around you. And we're always ready for a game of hoops, we Blue Skys." He grinned at his son. "If you don't overdo the noodles."

They took Crybaby for a short walk along the river after supper, enjoying the newness and the surprising ease of being three together, caring for the moment by not pushing into the future. It was too fragile for plans.

But when Sidney disappeared to get ready to go to the gym, the talk turned to intrigue. "What about this dealer who just quit?" Reese asked as he handed Helen the dinner plates he'd dried.

"Disappeared." She stowed the dishes in a cabinet. "Peter Jones. He was running a scam that should have been caught by Security. Carter should have seen it himself long before I told him about it."

"But you did tell him."

"I did." She sounded as though she shouldn't have. "He said he was going to bust him, but the guy didn't show up for work after that. He didn't exactly turn in his notice."

"Why do you think Carter missed seeing it? You think he wasn't paying attention?"

She shrugged, avoiding his eyes as she claimed two glasses from him.

"I want to know what you think, Helen. In your professional opinion, is my brother screwing his own people?"

"I don't know." She sighed as she set the glasses on the shelf, still withholding. She wouldn't let him see her eyes. "He's treading on thin ice."

"That's all you're gonna tell me?"

"I've told you all along that my job is spotting card scams. I work for the BIA, not the FBI, but they'll soon be involved." She turned to him now. "And I won't be."

"The FBI is supposed to be involved with finding out who killed my father. I guess you know we're pretty cynical about—"

"Government agencies and federal agents. I know, and with good reason. A long history of good reasons, going all the way back to Indian agents selling rations and letting children go hungry. And I won't say that's all *past* history. I understand it still plays its part. I understand better than most white people because the history affects me in a personal way." She leaned back against the edge of the sink, crossed her arms. "You know what this Indian Gaming Regulatory Act reminds me of? You're a student of history now, right?"

He smiled. "Just like you and the ol' man."

"Okay, bear with me, because this is a stretch. During the Middle Ages, the Jews in Europe were pretty much shut out of the mainstream economy because they couldn't own land. But the Church forbade moneylending, charging interest, so here was a business that feudal society said the Jews could have, and welcome to it. It was repugnant, sinful, and it didn't amount to all that much then anyway. Much like gambling."

She gave a graceful sweep of the hand. "Okay. Unofficially, America feels somewhat guilty about the taking of land, the reservation system, taking the children and marching them off to boarding schools—" She'd caught the look in his eye. "Yes, Reese, I know the reasoning behind the Indian Child Protection Act. Indian children were taken from their parents well into the 1960s, even the '70s; I know that. Adopted out, it was called recently, and certainly it wasn't always a bad thing. I mean, a good home can't be a bad . . ." She cast about, searching high and low for the compartments, good and bad.

They weren't there. They both knew that, but every time she backed off and said "Okay," she started looking for them again, arguing with herself. It amused him to watch her do it.

"Okay, okay. You're right. My people always think they know what's best for your people. But now that we have a son, it's more like *our*—well, at least—"

He churned the air with a rolling hand. "I'm still reaching for the 'much like gambling' part."

She recovered from her stammering so quickly it made him smile. When she was instructing, she hardly missed a beat.

"Well, of course, we keep trying to find ways to fix what we've done without giving up any significant part of what we've gained from it. In the 1980s, when high-stakes bingo began to spring up on the reservations, no one took notice except the churches. Some opposed it on some sort of moral grounds, and others—irony of ironies—said it was cutting into their Wednesday night fund-raisers."

"Then some California Indians decided to add slot machines," Reese recalled, "and the Supreme Court acknowledged that in states where gambling is legal, the Indians had the right."

Helen nodded. "When they passed the Indian Gaming Regulatory Act in '88, it was like all these Puritans in Congress saying, Okay, let's let them have gambling. It's repugnant and sinful, but it's a way for them to make a little money. It's a business we don't want flourishing in our backyards. Indian reservations were pretty isolated in their original design, so this sounded like a fine idea. It would be an extension of charitable gambling, right?"

"We could become America's favorite charity," he acknowledged, "if only we had a telethon."

"But the BIA was not prepared for the industry to spring up overnight. Suddenly the money was there for Indian enterprise because non-Indian businessmen, domestic and foreign, saw the potential for huge profits. And there were few regulations in place. So these casino management companies continue to make out like, well, one-armed bandits. But . . ." She laid a hand on his arm. "But, Reese, some of these people have no sense of humor."

"So I'm told."

"And there are many people—powerful, well-heeled people—who would like to see IGRA, the gaming act, repealed. Corruption in tribal government is good press for their cause. They can say, See? Just goes to show that we shouldn't have any laws that give unfair advantage to one group over—"

"Jesus, tell that to the oil companies. Mining companies, logging, how about—"

"I know." She nodded, smiling. Standing next to the sink, they could hear water running elsewhere. Sid was showering. "Men take their games seriously. Your father told a wonderful story about Iktomi, the spider, who challenged Coyote to a game, then laid down the rules and proceeded to cheat at every turn. When Iktomi collected the bet, Coyote said, 'Of course you won. You must be playing by different rules.' Iktomi said, 'Not only that, cousin. I'm playing a different game.'"

Reese laughed. He had forgotten the story, but he would file it away this time, and he would give credit when he used it. *This is what my father told my . . . wife.*

"So how long do you think the IGRA is good for?" he asked her, his secret thoughts spawning within him a secret smile.

Her smile was apologetic. "I'd say, don't put all your profits back into the casino business. Like your uncle Silo said—"

"What profits?"

"The profits you would be making if Ten Star were working for Bad River instead of for Ten Star."

"Or if people had listened to my father."

"They are." She put her hand on his T-shirt-covered chest, splayed her fingers, made his flat nipple jump to attention. But she went right on talking without even saluting. "They're still hearing his warnings, but now you've begun to add your voice to his, questioning some irregularities. These Ten Star people have a way of cushioning themselves, though, Reese. So in answer to your question about my professional opinion about—"

"Did I have a question?" He was a smiling, tingling, love-happy fool, no question. "Oh, yeah, waaay back there."

"About whether your brother is screwing his own people, a question for which there is no simple answer."

"No shit," he muttered, rolling his eyes, still smiling.

"Deep shit, actually. And if there's one thing I know for sure about being in shit that deep . . ." She frowned as she ran her fingertips over the neck band of his T-shirt, as though she wanted it to lay just so. "Screwing people is a side effect, but it's not what you're about. You're too busy treading shit, you see. That's all you can manage." Her eyes suddenly claimed his, and she finally smiled. "Have I just ruined my image?"

He grimaced. Not even the word belonged on his Helen's lovely lips. "But if I'd come along when you were treading . . ."

She laughed. "You would gag, choke, retch, *no dogs in my house.*"

"The hell," he said indignantly to Crybaby, who was lying on the floor a few feet away. "Would I say a thing like that? No way. I'd pull you out. I'd reach right down there, shit or no shit, wouldn't bother me."

She was laughing at him, shaking her head, rudely doubting his heroic boast. Had him laughing at himself.

"You want my answer or not?" she said, getting serious.

"I want your answer."

"I think it's very possible that, because of his debt, Carter's required to overlook operators like Peter Jones."

He glanced ceilingward, took a breath. "What about murderers?"

"That I don't know. Maybe he can't see what he doesn't want to see." She spoke quietly now, respectful of his worst fears about his brother's involvement, those he gave neither voice nor credence to. "I've reported Jones's disappearance," she said. "In fact, I'm waiting for a call on him. They're trying to find out who he is."

"Could you use his personnel file? If we can get our hands on it before somebody slips it into a shredder?" She nodded and so did he, with a wink and a promise as he traced the shoulder seam of her blouse with two careful fingertips. "I'm thinking if we can put the people you're working with in touch with the people who are supposed to be investigating my father's death, maybe one hand might be inspired by the other."

"The way mine are inspired by yours?"

He touched her chin, smiling. "How does that work again?"

A door opened on the other side of the apartment.

She answered, smile for smile. "Your son is out of the shower."

"Why did he think he had to take a shower before we go to the gym?"

"Because he's going with you. And he's very excited. And he wants to be clean. In the last six months *clean* has moved up on the priority list several notches."

"Maybe I should shower," he said, slipping his arm around her. "Do I smell okay?"

She laughed, closed her eyes, inhaled deeply. "You smell wonderful."

"You guys are way too weird." Their slick-combed and squeaky-clean son was ready to go. "What time do they start?"

"When everybody gets there, and we know of at least two guys still missing." Boldly Reese gave Helen a quick kiss. It was not the kiss he'd had in mind, but it was a kiss. "You're waiting for a call, right? Then you're coming over to the gym?"

She nodded. "If I'm not there by the time you're finished, come on back and we'll have some strawberry shortcake."

$\mathcal{R}$eese's high school alma mater had been remodeled for middle school. What was now "the old gym" had been available for public use since the new high school had been built, but when Reese was in school, it was *his* gym. The only gym. The first one in which he had dazzled basketball fans. His name was enshrined on plaque after plaque on the south wall, as Titus Hawk was quick to point out when Reese proudly introduced his son. He wanted to make a big deal of Sid, but Titus was too busy extolling Sid's dad. Reese noticed the boy's sudden shyness, and he realized that Titus's glib use of "your dad" hadn't quite clicked with him yet.

First chance he got—after he'd introduced Sid to his cousin John Bull and son, Glen—he grabbed Titus and buzzed in his ear while the Bulls asked Sid about the injured dog he'd brought in on a leash. "Don't make a big deal of all this stuff, huh?"

"What do you mean?"

"He's just getting used to me. You're calling me his dad— hell, he doesn't know what to call me. Haven't even heard him say my name yet."

"What do you want him to call you?"

"Whatever he's comfortable with. I want to be his father."

"You want him to call you Father? That might take some getting used to. I know I'd have trouble keeping a straight face." Titus punched him in the shoulder, and they both laughed. "Relax. Shouldn't be too hard for him to get used to being your kid. Now, if he'd just found out he was Dozer Junior, that might be a shocker."

Dozer deflected a ball somebody had lobbed across the gym as he approached them. "Somebody call my name?"

Reese surveyed the gym. Some guys were shooting baskets, others just arriving or coming out of the locker room, many of them wearing Law and Order sweats or T-shirts. This was going to be a big game. They'd have to run several lineups to give everyone a chance to play. He waved at Gene Brown, then clapped a hand on Dozer's back. "What I wanna know is, who's protecting our streets?"

"From what?" Titus scratched his chin, stroking his scraggly goatee. "We've got most of Bad River's baddest right here."

"I'm on duty, but even cops get breaks." Dozer tapped Reese's chest. "Hey, they know where I am. I've got my Dick Tracy two-way wristwatch right here, and if that fails . . ." He nodded toward Skeezix Ghost Horse, who was sitting on the wooden bleachers, elbows on knees, radio in hand. "Dispatcher."

"Did you hook up with the FBI?"

"I did. Turned the item over to the agent in charge. He'll be getting back to us. He said he could get a make on a vehicle, which would be a good lead. More than he had. I told him why I was delivering it personally. He said he understood where I was coming from." Dozer laughed. "What do you 'spose that means? Maybe he's paid us a visit?"

"You think he'll do anything?"

"I think if we don't hear right away, you and me both go see him. I dropped your name, but dropping your butt in his chair might be even better. Plus, Titus—" Dozer plucked Titus's shirt. "Tell Blue what you brought him, hey."

"Yeah, I've got that file you were asking about. Don't let me forget. It's out in the car."

"What, you just—"

"Lifted it right out of the drawer," Titus reported with a grin. "Didn't even have to be too sneaky. Hell, I'm on the gaming commission, man."

"I'll get it back to you," Reese promised.

"Hey, Gene!" Dozer elbowed Reese as the big man with the shaggy black mane ambled across the floor. "Don't say anything," Dozer muttered. "Just be friendly."

"Without saying anything?" Reese stuck out his hand. "Hey, Gene."

"Hey, Blue. Sorry about the ol' man."

Reese introduced Sidney, who was sticking close, hanging onto Crybaby for security.

"Jeez, you're gonna be as tall as your dad and a whole lot better-looking," Gene said as he shook Sid's hand. "Sorry about your grandfather."

"Thanks." Sid looked up at Reese, as though checking to see whether he'd done right by the condolence.

"We haven't given up on finding the sonuvabitch that—"

With a fierce snarl, Crybaby suddenly lunged, snapping the leash taut, hauling on Sid like a sled dog. Caught by surprise, Sid watched his arm shoot out in front like something that didn't belong to him as he was towed behind a yapping, snapping Crybaby. The dog bristled like a porcupine. Reese shouted at him, but the shepherd was fully focused on the man who'd just come out of the locker room.

Earl Sweeney was terrified. He scrabbled up the bleachers, hollering, "Whoa, whoa, mad dog! Get him away!"

Reese lent his son a hand, hauled back on the leash, and scolded Crybaby. "What the hell is wrong with you?"

Face drained of color, Sweeney waved a hand as he scuttled up one more level. "Get that mad dog—I'll kill him! I'll shoot the fucker!"

"He's okay," Reese assured the man despite Crybaby's bared canines and continued snarling. "He'll be okay."

But people were laughing. There was even a hoot and a

couple of howls. Sweeney glowered across the gym, glowered at the dog.

Gene Brown was holding his sides. "Damn, Sweeney, that dog sure don't like you much."

"He's a mad dog, that's why. Look at him!"

"I'm sorry, Earl. I don't know what got into him. I've never seen him do that before." Reese helped Sid get a firm grip on Crybaby before he approached the cowering man. "Did he bite you?"

"It's just you, Earl," Gene said gleefully. "You wearing your skunk oil tonight?"

"I'll take him out," Reese said.

"That's all right, just hold him back." Rather than stand up and walk, Sweeney slid to the near end of the bleacher seat, then skittered down like a crab. "That's all right. I wasn't gonna stay long anyway. Guess I won't stay at all. Guess I've got places to be." He shook a finger as he backed around the end of the bleachers. "But you'd better get a muzzle for that dog, Blue Sky. He's liable to bite somebody."

"He's had a series of traumas lately, Earl."

"Tumors, hell. He oughta be muzzled."

"Aw, now, look, you've got him crying," somebody said, and sure enough, Crybaby was whining, drooling, licking his chops. He wanted a piece of Sweeney.

"This is Blue's father's dog," Gene said. "He was there when we found him, Sweeney, remember? Watching over the body and watching that gate."

"Did he go after you then?" Reese wanted to know.

But Sweeney was making a beeline for the side door, humiliated by the laughter and showing no interest in Gene's recollections or Reese's questions.

"Nah, he didn't go after anybody that night, but Sweeney's scared shitless of dogs, and they can smell it on him," Gene said as he let Crybaby sniff his hand. Once he had the shepherd's approval, he scratched his head. "This is quite a dog. He knows his job. That night he wasn't letting those horses out of the pasture, no way."

"The gate was open?" Reese sat down on the bench, glanced at Sid—who was all ears since he hadn't heard anything about how his grandfather's body had been found—then peered at Crybaby. "There was no stock out, I was told. No reason for him to be out on the road."

"There wasn't any stock out, but there would have been if it wasn't for this dog." Crybaby whimpered, and Gene scrubbed his head some more.

"But the gate was open," Reese repeated.

"I closed it, yeah." Crybaby licked Gene's hand. "I don't blame you, boy. You're a hell of a dog, and Sweeney's a sorry excuse for a cop, so . . ." Gene looked at Dozer. "But I guess I am, too."

"Yeah, but you're not a bad guard," Dozer said. Gene frowned a little, and Dozer indicated the basketball court. Gene gave a wan smile.

"Dozer," Reese said, signaling with a jerk of his head that it was time for a two-man huddle. Crybaby wanted to come, too. "Sid, hold onto him. He won't do that again."

"You sure?"

"He'll be fine. Gene, introduce my son to—" Reese gestured toward the court. "We're gonna have a game here in just a minute."

"What's up, Blue?" Dozer wanted to know when they reached the cove the partially opened bleachers provided.

"Your break time," Reese said. He glanced at the EXIT sign above the door Sweeney had used. "I'm betting a crime's about to be committed, but if you hurry, I think you can catch him in the act." He pointed at Crybaby with a chin jerk. "You're looking at the sweetest dog this side of the river, Dozer."

"The Bad River? We've got some mean rez dogs—"

"He ain't one of them. Now, why do you suppose he'd be trying to eat Sweeney's liver?"

"Sweeney?" The answer dawned in Dozer's dark eyes. "Swee-neeey."

"Whoever it was, he came up empty the last time. But now I'm here, and the dog's here. And we're gonna be here for a while, along with most of the Bad River police. And Sweeney's got places to be."

"You're right, Blue. Damn, I just bet you're right." Dozer

checked his watch. "According to my Dick Tracy watch, my break time's up."

"Maybe you'd wanna take somebody else?"

"Hell, yes, you can ride along. This could turn out to be more fun than—"

Reese saluted his friend, fist to fist. "This is your game, *kola*. Yours and Gene's."

"Gene?" Dozer glanced at the other cop, down on the floor now with the dog, while Sid stood next to them, looking a little lost. "Good idea. Damn, you'd better be right, Blue. I was gonna play on the other side to keep you from scoring."

Reese grinned. "I'm playing for my son tonight. Nobody's gonna keep me from scoring."

And hardly anyone did. Soon after Dozer and Gene left, the visiting players were assigned to teams and the game began with a tip-off. Reese played for a good time, played for the old times, played for the joy and the camaraderie. For the sake of all those things, he played the facilitator. He fell naturally into the role of coach, getting everyone into the act, all ages, all skill levels. Inclusion was his gift. But because he was Reese Blue Sky, he was expected to perform, and he couldn't disappoint. He couldn't resist throwing in the occasional professional moment, the move no one on the floor could match. He played to entertain, always had, because he had always understood what he was getting paid for.

But this time it felt different. For the first time in his life, he knew his son was watching. His heart thrilled when he caught the look on his son's face after Sid watched him snake his way to the basket, handling the ball as if he'd cast a spell, pulling a trick out of the bag that still hadn't come up empty, sinking an impossible shot. He'd done it for Sid.

"Blue Sky is *in* the house!" Titus shouted the moment Reese's feet touched the floor.

Yeah, he sure was, and he looked right at his kid, who was in the house with him. His kid was dazzled.

When the teams changed, the two sat side by side on the bench and shared Reese's bottled water. Reese's hair and T-shirt were wet from his exertion. Sidney glowed with kid dew. He made a project of petting the dog, but Reese could feel the looks he was getting from the boy, the unabashed staring that was rude in his culture.

"Didn't your daddy teach you not to stare?" He tried to let the boy know with a look that he was teasing, inviting, and explaining all at once. "Indian people don't—"

Sidney dropped his chin to his chest and kept on petting the dog, but Reese saw the sudden flush of embarrassment.

"Hey, I was just kidding." He squeezed his son's shoulder, rocked him gently. "What's on your mind, Sid? The way you've been looking at me, you gotta be thinking up a storm."

"Just watching you play is so amazing. You're so good." The boy looked up, still red-faced. "I'm just thinking I can't believe you're my father, and I'll never be that good."

"You might be better, if that's what you want, but you don't have to be. You like the game? Great. Enjoy it. Play it with me for fun."

"You looked at me funny when I missed that easy shot."

"Did I? Show me how I looked at you."

Sidney re-created a slightly pained grimace.

"Get outta here," Reese said with a laugh, rocking the kid's shoulder again. "I looked like that? Must have been gas, huh?" He'd seen some version of that expression on another Blue Sky face, and he had to wonder, now that the tables were turned. Maybe it hadn't meant quite what he'd felt it meant. "You ever see that look on my face, you flash it right back at me."

The boy nodded, then flashed the look. They both laughed as Sidney attended to the dog again. Reese had been right about his son and the dog. They were a natural pair.

But what about . . .

"Don't you want to believe I'm your father, Sid?"

"It's just too unreal. You know, watching you."

"I kinda feel the same way, but I think we'll get real after a while, don't you?"

The boy shrugged. "You're still really good. Why did you retire so young?"

"It's a long story, and I'll tell you about it when we have more time. Okay? I'll tell you everything you wanna know if you'll return the favor. Because I've got a lot to learn about you." He glanced at the clock, then turned and signaled to the man a few bleachers up. "Hey, Skeez, have you heard anything from Dozer since he left?"

Skeezix shook his head, froze, lifted a finger—wait a minute. His radio was squawking to him. "Hold on, here's . . ." He listened for a moment. "He's out to your place, Blue. Possible break-in in progress, sounds like."

"Good."

Skeezix did a double take. "Good?"

"Good timing." Reese laughed, then affected a *Dragnet* voice as he turned to Sid. "Don't worry, son. Dozer Bobcat's on the case."

Dozer killed his headlights and radioed in, reporting that he was investigating a complaint and he'd be back with the specifics. He'd already asked Gene flat out if he'd have any problem turning Earl Sweeney in if they caught him in the act. Gene was a little confused until Dozer told him about the earlier break-in and the attack on Blue's dog. Gene was tired of Earl's throwing his weight around anyway, but it was the part about the dog that really got to him. He sure liked that mutt.

Dozer eased the dark patrol car onto the Blue Sky approach. He was counting on Blue's new air-conditioning for some white noise inside the house. When they got close enough to identify Sweeney's pickup, Gene's face lit up as if he were the kid who'd just tagged home base.

Then it clouded over again.

"We gotta catch him in the act of doing something he can't worm his way out of," Gene said. "He could be checking something out here. Maybe he was driving by, and he thought he saw a prowler." Dozer gave him a get-real look, and Gene shrugged. "Well, you know he's ready with some excuse if Blue comes home."

"He cut the screen before."

"He'll say it was already cut. You don't think he'd actually go in through a window, do you? *Earl?* Hell, he was just makin' it look good."

"Don't look too good right now," Dozer remarked as he slid out of the patrol car and eased the door shut.

The back door was open. Dozer signaled Gene to cover it while he circled the house. He saw a flashlight in use in one of the back rooms. He decided to send Gene to the front door, and he took the other one, the probable exit. They waited. Dozer was beginning to worry about what Sweeney might be up to—possibly messing with something important—when Gene appeared at the corner of the house.

Dozer motioned him closer. "What the hell is he doin' in there?"

"Sweeney's such an asshole, he's probably takin' a crap in the middle of his damn burglary," Gene whispered. He scanned the length of the house, caught a glimpse of light.

"Maybe we should go in."

"I'll go see what I can see through that front bedroom window. The ground's higher on that side." Gene returned in little more than a heartbeat. "Holy Christ, he lit a match!"

"Goddamn, we're going in. Take the front." Dozer gave Gene a few seconds to get into position before he entered through the back door. "Police! We know it's you in there, Sweeney. Put out the damn—" Dozer could hear the scrambling at the other end of the house. He smelled the smoke. "There's no way out except through me."

It was too dark to see who was barreling down the hallway, but the voice yelling "Fire!" was unmistakable. Dozer knew the house and remembered a trick Reese had used on him when they'd been chasing each other in the dark: fake left, jump right, throw the pantry door open behind you.

Ka-boom!

In the dark, Sweeney ricocheted around the kitchen like a ball on a bumper pool table, colliding with the pantry door first, then falling back against the refrigerator before he toppled over a table, taking what sounded like the whole room down with him. Dozer hit the lights just as Gene hurled himself through the door.

Dozer tossed him a set of handcuffs and started toward the bedroom. "Arrest him. He set the place—"

It wasn't much of a fire yet, but enough smoke to sting a guy's eyes and set him coughing to beat hell. Flames were just beginning to curl around a pile of folders and papers in the middle of the bed in the back room. Dozer flopped the blanket over on itself, then beat on it with a towel. He finished it off with a wastebasket full of water from the bathtub. He opened a couple of windows and turned the air conditioner in the other bedroom on Exhaust before he headed back to the kitchen.

Gene had gotten Sweeney on his feet and cuffed his hands behind him. "Says he was just lighting a cigarette in there when you scared the shit out of him, Doze."

"What cigarette?" Dozer wiped his face on his sleeve. "All I saw was a bunch of what looked like mail and papers."

Eyes popping and jaw jacking up and down, Sweeney looked the same as he had when the dog had cornered him. "I saw something . . . somebody . . ."

"What I saw was you setting a fire back there, Sweeney. Now, you've got a right to remain—"

"Don't start that shit with me," Sweeney croaked. "This ain't funny, now; take these damn cuffs off."

"Are you gonna try to tell us our eyes deceived us?" Dozer challenged as he surveyed the mess on the kitchen floor. A sheet of plywood with chicken wire and broken green plaster, a bunch of toy horses, and all kinds of little men were scattered across the room. He didn't know what this had been, maybe something for Blue's new kid. He shook his head and turned to Sweeney. "Why didn't you answer when I told you who it was?"

"You're trying to trap me. You set me up, didn't you?"

"Are you nuts? Why would we be setting you up? You set yourself up, you asshole."

"It wasn't me," Sweeney claimed.

Dozer and Gene looked at each other and laughed.

"You can't prove anything, and I've got nothin' more to say."

"That's fine by me. Proving comes later, anyway," Dozer said as he opened the back door and signaled Gene to bring the prisoner through. "It's the hauling you in that's the fun part."

"My brother isn't gonna like this."

Gene laughed again.

"I don't imagine he will," Dozer said.

Hauling Sweeney in was definitely the fun part. It brought a lot of wide-eyed stares at the police station, generated several what-the-hells, both silently mouthed and loudly voiced. Sweeney cursed them roundly, but they booked him anyway. He insisted on calling his brother before they put him in a cell. Dozer called the gym and told Skeezix to tell Reese that his house had in fact been broken into again, but this time they had a suspect in custody.

Reese dropped Sid and Crybaby off at Helen's, along with the personnel file Titus had provided on the elusive Peter Jones, whom Helen suspected of being part of a card scam. But so far, according to her superiors, there was no Peter Jones. He was not licensed as a dealer with anybody anywhere. She said the photograph of the man would be especially helpful.

Reese promised to stop back after he paid a visit to the police station. And when Sid overheard the bit about a break-in, he was dying to go with him. But Reese didn't figure this particular excursion to be the best way for the boy to get acquainted with his roots.

Dozer and Gene took Reese back to the drunk tank, which was where they had put Earl Sweeney. The padded cell was separate from the block, so it afforded him some privacy. More consideration than he deserved, Gene said on the way down the hall, but he was a fellow cop.

Sweeney sat cross-legged on the mat on the floor, which was all the drunk tank provided other than a toilet. He looked up at the three men, one at a time, letting each read the contempt in his eyes. He leveled the bulk of it at his partner, Gene, who turned it around like the refection in a mirror.

Dozer wasn't one to waste an opportunity to salt a genuine jerk's wounds.

"I don't know why anybody'd be trying to burn a bunch of mail and a bed, unless it was love letters. Damn it, Blue, have you been leadin' poor ol' Earl on?"

Reese knew about the fire, but he hadn't heard about the bed. "He set my new bed on fire?"

Dozer shook his head. "Didn't look too new."

"My dad's bed?" Reese grabbed one of the cell bars, leaned closer, peered at the prisoner in disbelief. "What, Earl, you're trying to help me out, burning his stuff? You did this out of respect, right?" He glanced over his shoulder at Dozer. "The old way, I would have torched the house. Earl must be more traditional than I am. He was offended by my pitiful half-assed ceremony." He turned back to the brown bug on the floor mat. "Right, Earl?"

"I ain't sayin' nothin' till my brother gets here."

"What you were after wasn't there, Earl, so you made an ass out of yourself for nothing," Reese said. Sweeney challenged him with a stare. "My father's papers, *Earl*. They're not at the house. See, I committed his records and ramblings to memory. I know it all by heart." He chuckled as he spread his hand over his chest. "So I guess you'll just have to get rid of me."

"Ain't tryin' to get rid of nothin'," Earl spat. "There was somebody prowling around your place. Somebody broke in again, and it wasn't me."

"Again?" Reese looked at Dozer. "*Again?*"

Dozer shrugged innocently.

"What's this all about?" Preston Sweeney demanded as he rounded the corner, ready to take over. He pointed an imperious finger at his caged and downcast brother. "Keep your mouth shut, Earl. You're digging yourself in deeper." The finger arced forty-five degrees. "Dozer, you tell me why you've got my brother locked up."

Dozer was more than happy to step up to the plate and tell the story, judiciously omitting any mention of the game plan he'd made with Reese.

"Okay, look, it's obviously a big misunderstanding," Preston said, converting the emperor's tone to the politician's. "I tell you what, Blue, this guy worships you. Now, I don't know what he thought he was doing—"

"Investigating—"

"Shut up, I said!" Preston barked. Then, down a notch, "You're being stupid, Earl." And for Dozer, Sweeney did a quarter turn, lowered his voice another notch. "That's all it is. Just Earl being stupid. He'll pay for any damage he caused."

Finally, for Reese's benefit, another quarter turn as he became the picture of reason. "You don't wanna press any charges here, Blue. You've got a brother, I've got a brother. They both make mistakes, but this one, sounds like these guys got there before it got out of hand."

Preston was so slick, such an artful shape-shifter, that Reese was truly tempted to applaud.

"I'd say breaking into my house and setting the bed on fire was Earl being stupid. But shooting my dog—"

"You can't prove—" Earl met Reese's cool glare with childish hostility. "I *will* shoot that sonuvabitch the next time!"

"Shut up, Earl," Preston said with a sigh. "Like I said, Blue, this guy's worshipped you since day one, and I don't think that's always healthy. Who knows what he was looking for? Maybe a souvenir."

Dozer nearly gagged.

Preston turned his back on the cell, blocking Dozer and Gene for a one-on-one with Reese.

"Listen, we've both got brothers. Yours is a hell of a lot smarter than mine, and it takes a smarter man than Earl to commit any real serious crime, you know what I'm saying? But he's the only brother I've got." He lifted his head, kept his gaze and his voice steady. "A man has to look after his own."

"Does he really," Reese said tonelessly, but he was thinking he had to hand it to the little twerp. He had balls. Conveniently located at Reese's knee level.

"Damn straight." Preston stepped back quickly and buttoned his sport jacket, as though he'd caught somebody ogling him.

Reese laughed.

"You can just sit here for tonight, Earl," the tribal chairman said as he moved away. "Tomorrow you can tell me what the hell you thought you were doing, walking into Reese Blue Sky's house and playing with matches. Right now, I don't wanna hear it. It's bound to embarrass me."

Preston Sweeney gave Reese a parting look, an unmistakable warning, before he took his leave.

"What happened to the evidence you found when my dad

was killed?" Reese asked Gene as they left the building with Dozer, headed for separate vehicles.

"They said it was nothing, and maybe—"

"Who's *they*? The Sweeneys?"

The three men stood on the corner of the quiet street. Under the streetlight, big Gene's chagrin took on a soft, sad glow. He hung his shaggy head, shoved his hands in his pockets. Reese wanted to tell him to forget it, go in peace.

But he couldn't do that without first asking, "Do you think it was off the pickup that hit him?"

"I don't . . ." Gene shrugged. "Probably. But it's gone now. You get to thinking sometimes that there's no justice anyway, so . . ." His eyes were glistening. "Well, you gotta hold onto what you got, you know? You try to say, 'Hey, I think I got something here I found in the grass,' and they say, 'What you got don't mean jack. If you're smart, you'll forget it.' Which oughta be easy, you know? Be smart, play dumb." He pressed his lips together and glanced away, into the dark where the cottonwoods rattled in the night breeze and the crickets hummed peacefully.

Go in peace.

"I make some dumb-ass moves sometimes," Gene said.

Reese clapped a hand on the big man's shoulder. "Who doesn't?"

Gene smiled sadly. "Nobody ever thought you did, Blue, but a guy's gotta wonder. What's Reese Blue Sky going to council meetings in Bad River for when he could be living the high life out in Minneapolis?"

"I thought I owed my father." Reese lifted a shoulder. "I think it's more like I owed myself. I'm here for myself." He squeezed Gene's upper arm. "Just like what you did tonight. You did that for Gene Brown. The one who couldn't carry a badge if he'd really given up on justice."

"Oh, yeah," Dozer chimed in, grinning. "Damn, that's . . . man! You gonna run for a full term, Blue?"

"You'd like that, huh?" Reese elbowed Dozer, and they all laughed. Then, to Gene, "Tell you what, if every guy who ever made a dumb-ass move decided to let that be his signature play, we'd all be go-to-hell."

"Yeah, well . . . I used to be a pretty good cop, you know? But they got all these damn procedures now, I don't know whether I'm comin' or goin' half the time."

"Neither does your ol' lady," Dozer said.

"Listen, before this gets too deep here . . ." Reese nodded over his shoulder at the police station. "I don't know if we can make any charges stick, but I'm pressing."

"Full court, huh?"

"Full court pressure."

"Hot damn." Dozer clapped his hands and rubbed them together. "I'm on duty, so I'd better get back to your house and gather up the evidence."

"I'll be there soon as I check in with—" The guys were both looking at Reese like he'd said he had to ask permission. He laughed as he started across the street toward his car. "Hell, you gotta let 'em know whether you're comin' or goin'."

"Hey, Blue," Dozer called out. "I really liked that part about not giving up on justice. I never knew you could talk so pretty."

Reese crossed the street still laughing.

Helen and Sid were watching TV, but he could tell they'd been waiting for him. He liked that. He wished he didn't have to turn around and leave right away.

"Would you mind keeping Crybaby with you tonight?" he asked his son. "I have to go out to the house with Dozer and try to help him figure out what Earl Brain-In-His-Butt was messing around with."

"Sure," Sid said, but he liked his idea better. "Unless you want me to go with you and help. I saw your house from the outside. Is it a ranch? We drove by it on the way to Wall Drug, and I saw the sign for . . ." He looked down at the dog sitting by his feet. "The Blue Sky sign." With his grandfather's name on it.

"On the way to Wall, huh?" Reese flashed Helen a knowing smile. A little out of her way. "You can see the place tomorrow. Dozer wants to snoop around some more, and I don't know what kind of a mess it is now." He put his hand on the boy's shoulder. "But thanks for the offer."

"It was that guy Crybaby tried to tear into? He tried to set your house on fire?"

"Sure looks that way." Reese squatted next to the dog, checked his bandage—looked as though the shepherd had done a little chewing—and scratched his belly. "Tomorrow we'll change this. You keep him close, okay? Your mom's all for keeping dogs in the house anyway, and he's a good watchdog. If he has to go out, he'll cry. If he's hungry, he'll cry. If he's thirsty, he'll cry. He's a big baby. Aren't you?" He ruffled Crybaby's ears.

"Not if he sees somebody he doesn't like," Sid said.

"That jackass is out of commission for tonight." Reese eyed his son. "You keep this guy close." The dog whined. "That means he's gotta go out. But you stay—"

"Close, I know. Come on, boy."

After the door whacked shut, Reese turned to Helen. Wordlessly he took her in his arms and held her, inhaling deep gulps of Helen-in-lilacs, inviting her scent to live in him, be the breath within his body. He felt bad about the ballplayer smell he shared in trade as she snuggled underneath his chin, but she didn't seem to mind. She slid her hands up his back, hugged him close, made him forget why in hell he was planning to leave her now.

Then he noticed the file he'd given her earlier, lying on the lamp table.

"Did you find out where this Jones came from?"

"I'd really like to know where he *went*." Reluctantly she withdrew from his embrace and reached for the file. "This has a lot of holes in it. He's worked at a number of casinos, but he doesn't seem to stay very long. His license hasn't been approved, so I don't even know why Carter would let him deal. But the good part is . . ." She waved a mug shot under Reese's nose. "We have a photograph. I tried to get him in a group picture a few weeks ago. I was—well, it's part of my job."

"Dealing face cards," he said with half a smile.

"Sometimes they can pick up on a known con with a picture, or, as in this case, the picture might come in handy later if the person skips out."

"*They* meaning . . ."

"The agency," she said matter-of-factly. "Usually I can get people to pose when I tell them it's for my memory book, but Jones wouldn't be charmed."

"The man is definitely suspect," he said, looking at the stringy hair in the picture, the half-mast eyes, obviously half blind if he was unreceptive to Helen. "I don't know how deep the Sweeneys are into all this, but right now, I can count the people I really trust on one hand. Well, maybe two. No more than that." He put his arm around her again. "How about you?"

"I'm down to three fingers. You're this one." She tapped his chest with her index finger.

"When does Sid go back? Day after tomorrow?" He closed his hand around her finger, enveloping her hand as well. "I'd feel better if you were both getting out of here right now."

"I have a part to play here, too, Reese. It's a small piece of the puzzle, but I think it might just be a corner piece."

"We'll get him back to camp, safely out of the way, and then we can fit our pieces together. See if we can make some—"

Sid pushed the door open and followed Crybaby inside.

Reese cleared his throat. "Did he take care of business for you?"

"Yeah." The boy had gone sulky.

"Tomorrow you'll come out, and I'll have all kinds of stuff to show you. Your mom says you like horses? Wait'll you see Blackjack and—can you believe a horse named Jumpshot?"

"I guess."

"What's wrong, Sid?" Reese laid a hand on his shoulder. "Hey, I gotta tell you. Playing ball tonight with you there at my old gym?" Sid looked up, guarding himself but hopeful. "It was great. I've never enjoyed a game more than I did tonight."

18

*D*ozer collected what was left of the burned articles as evidence while Reese shook his head in wonder. With each charred chunk of junk mail, bills, and bank statements that Dozer bagged, they looked at each other and laughed. "Maybe this was part of Earl's plan to win one of these sweepstakes this year," Dozer suggested. "Destroy the competition."

"I doubt the ol' man ever entered," Reese said. "Probably kept the stuff thinking he would. Everybody's got plans."

Reese figured the references he had made to his father's records during the council discussions must have aroused somebody's interest in the collected works of Roy Blue Sky. Apparently *somebody* wasn't much of a reader.

"Earl couldn't find what he was looking for right away, is what it looks like to me," Dozer said. "So he decided that burning the place down would have to take care of it. That works, huh?"

"It would if what he was looking for was here," Reese said with a wry smile. "And if you guys weren't."

"I ain't afraid of them slippery Sweeneys. If push comes

to shove, bet you anything Preston walks away and leaves his brother with his ass in the skillet."

"Ouch! You don't think he'll *take care of his own*?" Reese asked, mimicking Preston.

"Well, sure, his own ass." They'd moved to the kitchen. Dozer knelt to gather a few little plastic people off the floor. "I'm sorry about this mess, Blue. What is this, anyway?"

"This? This is a famous battlefield." Reese squatted next to the battered plywood model, standing on end against the wall. "You know which one? Give you a hint, Doze." He ran his finger along the blue-gray river of painted plaster. "The Lakota warriors said this was a good day to die, and then they headed across the river and kicked ass."

"Little Bighorn," Dozer answered as he extended a handful of soldiers and braves. "Damn that Earl, he busted up the whole camp here."

Reese plucked from Dozer's brown palm a blue-and-gold cavalryman, his legs bowed as if he'd gone into rigor mortis astride his horse. "They wore our old school colors," he said, and Dozer snickered. Reese rubbed the tiny leg between his thumb and forefinger, making the figure twirl back and forth. "This mob came into the valley with their guns."

"Mob?"

"Organized. This was going to be an organized crime. Custer was out to kill Indians, plain and simple. This was about gold."

"They wanted the Hills."

"Damn right. They always talk about the numbers, how the Indians outnumbered the soldiers, but the soldiers only had themselves to think about. These guys," Reese said as he picked up a small plastic tipi and a couple of Indians wearing red and yellow feathers. "Look at all the people these guys had to look after, right here within range of those guns. This is how you earn some serious bragging rights for looking after your own."

"They gotta be lookin' down the barrel of a gun with you?"

"It kinda ratchets the risk factor way up there. It's a lot simpler when it's just you."

"In your experience?"

"In my . . . pitifully limited experience." Reese braced

hands on knees and stood. "How soon will we know something about that headlight piece?"

"*They* might know something now," Dozer said, rising to his feet. "How soon will *we* know? When they get around to telling us."

"That's not good enough, Dozer. Whoever murdered my father could be sneaking around the coulees here, setting up to do more damage. It's all tied up with this casino business, and so is Helen, so is Carter, so is Titus, so are the Sweeney brothers, so is the council." Reese's gestures reflected his frustration. "We don't know who to defend and who to go after. We need to dog those damn Feds until we get answers."

"I'm just the Bobcat to do the dogging, Blue. I'm your hound."

"I've got a hound." Reese clapped a hand on his friend's back. "You're more like a brother, you and Titus. Seemed like I almost forgot."

"It's good to have you back. You don't have to stay forever. We Lakota, we kinda like to move our camp from time to time." Dozer tipped his hand to pour Indians and soldiers into Reese's palm. "Always glad to have you back."

Dozer had helped him clean up most of the mess. His father's passion for the old days was scattered from hell to breakfast, but he wasn't about to toss it. His son hadn't seen it yet, and maybe they could repair the thing.

Reese stared at the familiar water-stained ceiling in his bedroom and remembered the times when he was a kid and cleaned up after the old man. Broken dishes, ashtrays, and flat beer, a smell he detested to this day. He'd gotten it down to a science: pitch the rubble, sweep and mop, go out and shoot hoops, get out of the old man's way. There had been no repairs back then. There had been changes, but no repairs.

Iktomi once persuaded the Elk Nation to adopt him, but the foolish one was such a pain in the ass, sounding his crybaby alarm every time he barely scratched himself, that the Elk Nation struck camp and moved one night without telling him. The foolish one woke up the next morning and found that he was alone.

Did you do that, old man?

313

I did what I did. I felt sorry for myself.

But you changed.

Did I?

Apparently.

Apparently. Apparently Iktomi set my bed on fire.

Reese laughed aloud. He and Dozer had aired the place out and removed the burned mattress, but he could still smell the smoke. He lay on his new bed, his long, bare body cooled by his new air-conditioning, watching a muted television and listening to CDs. Turning off the sound on the TV was an old habit. There was nothing he wanted to hear on late-night TV, yet the shifting images created the illusion that there were people close by.

He'd taken his contacts out, so the figures had fuzzy faces. Nice figures, though. It was an old musical flick, and the dancers were now tapping and twirling totally out of sync with Thelonius Monk's piano on the CD he had playing. Wee-hours-of-the-morning music, the kind that reminded him of hotel rooms with big windows overlooking cities that all looked the same. He remembered those faraway echoes, distant lights, watching the clock, breathing refrigerated, recirculated, regurgitated air, waiting for the next move. Mostly looking forward to it. He hadn't always waited alone, but he'd felt alone often enough, even if he'd had company in bed.

We like to move our camp from time to time.

Early in the morning the camp would smell of smoke from a fire gone dead, but there would be no music. And the people close by would not be an illusion. They would be family, people who belonged together in the intimate hours before daylight, within steps of each other, or, better yet, side by side.

The huge red numbers on the bedside clock taunted him. It was either too late or too early. They were miles away, and the doors were locked on his new family of three.

New family?

Newly discovered. *Re*discovered, but not if he dwelled on his losses. Maybe "recovered" was the word he was looking for.

I'm recovered. Finished in the world you know, all done, all complete.

It's just a word. Recovering, then.

Like this? You've been doing it this way for years. Cool stud with his cool cash, cool music, cool air blowing all around a big Blue Sky.

Reese laughed aloud.

Big cool lonesome. What's funny about that? I never thought it was too funny. A moment ago you dared to think about being part of a family.

Yeah, but they're all asleep, all safe. Let them . . .

Do I have to send Iktomi to light a fire under you?

He had to knock at the door where his family slept. Inside, Crybaby answered with a devoted whine. Reese tipped his head back and smiled at the fading night sky. A waning, pale white moon winked at him.

Helen came to the door in a nightgown as white as the one the moon wore, and his first thought was that he'd never seen this woman in a nightgown. She was the mother of his twelve-year-old son, and he'd never seen her in a nightgown. Not that he didn't have immediate visions of peeling it off her, but the delicacy of the garment touched him, the feel of cotton worn soft by her sleeping body.

But all thought dissipated when she reached for him, took him in her arms, and held him close again.

"My place smells like smoke. I'm sorry to . . ." He lifted her off the floor as he kissed her hungrily. "No, I'm not," he whispered. "I'm not sorry to wake you. I could say I didn't realize how late it was, but that would be a lie, too."

"I'm glad you're here." She hugged his neck, rested her chin on his shoulder, her feet dangling above his. "How bad was the damage?"

"Not too bad." As he carried her across the dark room to the sofa, he nuzzled the hair curling softly against her neck until his lips found skin to kiss. "Good ol' Earl performed a bed-burning, is all."

"And he intended to . . ."

"Burn the house down, I guess," he said, sitting her in the corner of the sofa as though he were putting a child down. " 'Course, he says he was after a prowler, but even he knows how ridiculous that sounds, so he'll be counting on his brother to get him out of it."

He sat beside her and started pulling off his boots, getting comfortable. "It all seems too outrageous to even talk about. I hate like hell for Sid to walk into this, Helen. I mean, here he is for the first time, and he wants to see his grandfather's house, and this asshole of a cop breaks in, sets fire to the place."

"We're on the right track, Reese," she said as he draped his arm around her shoulders. She cuddled against his side in the cool, sleepy half-light of early morning. "They're getting nervous."

"You wanna know the truth? I'm getting nervous."

"I know."

"I'd like nothing better than to walk away and forget the whole mess. Get out while the gettin's good, head back to Minneapolis, all three of us. Okay, four," he amended as Crybaby flopped on the floor near his feet. "We could have a good life there together, Helen. Right now, today."

"Before we have all the answers?"

"Before we dig up any more shit." He stretched out his legs, propped them up on the coffee table. Beyond the screened window a dove cooed, gently welcoming the new day. "I've got a beautiful place there, honey. You're gonna love it. It overlooks a lake. It's—" She was looking up at him, and he felt her stiffen up a little. "Hey, if you don't love it, we'll sell it. No problem. We'll pick out something—"

"I'm sure you have a wonderful home, Reese, and I'd love to—"

"It's not a home. It's just a place to stay. *You* have a home, you and Sid."

"We have an apartment, and it isn't fancy. In fact, it's pretty basic."

"You have each other," he reminded her. "You wanna head West instead? I'm ready."

"Okay." She leaned her knees on his thigh and tucked her bare feet up behind her on the sofa. "Coffee first?"

"Sex first. Then coffee." He caressed her cotton-clad thigh and her sweet round bottom. "Then we spend the day with

Sid, doing whatever he wants to do before *he* heads West."
He turned his lips to her forehead. "I'd feel better if you were
going with him."

"You would?"

He groaned. "I'd feel miserable, but I'd know you were
going to be safer there than you are here, and that's what
I want."

"Nobody wants to harm me. Nobody shot my dog and set
my house on fire." She sighed. "I'd like to send *you* to camp
with Sidney. Wouldn't those boys just love that? Then you'd
both be safe, and I could wrap up my investigation." She
clutched a handful of T-shirt over his flat belly, repeating the
important part. "And you'd both be safe."

"Half of your plan coincides with half of mine, which at
least takes Sid out of the line of fire." She drew back, looked
up at him again, and he added, "So to speak."

"I was just thinking . . ." She stroked his belly. "Already
you've started calling him by a different name. I've always
called him Sidney."

"It's a guy thing. Only his mother should call him Sidney."

"You don't like his name."

"I like Sid. Even better, Sid Blue Sky." The stroking
stopped. He lifted one shoulder. "Well, it's there for him. It's
his if he wants it. I won't push it on him. Around here it's a
good name, but you take it down Main Street, U.S.A., you
can't believe how often they say, 'Blue Sky?' " He dragged his
name out, simulating stupidity. " 'And how do you spell
that?' " He chuckled. "I'm just too damned obvious, I guess.
Blue Sky's too damn simple. I won't push it on you, either."

"You won't push Blue Sky on me? Or sunshine, or happy
days, or this cock-eyed smile?" She touched the corner of his
mouth and made him smile.

"Or a slightly screwed-up heart."

She ignored that part. "I love you, Blue Sky. I'd love you
if your name were Tommy Tornado."

"It would have to be Whirlwind. It's all in the translation."
He tucked his hand behind the hollow of her knees and
dragged her legs across his lap. "Do you want to start the
coffee first, or go straight to the sex?"

"Straight to the what?"

They both sat up straight as Sid appeared in the hall doorway in his underwear.

"Sacks," Reese said with a one-sided grin. "I brought over some sacks of . . . socks."

"I don't know whether to laugh or puke. Do you guys realize what time it is?" He folded his lanky arms. "Was the house still there? How about the horses?"

"We'll go out in a while, and you can check it all out for yourself," Reese promised.

"Good." Sid turned to retreat, but couldn't resist one last shot of twelve-year-old wit. "By the way, you're not married, so you can't be sharing socks. Or sacks. Now get to bed, both of you, or you'll be zombies. Come on, Crybaby."

The dog hauled himself up off the floor and followed the boy as though it was a lifelong routine. *Click, click, click* went the claws on the hall floor.

"He's sure got a mouth on him," Reese said after the clicking stopped.

"He's at his best when he's playing my own tape back at me."

"You should go back to bed," he told her.

"For what? There's no chance of falling asleep now."

"Wait." He snatched the remote for the TV off the coffee table. "This works great." He clicked, muted, ran the channels until he found some guy singing to a girl. Or she was playing doctor, and he was showing her his tonsils. "No sound. It's like an electronic hypnotist." He pulled a knitted afghan off the back of the sofa and unfolded it over their legs. "We got no rules against a guy watching TV with his girlfriend, do we?"

She looked down at her nightgown. "We have a dress code and a curfew."

"Not if we're over twenty-one." He drew her back into his arms, and she cuddled like a kitten. "I like the way you're dressed, but you need socks." He wiggled his stockinged toes. "See, I've got socks."

"I like your socks. Nice, big socks."

He was content now, pleasantly tired. He closed his eyes, snuggling, drifting, muttering, "I'm a nice, big man."

19

*B*oth her men were sleeping like angels.

Helen had tucked a pillow beneath Reese's head and covered the big stockinged feet with the afghan, which he'd already kicked off, but he slept soundly. He would sleep until she returned, and then she would make his coffee.

First, though, she had to go knocking on Titus Hawk's trailer-house door.

It was early, but he came to the door, yawning, surprised, then curious.

The morning sun glinted off the aluminum siding as she squinted up at Reese's friend from the wooden steps that led to his door. After greetings and apologies for the early hour, she balanced her stance between two steps and launched into her concern.

"I want to ask you about the file you gave Reese on Peter Jones. We're wondering, Reese and I, because we've been trying to put some pieces together with all these strange happenings lately and . . ."

Titus shifted his bare feet, scratched his scanty beard, took a swipe at his rooster tail, all the while looking to her for the point.

"Why wasn't his license approved?" she asked.

He told her he hadn't made coffee yet, but he stepped back and invited her inside.

She said she hadn't, either. "As a matter of fact, I'm not here. I want to ask you a few questions, but it's not exactly my job to ask these particular questions. I'm strictly an observer."

"Posing as a dealer?" Titus directed her to a kitchen stool next to the counter, then turned to the sink to fill his coffeepot with water. "You're not just posing with Blue, are you?"

"You've met our son," she reminded him as she took a seat.

The trailer was furnished mostly in brown, worn but serviceable seating. Helen recognized a couple of chairs from the old high school, where she'd taught. She knew that government castoffs were officially destroyed, and she was glad the chairs had been salvaged. Much of Titus's furniture looked like salvage, but she'd always been impressed by the way people in Bad River made do. It was a lesson she would have done well to take to heart before she got caught up in trying to turn twenty-dollar bills into hundreds.

Titus noticed her checking his place out, and when she glanced at him, she saw his knowing smile.

"He's a real nice kid," he told her as he set the aluminum coffeepot on the stove and turned on a gas flame. "If you've looked at the file, you know why Jones's license was on hold. His application is incomplete. They kept telling us he was okay, he'd worked for Ten Star, and his file was being transferred. I said, 'Hell, no, I ain't giving him a license to deal cards here until I know he's really who he says he is.' And that's where we are with it."

"But he's been working."

"Yeah, I know. They do this all the time."

"Ten Star?"

"We get this runaround, and pretty soon the guy moves on. I don't know how our commission is supposed to do its job without their cooperation." He set two brown milk-glass mugs on the counter and brushed some crumbs onto the floor. "Reese says his dad asked for an investigation, but he didn't tell nobody."

"And that was wise." She looked him in the eye. "So you've had more like Jones."

"Oh, yeah, a few. I went along for a while, but lately I've been denying licenses left and right. So Ten Star complains that they're short-staffed because the commission is sittin' on the applications. I say send over the right applications."

"Good for you."

"I know for a fact that our people apply for training, and they get put on hold. Guys like Jones, hell, they put those guys right to work."

"White guys."

"They say Jones is Indian, but I didn't see any documentation." He braced his hands on the counter. "I figure, they put my people on hold, I can put their people on hold."

"What did Carter Marshall have to say about Jones?"

"Not much. Darnell recommended him personally, though, like I'm supposed to approve his license based on that. I ain't gonna do it."

"What about Chairman Sweeney?"

"He wants to go along with Darnell pretty much. They say Darnell gave three hundred fifty horses for pretty-boy Preston." His expression would have been deadpan except for the twinkle in his eye. "Hell, I wouldn't give that many horses for Marilyn Monroe."

She blinked, frowned a little, pondered this strange bribe. "Three hundred fifty horses for . . ."

"A pickup. See, Indians used to give horses for—" He shook his head as he turned back to the stove. "Well, for a lot of reasons. Just kidding."

She laughed, but she knew it was too late.

Maybe not quite. He flashed her a quick smile as he poured her coffee. "They say Sweeney got his new pickup from Ten Star, but it's just a rumor."

"Are there rumors about Carter?"

"Yeah." He lifted one shoulder as he poured for himself. "I don't know anybody who's been out to his house in Rapid City, but there's talk that he's getting a lot of money from somewhere. Blue's got a lot of money, though, so maybe . . ." He returned the pot to the stove. "Carter runs the casino pretty good. The everyday operation, the way he deals with people. He's working hard, from what I can see."

"And he's Reese's brother."

"And you're investigating him," Titus said, joining her at the counter again.

"No." She read the doubt in his eyes. "I'm looking for people like Peter Jones."

"Well, you can sure have that guy."

"I wanted to understand why he was allowed to work without a license," she explained. She sipped her coffee. It needed milk, but she wasn't going to ask.

"Because Darnell put him in."

"With Carter's blessing."

"Darnell's still looking over Carter's shoulder. Carter might be the manager of Pair-a-Dice City, but Darnell's *his* manager. That's what I see." He set a box of sugar cubes in front of her and handed her a spoon. "I don't think Carter has a lot of blessings to hand out, you wanna know the truth. I think he's fresh out of blessings."

Helen returned to the apartment, scanned the documents and the photograph from Jones's personnel file, and e-mailed them to the area office. She also sent copies to her FBI contact. Then she made breakfast for her slumbering angels.

It was a joy to watch them together. They would steal looks at each other—such boys, hanging onto the cool facade—but anyone who loved them knew the wonder they both felt when they looked at each other and thought . . .

My own father. A man who knew things Helen didn't know, like why Sidney had missed a shot last night and why he had a blister on his foot this morning, who knew exactly where the blister was without being told.

My own son. A boy who held his fork overhand, exactly the way Reese did, whose dark, thick hair fell over his forehead the same way, and who flashed the same mischievous smile in his eyes.

How could she have kept them apart?

All her answers were as useless as her excuses, which were as useless as her regrets. Following their lead, she stole her own looks, tuned in on their "man talk," and savored the joy of seeing them together, eating the food she'd prepared, sitting at the table she'd set for them.

They made a plan to spend the morning at the ranch, then drive to the Black Hills, where they would spend the night and put Sidney on the plane the following day.

It was hard to tell, after they arrived there, what he thought of his grandfather's small house, the modest outbuildings, the rustic bower made of poles and cottonwood boughs. When Reese explained the ashes in the backyard, Sidney remarked that he'd rather visit his grandfather's grave than Mount Rushmore. Wordlessly Reese put his arm around the boy's shoulders, took Helen's hand, and led them inside.

"This is something he'd want you to see," he said of the ruined battlefield model on the kitchen table. "He put a lot of work into this. I'm sorry it got broken."

Sidney examined the chicken-wire-and-plaster construction. "I could fix it pretty easy. It's really cool, except . . ." He stole a glance at his father and gave a quick shrug. "Well, you could put this on CD-ROM, and then it would take up less space, and it would do things."

"*You* could?"

"Somebody could. Probably already has." He lifted a small Indian from the pile of bodies that had been dumped into the river, the low spot in the terrain. One by one, he picked up a soldier, a horse, a tipi. "But maybe this is different. If a computer crashes, I can't do anything to fix it, but I could always put this back together."

Then he said tentatively, "I don't have to go back to camp for the last session." He looked up at Reese, then Helen, his eyes suddenly bright with what he thought was a winning bid. "I could hang with you guys and do stuff around here. It's only a couple of weeks."

"Oh, but . . ." *But?* Helen wanted nothing more than to have him stay.

"Jeez, you know what, Sid? Things are really—" Reese glanced at her, and she warned him with a look. *Don't say risky. Don't say unsafe.*

He laid a hand on Sidney's shoulder. "But what I'd like to

do is drive out with your mother at the end of the session to pick you up."

Sidney's attention was fixed on the small figure in his hand.

"I was thinking we could even show up a day or two early," Reese said, looking to Helen for encouragement.

She couldn't offer much more than a tight smile. Reese was making the noble effort, and his cause was just. But she'd been a parent for twelve years and knew the signs. Sidney was quietly arming himself against disappointment, and nothing Reese could say right now would turn that around.

But Reese kept trying.

"I could maybe teach a little ball-handling if the folks in charge could fit me into the schedule. I put on clinics and do summer camps for kids all the time, so I know the drill." He patted Sidney's shoulder. "What do you think?"

"You don't want me to stay?" Sidney said to the little Indian in his hands.

"I don't want you to miss out on a great program."

"But I just . . . met you."

"You give me a chance to work things out with your mom, you're gonna see more of me than—"

"Work things out with *her*?" The boy looked up. "What about me?"

"Both of you."

"How're you gonna work anything out with me if I'm in Colorado?"

"You're gonna have to trust me when I tell you that I will. *We* will. We have the will, and we'll be looking for the way." He rocked Sidney back and forth, a buck-up gesture. "Meanwhile, you'll be finishing up this great wilderness experience out there, and your mom—"

Sidney tossed the plastic figure into the pile of bodies in the river and bolted for the back door. "Didn't you guys say something about horseback riding?"

Reese cast Helen a doubtful look. "We'll have to flip a coin to see who rides double."

"I'm not going unless I get my own horse," Sidney announced as he flung the door open. Crybaby was waiting for him on the back step. The dog had to scramble to get out of the way.

"Flip you for the saddle?" Reese suggested to Helen as they followed their son.

"That would be gambling."

"Right. You've ridden this range more recently than I have, so I'll just ride the rump and play backseat driver." He shrugged when she offered him a sympathetic smile. "Maybe I took a wrong turn already."

"No, you did fine."

But she knew they hadn't heard the last of Sidney's petition. He would turn his full attention on the horses as Reese showed him how to catch them in the pasture by shaking oats in the bottom of a feed bucket. But he would bring it up again when he'd thought of another approach. Helen knew her son, and she could see that he was just as determined to stay as he had been to leave a couple of days ago.

But for now, the meager conversation turned to bridles and cinch straps as they saddled the two horses in front of the barn. Helen noted the approach of Carter's flashy white pickup with its sleek custom topper.

"I need to talk to you," he told his brother with little more than a nod to Helen and Sidney. "It's important."

"Off the hook." Reese patted the black paint's rump. "You guys take a turn around the estate, but don't be telling too many stories behind my back. I don't want to miss anything."

Sidney was making a study of ignoring him, pointedly avoiding his eyes, and it wasn't out of respect. It was pure, heavy-duty adolescent pouting. Reese remembered exactly the way it was done.

Damn. He'd been thrilled to hear the boy say he wanted to stick around. He wished he could have explained the situation to him right up front, but listing the offenses they were looking at—murder, burglary, animal abuse, arson—just might spoil his summer a little bit. And those were the crimes they knew about so far.

He let them through the gate that would take them to the path that followed the creek and watched them disappear below the hill, the dog trotting along behind.

"You and your son on the outs already?" Carter asked as the brothers walked back to the house.

"Trying to get in a little quality time before he heads back to camp." Reese offered a seat on the back stoop. "What's up?"

Carter put one booted foot on the step. "I heard you had a little fire out here last night."

"Earl the Pearl must have been after the ol' man's papers, is all I can figure." At this, Carter gave him a strange look. Reese shrugged. "I took all that stuff out of here, though, so he came up empty-handed."

"What did you do with it?"

"Safekeeping." He spared his brother a smile as he sat down on the stoop. *Safekeeping* was all Carter was going to get right now. "You're supposed to put stuff like that in a library. 'Course, Bad River doesn't have a library." He quirked an eyebrow. "What would you think of the Roy Blue Sky Memorial Library?"

"That's a noble suggestion, Reese, and I'm sure you could finance it yourself, but I can't see—"

"What would you say if I told you I was thinking of running for a seat on the council?"

Carter's face dropped. "I'd say you'd either lost your mind or you were jacking me around. And I did come to talk ser—"

"How about chairman? Think I should take Sweeney on for chairman?"

"Jesus. Are you serious?" Carter shook his head. "You're not."

Reese shrugged. He didn't know how serious he was, but he'd decided to spread the rumor that he was thinking about it and see if he could rattle Sweeney's cage a little more.

"So what can I do for you, Carter?"

"Sarah took the kids and went home to Yakima."

Reese let a wordless moment pass, respectful of Carter's loss. Then he offered what comfort he could. "They've always come back."

Carter nodded. "I've . . . I think for now they're better off with . . ." He took his right foot off the step, switched it for his left. "What you can do, brother, what you need to do . . . what I'm begging you one last time . . ."

Reese lowered his gaze. "Jesus, Carter, will you give it up?"

"No, listen, please." Carter sat down, a step below his brother. He was determined to get the full begging effect. "All I need is your word that you'll ease up. Take a breath, step back, and get a little better perspective on—"

"Carter, Ten Star isn't doing us any favors. Somebody's making a hell of a lot of money, and it's not us." Reese gestured, pleading in his own way. "I don't need to take a step back. From where I'm standing right now, I can see that it's time to part company with that outfit, and I'm thinking you—"

"I'm asking you not to press this. For my sake."

"Nobody's suggesting that you haven't done your job. You're the only manager we've got. We need—"

"I need *you*, Bro-gun. I've never asked you for anything, have I? You've always been my super-stud brother going your own way, and I've been . . . whoever. Who the hell knows who I am and where I belong? Not dragging on your shirttail, that's for sure." Carter sighed and gestured in frustration. "So I've never asked, but I'm asking now. All it would take is for you back off. Just go along with . . . with what's already in place. Maybe it's not the best deal we could get, but it's not that bad."

"Not that bad?" Reese considered his brother's face for a moment. The brother he hardly knew. The brother his father had sent away and reclaimed. How much, he wondered, had that hurt, and which part had hurt more? And when would it be time for all the old hurting to be over?

"Carter, who killed Dad?"

"I don't know." Carter sighed again, this time on a shaky breath. "I don't ask. I accept it as a hit-and-run. Somebody out of the blue, somebody who came and went."

"They didn't come and go. They killed our father." He looked into his brother's eyes, seeking assurance that he was not *they*, or any part of them. "They came and stayed, like some big leech. They came and attached their greedy mouths, and they started in sucking."

"The business wasn't here when they came. They built it."

"Why here? They think this is like the Nevada desert, like

there's nobody here? Maybe we won't notice if they use us? We oughta be grateful, right?" He paused. Then, apprehensively: "What are you grateful for, Carter? What did they do for you?"

"They gave me a job with a lot of—perks."

"The Bad River Lakota gave you your job. That's who you're working for."

"I'm doing what Ten Star tells me to do. And they're telling me to try to talk some sense into you."

"What do you owe them? What do you do for them?"

Carter stood.

Reese stood taller. He turned his brother around by his shoulder, made Carter look at him. "What do you *do* for them?"

"I look the other way when they tell me to. That's all. I swear to you, Reese, I've tried . . ." The breath Carter drew quivered in his chest. He looked away from his brother as well. "I figure, we get this business built up, there'll be enough in it for everybody. They'll get what they require, and we'll have more jobs, more revenue, more—"

"Their price is too high, little brother. The price of your soul is too high. And yours isn't the only one, is it? They've got Sweeney, too."

Carter stepped away.

Reese let his hand fall to his side. "You don't really think they'll ever have enough, do you? History proves otherwise. The stories—"

"Forget the damn stories!" Carter whirled to face him, eyes full of fear. "If you keep this up, *I'm* gonna be history."

"Come on, Carter . . ."

"I don't know why I thought I could talk to you." He shook his head, backpedaling, wiping his hand over his lower lip. "You're just like . . . Damn, you should know better, but you've got your head up your ass, too, just like—"

"Nah, mine's in the clouds," Reese said calmly. "I like that much better."

"I'm telling you, people are gonna get hurt."

"People are already getting hurt. They have been hurt. They've been hurting for a long, long time." Reese extended his hand. "If it's money you need, just tell me how much. I'll stand you whatever—"

"Money won't pay my bill. I'm asking you to *stand down*. That's the only way you can help me."

"Stand down?" Reese gave a dry chuckle as his hand claimed his brother's shoulder again. "Hell, I've already retired once. We'll find another way. I'll stand by you, and we'll find another way."

"Yeah." Carter backed up a few paces. "You watch yourself, okay? And anybody you care about. Watch all the doors."

"Watch for what? Earl Sweeney? If these Ten Star people are outsourcing their dirty work, they should try enlisting somebody with half a brain."

"They probably will."

"Do you hear yourself?" Reese demanded incredulously. "This is like something out of a damn movie. But movies end. A couple of hours, and it's all over, case closed. We don't need this outfit, Carter. Their contract is up."

His brother wasn't hearing him.

Damn, how bad could it be? Carter said he had nothing to do with their father's death. As far as Reese was concerned, anything else could be repaired somehow.

Repairs could still be made.

"You let a killing threat lead you around by the nose, you can't live your life," Reese said quietly. "Believe me, I know this for a fact."

"I have to get over to the casino." Carter turned to leave, then paused. He looked at his brother. "I like the money they're paying me, sure, but I've tried to do a good job. Maybe it's not the best business, but I guess it's no different than selling other kinds of entertainment, and we're actually getting people to come out here for it." He drew an arc with a sweep of his hand, as though he were presenting Reese the prairie. "Way the hell out here, on a godforsaken Indian reservation, we built a glittering entertainment palace. And it ain't covered with colored corn, either."

"Hey," Reese said with an openhanded gesture. "I own a damn limousine service."

"The grand illusion, huh?" Carter smiled wistfully. "It's a

business, and it's growing. Given a choice, I'd rather create something besides winners and losers, but this is what we've got. I'd like to see you pull it out of the fire, Bro-gun."

"Help me."

"If Ten Star goes down, I go down." He shoved his hands in his pockets and watched the riders approaching through the gate Reese had left open for them. "Helen's undercover, isn't she?"

Reese ignored the question. "We could help each other, Carter. I've got money, and I've got influence. You've got information."

"More illusions, Bro-gun. You're liable to give yourself a heart attack trying to save us all."

"It could happen," he allowed, chuckling, easily shrugging the weight of that particular worry off his big shoulders. He started to add his usual line about getting hit by a truck, but that one didn't work for him the way it used to.

The phone was ringing inside the house.

"I'll get moving. You catch that, and I'll say good-bye to my nephew."

Reese went inside and grabbed the receiver off the hook. Without any preliminaries, the caller informed him that Helen Ketterling had left this number.

"Helen! Phone call. This guy's pretty insistent."

Carter relieved her of her horse and led the animal back to the barn. Reese started to follow, but she motioned him inside. He leaned against the kitchen counter and tried not to listen in, although her side of the conversation was pretty cryptic, anyway. But when she turned to him, she looked pale.

"The scan I sent of the photograph of Peter Jones?"

"They found something already?"

She nodded. "They found his body in Wyoming. Shot through the head."

"Suicide?"

"Murder." She stepped closer to him, bringing him more details. Her eyes told him the important part was still coming. "He was found in a pickup. Front end damaged. Headlight broken."

"The piece I found . . ."

"Fits. The tires match the impressions they took out here."

His mouth went dry, but he was sure he tasted blood. He reached back, gripped the edge of the counter behind him.

"He killed my father?"

"Somebody driving that pickup did. The only vehicle I ever saw Peter Jones drive was an old van, but that doesn't mean anything. He had friends, people who worked with him, pulling his scams."

"He had to be hooked up with Ten Star."

"I can't prove that at this point, but I'd bet on it." She laid a hand on his arm. "If I were a betting woman."

"Proving it isn't your job." He jerked his chin toward the phone on the wall. "That's his job, the guy who just called. The guy who should have been calling *me* about the pickup matching the tire tracks they found next to *my father's body*."

"The guy who called is my boss. He's not investigating either homicide. We're interested in Indian gaming. But he is working with the FBI, and yes, they see the connection."

"We're making some progress," he said eagerly as he pushed away from the counter. "My dad's files are full of newspaper clippings about Indian gaming, and there are a lot of success stories. But in some places these outside managers are turning out to be crooks, and some management companies are taking Indian people for a ride."

"But they pay a lot of bribes, and that's where some of the tribal officials get themselves in trouble," Helen said.

"Yeah. Loans, I guess they're called." He took a bottle of water from the refrigerator and uncapped it. "One case, the crafty manager plea-bargained with the federal prosecutor, turned in a bunch of Indians he'd given these loans to, and got off pretty easy."

She refused the drink he offered. "It could go the other way. Somebody who's taken a bribe could turn state's evidence."

"And ruin his life." Reese took a long drink, then passed the back of his hand over his lips.

"No. *Change* his life."

"My brother didn't have anything to do with my dad's death. It had to be this guy Jones. Or Darnell."

"That's not your job, either."

"I said I'd help Carter. If it's a loan, he can pay it back. I can give them their money back."

She shook her head. "That's not what they want."

"We're not giving them what they want, not anymore." He was heading for the door now, and she was right behind him. "I wish we could be up front with Sid," he said. "He thinks we're sending him back to camp because we don't want him around. But if we tell him things are a little hot around here, he'll be worried about you."

"He's very protective. He's been the only—"

She stopped. Reese stood at the edge of the yard, noting the absence of Carter's pickup, the tail-swishing horses grazing on the hill, the barn door left open, the perpetual humming of the cicadas.

And the dog trotting back down the driveway toward them.

"Where's Sidney?"

"Sid!" Reese called out. The cicadas droned on.

"Sidney!"

They circled the house, checked the barn and the machine shed, but they knew. The emptiness was unmistakable, a twisting in the gut.

"He must have gone with Carter."

"Shit," he spat. "Carter must have *taken* him."

20

*C*arter knew he had a stowaway in the back of the pickup.

The kid obviously thought he was fooling somebody, but whoever it was, he could forget putting anything over on Carter. He had kids of his own. They had a heck of a time keeping still when they were hiding. Carter had seen Sidney reach through the window and take the pickup keys earlier, undoubtedly thinking his uncle was thoroughly absorbed in unsaddling his mother's horse.

A bid for attention was obviously in the works. Carter was all set to put a stop to it, but Sidney merely unlocked the back of the topper and replaced the keys, piquing Carter's interest. The boy's sulkiness had suddenly reversed itself, and he'd been quick to turn his own mount back into the pasture. Sure sign of a scheme brewing in a kid's mind. "Be seeing you, Uncle Carter," he'd said as Carter was heading into the barn to unload the saddle. And Sidney appeared to be bound for the house.

The boy had climbed right into his lap.

The pickup bobbled twice on a pothole. In the rearview mirror Carter saw a displaced foot, then a hand bracing for balance. He took a two-handed grip on the wheel and stared at the road ahead, air-conditioning blasting his neck. He'd have to stop pretty soon or the kid was going to melt back there.

Or drive on, now that he had what he needed. *The boy had climbed right into his lap.*

He had his cell phone turned off. Cell phones were iffy out here in the wilderness, and he knew his dad's place wasn't accessible until you got up on a hill. Calling Law and Order and having them relay the message would be the decent thing to do. But for the moment, the boy had given him leave to perform ignorance rather than decency. He knew what he ought to do. He knew what he was inclined to do. But what he might have to do was something else, a disturbing idea if he thought about it. As disturbing as the boundless grass and barely traveled roads he'd never really gotten used to on the prairie. As disturbing as big brothers with big heads and grandiose ideas.

Carter had been directed to deal with his brother, the man who was supposed to play the councilman role like a cork, skimming the surface, bobbing his weightless head in agreement. All he was expected to do was play the game. But Reese couldn't get it through his head that the game was played according to Ten Star's rules. He'd treated Carter like a kid, when Reese was the one who had no idea what was at stake.

Don't worry, your brother's here now. Even less comfort than *Your father's not afraid of them.*

Either they didn't get it, or they just didn't care.

Deal with your brother, Carter. If he couldn't find a way, Darnell would. Keeping it in the family was thought to be the best way. *You people have strong family ties. You need to learn how to use them the right way.*

Use them? How could you use them the *right* way when Indians were crazy? *It's a good day to die,* they said, and then they'd paint lightning bolts on their faces and watch the sky for thunderheads. That was exactly what his father had done, what Roy himself had once described as "tweaking the bull by the tail while the white guys are fighting over who gets to grab it by the horns." Roy had been watching for thunder-heads instead of headlights.

Carter wasn't eager to claim either end of anybody's bloody bull. He wasn't crazy. He wasn't interested in getting himself kicked, gored, or run over. He didn't believe there was such a thing as a good day for dying, and if that made him an apple—red on the outside and white on the inside—then fine. He was an apple. Likely a rotten one, but at least he wasn't crazy. He wasn't risking his kids' lives. There was no way Darnell would get to them on Sarah's reservation if the management contract went south. He'd tried to warn Reese not to let that happen, but Reese was a stud. Reese was in charge. Like the announcer used to say when he'd make one of his game-saving shots, *Reese Blue Sky was in the house.*

Good enough. Now all Carter had to worry about was his own hide.

In his side mirror he saw the police car's lights flash. There was a little movement in the back, too. A long, lean, sun-blessed arm snaked up to the topper's side window and slid it open. Carter smiled and pulled over before the cop turned his siren on. Maybe Dozer Bobcat was about to do everybody a favor. If he searched the back of the pickup, the lost would be found. So be it.

"Looking for Sid," Dozer said as Carter lowered the window at the touch of a button. "Your brother's boy. Weren't you just over there? They thought maybe the boy jumped in with you."

Carter's nose looked huge in Dozer's mirrored sunglasses. "He said something about going for a run. Did you look along the road?"

"He said that? He was going for a run?"

"I think that's what he said. He seemed a little pouty."

"Like he might run away?" Dozer laid his arm on the roof of the pickup. "Shit. You think that's what he did?"

Carter shrugged. "I don't see how he could get very far, though, do you?"

"Unless he hitched a ride, but that quick? He'd have to be damn lucky."

"Where's Reese?"

"Where do you think? He's beatin' the bushes out to your dad's place looking for the boy."

"I'll give them a call as soon as I can."

Dozer nodded. "The kid'll come back on his own, probably, but right now, they're both pretty scared."

They had reason to be, Carter thought, using his side mirror to watch Dozer. Their son was in the company of a desperate man. Dozer peeked through the topper window. If he looked carefully, he'd see the boy's shoe. Look through the back window, Carter thought. He wants attention. I want . . . relief.

But Dozer Bobcat was not the man to relieve him.

Carter pulled the pickup back onto the highway, reached above the small rear seat, and opened the window between the cab and the box, which was enclosed with a custom topper. There was plenty to hide in back there—toys, boxes, a rack of Carter's clothes. Yet Dozer should have seen him. He should have forestalled this thing right there and then, while it was still an innocent child's prank. He'd had the chance.

"Did you hear any of that?" Carter called out after he'd watched the cop turn around and hurry back to his buddy Blue. "Sidney? I know you're back there. You might as well talk to me."

No answer. An invitation to save them both, and there was no answer.

"Either I make a U-turn right here, or—"

"Don't take me back, Uncle Carter," the boy pleaded as he shoved plastic crates and in-line skates aside, scrambling toward the cab. "All I wanna do is miss my plane."

"You were all set to turn around and head right back after—"

"It's stupid to go back to camp now." Sidney stuck his face through the back window and gulped cool air.

Carter could smell kid sweat. He turned and smiled at the soggy head.

But Sidney had used his quiet time to get wound up, and he wasn't having any patronizing smiles.

"No. I'm serious. It's totally stupid. I've gotta get used to the idea that I have a father. A real, live father, emphasis on the 'live' part. Just looking at him is, like, unbelievable. I know

I said I wanted to go back to camp, but I don't anymore. I wanna stay. And they wanna get rid of me."

"Maybe they want to get used to some things, too, like . . ."

"Sleeping together? Yeah, right. Don't you think maybe he oughta marry her first?"

"Maybe that's one of the ideas they're working on. When does your plane leave?"

"Tomorrow morning. What I'm figuring is, once I miss my plane—"

"They can put you on the next one."

"But they won't, because by that time—"

"They'll be so glad to see you they won't want to let you out of their sight. Have you run away before?"

"Once. I hid out at my friend's grandma's old place for a day and a half. I didn't want to stay with my grandfather while my mom went on assign—"

"Assignment?"

The boy pressed his lips together, sucked them in and clamped them between his teeth. He stared straight ahead.

"Your mother's talked with me about her work."

"I don't . . . I didn't mean *assignment*. I meant, just a trip."

"She's really got card smarts. Excellent candidate for her line of work, which I know you're not supposed to talk about."

"I just know she's a good dealer," Sidney said quickly. "So how about it? Can I stay with you until tomorrow?"

The boy had no idea how worried his parents were. Or maybe he did, but only in terms of how that would affect him. They'd be so relieved when he showed up, they'd give him whatever he wanted. Carter knew how well that worked. He'd used it on his father. He'd used it on Jane and Bob Marshall. He'd tried it on his wife, but he couldn't get it past her as easily. Times like this, when she and the kids were gone and he knew he couldn't just pop in the door with presents all around . . . oh, God, these were the times when all he wanted was to see them. Just that—just see them, hear their voices in the room, know they were close by—and he'd make sure they knew how pleased he was. This time he would truly experience the pleasure himself. He would believe in it and make it last.

But Sarah and the kids were safe now, better off without him. This boy would be safer at camp in Colorado, and his father knew that. Safer than he was with his desperate uncle.

"You should have driven off with the pickup," Carter said, chuckling for effect. "Then I wouldn't have been implicated."

"I can't drive. And I wasn't going to implicate you. I figured you'd probably go to the casino, and I was going to sneak out of here and get a room at the hotel. Under an alias, of course."

"Of course."

If he'd been in a better mood he would have laughed, and he might have told his nephew that the staff wouldn't rent a room to an unaccompanied twelve-year-old, even if he did look more like fourteen. And he would have been in a better mood if the notion that desperate times called for desperate measures wasn't rattling around in his head, knocking against the question of how to play this unexpected hand.

"All you want to do is miss your plane?"

"Mom's starting to worry by now, but she knows I can take care of myself. It's just a little game of hide-and-seek, is all."

"I know a place," Carter said, hardly believing the words were coming out of his mouth. But the hard part of him believed, and that was the part he would call on now.

"You'll help me?"

"I'll help you miss your plane."

Hell, he'd paid for the ticket.

Reese had been searching for several hours, and he was coming home empty. Sick-to-his-stomach empty. It was a helpless feeling, and he didn't want it plastered all over his face when he walked in the door. He took a couple of deep breaths before he turned the knob.

Helen was waiting by the phone, standing with her back against the refrigerator and her arms wrapped around her middle, as though she were holding herself together. The hardest of jobs, waiting.

She looked past him, hoping, but it was only Crybaby who followed him inside. He closed the door, apologizing with a look. She lowered her head.

He drew a deep breath, sick with heartache. The smell in

the house made it worse. "Can't get rid of the damn smoke in here," he muttered.

"I'm sorry," she said in a small voice. "It's me. I had to have a cigarette. I would have gone outside, but I was afraid I'd miss the phone."

"No, it's okay. I didn't know. I guess I've . . ." He started toward her, but he ran into the corner of his father's damned Little Bighorn disaster. Routed and smarting, he offered a wan smile. ". . . never seen you smoke."

"And you won't. I found a pack in the cupboard. Don't tell Sidney. I promised to quit for good, but sometimes . . ." A fluttery gesture seemed to embarrass her, for she quickly jammed her trembling hand back where she'd had it, nailing it down with an elbow as she hurried to explain that smoking wasn't all she'd been doing.

"I asked Jean Nelson to wait at my place, but so far, Sidney hasn't shown up there. I've tried the casino, tried Carter." She shook her head, breaking his heart with those fragile eyes of hers, like blue glass lying in the middle of a gravel road.

He wanted to reach for her, but he felt too damned powerless. He turned away, hating his empty hands.

"You can't get hold of Carter?" He went to the sink, flipped the faucet handles, plunged his hands under the water, and splashed it on his face.

"No. I've left several messages." She raised her voice above the noise of the water. "I don't want to tie up the phone. You don't have call waiting."

"We're lucky there's a goddamn phone!" He slammed the water off and stood there dripping into the sink. "I just don't understand why Carter didn't come back after Dozer stopped him."

There was no answer. She was gone. He felt her silent departure. He hung his head between his arms, braced on the edge of the sink, and he wiped his dripping chin on his sleeve.

Then he felt her hand on his back. Something quivered deep in his gut. When he turned, she handed him a towel, and he used it only because she had brought it for him.

"He hadn't been gone that long when Dozer caught up with Carter," she told him. "Nobody else is going to get too upset until he's been gone a while. He's twelve years old. Kids go off, they hide sometimes when they're . . ."

Her voice failed her, just as he was doing. He could only take her in his arms, apologize for snapping at her, and make promises like "We'll find him."

She allowed herself a few tears before she gathered herself up like a string purse, tucking her raw parts inside. "I think he got in a car with someone."

"Would he do that?"

"No. I don't—no. Not by choice. Unless . . ."

"Unless what?

"Unless he was so angry he just wasn't thinking."

Reese nodded. He'd been there, so angry all you can do is run. "Soon as we get him back I'm gonna . . ." He gripped her shoulders. "Hang onto him. I've been trying to be cool around him, only had my arms around him once, but after this, I ain't lyin', he'll be calling me the ol' ball and chain."

"I think he's hiding somewhere. He's probably sitting up in a tree, watching to see how crazy he can make us. You checked—"

"Checked the shelter belt, checked the out buildings. You're probably right. I'll go out and cover all that ground again." He smoothed her hair back, swept tears from her cheeks with his thumbs. "I know it's hard, honey, but we've got the cops looking. You've gotta stay by the phone. Keep trying Carter."

Carter didn't much like what he was doing, but he was running low on choices. As long as he was the only one who knew where Sidney was, the boy would be safe. Tucked into the rugged moonscape of the Bad River Reservation's outlying piece of the Badlands was an old cabin Reese had shown him once after they'd borrowed the ol' man's pickup to go to a football game. A good place to be alone or take a girl, his new brother had told him, but Carter wasn't having much luck with girls at the time, and he remembered Reese confiding that he wasn't, either. He'd cherished that confidence.

They had been on the verge of going their separate ways again. Reese was leaving for college, and Carter would be going back to prep school. Reese had asked him what that was like. It was the first time and only time he remembered his brother asking him for any insight, and he remembered thinking, *My God, the Big Man is actually scared.* He'd desperately wanted to say something wise and memorable, but all he could come up with was, *Hell, it's easy, man.* He'd thought Reese was asking about school, which, for Carter, had always been easy. He'd forgotten that Reese had never been away from home. If his own young heart had been in better touch with his mind back then, he might have told him that that was the part that wasn't so easy.

He had returned to the cabin many times. He'd never taken a girl. He'd never brought anybody before today, but now he had taken his brother's son to the cabin. The boy had deemed the place a cool hideout, better than his friend's grandma's house. Carter had left him there with a flashlight, a sleeping bag, a little food, and some bottled water.

Now what? How could you use a child to get somebody to do something he didn't want to do without actually doing harm to the child?

He decided that was Bill Darnell's department. He found him in his office at Little Pair-a-Dice, talking on the phone. Normally Darnell would have ignored Carter or dismissed him until he was finished, but this time he saw what he wanted in Carter, and it was the phone caller who was dismissed.

"You look like you've been wrestling with the devil," Darnell said with a smile. "I wonder who came out ahead."

Carter could only stare at the man. His gut roiled. A terrible clamor in his ears defied him to form the words he had come there to say.

"Have you found a tender button in your brother's scrawny gut?" Darnell rose from his chair, his detachment disintegrating. "You did, didn't you? You got your thumb on it now, and you're digging in on him."

"I have his son."

Darnell's eyes fired up. "What, you nabbed him?"

"Not exactly. The boy was trying to run away. He fell into my lap, more or less."

"What are you planning to do with him?"

Carter sank into a padded chair. "I'm planning to steer clear of my brother while *you* do something. Get some anonymous phone calls going or something."

"And what good is that going to do?"

"I can't threaten him. *You* have to threaten him. Tell him he'll never see his son again unless he gets that contract approved."

Darnell smiled. "That sounds good. I think I might have heard it somewhere before, but there's nothing really new under the sun, is there?" He moved to the front of his desk and sat on some papers, which was Darnell's favorite way to cover his paperwork. "But you'll have to tell him, Carter. You're the one who's holding the kid."

"I told you, I'm not exactly holding him against his will. Not so far, anyway, and if we work it right, I won't have to."

Darnell mocked him with malicious amusement.

"The cops are already looking for him," Carter said, evoking more twisted amusement. "But the Indian police, mostly they're Reese's friends. If you started the calls to him right now, tell him to keep the cops out of this and shit like that . . ."

"That's bullshit, all right. Hollywood bullshit. He'll know you're behind it, sooner or later."

"Threaten me, too. Tell him you'll ruin his brother," Carter offered. Darnell kept laughing, and Carter thought wildly that maybe he'd go along with it just for the laughs. He smiled, shrugged, knowing what a buffoon he'd become. "Tell him you'll mess me up really bad."

The last of the suggestions had Darnell tossing his head back and fairly hooting. His belly was still jiggling as he used his hand to wipe spittle from the corner of his mouth.

"Now . . . ah, you slay me, Carter. But, seriously, how is this going to work once we have the contract and he thinks we've kidnapped his son and, uh . . . threatened to mess his brother up real bad?"

Darnell stood, unconsciously clenching and unclenching his fists, and Carter began to imagine what it might be like to be messed up real bad.

"You haven't thought this through very well, have you,

Carter? You know, for such an intelligent man, you are one dumb fuck."

"You told me to find a way to—" He glanced away from his overseer, his damned puppeteer. "You told me to use the kid or the woman."

"And now you have the kid. I don't have the kid. *You* have the kid."

"I can't . . ." Carter stood also. He was almost surprised he had enough backbone to get himself out of the chair. "I won't hand him over to you."

"Did I ask you to? I really don't want him. This is your show, Carter. It'll be interesting to see how you handle it." Darnell whacked Carter's chest with the back of his hand. "I'll give you a hint. If you want to get away with this, you have to be willing to off the kid." He smiled. "That's another expression you might wanna throw into your little script."

Carter blanched.

"No, I didn't think so," Darnell said. "Did you hear about Jones? Funny name for an Indian guy, Jones. Marshall ain't much of an Indian name, either. If I could have a name like Blue Sky, I'd be on it in a minute." He turned to the window. "It's just . . . *Blue Sky.* Saying it makes you feel good.

"And when you see it in print, like in a newspaper or something, you know they're talking about a redskin, don't you?" He looked at Carter again, his eyes fairly glittering. "And I ain't talkin' football, either. Think about it. Who else would have a name like Blue Sky? So everyone knows when they read about what's going on at Pair-a-Dice City—the whole world knows that it's the Indians who fucked it up. Oh, they'll probably say 'tribal member' or some kinda language like that, if that's part of the story. But you guys are taking bribes. We try to put you in management positions, and these card sharks come in and rob you blind.

"And you can't make any money for the Bad River people, running your business like that. Your father knew that, but he's dead. Now we've got your brother. What kind of head-lines do you suppose we could make with him?"

Carter was flabbergasted. Darnell had just laid out his cards as if the game were over. And damn if he didn't have a startling hand. The funny thing was, Carter had been wrong about the stakes. Ten Star wasn't nearly as interested in profiting from Indian gaming as they were in destroying it.

And the only reason Darnell had laid it all out for him now was that Carter was the ultimate pawn. He had taken a decisive step today. He had screwed his own brother.

"What about Jones?" Carter asked.

"Oh, poor Jonesie's dead. Took a bullet in the head." Darnell's bug-eyed smile made him look like a bullfrog. "You like that? It rhymes, doesn't it?" He shrugged. "He'd gotten in with shady characters before. I had to deal with him myself at a casino we opened up in Wisconsin. Indian casino. He lost his gaming license, but I believe in giving a guy another chance, don't you? Especially when he can be useful.

"Funny thing is, they found him in a pickup truck that didn't belong to him. You know who it's registered to? Officer Earl Sweeney. Another dumb fuck. And the tires on that truck match the tire tracks—"

Carter felt sick, and it showed.

"That's right, the truck that killed the old man. Sonuva-bitch, huh?" Darnell laid a clammy hand on Carter's shoulder. "Come on, Carter, you didn't think that was a random hit, did you?"

"I tried to get him to back off," Carter said tonelessly. "I've tried to talk to my brother."

"And that's the way it should be handled. Keep it in the family. Take care of your own. You Indians are supposed to be good at that."

"I like the gaming business." Carter was talking to himself now, pulling himself away from Darnell. "I love managing Pair-a-Dice City. I could have been good at that."

"Maybe. Hard to tell. This wasn't much of a test, since I've been managing you." Darnell rapped his knuckles on top of his desk a couple of times. "And Sweeney, and a small operation within the operation. Gotta have a few card cheats to make life more exciting."

He folded his arms across his barrel chest. "So now that you've added kidnapping to your offenses, what are you gonna do with the kid? Do you want me to take him? I'm not making any threats *for* you, Carter. Not while you're holding a witness." He withdrew one hand from the crook of his elbow and made a "gimme" gesture. "Turn him over to me, and go commiserate with your brother."

Carter shook his head. "Right now, he's just playing a trick on his parents. And I'm in for a little grief from my brother for going along with it, but that's about it. If you lose the contract, so be it."

"*So be it?*" Darnell laughed and wagged his head. "Carter, between you and Sweeney, I can't lose. You're all the insulation I need. You've sold the Sioux down the Bad River. But all I need is one of you, and I don't care which. The other one's a cushion, totally expendable." His smile was chilling. "Do I get the kid?"

"Let me think about it."

"Don't take too long. No point in feeding him if you're turning him over to me."

With Darnell's sick laugh following Carter out the door, he realized that maybe there was such a thing as a good day to die.

Helen had thrown the cigarettes in the trash, retrieved them, then thrown them away again. But she'd kept one out, and now she was dragging deeply on it. *Come back this minute, son, and you can catch me red-handed.*

She nearly jumped out of her skin when the phone rang. She reached for it, hesitated, then ripped it off the hook in the middle of the next ring.

"Let me talk to Reese."

"Carter?" *Finally.* "He isn't here, but we've been trying to get hold of you all afternoon. We can't find Sidney. We haven't seen him since you were—"

"Don't worry about him. He's fine."

A casing of measureless weight cracked and fell away, leaving her breathless, dizzy. She tipped her head back, resting it against the wall.

"Helen?

Where was her voice? "H-he's with you?"

"Yeah." There was a long and terrible pause, then a sigh.

345

"Yeah, more or less. He stowed away in the back of my pickup. He's fine."

"Oh, thank God." She felt giddy, actually gushed. "Oh, that boy, that rascal of mine. He hid in your pickup?"

"Helen, I need to talk to Reese. Did you know about Jones?"

"I know he's dead." Calm down now and get the facts, she told herself. "Carter, where are you? Where's Sidney?"

"He's . . . I've got him in a safe place, and for now he's fine. What do you know about Bill Darnell? What do you know about Ten Star?"

"I don't know very much, Carter. I really don't. I—" Why was he asking her these questions? What did it matter what she knew, and what did he mean by *for now he's fine?* "Please don't hurt my son."

"I need to talk to my brother."

"He's been out looking everywhere, and they've put out police bulletins, and people in town are . . ."

Her heart had vaulted into her throat, and the tears were rolling again. She hated it. She hated that she was shaking so. She had to calm down and give the man any assurances he might want.

"Carter, whatever you owe, I'll find a way to pay. What good can it do to hurt a child?"

"I won't hurt him, and I don't want him to get hurt. I want . . ." She could hear him breathing heavily, as though he was running. "I want to talk to my brother, Helen. I'll call back in an hour."

He hung up on her.

It would be dark soon. What should she do? Call the police?

What police? The tribal police were already there. Dozer Bobcat had been prowling every dirt road and cow path within a ten-mile radius.

Carter sounded scared. Kidnapping, was that what this was?

Obviously he wasn't going to tell her. She had to find Reese.

21

*I*t was almost nightfall. Carter was pretty sure he'd been followed on his way back to Pair-a-Dice City, which was why he'd avoided the switchboard and called Helen from a pay phone downstairs. Then he'd slipped into a different suite. The hour dragged by. He tried to think only of the boy, who was a tough one, much like his father.

Unlike his uncle. Carter tried to think only of the boy, but his thoughts quickly returned to himself, to what a pathetic fool he'd been, to all the promises he'd broken and all the people he'd let down. Ten Star had used him. He'd been disgustingly easy to use.

When the time finally came, he made the call again.

"Carter, where's my son?" Reese demanded without preliminaries.

"I'm going to tell you where he is, and I want you and Helen to pick him up and then keep on driving. Don't look back."

"What's this all about? Helen said he hid in the back of your pickup, and you—"

"He did." Carter closed his eyes, took a deep breath, saw

the faces of his own children. "He wanted to miss his plane so he could be with his parents."

"Carter, I don't interfere with decisions you make about your kids."

"I don't think we need to discuss child-rearing right now."

"Then tell me where the hell you've got my son!"

"He's safe. And, Reese, he doesn't know . . . He thinks this was all his idea and I'm just helping him out, which I swear I wouldn't have done if I hadn't been so damn scared."

"Scared? You don't know the . . ." Reese paused, calling on his considerable self-control. "Tell me, Carter, please."

"You have to be careful. They've been following me. They'll probably stay with me for a while at least."

"Who's following you?"

"Either Darnell or somebody who works for him. I thought they were going to kill me, but I'm not so sure they're willing to do me that service."

"Service? Carter, *where is my son?*"

"I couldn't hurt him, but I thought I could use him to get you to—"

"What do you want, for crissake? I offered you—"

"Money, I know. I appreciate that. Listen, I have a son, too." Carter rubbed his temple with quivering fingertips, trying to erase the image. But it wouldn't go away. "And a little girl. And a wife."

There was a long pause. "They'll come back to you, little brother. You know they will. I'll . . ."

"You'll look after them?"

"Where are you? Is Sid with you?" Reese waited for answers, and when he didn't get them, he offered to save the day. "Just tell me where you are. I'll get there as fast as it's humanly possible, and we'll take care of everybody."

"You probably could, too." Damn right he could. He was the Big Man, the Big Gun. "I'm asking you to look after my family, Bro-gun. Promise me that, and I'll tell you—"

"Anything, I swear. Whatever they need me to do or provide, I'll see to it. You have my word. Now where is he, Carter?"

"Remember that night you took me out to the Badlands? It was just before you left for—"

"He's at that cabin?"

"Cabin? Where?" Helen piped up in the background.

"Yeah," Carter said softly, imagining the look on her face, the ache in her heart. "And he's alone."

"Shit. Carter, I don't know if I can find that place anymore. Where are you?"

"Doesn't matter. I'm leaving here anyway. I'm on my way home, and I figure I'll be taking my tail with me, so you should be okay. Sidney should be okay."

"Listen, you meet me—"

"You'll find it, Bro-gun. You've got a sensitive heart. You follow that." Carter smiled. His throat burned like hell. "You're my hero. You know that, don't you?"

"Carter!"

Reese slammed the phone down and turned to Helen, who was ready to bowl Dozer down and fly out the door. "He hung up. He's—God, I hope he's not shittin' me about that cabin." He looked at Dozer. "Why can't somebody arrest that sonuvabitchin' Darnell?"

Dozer's eyes lit up. "On what charge?"

"Being a goddamned sonuvabitch!" Reese shouted as he grabbed the nearly useless cell phone somebody had loaned him off the counter.

"Works for me. Did he take the boy?"

"I don't know what happened. I just know my brother's all messed up, and I pray to God he's telling the truth about where Sid is." He ripped into the kitchen drawer that was the repository of keys. "Dozer, I want you to stay here. I don't know where Carter was calling from, but he said he was on his way home."

"If he's coming this way, you'll pass him."

"Then I'll pass him. You catch him. Send somebody out to the casino, see if they've seen him. Anywhere you can think he might . . ." He glanced at his friend. "Remember that cabin back in Gray Horse Canyon?" Dozer nodded. "That's where we're headed. I hope the ol' man left me some gas in his pickup for once."

It was the first time he had touched the pickup. His father hadn't been one for keeping his vehicles tuned up, never one for getting gas until the gas gauge was on Easy. But still it didn't surprise him that the old Chevy fired right up. He gave the *wanagi* a thumbs-up when the needle floated all the way up to Full, probably for the first time in Blue Sky history.

He went back in the house for his father's .22 pistol, glanced at Helen as he tucked it under the front seat, and muttered, "Rattlesnake insurance."

To her credit, Helen didn't ask too many questions he couldn't answer. She'd heard his end of the conversation with Carter, and there was only one question that mattered. The answer, he fully believed, was yes, their son was all right.

Purple dusk descended slowly over the weathered gray earthen bones of the Badlands. If the Black Hills sheltered the heart of the earth, if that sacred place had given birth to the first Lakota, then the Badlands must have been placed close by to complete the circle. The eerie moonscape was surely the image of death, a haunting visual testament to the spectrum of the journey. The Badlands were especially beautiful at dusk, all stark angles and smooth planes, a clean clay canvas stippled with purple shadows and mystery.

But it was a frightening tableau for the mother of a twelve-year-old boy. She was sitting so far away, she looked almost like a child herself, lashed to the seat and huddled close to the window, looking anxiously for signs from the land and from her lover.

"Is it . . . any of it familiar?" she asked him finally.

"Oh, yeah. Familiar as the back of my—"

Ass. Which he had seen exactly once in a picture some idiot had snapped in a locker room. Real familiar.

He tried to comfort her with a small smile. "It's been a while, but I know where I am. We'll find him."

Follow your heart. Great line for a fairy tale.

"It's getting dark," she whispered, and all he could think of was more fairy tales, the kind with little girls wandering through big woods. She perked up, returning his sad excuse for a smile. "But he's had all kinds of wilderness experience this summer. He's been telling me, every time I talked to him,

350

about these excursions they'd go on for two or three days at a time."

"It's only been a few hours. He'll be fine, as long as he stays where he is."

"If he's at the cabin."

"He is." Reese slowed the pickup. The shape of the horizon matched something less distinct than memory but far more urgent. "I'm feeling a strong pull."

The road had never been more than tire tracks, and even that was largely overgrown. He prayed he was going the right way, but he kept those prayers silent. Jesus, had the cabin been this far back?

Christ, he'd run out of ruts.

Goddamn it, where was the road?

Sweet Jesus, show me the way.

There it was at last, a ramshackle cabin made of Black Hills pine, tucked between the huge clay paws of a formation he had long ago dubbed "the Sphinx."

"There's no light," Helen said. "Would he leave him without a light?"

Reese had no answer for that. This stuff happened only in fairy tales, where the wilderness was always dark. Fairy tales and Iktomi fables. It occurred to him that he might be leading Helen into some kind of coyote's lair, some shape-shifting spider's snare.

"It doesn't look like . . ." Her face was inches from the windshield. "Would he send us on a wild-goose chase?"

Shit. Would he?

"Reese?"

"No!" He slammed on the brake and the clutch, threw the gear into Park. His heart was pounding like an old windup bedroom clock. He reached under the seat for the flashlight and the .22. "I guess we'll find out, huh?"

Her eyes widened at the sight of the pistol. "Reese, you'll scare him!"

"Snakes. Just in case." He grabbed her hand when she released her seat belt. "Listen, I want you to stay in the pickup. Keep it running, but stay put until we know what's here."

"My son's here. He has to be."

"*Our* son." He squeezed her hand. "He's our son, Helen."

"Our son," she whispered. She knew what that meant. She accepted it.

He touched her hand to his lips, then got out of the truck and trotted to the cabin, pushed the door open and wielded the flashlight with his left hand. He carried the gun in his right. "Sid? Are you here?"

The night was still. Not even a damn cricket greeted him.

He stepped inside. "Please be here, son," he whispered. "Please be okay."

He checked behind the door, flashed his light into each of the four empty corners, played it over the dirt floor. There was nothing there. No mice, no gum wrappers, nothing. Disappointment rattled in Reese's aching chest.

"Reese?"

He stepped outside to meet Helen. "It doesn't look like anybody's—"

"I'm here."

Sidney appeared at the corner of the cabin, dragging his sleeping bag like a shy and humble Linus emerging from his hiding place behind a dugout somewhere in bumfuck Egypt.

Reese laughed with pure joy and blessed relief. Helen swooped down on the boy with wings outstretched like Mother Goose.

"I could tell it wasn't Uncle Carter's pickup," Sidney explained quickly.

Reese flipped the pistol's safety latch and tucked the weapon into his belt. He remembered his vow to hang onto the boy, hang on tight next time he had the chance. But Sidney's mom had first dibs. Reese managed to get a hand on his son's small shoulder. "This one was your grandfather's."

"Well, I didn't know who it was, so I quick shoved my stuff out the back and hid." Sidney stepped back when his mother released him, hanging his head. "I'm glad you came. Uncle Carter said he'd be back for me tomorrow, but, um . . . I'm just glad you came tonight. I was getting a little scared."

"*We* were getting a lot scared," Reese said.

"So you're not gonna send me back to camp now, right?"

"We've got a lot to talk about, but—"

"You don't have to go back to camp if you don't want to," Helen put in quickly as she maneuvered Sidney back under her wing. "But I don't want you to think it's because of this. You should have told me . . ."

"I did."

"No, I mean—"

"Sid, I gotta tell you, this was a real dangerous game for you to play," Reese said. "If you ever pull a stunt like this again, you'll be paying serious consequences."

The boy looked up at him, ready to take his medicine right there and then. Reese had all he could do to keep from praising him for it. He was so proud of the kid his chest hurt. Later he'd sure tell him what a smart move it had been for him to hide, not only himself but any sign that he'd been there.

He put an arm around both of them and steered them toward the pickup. "But this time I guess we can figure, with all the surprises we've had recently, we're all about half a bubble off plumb."

"Huh?" Sid said.

"Haven't you used a carpenter's level?"

"Uh-uh."

Reese and Helen buckled their son into the space between them on the bench seat, and then they headed for the highway, letting silence reign over the jolting ride. Explanations would come. Apologies would come. But right now, relief simply felt so good.

The way out seemed much shorter than the way in. The night sky was far brighter now that the stars were popping out. Reese couldn't get over the dizzying high that the flurry of discovery had provoked. As they approached the fence line along the highway, he imagined his father stretching wire. It must have been the mention of tools that had him seeing such things in the dark.

"Damn, I wish your grandfather was still here," he told Sid. "He was real handy with stuff like carpenter's levels."

"Should we fix up his battlefield?"

"We should, yeah. And then we should build a room big enough to—"

"Where are we going?" Helen asked.

He hadn't made a conscious choice, but they weren't headed for the Blue Sky place. There was something else he had to take care of.

"How about we spend the night in Rapid City?"

"That's where the airport is," Sid said. "If you're sending me back, I don't have my stuff."

"Your mom said you weren't going back, and that's fine with me, but . . ." He glanced at Helen. "I've got a bad feeling about Carter."

"I'd rather not deal with him now. We don't know—"

"He said he was going home." Reese reached across the dash for the cell phone. "He said some pretty strange things. I can't explain it exactly. I wasn't even thinking when I turned west instead of east."

"What are you thinking now?"

"I'm thinking . . ." Of getting in touch with Dozer. Of Darnell and the chances of getting him convicted on sonuva-bitch charges. Of his dumb-ass brother. "He called and told us where to find this guy, and I'm grateful to him for that."

"And what else?"

"I'm a little worried about how far off his bubble might be."

There were lights on inside the house, but the front door was locked. Reese rang the bell. There was no answer, but he was sure he'd seen some movement in the window. He remembered the key Carter had hidden under the seat of a porch bench—a practice he'd warned his brother against. Fortunately, his warning had been ignored.

Reese called his brother's name. Again there was no answer.

The light was coming from the master bedroom at the end of the hall. The house was quiet.

"Sid, would you take your mom outside and wait for me in the pickup?"

"What's wrong?"

"Just do that for me." He looked at Helen, reached behind his back, and touched the .22 he'd tucked in his belt again. "Please."

"Let me call the police," she said.

"Not yet."

"How will I know?"

"All right, wait by the door." He glanced at Sid, then jerked his chin toward the door. "You go out to the pickup and man the cell phone, okay? If there's a problem, call nine-one-one." The boy nodded.

Reese headed for the rear of the house, announcing himself when he entered the bedroom.

"Bro-gun?" Carter's voice, coming from the master bathroom, sounded thin and taut.

"Yo, it's me. Hey, listen, thanks for—"

"Are you alone?"

The bathroom door stood open. He could see Carter's face in the mirror above the sink, and he figured he had to be sitting on the edge of the big marble bathtub.

"I sent them out."

"Was there a car in front of the house?"

"I didn't see anything." He moved in closer, trying for a better view in the mirror. "Carter, what's going on?"

"I'm on the can, and I don't need company right now. Stay—"

The hell with the sneak-up dance. Reese walked in. Carter was sitting there in jeans, no shirt, one hand on his knee, the other behind the rim of the tub.

"Where's the water?"

"Stay out, big brother." He sat there like a plumbing fixture, inanimate but for his dark, desperate eyes. "Listen, you've gotta get out of here. Take your family and get as far away from this business as—" The hand came away from his knee for a gesture. "They followed me here. Then they just sat there in front of the house. Didn't come after me, nothing. I'm their—" The hand became a stop sign, the eyes lowered, as though he'd been caught with his pants down. "Don't, Reese."

Reese took a step closer. "You're their what?"

"I'm . . . I'm their monkey on a string. Me and Preston both, we walked into this show of theirs and played the roles just as they wrote them for us. There's no way I can . . ." He showed his hand now, filled with a snub-nosed .38. He stood

355

slowly. "You've gotta get out of here right now. Or I'll do you first, then me."

"No, you won't."

Carter pointed the gun at Reese.

The barrel wavered, but its black hole said, *O, yes.*

"Stay away," the unsure voice said.

But the black hole said, *O, I'm dead sure.*

"Put it down, Carter. You asked me to look after your family. You're not going to—"

Carter turned the menacing hole to his own temple. "Stay away."

Reese swallowed. His was feeling a little unsteady himself. His heart careened within the walls of his chest like a jalopy that had just blown a tire.

"Carter, please listen."

Oh, Jesus, it was Helen. Reese didn't flinch, couldn't take his eyes off his brother, but he could see her out of the corner of his eye. What the hell was she trying to do?

"Carter, I know how you feel," she said as she approached. She had the view in the mirror now. She could see her boss holding a gun to his own head, yet she spoke calmly. "Believe me, I've been exactly where you are. Up to your eyebrows in debt, right?"

"Helen, please go out."

"I understand Carter's problem, and I think I can—"

"No, you don't, Helen. Don't bring your Gamblers Anonymous shit in here. I don't need . . ." He turned the gun on Reese again. "If you care about her, get her out of here."

"Carter, I know because I've been there, and the only thing that kept me going was the fact that my son needed me," she said, her voice as soothing as warm water. "Just as your family needs you."

"They'll be better off without me." Carter shook his head, his eyes growing wilder by the second, his gun hand unsure of its target. He jerked the weapon back to his head. "I'm really too stupid to live, you know? I walked right into Ten Star's scheme to fuck up the Indian casino business."

"What are you talking about?" Reese asked. "They have the management contract."

"They want us to hang ourselves on a gilded rope. They just kept loaning me money. I could never repay it. But I took it. I took everything they offered and asked for more."

"We'll get Darnell behind bars."

"If he doesn't kill me, he'll turn me in for taking bribes. Me and a few others. Indians killing Indians, that's what they want." His eyes went wild again, popping open and shut like screen doors, as if he were having trouble staying awake.

His hand twitched.

Reese's stomach lurched.

"Am I really Lakota, Bro-gun? Is this a good day to die?"

"It's not a good *way*." Reese had to keep Carter's eyes fixed on his. It scared him when he closed them. Had to keep talking, try to come up with something he wanted to hear. "Yeah, you're Lakota. You're Roy Blue Sky's son, just like I am. And we've all three had a hell of a time finding the red road. A good way to live, little brother. That's what our traditions are about."

"I'm not headed that way. I've gone too far. I can't . . . turn . . ."

"You can turn state's evidence, Carter," Helen said. Carter's eyes glinted, pleading with Reese to get her out of the room. But she hung in there with a woman's strong presence, a woman's quiet bid for life. "Tomorrow we'll get you a good attorney. We're already building a case, Carter, and you can be part of that. Beat them at their own game."

"She's right, Carter. You can turn the tables. Do us all a service."

"I want you to know one thing, Bro-gun. I had nothing to do with Dad's death."

"I believe that." Reese was feeling so damn dizzy, he wasn't sure where his next breath was coming from, but the mention of his father . . . the image of his father amid flashes of light and splashes of black . . . "I also believe he made me come here tonight. I ain't lyin', little brother. I've been trying to do everything the way he'd want it, but he still won't leave me alone." Reese had to move or he was going to drop. "And I don't believe you want to shoot anybody."

"Nobody else, just . . ."

"Just nobody." Reese caught himself, felt the cool tile on the wall. "You're not leaving me without a brother again."

"You've got plenty of brothers."

"I want *you*," he said, moving slowly, concentrating on the bits of life, the light, his brother's eyes and the tears on his face. "You're my brother, the one who was taken from me. Nobody's taking him from me again. Not even you. So put it down." The gun was down by the time Reese reached him, and it slid from hand to hand. The best Reese could do was find the safety latch with his thumb and let the thing drop into the sink.

He staggered like a lush, draped himself over his brother, rested his forehead against Carter's, and whispered, "I need you to take me to a hospital now."

Carter caught him in his arms. "What's the—oh, God . . ."

"Don't . . . make a big . . ."

"Helen, call an ambulance," Carter shouted, loud enough to wake the dead. "Now! Get nine-one-one and ask them what to do for him. It's his heart!"

Reese fought for every breath. He was as light-headed as he'd ever been with this crazy condition of his, but he was pretty sure he was still conscious. Somewhere along the line, one of the drummers in his chest had gotten himself loaded, and there was no rhyme or rhythm to his heartbeat. But there was volume. He could hear it in his head.

"You still with us, Bro-gun?"

"Gun," Reese muttered, leaning heavily on Carter as they moved to the bedroom. He still had his legs under him. He was pretty sure he did. He saw Helen, and she looked scared, and he didn't want her to worry. *Give her a job.* "Can you get the . . . gun and put it . . . away somewhere?"

"The ambulance is coming. We're going to lie down now."

"Tired," he said, and he was congratulating himself for being in control, still breathing, still conscious. "Been a long day."

Helen's sweet face hovered over him. Some of it was gone, but most of it was there. "You got the gun?"

"Don't worry about the gun," Carter said. "Just don't black out, okay?"

"Drummer's all fucked up. Makes me dizzy, trying to keep up. Can't do that step." But he didn't want to lie down. He was afraid he wouldn't get up.

"Should he be talking? Save your strength, my love."

"Just sit," he said, but he might have been down now. He wasn't sure. His body wasn't all his. "Say that again. *My love*."

She said it over and over again while he concentrated on her blue eyes the way he'd focused on his brother's.

"Mom? What's wrong?"

Sid. More light. More bright spots than black spots.

"It's not as bad as it looks." He waved his son's voice closer. "Don't be scared. It's happened before, and I'm still . . . around to tell the tale." Ah, there was Sidney's face. Reese touched his fist—he thought it was a fist—to the boy's arm. "I'm sorry."

"Don't be sorry. I'm the one who's sorry. I shouldn't've . . . Don't die, okay? Okay—Dad? Can I—can I call you Dad?"

"Please . . ." Reese hooked his arm around the boy's neck and drew him close, head to head. He felt giddy, like he was half drunk himself. "Lemme hear it again . . ."

"Dad," Sid chanted fervently. "Dad, my dad, don't die now, please?"

"Not today. Not a good day for it. When I go, it'll be . . ." He tried to snap his fingers, but they were like rubber. "Damn. Weak as a . . . kitten."

"They're here, Reese—the ambulance," Helen said, and only then did he recognize the sound of the siren. He'd thought it was the singers. "Sidney, go tell them," she said.

"Nah, come on, no ambulance. I don't need . . ." He was looking at his brother, but behind his brother's shoulder, another face appeared.

Take your brother with you, his father said.

Take him?

He has no will of his own right now. He needs some of yours.

Mine? I can't even will my heart to beat steady.

You have what your heart needs. Share that with your brother.

Helen was close by, but she'd brought strangers. Two white guys. "Carter?" He grabbed a blue shirt. "Let my brother ride with me."

"I'll be along, Bro-gun. You've got—"

"You're staying with me." He fought off the little white guys until Carter appeared. "For instructions. Just in case. You've gotta . . . do this for me." He looked at Helen for help.

"Please don't argue with him, Carter. He needs you."

Helen knew exactly what Reese was up to. He had to get his brother to the hospital. Carter was too unstable to be left alone, even though he now had the presence of mind to explain Reese's condition as he and Helen both followed the gurney down the driveway. After Reese was loaded into the ambulance and Carter climbed aboard, Helen confided to one of the paramedics that Reese had just kept his brother from committing suicide.

"Pretty remarkable for the shape he's in," the man shot back at her as he climbed into the driver's seat. "Preventing a suicide while you're having a cardiac episode takes some heroic effort."

"What I'm saying is, you need to admit them both."

It wasn't that simple. She would have to report the incident anyway, but in the end, Carter agreed that he needed help. He sat with her outside the ICU, watching through the window while Reese was hooked up to machine after machine. Since nobody would tell them much of anything, the three of them held hands and looked at each other and talked quietly.

She told Carter that debt wasn't insurmountable. She knew how scared he was, how sick he felt about the stupid things he'd done, how bad he felt about taking his family for granted, how much he missed them. "One step at a time," she told him. "The first step is surrender. Right here and now, sign the papers and let these people help you." Otherwise she would call the police and report the suicide attempt herself.

But she didn't have to. Carter referred himself and was admitted to the psych ward.

Sidney was asleep in the waiting room, and Reese was asleep in the ICU when Helen was finally permitted to sit beside his bed. The nurse suggested that she find a bed and get some sleep herself, but she refused to leave him. She'd left him once before, and he was going to have to drive her away with a stick this time. She was determined to be the first person he saw when he woke up.

She was, but it was fourteen hours later when he woke up with a sweet, bemused look. "Did I black out?"

"You're exhausted. You've been asleep for a while."

He eyed the monitors, the IV bottle, the daylight leaking through closed blinds. "So it's tomorrow, huh?" He looked at Helen. "What's tomorrow good for?"

"It's no better for dying than yesterday was."

His mouth twitched. "How do you know?"

"The doctor told me."

He nodded. "Heard the same thing from my father. He sends his best."

She stared at him.

He managed to smile. "So did I black out? I know I was pretty light-headed, and I remember the ambulance, the emergency room." He started to sit up. She offered to crank up the bed, but he waved the suggestion away and dropped his bare feet over the side of the bed. He groaned. "I need sex."

"Now?"

His smile was improving. "Socks. And boots."

"You need rest."

"Had that. Still a little light in the head, so I'm just gonna sit for a minute." He shook his head as if to clear it. "Syncope. That's what they call it if you black out. That's not good."

"Do you have blackouts often?"

"No, I don't. I get the palpitations once in a while, the breathlessness, sometimes at night. But I don't hardly black out, and that's good." He looked at her, as though she doubted his worth, or that of his word. "It's only happened to me twice. That's all. It's not as bad as it looks. Where's Carter?"

"We reported his suicide attempt. He's here. He agreed to check himself in."

Reese nodded, staring down at his toes. "Sid?"

"Getting something to eat in the cafeteria. He slept on the sofa in the waiting room." She smiled. "He missed his plane."

"This doesn't happen much," he told her, as though she were considering his application for a laborer's job. "I'm mainly pretty healthy. I'm lucky. This thing was diagnosed, and I know about it, and I understand it pretty well, and according to the latest studies, my prognosis is pretty good."

With a nod she took his big hands in her small ones.

"But I could just drop dead one day," he said quietly.

"And I could get hit by a truck."

He gave her hands a quick squeeze. "Don't say that."

"Oh, it's okay for you to say it, but not for me. Walking away from each other the way we did before amounts to the same thing, doesn't it?"

"It would kill me, for sure."

"Me, too." She sat next to him on the bed, and she lifted the IV tube over her head as he put his arm around her. "What are we going to do, then?"

"My son won't let me sleep with his mom unless I marry her first. Now, I don't know what kind of arrangements have to be made, but I'm making my first vow right here and now." He raised his unpunctured arm. "From where the sun now stands, I will sleep no more without her."

She was looking at him, smiling.

"So you'd better get your affairs in order, lady."

"My affairs?"

"You've got a history, I've got a history."

"We've got a history together."

"We ain't gettin' any younger, and we don't know how much time we've got." He glanced at the clock visible above the nurses' station outside. "To get the license and stuff. But they can do the blood tests right here, and I'll bet they've got a chaplain."

She glanced, too, and noticed two nurses staring right back at them. "At about a thousand dollars an hour, they're going to be kicking us out of this little honeymoon suite any minute."

"Hell, any minute we're going to become the best show in town." He lowered his head for a kiss while he dragged her hand across his sheet-draped lap. She squealed, and he smiled against her lips. "This unit needs intensive care," he muttered.

"Eunuch, my—"

"Shh. Behave yourself, woman. I think this room is bugged." He smiled at the two nurses, who smiled and waved.

"Are you ser—"

"I'm a man of my word, honey. I'm not going to sleep again unless your head's on the pillow with mine."

She drew his head down for a kiss. "Far be it from me to keep a sick man from his rest."

"Far be what from you?" He kissed the corner of her mouth. "Not this man. No matter what happens, I'll never be far from you again."

"*H*ey, Blue!"

Sid peeked through the doorway of the new master bedroom at the recently remodeled Blue Sky Ranch. Reese was still fussing with his tie. He'd begun with a silver bolo, thinking he needed a Western touch. He'd jerked that off and grabbed a tie. He wanted to start this off right. He wanted to be taken seriously from day one.

"Mom says we shouldn't be late for our first day. Especially *you* shouldn't be late." Sid whistled. "Pretty sharp threads, there, Coach."

"Too much? Should I lose the tie?" Reese undid the knot and pulled the silk tie from his collar like a loose thread. "I could let you have it for a belt. I'd hate to see you lose those pants on your first day, Sid Roy."

Sid leaned his shoulder against the doorjamb. Tall and lean as a cottonwood pole, he'd grown four inches in the past year. And like the tree in the dancers' bowery, he stood in the center of his parents' world. "Nobody wears tight pants," he said, shaking his head at the offer of the tie, which Reese then tossed on the bed. "Not even here."

365

"You okay with *here?*"

It had been an issue, and the decision had been made over time. Trial and error. Once they'd discovered each other, any time they'd been forced to spend apart had been a trial. And trying to build a life together without compromise would have been an error.

Sid grinned. "As long as I get to suit up when basketball season starts."

"You'll do more than suit up."

"Gentlemen, I have already started your engine." Helen now filled the other half of the bedroom doorway. She wore a pale yellow dress and a sunny smile. "You both look wonderful. The handsomest set of bookends I've ever taken to school with me."

"We won't be sitting on your shelf."

"You're right about that. You're going to be hopping, Mr. Blue Sky. It's been a long time since I've had a student teacher."

The look he gave her was innocent enough, but she read the reminder in his eyes. She'd had one last night, right there in the longest bed in the state of South Dakota. There wasn't much space for anything else in the room, but they had each other, and there was no need for television or for the illusion of companionship.

"Be gentle," he said, his eyes twinkling, for he'd whispered the same words to her only a few hours ago, and her joy had bubbled, warm and husky within her lovely throat.

"Yeah, Mom. Don't get him nervous." Sid looked worried. It had been a year since Reese had experienced a cardiac episode of any kind, but the boy was a worrier. "You're not nervous, are you, Dad? It's just school. School's easy."

"You sound like your uncle Carter. School's easy. Nothing to be nervous about." Reese chuckled, glancing at his wife as he shrugged into his navy blue sports jacket. "Yeah, I'm a little nervous."

"You've got your pills with you, though, right?" Sid asked.

Reese signaled for an about-face. "I've got everything I need."

"I think you should show one of Grandpa's videos the first

day," Sid advised as they trooped downstairs. A second floor and a whole new wing had been added to the house, along with an attached garage. "Videos are great to start off with."

"I've got a plan for that unit." Reese gave a passing nod to what they were calling the activity room, for want of a better term. The Little Bighorn battlefield occupied a spotlighted, custom-built niche in one corner.

There was no TV in this room, either. This was where the books lived, along with the music, the fireplace, and the big easy chairs. There was a game table for chess and Monopoly. And cards, of course. There was a card shark in residence.

"She's got you doing the lesson plans, too?"

"I figure it's like setting up the game. You play to your strengths. Your mom does the Constitution, and I do the treaties. Then we talk about dual citizenship and a nation within a nation and how Indians have a unique status—like it or not, America, you gave us your word—and how I never used to care much about it myself, and some of us choose not to, but now that I've come full circle . . ." He laid his hand on Sid's shoulder, guiding him through the new kitchen, trying to keep up with Helen, who was an incurable clock-watcher. "And now that I have a son, it means more. The future means more."

"So what about Grandpa's videos? You gotta get those in there."

"Oh, yeah, we will. After we build the battlefield model in class."

Helen glanced over her shoulder and rolled her eyes. She'd warned him that he was asking for a mess.

"And before the two-day field trip to Montana for the reenactment."

She groaned. He laughed.

"Cool," Sidney said as he let Crybaby out the back door. The dog's domain had been remodeled, too, with a new fence, a new house, and a new mate on order from a Minnesota breeder. "They let you take field trips like that here?"

"We'll have some casino profits going into education this year." Reese reached past Helen to open the door to the garage. "But I'll provide the transportation. Blue Sky Limos in

Big Sky country. The kids from Bad River High School will be pulling into that Little Bighorn parking lot in style."

"Can't I take that class this year?"

"Don't be in such a hurry, okay? Give your ol' man a break. The fact that you're starting the eighth grade is hard enough to take."

"Oh, the pressure. You guys need to have another kid." Sid flashed a warning look at his mother. "And don't say you're too old. You're not too old."

She smiled innocently as she slid into the car. "I didn't say anything."

She knew better. They both wanted another child, but Reese was dragging his heels.

They'd been married almost a year, which everyone agreed was a fine first step toward building a family, even though they'd often been separated in those first few months. Reese had felt duty-bound to stay involved in tribal politics, at least for a while. With the death of Roy Blue Sky, the fall of Preston Sweeney, and the removal of Ten Star, some important holes in the community fabric had to be patched up quickly. Reese had helped Titus Hawk get elected tribal chairman, and then he'd accepted an appointment to a new gaming committee.

With support from the Bureau of Indian Affairs, the committee had worked tirelessly in the past year to reorganize the tribe's casino business under new management. Sid and Helen had gone back to Denver for school. Reese had spent as much time with them as he could. The remodeling project at the ranch had driven him into the hotel at the casino when he was in Bad River, and they enjoyed spending holidays at his condo in Minneapolis. But there had been too many nights when the pillow next to his was empty.

In June he had celebrated his son's birthday for the first time ever, but Sid was not a year old. He was thirteen. That was the day when dreams had collided with reality at one of life's inevitable intersections. It was the day the results of Sidney's DNA tests had come back.

The tests confirmed that Sidney carried the gene for hypertrophic cardiomyopathy. Physical exams indicating no sign of hypertrophy, no abnormal thickening of the muscle, had given the family reason to hope that the boy would never have to worry about the problem. But Reese was sick with the thought that his first gift to his son had been a defective gene. He hadn't said as much, but his reaction must have shown, because Sid had ordered both his parents to cheer up. He'd done some research on the disease on the Internet, and he'd discovered that you never heard much about the people who *lived* with the disease. All you heard about was the people who died suddenly on the field or on the court. He cheerfully pointed out that early detection gave him more than a fighting chance. What the heck, he'd take the gene along with his father's shooting arm.

He would take his father, period. He would be his father's son. Like his mother, he had chosen to take his father's name.

Reese's doctors had deemed Sidney the perfect candidate for an experimental program aimed at preventing the development of hypertrophy in HCM gene carriers. They all understood that no treatment had been demonstrated to restore the hearts of HMC patients like Reese to normal, but that advances were being made all the time with drug therapy, the use of pacemakers, and surgical procedures. Sidney was going to get to know his new second home in Minnesota very well. Some of the best heart specialists in the country practiced in that state.

So did the Minnesota Timberwolves and the Minneapolis Mavericks. Sid had dropped his allegiance to Denver like a hot nugget the first time Reese had introduced him to the Target Center locker room.

The early-morning mist drifted above the Bad River like a congregation of *wanagi* the sun had chased from the plum bushes along the riverbank. Up from the meandering river stood the new high school. Not far away, the "old school" and the elementary school building faced each other across the street. Kids alighted from vehicles of all shapes and sizes—big yellow buses and small, battered Chevys. Cars circled, others idled, waiting for a parking spot, parents there with their children. It was a good day for beginning, a good day for continuing on.

The Blue Sky vehicle rated a spot in the gravel parking lot's teachers' corner. Reese recalled playing a few pranks in that corner, including helping Titus and Dozer carry the typing teacher's VW across the street, where they'd deposited it in front of the side door, next to the typing room.

"I remember your typing teacher," Helen said. "She was still here when I came. We called her Joyce Legs."

"So did we. I hear they called you Helen of Troy." Reese winked at his son. "Pretty enough to start a brawl over."

"I wonder what they'll call—" Helen's arm shot up in the air. "There's Sarah and the . . . Sarah!"

"Hey," Reese said as he ruffled his nephew's hair. His niece would not permit any such mussing on her first day of school. "How's the old man doing?" he asked Sarah.

"We left him at home."

She cast a wistful gaze toward "Dodge City," where the boxy streets were in need of fresh asphalt and the paint was peeling on public housing. It was a comedown for Carter, but he still had his family. He had his life back. With those gifts, there would be more chances. Now he would learn the things that no school could teach him. He needed to understand the true value of his fine education and his skills.

Sarah had come back to her husband as soon as Reese called her, and she'd put the house in Rapid City on the market before Carter was released from the hospital. There was no keeping "the palace" with the kind of debt they had to contend with, and Sarah had no trouble diving into contention. She didn't mind leaving it all behind and starting over in a good way, in a humble place. She reminded her husband that this was where the people lived, and the profits from the casino were needed there.

Reese, of course, wanted to bail his brother out financially, but Helen advised him that Carter's life was endangered by madness, not the Mob. In the end, Carter was going to have to bail himself out. It wouldn't happen overnight, but he had a chance. He was working on it.

And he wasn't alone.

"He has his good days and his bad days," Sarah reported. "Today I'm starting a new job. The kids are starting in a new school. Carter gets depressed about things changing. Sometimes he doesn't want to get out of bed in the morning."

"He's been in court so damn much in the last few months. That, and all the counseling. It's bound to make a guy . . ." Reese's heart drew his eyes to the other end of the street and to his father's old pickup, just turning the corner in front of Big Nell's Café. Reese smiled. "Looks like he's up and dressed now."

"I don't know what I was thinking," Carter called out as he closed the pickup door. Alicia hurled herself at her father's legs, abandoning all her small-woman reserve as Carter lifted her into his arms. "My daughter's first day of the first grade, and I'm hanging around the kitchen in my underwear. What's wrong with that picture?"

"I don't know." Reese grinned. "Boxers or briefs?"

"What are you endorsing these days, Bro-gun?" Carter turned to Sidney. "Did you know that your dad did a commercial for underwear?"

"It was actually socks," Reese averred as he slipped Helen a sly wink. "Tube socks."

Sid eyed his father skeptically, then his uncle. "You're kidding, right?"

"What I socked away from those socks will pay for your college education, so don't laugh. I don't endorse just anything, but I do know socks."

"Hey, there's Dozer," Helen said. She waved at the patrol car. Dozer honked and waved back.

"Don't ever say anything to Dozer about the socks. I'd never live it down."

"Nothing wrong with socks," Carter said. They started across the street, a cozy Blue Sky cluster. "You nervous about your first day of school?"

"Damn right I'm nervous, and don't tell me school is easy."

Carter laughed. "I was asking my daughter." He set her down, took her hand, and walked side by side with his brother. "Titus offered me a position as special consultant on casino operations. He wants me to work for the tribe. Did you put him up to that?" He glanced down the street. "Is it really a job, or just a title?"

"Nobody's getting any more meaningless titles," Reese

371

said. Carter looked skeptical. "You're on probation, little brother. You have to prove yourself all over again."

They had reached the front yard of the old school, where much of the community would soon gather for a school-opening ceremony, which would be conducted by tribal elders.

Reese laid a hand on his brother's shoulder. "But not to me. I know you. You're my brother."

Carter shoved his hands in his pockets and squinted one eye against the morning sun. One corner of his mouth twitched. "Meaning I ain't heavy?"

"I didn't say that." Reese chuckled, gave his brother's shoulder a quick squeeze. "You helped us get Bill Darnell behind bars. I don't care who was driving that pickup, I know damn well Darnell was responsible for Dad's death."

"Plus I helped secure the total humiliation of the Sweeney brothers."

"They had it coming," Reese said. Like Carter, Preston Sweeney had cooperated with federal prosecutors, but Earl had gone to jail. He'd insisted that Peter Jones had bought his old pickup and that he'd had nothing to do with the hit-and-run. The title to the pickup had never been transferred, but there was evidence that Jones had taken possession of the vehicle. Earl had admitted to withholding evidence.

"So do I." Carter hung his head, his mood reversing quickly, which happened often lately. "I screwed up. I don't know why you guys stuck by me."

"You're the smart one in the family, Carter. You can't figure it out?"

"If it's beyond reason, it must be love," Helen put in quietly. Carter looked at his sister-in-law in gratitude. She understood him better than anyone.

"We need you," Reese said. "Pair-a-Dice City is in pretty good shape, thanks to you. Ten Star tried to convince us we couldn't tie our shoes without their help, but once we kicked them to the curb, we were able to get favorable terms on slot machines and contract for services at about half of what Ten Star was taking. And that was at least partly because the restaurant and the hotel were running smoothly."

"And you run an honest game as far as the public is concerned," Helen added. "A reasonable percentage of the take is paid out to winners."

"If it hadn't been for Ten Star's scams, the way they were working both ends against the middle, which is where the people live . . ."

"The tribe would have seen more profits," Carter admitted. He nodded, as though the question had been settled there and then, on the first day of school. "I'm taking the job. It's like starting over, but if they're willing to trust me, I know I can do a good job."

"I know you can, too. I know you will. And you know what else?" Hand still on his brother's shoulder, Reese guided the group toward the glass doors that led to the red tile lobby outside the gym—the red road to a place that felt like home. "You're gonna be a guest speaker for us this fall. I'm booking for Mrs. Blue Sky, who's looking to work my tail off, so any points you can get me . . ."

"You did very well, you know," Helen told him late that night as she stroked his long, sleek, dewy torso after they'd made love. "For a beginner."

"Thank you, ma'am. I know I need lots of practice. What part of my game would you have me brush up on?" He traced her form from hip to belly to the soft underside of her breast. She caught her breath when he made a bead of her nipple. "This part?"

"Mmm, I meant teaching."

"*Practice* teaching. I'm willing to make a career of practice teaching."

"I'm not. You're good. Much too good." She cuddled against his side. The skylight above their bed was like a jewel box filled with Dakota stars. "I remember when you were shy and quiet, hardly said a word."

"Takes me a while to warm up. Did you like me better that way?"

"I loved you then, love you better now." She spread her hand over his chest. "But you really must stick around until tomorrow. Tomorrow I'll love you the best ever. Wait till you see what my best love ever is like."

"You've got a deal, Mrs. Blue." He reached past her for the clock on the nightstand, turning the red digits in their direction. "Well, will you look at that. It *is* tomorrow."

She laughed as she hung her arms around his neck and drew his head down for kisses and covenants and the most exquisite connections. They had something too often missed.

They had today.

Acknowledgments

I wish to thank Chandler Eagle, who serves on the gaming commission of the Standing Rock Lakota Nation, for sparking ideas and providing me with information about the Indian Gaming Regulatory Act. Any mistakes or discrepancies are strictly my own doing. I have set this story on a fictitious reservation in order to avoid any suggestion that the characters or events actually occurred anywhere in the real world. I do believe, however, that Indian gaming is largely misunderstood by mainstream American society. Indian casinos have not made most American Indians rich. As far as I know, unless they are employed *by* a casino, relatively few American Indians receive a direct personal income from casino profits, which are generally used for much needed community projects and improvements. Like so many of the laws we have enacted over the years in our feeble attempts to make amends for injustice, both the Indian Gaming Regulatory Act and the Indian Child Protection Act are double-edged swords. But I guess they are better than taking the land, spiritual practices, tools, and children away, as we have done in the not-so-distant past.

I am also grateful to Dr. Tom Nelson for his generous help with the research for this book. Hypertrophic cardiomyopathy turned out to be a far more complicated topic than I envisioned, but Tom provided me with volumes of material and with his most helpful translations of the material into layman's terms. His interest in my books initiated an e-mail correspondence that I have enjoyed and taken shameless advantage of in getting the medical background for this book. If you find any mistakes, they are my fault entirely.

Although the Bad River does run through South Dakota, there is no Bad River Reservation there. The Bad River Lakota do not exist.